# DIGGER

## ARJAY LEWIS

MIND
BENDER
PRESS

Cover Design: Marianne Nowicki, PremadeEbookCoverShop.com
Editing: Libby Broadbent

ISBN-13: 978-1737838111

Published by:
Mindbender Press
474 South Main Street
Phillipsburg NJ 08865
www.mindbenderpress.com

# DEDICATION

To Marvin Kaye
Mentor and friend
no longer with us.
A man who enjoyed a good, scary tale
As much as I do.

# ARJAY LEWIS

"Death and burial were a public spectacle. Shakespeare may have seen for himself the gravediggers at St Ann's, Soho, playing skittles with skulls and bones."

—*Catharine Arnold*

"But the reason why the grave-digger made music must have been because there was none in his spade"

— *Herman Melville*

**ARJAY LEWIS**

# PART ONE:

# ON THE

# TRAIL

# ONE

I was seven when I learned monsters were real.

October was always a strange month growing up. My birthday was on the twenty-ninth, and my Poppa tried to make it fun, but he always acted strange on the day of Halloween. He took me trick-or-treating, but only during the day. Once the sun went down, he refused to allow me to go outside. We stayed in the house and he scanned our property from a window, taking sips from a pint of Wild Turkey.

It was a moonless night in late October. Poppa and I went out to gather wood for his fire-pit. We lived on a few acres of land in Alpha, New Jersey. Poppa constructed the fire-pit about a hundred yards from our house from bricks and an enormous metal truck wheel.

Gathering sticks in the deepening shadows, I watched as Poppa lit the fire, settling himself into one of the chairs surrounding it. The two of us were alone, ready to take in what the night offered.

That was the year I finally asked my dad the question that had been burning inside me: why didn't I have a momma like everyone else? He had told me that my mother had passed away when I was born, but I knew there had to be more to the story. That night, I hoped he would tell me more about her.

Born with Waardenburg Syndrome, a genetic disorder, I had moderate hearing loss. I also had another symptom called heterochromia iridis — eyes of two different colors. People often gave me strange looks when they noticed my eyes for the first time — one brown and the other a bright blue.

An African-American man with blue eyes was unusual, but having only one blue eye was downright odd.

My father was the successful owner of a fuel oil company business. This meant he could provide me with hearing aids and the special education I needed to attend school alongside my peers.

Poppa seemed anxious as we sat in front of the fire. He glanced around and stared into the night as if he was expecting someone — or some *thing* — to appear.

The night was chilly, and Poppa had brought a blanket for me, which I wrapped tightly around myself as he stirred the fire with a stick.

"Poppa, can you tell me about my momma?" I asked, my gaze shifting to the firelight glinting on the prosthetic hook that replaced my father's left hand.

His gaze met mine, surprise evident in his expression. "Not tonight, son," he said, shaking his head before returning his attention to the fire. "Can you sense something in the air?"

"I guess. It's like I'm scared, but don't know why."

A grim smile appeared on his face. "I was told those eyes of yours meant you can see things other folks can't."

I focused on his lips as I was still honing my skill of lip-reading. Having this ability was a great complement to my hearing aids. "Who told you that, Poppa?"

He looked down at the hooks that replaced the fingers of his missing left hand. The metal stud that worked as his thumb glinted in the light. His smile faded as he thought of the past. "Your momma, back in the day."

I whispered, "Before she died." I had a million unanswered questions — which included not knowing her name.

"Yeah," he said. "Something might be comin'. That's why I brought you out here with me — so I could look right at you." He leaned closer and spoke in a low voice. "Now, let's get this straight. If I tell you to run, you go as fast as you can into the house and you lock the door. You don't open it for nobody, not even me."

This confused me. "Not you, Poppa?"

"I've got my key, but something that looks like me won't," he said, his face deadly serious.

Gazing at the flickering shadows cast by our fire, a wave of vulnerability washed over me, sending a chill down my spine and raising goosebumps across my skin.

Something moved in the woods nearby.

I jumped in surprise, and my poppa's head snapped up. He reached into his coat and pulled out a small cloth bag, dark brown and securely tied with leather laces.

"What's that, Poppa?" I hissed.

"Never you mind," he murmured through clenched teeth. "Remember what I said: when I tell you to run, you run."

I remained still, silently nodding in agreement.

I heard snapping branches and rustling leaves as if something big was moving through the forest. When I looked in the noise's direction, however, I couldn't see anything.

I held my breath, fearful that some kind of nocturnal predator lurked nearby. I glanced over at my poppa as he placed his index finger to his lips, silently warning me not to make a sound.

I tightened my grip on the blanket, preparing to run and suddenly feeling colder than before.

Poppa grabbed the cloth bag at his feet with his prosthetic hand, untying the strings that kept it shut. He pulled out a gleaming piece of metal.

To my seven-year-old eyes, it looked like something magic. It glowed a brilliant gold in the firelight, and I saw symbols and odd letters covered it. The main part was a straight tube my father grasped with his good hand. At the base, it ballooned into a round, bell-shaped ball and a circle of metal about an inch thick crowned the top.

I could not take my eyes off it.

The sound of a branch breaking like a gunshot jerked my attention back to the present. My father's face was grave as he shouted at me. "RUN!"

Without a moment's hesitation, I dropped the blanket and sprinted toward our home, a hundred yards away from the fire pit. I heard my Poppa speaking, but I couldn't make out his words.

I stumbled over an old, gnarled tree root in the pitch-black darkness and landed with a thud on the ground. I scrambled to my feet, only to realize that everything had gone completely silent.

My hearing aid had fallen out of my ear. I snatched it off the ground and glanced back at my father in a state of panic.

He stood grasping the metallic tube, his right hand around the hilt with the hooks of his prosthetic hand giving support. An intense two-foot high flame erupted from the end of the cylinder, blazing brighter than the campfire.

I had seen the original Star Wars on TV, and all I thought at that moment was that all would be well because my poppa had a light saber.

—but this wasn't a light saber. As he waved it, the flames coalesced into a solid blade.

A flaming sword.

My father thrust forward, brandishing the weapon at the empty air. He lunged with a powerful swing, and the flame hit — something.

A brief flash of light flared from the contact. At that moment, I glimpsed a creature the size of a man, but with an upper body shaped like a woman. Below the waist, it was long and scaly, writhing up from the ground like a giant serpent. As quickly as it appeared, it vanished back into the darkness.

My father wasn't moving like he normally did — he was confident and agile, shifting quickly on the balls of his feet as if he was ready to sprint at any moment. He constantly changed direction, moving forward and back without pause, the flaming sword firmly in his grasp.

He raised his blade again, and in the darkness, a semi-transparent female figure lurched forward. Her hand connected with my father's chest, sending him reeling.

He collapsed backward with the fiery sword still aimed at the unseen foe.

I scrambled toward the house, like Poppa told me.

I gasped for breath as I tore open the door, slamming it shut behind me and flipping the lock. Racing to the window, I peered out into the backyard.

My heart pounded as I scanned the backyard. I pressed my face to the window, desperately trying to get a better view of the scene. But all I could see was the fire pit, with no sign of my father or the snake-like creature that had attacked him.

A knock echoed through the room. I rushed to the door to peek through the small window.

It was Poppa.

He was gazing down at the door handle.

I let out a deep breath as I reached for the lock, but my father's words echoed in my mind.

*"You don't open it for nobody, not even me."*

Poppa's mouth moved. "Son?"

I couldn't hear him, with my hearing aid still clutched in my hand, but I watched his lips form the word. I stepped away from the door, slipping my hearing aid back into my ear.

"Let me in, son," Poppa said. It was *his* voice, yet it made all the hairs on my body stand up.

"You told me not to, Poppa," I croaked, surprised how scared my voice sounded.

"Never mind that," he said, sounding angry but not looking up. "Open this door."

I trembled, a part of me wanting to do as I was told, but knowing that if he had instructed me not to open the door, there must have been a good reason for it.

"No, Poppa," I finally blurted. "You have your key."

He raised his eyes, and my breath caught. His gaze was no longer human. He glared at me with the eyes of a snake, dark yellow with the vertical slash of black pupils.

The thing masquerading as my father raised its arm and drove its right fist through the window. The glass shattered and showered me with thousands of tiny fragments.

It thrust through the opening with its left arm, reaching down. The hand — which my father didn't have — was fully intact.

The fingers writhed bonelessly like snakes, growing and extending, clawing for the lock.

I grabbed the kitchen knife out of the dish drainer. With unsteady hands, I held it high and moved to the door.

The creature's left hand extended far beyond the reach of a human arm, its wriggling digits resembling worms crawling and slithering. Its fingers were almost long enough to reach the lock.

I slashed with the knife, and an inch of one finger fell to the ground.

Whatever the thing was, it didn't cry out, but the severed finger restored itself as I gaped in horror. The piece on the ground no longer resembled a finger, but the scaly skin of a snake.

Its fingers slowly wrapped around the latch, and I felt my back hit the wall. I clutched the knife tightly in my hands, my knuckles turning white. I sank down to the floor, frozen with terror.

There was a flash of fire, and my Poppa's head — no, the creature's head — toppled out of sight. I screamed. I didn't know what to do or say. None of this could be real.

The crawling arm yanked back, disappearing from view as the body crumpled to the ground.

My poppa, my *real* poppa, was looking in through the broken glass. His eyes were normal, and he gripped the blazing sword tightly.

"You okay, son?" he asked.

I nodded, unable to speak.

He looked at the knife in my hand and smiled. "My brave little man. You stay in there. I've got some clean-up work to do."

The flame in his hand flickered and died, and I ran to the window to see him retrieve a powerful flashlight from the shed, as well as a hefty shovel.

I hardly believed what I was witnessing. My father dragged an otherworldly creature across the lawn, its long serpentine body curling behind him as he moved. The sight was both terrifying and mesmerizing, and I was powerless to look away. I had no idea what this creature was or what my father intended to do with it.

He picked up the severed head, allowing me to get a closer look. What had been my poppa's face was now a woman's — beautiful, even in death. Where her hair should have been, scales covered the top of her head and neck.

A pair of fangs extended from her mouth, dripping with liquid. When I wondered whether it was blood or drool, it made me shiver.

He walked past the fire pit, the bag with the golden sword hilt swinging from his belt, and he began to dig.

Poppa dug a deep hole with practiced skill. He dragged the dead creature over and rolled it in to the makeshift grave. With a speed that surprised me, he covered it up with dirt in half the time it took him to dig it.

I still gripped the knife as the sound of his key turning in the lock filled the room, followed by the creak of the door opening.

My father was dirty and bathed in sweat despite the chill. "Joshua, you can put the knife down now, son."

He tenderly removed the knife from my trembling hands and laid it in the sink. He pulled me close into a tight embrace.

"There, there, it's all right now," he said.

"Poppa, what was that?" I choked, fighting tears.

"A creature called a Lamia," he stated, as if this were the most natural thing in the world. "It's able to change its shape."

"Why was it here?" I asked.

He exhaled. "It attacks children, son."

"Was it here for me?" I gasped.

He patted my head. "Don't worry, I'm here to protect you." He glanced over at the knife in the sink. "I got me a feeling you can protect yourself if it comes down to it."

# TWO

No one ever knew about the mysterious carcass buried in our garden, and I worked hard to forget the strange face I'd seen. Keeping myself busy with homework and TV usually did the trick, but I would still dread the night. Images of that scaly reptilian head and its dripping fangs haunted me as I burrowed beneath the sheets to find comfort.

As a child, I did not know that my Poppa was courting Elizabeth Baron, who was our part-time housekeeper. So they pleasantly surprised me when, at age eleven, Poppa revealed they were getting married.

She became a full-time caretaker for both Poppa and me.

Lizzie was a woman of outstanding wisdom, strength, and kindness. She never asked that I address her as "Momma," because she knew my mother had passed away and it would be inappropriate to replace her. She had a steady character and could be stern when the situation required it. The stability Lizzie offered improved my young life, and she also taught me the value of self-discipline and self-control.

Poppa would often retreat to the fire-pit and Lizzie always sensed when he was in one of his dark moods. She observed him from the safety of the kitchen, yet never joined him outside.

"Lizzie, why don't you ever come out to the fire?" I asked one night when Poppa was out back, silhouetted by the flames.

"Because I can't be with your poppa when the shadow's on his soul," she said. "That's why I send you out there." She smiled and touched my cheek. "Because you are like a bright light, Joshua. He can talk to you, and you push that shadow away for a time."

Usually, I would go see Poppa by the fire, but sometimes if he was sipping a pint of Wild Turkey Bourbon with a haunted look in his eyes, I would stay away.

Those nights, he wore the look of a man who had seen too much.

If I dared approach, I would do so cautiously, fearful that he would not return from whatever dim abyss he had ventured into.

Sometimes, we'd simply gaze into the flames of the fire. Other times, my poppa told me stories of dead things that refused to stay in the ground. He'd speak of mysterious creatures from ancient tales and legends that had been around since the start of time.

That's when I learned that before I was born, Poppa had traveled with a man he called Digger. His name invoked a sense of awe in me.

As a child, I never questioned why he was called Digger. I simply accepted it and hung on every word of Poppa's fantastic stories. Each one began with something like, "Back when I was up in Maine with Digger..." or "I was down in Georgia with Digger..."

He told stories of monstrous creatures that lurked in the shadows, recounting the battles he and Digger had with them. These tales were always dark and captivating.

As he talked, his gaze would drift to the prosthetic hook at the end of his left arm.

My father regaled me with tales of epic battles, full of mythical creatures that he encountered. His vivid descriptions of these creatures piqued my curiosity, so I would often do my own research, exploring websites dedicated to mythology. I kept meticulous notes of Poppa's narratives, including the locations and dates he mentioned.

Lizzie was aware of my passion for capturing my father's tales, so she gifted me a journal to write them all down in one place.

For my entire life, my father had been the proud owner of the Alpha Fuel Oil Company. He supplied homes with their heating needs and provided me and Lizzie with a comfortable lifestyle.

Thanks to my father's business acumen, I had access to hearing aids and speech therapy. I mastered hearing technology, sign language, and lip-reading skills before leaving elementary school.

Even without my devices, I could follow my poppa's stories — the movement of his mouth captivated me in a way that was eerie. His tales of the undead were almost hypnotic, the hushed silence of my impaired hearing making the tales even more intense.

Since I grew up listening to his stories, and putting them in my journal, the written word became a source of joy.

At age fourteen, my dad enrolled me in a series of self-defense classes. As I entered high school, I explored various martial arts such as karate and aikido, as well as a street-fighting course. When I was a junior, he signed me up for fencing. I loved it and in my imagination; I was wielding my father's blazing sword rather than an épée or foil.

I had to focus intensely during those classes, as wearing a hearing aid wasn't a good fit for the robust physical activity of self-defense. I had to watch the teacher's mouth carefully for instructions.

In high school, I excelled in English and wrote for the school newspaper, getting high marks. My hard work paid off, as Rider University accepted me and I pursued a degree in journalism. Although the university encouraged me to move into the field of Broadcast Journalism, I was determined to hone my skills in writing. To my surprise, my professors pushed us to not only report stories but also become advocates for certain causes.

I did well, though I was worried about my father without me at home to keep him company by the fire-pit. But Lizzie assured me he was doing all right and kept the darkness away.

On the day of my graduation, Poppa and Lizzie were there to share in my success. They were both beaming with pride, and it filled me with a sense of warmth and accomplishment. I had been interning at a newspaper in Philadelphia throughout my college years, and to my delight, they offered me a paid position upon my graduation.

On the eve of moving to a small apartment in Philadelphia, my father was sitting out at the fire pit. I joined him and spent one last night under the stars.

"Y'all packed?" Poppa asked.

I nodded and saw that his jaw was tight. "You doing okay, Poppa?"

"I'm worried, son," he said. "I hope I prepared you for what's comin'."

I frowned. "Working at a newspaper? I think I can handle it."

He met my eyes. "Son, I gotta feeling that you're going to have to face some things — like Digger and I did."

At that point, it had been several years since Poppa had told me one of his Digger anecdotes. "I doubt I'll run into anything like that."

He sighed. "After you were born, someone I trust predicted that you would have to face dark creatures once you became a man." He looked me over from head to toe. "And here you are, all grown up."

"My biggest worry is getting a paper cut," I joked.

He shook his head. "The fates maybe have other plans for you."

He dropped the conversation, and instead of discussing anything important, we focused on simpler topics, mainly my move and how I hoped to build my career.

I never imagined that our goodbye would be our final farewell — as it was the last time I would see my dad alive.

For the next six months, I threw myself into my new career as a full-time reporter. I ventured out into the world and documented the events that I witnessed firsthand. I committed myself to reporting the truth, no matter how hard it was to uncover.

I hated it.

I had expected to work with honest journalists. Instead, I found people more interested in micro-aggressions than facts, and spin instead of meaningful ideas. They preferred to push an agenda rather than meaningful arguments, and used anonymous sources to discredit others.

It took me aback to discover that it wasn't only journalists who were unethical, but editors, management, and everyone else. Despite the turmoil, I stayed focused on my tasks and strove to report events in a truthful and unbiased manner.

I confronted an editor because he completely rewrote one of my stories. He had not only manipulated the facts, but he also altered my language and writing style, leaving it hollow and disjointed, yet with my byline on it. Despite my complaints to management, they refused to take any action, instead assigning me to write puff pieces and obituaries.

Not quite the dream job I had envisioned.

After a strenuous day covering obituaries, Lizzie phoned me in tears with devastating news.

Poppa had passed away.

I was in disbelief as I held the phone, unable to find the words to express my confusion and grief. "How...?"

She told me he died the previous night — by the fire pit. He hadn't returned to their bed, and when she woke up and ventured out, she discovered his lifeless body lying in the chilly morning air.

"He was so very pale," she said. "He had a circular mark on his neck, and Joshua, he looked — terrified."

I rushed home to meet with the coroner and uncover the truth. The autopsy showed that Poppa had lost a large amount of blood. The medical examiner wrote it off as blood loss from an injury, with the blood soaking into the ground.

The events from when I was seven flashed through my mind. Had one of the sinister creatures my father spoke of finally tracked him down to exact revenge?

Though my heart was heavy, it forced me to focus on what needed to be done. I escorted Lizzie to the closed-casket funeral for my father, where many people came to pay their respects. My father was more than just an employer, he was a well-liked and respected member of the community. I heard countless stories about how he had been generous to so many people.

I served as a pallbearer, accompanying my father's closest friends in carrying his coffin. We laid the box down on the webbing and watched it slowly lowered into the cold ground.

At the gravesite, a mound of freshly dug soil lay atop a sheet of plywood, draped with a white plastic tarp. This soil would soon fill the grave, entombing its occupant forever.

At the graveside was a hefty man in jeans, standing back and contemplating the service. He was Caucasian with a short white beard, but his jeans were spotless and new. He had on a green army peacoat, and as the coffin was being carried to the burial plot, he took off his hat to reveal a balding pate with a short white ponytail.

Once the coffin was in place, I asked the funeral director about the man in the peacoat.

"Him?" the somber man asked. "He's just the gravedigger."

"Who hired a gravedigger?" I said. "I thought you just used a backhoe."

"He arrived with the correct papers," the director explained quietly. "I assumed your stepmother requested it."

I asked no more about the man, but stood by Lizzie for the graveside service. Some people wept openly, but Lizzie remained dry-eyed.

"You okay, Lizzie?" I whispered to her, surprised by her stoicism.

She nodded. "He's finally at peace, Joshua. Finally."

I kept stealing glances at the gravedigger. He seemed to be in deep sorrow, his head hung low and hat in hand. I couldn't help but wonder…

After bringing Lizzie home, I went back to my father's grave for a moment of solitude. I parked down the hill and walked up to the gravesite. The weather had changed, and the sky was now overcast and the wind howled through the graveyard as I trudged across the grass.

I was stunned to discover that someone had filled in the grave and removed all the tools and plywood. There was no sign of the mysterious gravedigger. To my surprise, someone had placed a vibrant bouquet of flowers atop the grave, adding a touch of life and beauty to the solemn spot.

It surprised me that the older man I'd seen could fill in a grave in less than an hour, with nothing but a shovel.

My gaze swept across the cemetery, taking in all the other graves. The sorrow and pain I'd held back for the last few days threatened to overwhelm me, but I pushed it away. A rumble of thunder in the distance seemed to echo my feelings, and I looked up at my father's gravestone.

"I promise, Poppa. I will find out what did this to you and make it pay."

Poppa had said I might have to fight dark creatures. Now I would have to learn how.

The following day was the reading of the will at the lawyer's office. It stunned me to learn that Poppa had a variety of successful investments, and his will divided them between Lizzie and me.

I realized I inherited enough money to never have to work again.

I departed the lawyer's office in a haze, taking Lizzie out to the Alpha Family Restaurant. It was a quaint diner that had not been updated since the 1960s. We enjoyed a breakfast of grits and eggs in a booth away from the rest of the patrons. As we ate, I tried to process the reality that I was now financially secure for life.

"What's going to happen with Alpha Oil?" I asked.

"Several of the men who worked for your poppa are going to buy us out, which is fine," Lizzie said and smiled at me. "I know nothing about the heating oil business, so I think it'll be better in their hands."

"Will you be all right, Lizzie?"

She nodded. "I was alone before I met Ephraim. I'll be fine. How about you, Joshua? You going back to the paper?"

"Not me," I said. "I've hated that job ever since I started it, and I want to get away from people with agendas trying to control the way I write my stories."

"What will you do?" she asked. "You're too young to retire."

I took a forkful of grits and looked at them, trying to control my anger. "I have some ideas."

Lizzie became concerned. "What are you thinking?"

All those stories Poppa told me flashed through my mind. If I could find out the truth of those tales, maybe I'd know who, or what, killed him.

"I'd like to find out more about the stories Poppa used to tell me," I said.

She shook her head, putting her fork down. "I have no idea how you'd go about tracking down any of those."

I grinned. "I do. Research. I have dates and places. Remember, I used to write things down after Poppa told me one of his stories."

Lizzie smiled sadly. "You were a journalist even back then. But if you track down these stories, what good will it do?"

I looked around the room and spoke in a harsh whisper. "Maybe I can find out what happened to Poppa — what killed him."

She appeared incredibly sad and took my hand. "Josh, revenge is never a good path."

"Poppa said I had some kind of destiny — if I can find his old partner, maybe he can help me."

"I'm worried, son," she said, her eyes wet. She had never called me 'son' before. "I lost Ephraim, and I don't want to lose you."

I took her hand. "You won't, Lizzie, I promise."

At that moment, the morning sun shone through the many windows in the restaurant, casting a glistening light on the room. A look passed over her face, and she reached into her massive purse. "I guess you've decided. One thing your poppa told me was that if anything happened to him, I had to give this to you."

She retrieved a bag from her purse that I hadn't seen since I was seven. She placed it heavily on the table. It was made from a soft leather material, almost like chamois, and I carefully untied the leather cords. As I glanced inside, I saw a glint of gold. Without hesitation, I swiftly moved the package to my lap.

"Are you sure, Lizzie?" I whispered. "This is probably worth a lot of money."

"Your father said you were to have it, that he meant it for you," she said, her jaw set. "And if you're gonna go find out about these things your father tol' you, I think you're gonna need it." She looked around the restaurant, but no one was paying attention to us. "You got any idea where to start?"

I considered this. "If anyone knows the truth about Poppa's stories, it would be Digger," I finally admitted. "Problem is, I don't know his real name, or where he lives, but I think I saw him at the funeral."

"So how you gonna find him?" she asked.

I set my jaw. "Any way that I can."

I left my life in Philadelphia behind me, packing up the contents of my small apartment and placing the items I didn't need into storage.

Traveling back to my hometown, I contacted the funeral home. They had paperwork for my father's grave, but no information on the name or the location of the gravedigger himself.

Spending the next few days at home, I retrieved my hand-written childhood journal and spent time re-reading it.

If I accepted Digger was indeed real, then I needed to talk to anyone who had seen him, no matter how bizarre their stories may be.

Doing extensive research online, scouring newspaper archives for accounts of events that occurred at the right times. I reached out to people I located who could provide information about the events. I was eager to have conversations with anyone who would share their knowledge.

After making the necessary connections and scheduling my interviews, I was ready to hit the road.

I said my farewells to Lizzie and hopped into my newly gained ride, a pre-owned Chevy Trax, and headed north.

Starting in Connecticut, I set out on a quest, relying on my instincts to get me closer to the truth. My father had told a story about himself and Digger in a town called Griswold, Connecticut, about thirty years earlier.

Back then, after a minor earthquake, the local children were curious and investigated the damage. When they peered into the hole it created, they discovered a human skull. One child took it home to show his mother, and she contacted the authorities.

At the same time, police were searching for a serial killer who was terrorizing the area for several months. Initially, they feared that the skull may have belonged to one of his victims.

It turned out that the bones were more than a century old. They called in an archaeologist to investigate. Upon further examination, he determined the graves were part of an old, forgotten family cemetery, dating back to the early 1800s. Such unmarked cemeteries were not uncommon in the area, and the burials were typical for that time period.

The archaeology team carefully excavated the site, expecting to find just rotted wooden coffins. Instead, they uncovered an empty stone crypt. The soil was loose, and the uppermost stone broken. Dirt had filled the sepulcher, and there were no remains — no bones, no hair — just scraps of deteriorating old clothes.

The team concluded that something disturbed the crypt prior to the earthquake. The tremors had merely revealed the damaged burial chamber.

I met with the retired archeologist, Lincoln Moss, who worked on the case.

He greeted me at the door of his home, a diminutive man with snow-white hair and round spectacles. Dressed in a blue corduroy coat over a crisp white shirt, with a pair of khaki trousers, he wore dark brown loafers and a pocket watch tucked into his pocket.

I presented my newspaper ID to him, a credential I had yet to surrender even after I resigned.

"You work with the Philadelphia Examiner? Why are you interested in things that happened up in Connecticut thirty years ago?" he asked, squinting at my ID.

"Research. For a story I'm working on."

He carefully poured the tea, its aroma filling the room. The porcelain cups, a soft pink hue, glimmered in the light, their interiors crafted from mother-of-pearl.

He shook his head. "That entire case was crazy, totally insane. A stone crypt in an unmarked cemetery? It was a rare archeological find, I'll tell you."

I nodded sagely. "It's that the crypt appeared to have been dug out from the inside that interested me."

The older man sat back in his chair and sipped his tea. "That should never have ended up in the final report. One of my teaching assistants got it into his head that there was something supernatural going on." He uttered the word "supernatural" with a scowl, as if it left a foul taste in his mouth. "You're not one of those ghost-chaser people, are you?"

"Just a reporter, sir," I said with a reassuring grin.

"Well, they're bad enough these days."

"I may agree with you on that," I told him. "There were a lot of strange theories being thrown around back then."

He sighed. "Yes, ridiculous theories about the Jewett City Vampires, if you can believe such foolishness."

"Can you enlighten me?"

"Newspaper accounts from the 1850s suggested that Lemuel Ray, a member of the Ray family, had died from tuberculosis. Soon after, his father and brother also died, and the community believed that Lemuel was returning from the grave and killing off the rest of his family. This caused a great deal of panic, leading some to suggest that he had become a vampire, of all things."

"Why would they believe that?"

He ran his fingers through his short, white hair. "Back then, witchcraft and superstition were more widely believed. Not to mention tuberculosis — it's a nasty little bacteria. Many people don't even show any symptoms, yet it still kills half of those it infects."

"But, vampires?" I repeated.

"In the 1850s, rumors of a vampire roaming Jewett City were rampant. Even thirty years ago, people believed the earthquake allowed an ancient creature to escape from its stone crypt."

"I still don't see the connection," I said.

"Think of it! The vivid symptoms of tuberculosis! Pale skin, blood on the mouth from coughing, an emaciated body, cheeks a livid crimson, sunken eyes and bad breath. It isn't hard to imagine people might think something was draining the life out of someone."

"So, between the empty crypt and the serial killer, the suggestion was that the vampire had returned."

"People were so scared that they resorted to desperate measures like nailing crosses to doors and windows," he said, rolling his eyes. "The only silver lining was that churches experienced a surge in attendance and the Catholic church had a record year for holy water requests."

"Then a man came to town," I said, and opened my reporter's notebook as if I had to check. "A man called 'Digger'?"

"Yes, he showed up with an impressive African-American fellow."

"And they said they could solve the problem?" I asked.

"Of all things! This Digger fellow insisted that the archeology team leave the site so he could examine it," Moss said and shook his head. "He acted like he was some kind of expert, and I assumed he was an archeologist. Only later did I learn he possessed no degree of any kind."

"And that upsets you?"

"I'm a scientist. I was running the examination and excavation of a historic site," he said, offended. "The last thing I needed was a pair of ghost hunters, or whatever they were, mucking about my site!"

His face had gone red with the memory.

"How long did they take over?" I asked.

"Only a day or two, but they remained in the town for the next week," Moss said. "Then, just like that, they left."

"And — the murders ended?"

"Well… yes…" he snorted. "I think it's more likely the killer or killers moved on. It shocked me to learn months later that the town paid this Digger person a rather sizable sum."

I paused at this. "A large sum? What for?"

"I do not know," he said with a shrug. "We finished our investigation, and I went back to teaching. Never saw that man again."

"Any idea where this Digger, or his companion, came from? Or where they went when they were done?"

"The stories were that he lived in Maine, but my guess is that he came from the New York area."

I smiled at this. "What makes you say that?"

"The regionalisms he used when he spoke."

"You know phonetics as well as archeology?"

Moss raised his chin. "I know many things, Mr. Bennet, I assure you. What I do not know is who this Digger was, where he came from, or what he did to earn an enormous sum of money investigating a broken crypt in Connecticut."

I closed my notebook. "Thank you for your time, sir."

"I still don't understand how this could help with something in Philadelphia," Moss said as he escorted me to the door.

After returning to the hotel, I sat in my car and jotted down my thoughts. I never questioned why my father owned an oil delivery company — he had done that since I was young — but for the first time, I pondered how he gained the funds to start it.

The town had paid my father and Digger a hefty amount of money, and I knew it wasn't for peering into a tomb. The reason I looked up Moss and the entire incident was because of a tale

Poppa had once told me about him and Digger vanquishing a ferocious vampire.

He neglected to tell me they paid him to do it.

I did not know what his work with Digger entailed until now. Could my father have been a mercenary, killing monsters and earning money for it?

Was that why my father had been so secretive about it?

# THREE

I ventured north to Portland, Maine, for my next journey. Before I was born, the area experienced an event linked to demon worshippers, and I had arranged an appointment to meet with a witness. I was also eager to learn more by talking to the locals.

A short three-hour drive led me near the Casco Bay at the top of Portland's Munjoy Hill. Just across from my lodging was Fort Gorges — an old nineteenth century U.S. military fort on an island, now converted into a public park accessible only by boat.

Driving into the small city, past the aging brick warehouses as I exited the highway. My GPS led me to my Air BNB. I easily found a spot for my car on the street in front of a grand house a few hundred feet away from the shoreline of the bay.

I found a lockbox hung on the doorknob when I reached the side entrance. After entering the four-digit code, I was soon inside the house, carrying my luggage and laptop bag into a spacious room at the rear.

The room had a bed and a desk, and another room with a bathroom and a shower. The house was a big Victorian, and I had a good-sized space, although I didn't like the fact that there was only one entry. I reassured myself that I was on the first floor, so I could go out a window in an emergency.

I was experiencing a strange sense of paranoia since I'd begun my search and it seemed to intensify. Why would I need an escape route? No monsters were coming after me.

The creature that had imitated my father's face with its snake-like eyes flashed through my mind. I decided that a little paranoia couldn't hurt and perhaps things to be feared were lurking in the shadows.

My visit to Connecticut proved Poppa had been there. It left me wondering if he and Digger had really defeated a vampire.

Poppa's story was about an epic battle with a monstrous creature, long-buried in the earth's darkness, driven mad from the years of isolation.

I always thought vampires were like Bela Lugosi from the old films — elegant and sophisticated, with a gentlemanly thirst for blood. But my father informed me that vampires were extremely hazardous. Their craving for blood pushed them into insanity and stripped them of their human qualities.

"Vampires ain't classy, Joshua. They ain't classy and they ain't pretend either." I remember Dad rubbing the stump of his wrist, his gaze grim. "Those fuckers will plunge their fangs into your throat in a heartbeat, no different from a wild animal. No remorse, no hesitation — and no guarantee that you'll stay dead, neither."

I shivered in the warm air, my mind flashing back to my father's death. He died with much of his blood removed — but vampires left puncture wounds on the neck. The mark on my father's flesh was a circle the size of a silver dollar.

I was determined to know what kind of creature could do that.

I ventured to Portland to uncover the truth about Digger and Poppa's battle with the alleged cultists.

Intending to gain more information, I went to the Front Porch, a local restaurant. The place boasted only a few customers, and my waiter soon came over. He was a kind-faced man in his fifties with twinkling blue eyes that sparkled when he smiled. He was of average height and had a slender figure with a slight belly. I figured he was the perfect age to recall any rumors of the incident.

I asked him if he knew anything about the old fort.

He frowned at this and with his heavy New England accent, he asked, "You're not planning to go out they-yuh tonight, are yah?"

I smiled. "No, sir. I won't go out there at all. I was just curious."

"That place is bad news. Have yah been told any of the stories?"

"A few. What have you heard?"

He shrugged. "One tale from a fisherman who went across they-yuh with his friends. Must've been back in ninety-something."

"So, a while ago?"

"Ayah. He claims they all had a bottle of whiskey with them and intended to make a night of it. When they got they-yuh they thought they saw a woman in white walking around the stone corridors. Y'know, the old fort, she's just a bunch of corridors in a big circle around the entire island, right?"

"That's what I've heard."

"So, them bein' young men, he and his friends try to follow this girl. They went deeper into the fort, trying to find her again, but she weren't nowhere to be found. Nightfall sets in, they turn to go, but suddenly they're paralyzed — lost the ability to move."

"Couldn't move?" I repeated.

"Ayah. For a couple minutes or so, somethin' froze 'em in one spot."

"How'd they get away?"

"They ain't sure, but according to what this fell-ah tells me, they began cursin' about that woman, sayin' it was her fault, and callin' her all kinds of nasty names. Somehow, that broke the spell. They ran off to their boat and got out of they-yuh, let me tell yah."

"Quite a tale," I said. "I'm more interested in the incident that happened on Halloween with the people from the cult."

The server paled. He suddenly noticed other customers that needed attention. "I'll get back to yah, sport."

While I was eating, a large man came up to my table. He was tall, with a broad frame and a bushy mustache, dressed in an old-fashioned three-piece suit. He introduced himself as the owner and did not look pleased.

"Look he-yah," he began, growing red in the face. "What is yah interest in the old fort, anyway? You a reportuh or something?"

"Actually, I am," I confessed, though I wondered why I had to validate myself. "Just doing some research and I don't have anyone interested in buying the story. I don't expect anyone will publish it."

I tried to sound relaxed, but this did not calm the owner.

He looked around the other tables and spoke in a low voice. "Look, we don't want any of that bein' brought up."

I leaned in to speak softly as well and tried to look like I shared his concern. "I doubt it would cause much of a stir after all these years."

"You not from around he-yuh, are yah?"

"No, I'm from New Jersey."

"Figures. We don't get many folks of your persuasion round he-yuh."

I felt my jaw tense. "What is that supposed to mean?"

"Look, we don't need no more ghost hunters comin' round stirring up things, making people upset."

I sat back and crossed my arms over my chest. "I am looking into those events, sir. If a few people become upset, I don't really have a problem with that. I think it should upset people."

His expression darkened. "You openin' a can of worms. I hope yah have the sense to know when to quit."

I pushed the plate of food away from me. "Could I have my check? I seemed to have lost my appetite."

He gestured gruffly to my server. "Find yourself another place to eat. We don't like ghost hunters in he-yuh."

I glared up at him.

His mouth became a tight line, and he stormed away. I polished off my wine in one gulp as the server placed the billfold on my table.

"I'm sorry about that," the server said.

Our eyes met, and I could tell that the situation had upset him.

As he stepped away, I opened the leather folder with my bill. On top was a handwritten note torn from a piece of scrap paper.
If you want to find out about the fort,
and that Halloween
meet me at the corner of Beckett and Congress
at 11:20

As I walked the few blocks to my Air BNB, I felt the suspicious glances of passing pedestrians. I was more than just an outsider looking into a mysterious event that the locals seemed determined to keep hidden. I was African-American, and I was a reporter, invading their space, and they didn't like it.

I had several hours before my server was free, and I went back to my rented room and read over the newspaper reports I downloaded from the 1990s. The headlines blared their gruesome tales:

**Cultists Commit Human Sacrifice**
**Deadly Cult Responsible for Abductions Ended**
**Fort Gorges Bloodbath**

The papers filled the stories with what they were allowed to release, presented in a lurid manner that lacked detail. I made notes of the facts that were written in the papers:

**1. A "so-called cult" had abducted over a dozen people — mostly young women.**

**2. The cult members brought their prisoners to the fort by boat on Halloween.**

**3. Law enforcement interrupted the cult's ritual, but only after they sacrificed several of their prisoners.**

**4. The police killed all the cultists to free the captives.**

The authorities presented the facts; the press reported them and law enforcement monitored them. No one investigated any other theories aside from the ones given by those in charge.

For years, conspiracy theories circulated that suggested mind-control and government experiments took place. Some even suggested there were other people at the fort besides the police who fought the cultists.

No source mentioned the name Digger or Ephraim Bennett.

I had heard the tale from my father on one of those dark summer nights sitting around the fire pit at home. He asked if I was sure I wanted to hear the tale, as it was 'disturbing.'

That night, he captivated me with his story. In the years that followed, I couldn't help but doubt its authenticity, as it seemed too extraordinary to be real. I embarked on this journey to speak to someone who witnessed the events recounted to me, to see how accurate his version was. I hoped that this might provide a hint as to the whereabouts or identity of Digger.

I scheduled my interview for the following day, so I had tonight to ask the waiter if he knew any helpful information.

At about eleven PM, as I ventured outside and was welcomed by the refreshing touch of the late spring wind. I could detect the briny sea air as I headed toward our meet-up location. Pulling my jacket close, I embraced the chill of the night and hurried on my way.

I crept into the shadows, scanning the area for any suspicious figures lurking in the night, as I reached our meeting place. I felt anxious as the clock ticked to 11:20 and then to 11:30 — was I tricked into coming here?

Or was I just being paranoid again?

A figure walked towards me. It seemed to be the right height and size, so I lifted my hand to give a friendly wave.

He kept walking and as he approached, hissed, "Turn and walk with me, will yah?"

I did so. "Where are we going?" I asked as I strode to keep up.

"A place I know. It's not far."

We strolled a few streets, and he stopped at a bar. If I were being kind, I'd call it a dive, but I think that's being generous. As we stepped inside the grimy bar, the inside was dark and poorly lit, and at the bar sat a couple of burly, rough-looking men.

My new companion led me to an out of the way table, then went off to the bar and came back with two cold beers. He placed one before me and settled into the chair opposite.

He glanced back at the room to make sure that nobody was paying attention to us.

"The name's Kelly," he began.

"I'm Josh."

I took a big gulp of the beer, and its wonderful flavor amazed me.

Kelly smiled. "Good, t'aint it? The bartender they-yuh, he's the owner. Brews it up himself."

I looked at the glass again. "Really?"

"Ah-yah. The place don't look like much but the be-yah is good. Now, I have got to ask you an important question, if yah don't mind."

"Sure," I said, surprised by his tone.

"Back on that Halloween, there was a fellah who came to town. He was a black fellah and worked with a man who said he was a gravedigger."

I nodded.

"Was that fellah someone important to you?"

I let out my breath, shocked that I'd been holding it. "He was my father."

"I knew it," Kelly proclaimed. "I knew it the minute I saw you. You look just like him."

"You know what happened to my father? And do you know about Digger?"

"Digger?" he repeated. "Ay-yah, that was what the man was called."

"What do you know about that Halloween? From my research, local officials tried to keep everything under wraps."

"I have to tell yah, maybe right they did that."

I frowned. "Why do you think so?"

"'Cause I was they-yah. I wasn't always a waiter. In fact, back then, I was a rookie."

"A cop?" I said in shock. Kelly certainly didn't have the hard edge of a police officer.

"Ay-yah, and what I saw that night made me leave the force. Been waitin' tables ever since. Ain't as prestigious, but I nevah have to see the horrors like that night." He looked away from me. "I still get nightmares, sometimes."

"What can you tell me about the night of the incident? My father told me stories, but they sounded pretty unbelievable."

"The basic facts are right if you've read the headlines…"

"I have."

"Good, that will make this easy-yuh." He looked at his beer and seemed to grow younger as the lines on his face fell away, and time appeared to reverse for him. "Like I said, I was a rookie, wearing my new uniform and all spit-and-polished. That man, Digger, showed up with his friend, your fath-tha. Somebody had brought him in to dig a grave, nothing more than that. First thing, he went to police headquarters and gave copies of certificates showing that he was bonded and insured."

I frowned. "Was that common back then?"

"We all talked about it, as everyone thought it was a big laugh that this he-yah fellah got himself fancy paperwork just to dig a hole in the ground." He stared at his beer again. "Course, later on, we understood why he'd come by to give us those papers. They came in handy after everything that happened."

"Whose grave was he there to dig?"

"Some rich fellah had it in his will that his grave was to be dug by hand in the Evergreen Cemetery. But turns out this Digger fell-ah was investigating vandalized graves."

"Vandalized graves?" I repeated. "You had grave-robbers in Portland?"

He met my eyes. "Back then we did, all of a sudden. Someone was opening graves and stealing bodies of the recently deceased. Some folks 'round here said they heard strange noises coming from the graveyard. Other people whispered they saw dead people coming out of their graves all by themselves."

I looked down at my beer. "What can you tell me about that night?"

"Let me get another be-yah first. I know I need one," Kelly said and rose. He went to the bartender, and the man drew another large mug.

Kelly returned to his seat and glanced over his shoulder at the two fishermen still seated at the bar. He gulped down a large mouthful of his drink and set the glass down, watching as the liquid sloshed around inside.

"That night, that Halloween," he said in low tones. "The Maine Marine Patrol let us know about boats headed out to the fort. Everyone thought it was a joke, just teenagers givin' themselves a scare on Halloween. So, we headed out to the island in police boats to check it out."

"But that wasn't what you found," I said, and sipped my beer. My mouth was dry and my throat tight.

"As we headed out, the only sound was the waves hitting the boat, and the sound of the motor. But the further we went, the more uneasy we became. Suddenly, we heard a faint shriek in the distance. All of us men, we looked at each other, trying to figure out what it was. As we got closer, the shriek turned into full-blown screams. Let me tell you, those of us who heard it were pretty shook by that. The sergeant immediately radioed for backup."

I nodded.

"So we get to the island, and we come off the boat with weapons drawn, ready to face whatever was they-yuh. Couple of fellahs got themselves shotguns. Now that building is all cut stone, and torches were all set up in the center of the courtyard. Stuck into the ground like tiki torches, ya know what I mean?"

"I do," I responded.

"Well, they-yuh were bodies lying about everywhere as we came in, many of 'em missin' their heads. I couldn't believe what I was seeing — it was like a scene right out of a horror movie. In the center of the open courtyard was this big stone altar."

"A stone altar?"

"Ay-yah. All covered in a thick layer of drying blood, and that gave me the shivers. I can't imagine how they got it they-yuh, as it was too big for any of the boats to bring over, I'll tell yah. They had to use a ship with a crane to remove it afterwards. So, the folks still alive, they're dressed in ragged clothes, sitting on the ground and some of them were weeping. I felt a sense of dread coming over me as I continued walking, unsure of what else we might find."

"Those people you found — they were the ones abducted?"

"Ay-yah, some of them were not in good shape, thin like they didn't have enough to eat and weak. They were pretty scared, I'll tell yuh."

I went to take another swig of beer and discovered that I had emptied my glass.

Kelly leaned in close. "It was the dead bodies laying all about. They weren't normal."

"Because someone separated the heads from the bodies?"

"That wasn't the weird part. They had rotted faces, hands all withered, like them zombies yah see on the TV shows where dead people go walking. Yet they-yuh they were, and the witnesses said they'd been moving about."

I peered over at the men at the bar to make sure we weren't being overheard. "That must have been a problem."

"None of that ended up on the official reports, and they buried those bodies as quick as they could. Digger helped with that while your father was in the hospital."

"My father was in the hospital?" I asked.

"Don't really know all the ins and outs, only what I saw that night."

Something else I had to find out about. "So — why did you quit the force?"

"Cause those bodies, the ones who'd taken the folks captive? I'd heard stories of such creatures, but never expected to see them in real life. Y'see, the coroner said that some had been dead for months, best he could tell. And the witnesses said they had been... eatin' people."

# FOUR

I tossed and turned in my bed, unable to get Kelly's words out of my mind. I was taken back to my childhood, standing before the fire pit with my father, riveted by the story of those people kidnapped by a horde of the undead, destined to be offered as a sacrifice on a stone altar.

In *Night Of The Living Dead*, zombies attacked humans, and that film created a new genre of animated corpses depicted as brain-eating monsters.

My father made it very clear this was not the case. When someone reanimates corpses as zombies, they were mindless servants who operated like automatons. Creatures that were undead and ate human flesh — the movie's brain-eaters — were ghouls.

That was what Kelly had seen on that island. It was human sacrifice using a group of ghouls to keep the victims in line, and to feast upon the remains of those murdered.

Digger and my father had stopped them.

It was his last mission with Digger, and I was born the year after. In my personal tragedy, my mother did not survive my birth. Losing his wife left Poppa with no choice but to change his life.

I did not know where my father's money came from. Was it a government entity that was paying him for his silence? Or was there a secret benefactor who had given money to both my father and Digger to prevent something worse from happening in Portland? I had no answers, but I was determined to find out.

I awoke with a foggy head and the beginnings of a hangover. The combination of wine and beer I consumed the night before had been more than my limit.

I was thankful to Kelly, so I'd handed him a twenty when we left the bar. He said he was just happy to have encountered me, and that my father and Digger had thwarted those creatures.

I didn't explain to him about ghouls.

I showered, shaved, and dressed, and got my hearing aid off the charger where it spent the night. A grabbed egg sandwich was breakfast, and I drove off to make my appointment with Julia Scalia.

Through painstaking research, emails, and phone calls, I located one of the few remaining witnesses of the fateful night. It took me a while to get Julia to agree to a meeting. She'd become a shut-in. Only when I mentioned my father and the connection he had to Digger did she finally consent to talk to me.

I drove out to an area known as Sagamore Village in greater Portland, and the address she gave me led me to a small gray house on Taft Street. Parking the car on the street in front of her home, I approached and rapped on the door. There were several deadbolt locks, and I heard the loud clicks as each one was unlocked.

The door opened the length of a security chain. "Mrs. Scalia?"

"It's just Miss," she said from the shadows, and then the door closed, and I heard the chain come loose. The door opened to a woman in her late forties, solid but not heavy. Matronly would be the best description. She stood in the doorway in a formless maroon house dress covered with dark flowers, slippers on her feet, her greying hair tied back in a bun. She clasped her hands, and her knuckles were white with tension.

She gazed at me from head to foot, nodded and said, "You look a lot like your father. Except for the eyes. You got one blue one."

I smiled as best I could. "I know that, ma'am."

"Come in," she said and stepped aside to allow me to enter the dark house. She kept the curtains shut, allowing in minimal light. She led me past the dark living room into a corner table near the kitchen.

Next to the table stood a carpeted cat tree. At its top, almost at eye level with me, a black cat stared with an expression of disapproval and suspicion.

Miss Scalia pulled back a curtain concealing a large glass sliding door, allowing the light to banish the gloom. This did not please the cat, who dashed into the comfort of the dimly lit living room.

Julia poured herself a cup of coffee as I sat down and took out my notepad.

"You want coffee?" she asked, her voice barely audible. I reached up to adjust my hearing aid, ensuring I could hear her properly. I didn't want to rely solely on lip reading for this conversation.

"Yes, please. I take it black."

This made her grin. "Just like a real reporter, huh?"

I smiled. "Just like one, ma'am."

She put our cups on the table after she'd added a little cream to her own. "You hafta excuse me for the drapes and keepin' the house so dark and all. It's just that since that ... night... I don't like anyone looking in."

"You live alone?" I asked, pulling out my pen.

"Pretty much, just me and Whiskers." She took a sip of coffee and considered it. "It's kinda hard to have relationships after the kinda thing I went through."

"I appreciate you being willing to talk to me," I said.

She declared, "I'm only doing this because your dad and Digger saved my life. After the incident, I went to every place I could think of to share my story — newspapers, television stations — but no one believed me. They thought I was crazy, so a doctor prescribed me medication for my anxiety and depression — and now I'm on disability."

I nodded. "That must be tough."

She shrugged. "It ain't so bad. My mom left me this house, so I don't have a mortgage. I get by."

"About the incident..."

"Is that what you're calling it, the incident? I'd call it the apocalypse — everything I ever believed died that night."

"Please start from the beginning," I suggested.

She opened a cabinet to retrieve a pack of cigarettes and an ashtray. "You mind if I smoke? I don't think I can get through telling ya if I don't have a smoke."

"It won't bother me," I told her.

She slowly reached into the pocket of her housedress, taking out a lighter. Clicking it open, she lit the cigarette and took a deep drag; the smoke curling away from me.

She turned to gaze out the glass door as she spoke. I kept my eyes glued to her lips, not wanting to miss a single syllable.

"Back then, I was seventeen. I was something in those days, a trim figure, big boobs, and I was pretty popular." She sighed. "Well, isn't that what they say? Youth is wasted on the young."

I checked my notes from my research. "From what I found out, they abducted you after your car broke down on the side of the road. Am I right?"

She nodded and took another drag. The tip glowed red.

"Yes," she said with a nod. "I was driving back after visiting a boy I was seein' down in Scarborough. On my way home, the sky opens up and there's this downpour. My engine goes wonky, and I pulled into the parking lot of a warehouse there on Route Nine."

"When was this?"

"It was October eighteenth, about ten-thirty, maybe eleven at night."

"A van approached your car. Is that correct?"

She nodded. "This van pulls into the lot and blocks my little car from view of the highway, and you know, I'm young, cute, and brainless. I figure it must be someone who wanted to lend a hand."

"You didn't think it was suspicious that it blocked your car?"

"I told you, I was seventeen. Who thinks they're in danger at seventeen?"

That was true. When we're that young, we think we're invincible and that somehow God, fate or good luck will protect us from our own foolishness.

"This guy comes around and taps on my window. He wasn't scary at all. Like, thirty-five with a weird little beard and mustache. He was kinda cute, in an older guy way."

I checked my notes. "That was Alexander VanWry?"

"Yeah, but I didn't know it," she said, taking another drag on the cigarette, now getting close to burning her fingers. "Tell me, was he... like the others... y'know, dead?"

"From my research, we believe he was the one who animated the creatures you saw."

She considered this, shaking her head. "What was he? Like, a wizard or witch or something?"

"Or something. You got out of the car because VanWry said he would help you?"

She crushed out the nub of her cigarette in the ashtray. "Yeah, I get out of the car and he asks what went wrong. Next thing I know, a pair of arms grab me from behind, and I look down and the hands are decaying, with black fingernails, the fingertips all dark and the skin gray. I look over my shoulder and there's a guy

—" She paused for a moment to collect herself. "'Cept he wasn't a guy. His face had rotted, his cheeks had all collapsed, and his hair had become all wispy. But his teeth, his friggin' teeth, were all pointy and gleaming."

"What did you do?"

"I pulled in a big breath, because I'm about to scream my freakin' head off. But this VanWry guy, he sprays something sweet in my face, just as I suck in the breath, and I'm falling and everything is going black."

I made a careful notation on my pad. "Where did you wake up?"

"I was in the back of that van when I came to, and I heard someone sobbing, another girl, like me."

I looked at my notes again. "That was Katie Windell?"

"Yeah," she said, staring at her now-empty mug of coffee. "We got to be friends over the next twelve days." She looked at the smoldering cigarette butt in the ashtray. "She didn't make it."

I nodded solemnly. "And in the van, there were two of the... creatures?"

"Yeah," she said, as she pulled another cigarette from the pack and lit it. "They just sat there, and they... didn't look real. I mean, they were all dark and wrinkled, like guys wearing Halloween masks. But I could see it was their faces."

"How long were you in the van?"

"I don't know how long I was out. Finally, when we pulled over and stopped, the two dead guys get up like nothing happened, and they grab me and Katie, and pushed us out. We step outside to this friggin' castle, like this VanWry was Dracula or something. Turns out it was this abandoned amusement park, and this VanWry guy bought it or — I don't know — just moved in."

"That was where you saw the others?"

Her face grew pale, and she sucked on the cigarette to get her bearings. "Yeah. Some of them had been there for weeks. Their clothes were dirty, and they were really thin and stuff. There wasn't much food, and when we went to the toilet, one of those... things... went with us. And the rooms they held us in were all dark, because those guys couldn't go out in the daylight."

"That must have been scary."

"The scariest thing was, like, the look in the eyes of the others, the ones that had been there the longest. It was as if they'd already accepted the fact that they were going to die."

"They kept you there until the night of Halloween?" I said, wanting to keep her on track.

She nodded. "That's right. Like I said, there wasn't much food, and no showers or anything. One guy tried to fight back and those corpses, zombies, whatever you call them attacked him."

"What happened?"

"They smashed in his head with a pipe, killed him. Then the next day, he was back — as one of them."

"He was dead, but they... reanimated him?"

She nodded. The look in her eyes was chilling. "Yeah, and he had an opening in the side of his head where they'd cracked it open. You could see his brains poking out. He didn't talk, and he just did what he was told. It terrified Katie, I mean, that we could end up like that."

I looked at my notes again. "Halloween night, they put you and the others in a pair of vans."

"Yes, we were all huddled in together. There wasn't even room to sit down. We just kind of held each other up as the van drove down to — wherever we went."

I glanced at my research notes. "They drove you to Mackworth Island."

"Is that where the boats were?" She shrugged. "I don't know. It was dark. There were no lights except flashlights. We all got out of the vans and got into boats. I was there with Katie, and she was crying, like she knew we were going to our deaths."

I focused on her face. "What happened when you arrived at Fort Gorges?"

"We got off the boats, and I gotta tell you after all the weeks with those things… none of us resisted. We just did what we were told."

I frowned. "Even though you thought you were going to die?"

She nodded. "After twelve days with those monsters, living the way we did, in constant fear? I just… wanted it to end."

She put the stub of her cigarette in the ashtray and lit another.

"The creatures led you into the fort?"

"Yeah," she said, and blew out another stream of smoke. "They had all these little fires burning on the top of these metal holders — braziers or whatever they're called. They lit them in a big circle in the middle of the courtyard. That's when I saw the altar."

"The large rectangular stone in the middle of the courtyard?"

"Yeah, I can't imagine how they got it there. I mean, it was huge, wide enough to fit a big man. It was like someone just dropped it there with a helicopter or something, y'know?"

"And VanWry was there?" I asked.

She grimaced at the recollection. "He sure was, standing in front of that altar stone, dressed in black with this black hood covering his face." I could see the hate in her eyes as she went on. "He was all smug-looking and shit." She took another big drag from her cigarette and blew it out in disgust. "Then he makes this speech."

"Do you remember anything he said?"

"Not really. It was all a bunch of horseshit. Stuff like: tonight we release the ancient entity and our sacrifice serves a noble cause. You know, horseshit."

As she used VanWry's catch phrases, she wiggled her hands in front of her as if she were about to make a mystical incantation.

"Two of the dead guys grab Joe. Joe was a nice guy, always tried to keep our spirits up and stuff. They take him to the altar and lift him up and put him on top of it. A couple of people try to stop them, but the dead guys just slap them down. They rip open Joe's shirt, not like that was hard because he'd worn the same one for weeks and it was falling apart. Weird thing runs through my mind — I think, that's mean, 'cause it's chilly out here, and Joe might catch a cold."

I nodded and tried to reassure her. "It's not unusual to have odd insights during a stressful situation."

She looked at me, and I saw the anger in her eyes. "Oh yeah? Well, Ol' VanWry picks up this freakin' sword with a curved blade and he holds it up high — and plunges it right into Joe's chest."

She raised her hands, miming the horrifying action.

I sipped my coffee. It was cold.

She stared at her cigarette. "Joe screamed. Well, not for long. Everyone else screamed. Me too. Then VanWry pries open his freakin' chest and cuts his fuckin' heart out."

She pushed the cigarette out in the ashtray with such force the heavy marble tray jumped.

"But that wasn't the worse part," she said, her face drawn, and she looked much older, like a woman in her sixties or seventies.

I spoke quietly. "What was the worst part?"

"VanWry pushes the body onto the ground, and several of the dead guys rush forward, and tear him apart. They pull off his arms and his legs and they... they... ate him."

She swallowed several times, as if she might throw up.

I looked at the table. They were definitely ghouls, no doubt about that now. When my father told this story, it seemed all so unbelievable. Yet, here was this woman, an eyewitness, who was verifying the deadly tale.

She lit another cigarette. Sucking the smoke into her lungs, she seemed to recover a bit. "They killed another guy the same way. VanWry would plunge in the knife, pry open the rib cage and take the heart. The monsters, zombies, or whatever they were, would devour the remains each time. Then VanWry called for Katie."

"It must have terrified you."

"You have no idea. I mean, she'd become my best friend. The dead guys laid her out on that enormous stone, which now had blood all over it, and ripped off her blouse and her bra, and that made it worse, just exposing her like that. Like she wasn't human, just a thing."

"Was Katie killed on the altar?"

"No, that's when we all hear this voice, and everything stopped. It was a big, booming voice, like a guy who sang opera or something. He calls out: Gremory, this stops here and now! I look up and there's this guy standing up on the second level of the fort. I got no idea how he got there. He's got this bright light on him, like some kind of battery powered thing, but really bright. He's just this stocky guy with gray hair, a short beard, in jeans and a peacoat and holding a weird old book. Next to him is this good-looking black guy—" she paused and turned to face me. "It's okay that I call your old man good-looking, right?"

I smiled as best as I could. "It's fine."

"I hear Van Wry mutter, Digger, like he recognized the guy."

"What happened next?"

"Suddenly, the dead guys don't give a damn about any of us. They rush to climb up that stone outcrop thing—"

"A parapet?" I offered.

She shrugged. "Whatever. They're trying to get this Digger guy and your father. But your old man, he pulls out this handle thing."

"Handle thing?" I repeated.

"Yeah, it was all shiny, like gold or something. Well, the Digger guy reads something from that book, in his booming voice. I don't know what he was saying. It was, like, Latin or something, and a freakin' flame shoots out the top of the thing your father is holding."

I paused. I knew it well, and I even had seen it used.

"So, your dad, he jumps off the parapet like a goddamn superhero and starts swinging that flaming sword thing at the dead guys, and just slices their heads off."

I nodded. From the stories my father told me, that was the only method of killing a ghoul. Actually, it was a pretty useful technique to use on most of the undead.

"He's moving through the crowd, carving away with that sword. That fire blade took off anything it came in contact with: hands, legs, heads. And when those things died, there was, like, very little blood and what poured out was black, like oil."

"What did you do?"

"All of us were, like, backing away, because the dead guys are attacking your dad. So I go to Katie, and pull her off that freakin' altar. She's still surprised or in shock because she didn't move at all. So I help her up and say to her: 'Katie, we gotta run.'"

She lit another cigarette, her hand shaking.

"That's when that curved sword just punched out of her chest. VanWry came up behind her and shoved it right through her. He pulled the sword out of her because by this time your dad is fast approaching with that flaming sword, and VanWry needs to defend himself. Katie falls to the ground, blood pouring out of her chest and she just stares at me, her eyes wide, as if to ask, 'Why?'"

I nodded. I could tell this was a strain for her.

"Your dad is yelling: 'No!' as he comes near, and he lifts that flaming sword with his left hand. VanWry just swings that curved blade and in one move, cuts your father's hand clean off."

I sat back in my seat, fighting to not let shock come over my face. My father never told me this part. He'd always said he'd lost his hand in an accident. What other things had he kept from me?

"Your father's sword falls to the ground, and the flame goes out, and it's just this gold tube thing again. Your dad falls to his knees, screaming and holding the stub of his arm with blood spurting everywhere. VanWry steps back and lifts his sword like he's going to kill your dad."

I met her eyes. "What happened?"

She smiled slightly. "I grabbed his leg, and — bit him."

I stared at her. "You did what?"

She sat back in the chair, proud of herself. "I bit his damn leg!"

I smiled. "That's amazing."

"Damn straight."

"You're lucky he didn't slice you with the sword."

"I think he would have, but he just hit me with his free hand, and I let go. By then, that Digger guy was standing right next to me. He picked up the gold tube and the fire blade was back. He used it against VanWry's sword, and the two of them battled over us as I sat there with Katie. I thought he might not win, because Van Wry swung that blade, all ninja-like and stuff. But Digger backs up, flips the sword right out of VanWry's hand, and plunged that fire blade right into his chest."

I nodded, spellbound by her tale.

"VanWry screams and his body, like, all of it just bursts into flame, right there a few feet from me. Digger pushes him back and VanWry just burns away into nothing, screaming the entire time. He turns around and his sword thing is still on fire. He runs to your dad and tells him he needs to stop the bleeding from his... where his hand used to be. Your dad, he's in a lot of pain and he just nods his head. Digger grabs his left arm and puts the flaming sword to it as your dad screams and screams. I looked away, and when I looked down at Katie, she was dead."

We both sat there in silence for a moment.

"It's a miracle you survived," I finally said.

"There's one thing I never told the police, and looking back, I'm not even sure it actually happened."

"What is it?"

She shook her head. "When I looked up, right after Katie died, that Digger guy was busy with your father and all that. But in the distance, I saw this weird lady all dressed in white."

This got my attention. The waiter mentioned the young men following a woman on the island. Had it been around the same time? Could it have something to do with what happened?

"Why was she weird?" I asked.

"She was weird because she was standing up off the ground, on one of those outcrop things. I could swear she wasn't there before. I looked over at Digger helping your dad, and when I looked again, she was gone."

I nodded, trying to get my head around this additional bit of data.

"After that, the police arrived," she said and sucked at her cigarette, taking it down to the nub. "I told the police my story, everything I saw, and what happened to me. They didn't believe me."

I sat up. "What about the headless corpses and everything?"

"They covered all of that up," she said, lighting yet another cigarette. "Once they got me off the island, they had a psychiatrist tell me they'd drugged me and I was seein' things." Her jaw grew tight. "But I know what I saw."

She looked out the glass door at her small backyard. "I just wish I could forget that I saw it."

# FIVE

I was soon back on the road again, this time heading south. Everything Julia Scalia said correlated with my dad's account and my research — except for how he lost his left hand and the mysterious woman in white.

It explained why he'd stopped working with Digger. It filled me with curiosity, wondering why he'd neglected to tell me this part.

Those events, so early in Julia's life, meant she'd spent the last twenty-odd years unable to get close to anyone. After all, to whom could you tell such things?

What was the true identity of the mysterious woman in white? Was she a creature of the night or something else entirely?

My research on the published accounts told me that the total number of prisoners was twenty-six. Through my investigation, I found that twenty-six was 'the number of God.' The Hebrew letters that form the word for God, YHVH, which are also numbers, add up to twenty-six.

This VanWry guy was trying to increase his power through human sacrifice. Or was he attempting to release some demonic entity?

Out of the twenty-three survivors, only twelve remained, as the years have taken their toll and several have taken their own lives. Julia Scalia was the only one who would share her story with me.

I couldn't help but ponder what the consequences would have been if Digger and Poppa hadn't put a stop to VanWry's plans. My curiosity was further piqued by the mysterious flaming sword that found its way into my possession. Where did my father get it from?

Digger had a mysterious book, what secrets did it hold? Was it brimming with ancient spells and knowledge? Would it provide the answers on how to battle these creatures?

After the events of that Halloween in Portland, my father left Digger and more than a year later, moved to New Jersey with me to live a quiet, and sometimes haunted life. He did so with a great deal of money. Had he earned it during his time with Digger?

I still didn't have a name or a place to look, and I couldn't help but wonder where Digger was now. He had to be pretty old — he might even be dead. There was no guarantee that the gravedigger I saw at my father's funeral was him.

I was now even more determined to locate him.

After a long drive, I arrived in Duivelsmeer, New York after dark. The town proudly resided between Manhattan and Albany on the Hudson River and called itself the "Queen City of the

Hudson Valley." It derives its name from the Dutch word for a small lake with the fanciful title of 'Devil's Lake.'

Willem van Tienhoven, a local official, tragically took his own life in the lake in the seventeenth century. This was when tensions between the Wappinger tribe and the colonists had become unbearable during his time of leading the colony. Personally, I believe it was his own shortcomings that caused his suicide rather than any demonic influence.

When the English colonized the area, they kept the name, and the city flourished over the years. It went through an economic collapse at the end of the twentieth century, when factories and businesses moved out. But the town was now in a time of revival.

I made my way to the house I was staying at in the historic district. It was a grand Victorian house, with a tower that had its own distinct entrance. I found the lockbox and in moments I was carrying my luggage and laptop bag upstairs.

When I stepped inside my room, the spectacular view of the town from the rounded room amazed me. The bedroom was in the tower room, and there was an accompanying small kitchen and bathroom with a shower. Although it was a suitable space, I was concerned that there was only one stairway leading in or out.

After dropping off my suitcase in the room, I grabbed my laptop and set out. Over dinner, I wanted to transcribe my notes from Julia Scalia while they were still fresh in my memory.

As I walked to the Duivelsmeer Tavern, I couldn't help but feel a sense of anticipation.

I stopped on my journey to observe a once-grand Victorian domicile. The impressive front porch and curved outcropping on the second floor were now reduced to a mere shell, charred and destroyed by fire.

Reports from the local area suggest that the owner of this property was a member of the Church of Satan that had a local branch in the area. My research into the group revealed that most of them were relatively harmless. They were typically middle-class individuals who enjoyed the thrill of being seen as daring and rebellious. Some of them even practiced witchcraft and dabbled in spell casting and creating potions. In fact, a pair of them even opened a store to sell their special remedies and powders to tourists and customers online.

The locals called it 'The Halloween House,' but there was something sinister lurking beneath its exterior. No one would have known of the horrors that occurred within had it not been for the fire that exposed the owner's hidden, malevolent intent. Thomas Neill was not what anyone had expected him to be.

Someone set the house afire a mere six months earlier. I investigated because the home security system took a video of a man resembling Digger in the area on the night of the fire.

I intended to speak to Charlie Gillfeld, who knew the late proprietor very well. Police interrogated him after the discoveries found within the burned house. I decided he might give me a lead to Digger's true name and whereabouts.

I continued on my way, in the mood for a good meal and a couple of beers at the Duivelsmeer Tavern. I was fortunate enough to get a table right away.

I sat down with my laptop and started typing away as I drank my beer. I'm a fast typist, and already filled up several pages by the time the server arrived with my dinner. He was a young, lanky white man in his mid-twenties.

I asked him, "Do you know anything about the Halloween House fire?"

His eyes got very wide. "What are you, a reporter?"

I shrugged. "Just doing some research."

He leaned close and murmured. "Look, those people in that so-called church? They're really weird. Since the fire, there's been a whole movement to get them out of town."

I lowered my voice and looked around to make sure no one else was listening. "You mean, the people from the Church of Sat—"

He put his raised index finger to his mouth. "Really, best not to get involved."

"Thank you," I said, and let him get back to serving the other tables.

I sipped my beer and pondered his words. Fear still lingered in the air months after the traumatic event. Now the townsfolk were trying to drive out the Satanists? That was some serious stuff.

I'd done research on the Church of Satan, and it had a colorful history. Founded by Anton LaVey in 1966, he had led it until his death in 1997. Rather than revolve around a belief in a higher power, LaVey's faith system was atheistic because he felt the universe was indifferent. LaVey criticized other belief systems such as Christianity, giving the Church of Satan a secularist world-view. Despite its intriguing past, however, there had been no reports of murder associated with the Church.

This was all pretty white-bread, and a stark contrast to the tales my father spun about the undead and those who allowed them to come back to life.

And Digger. Every story Poppa told featured Digger.

From what my father said, Digger was part superman and part genius, with a vast amount of knowledge of the undead. However, after hearing Julia Scalia's story, I had to admit that my father was a pretty amazing guy himself.

I polished off my beer, settled my tab, and then made my way back to the residence where I was staying.

I shuddered as I walked past the scorched remains of the building. The gaping windows seemed to stare at me, like a silent warning of the devastation that took place. If the flames engulfed the entire block, it would have been impossible to uncover the dark secrets hidden within its walls.

My breath catching in my throat, I cautiously peered into the shadows of the house. I thought I saw a flutter of white fabric, as if someone moved within. I stood still, my heart pounding in my chest, but the figure was gone. Had I imagined it? I stepped closer to the picket fence, desperately searching for a sign, but dreading what I might find.

I heard no sound and as the breeze wafted by me; I was certain it was an illusion of the dark and the wind.

I nervously made my way back to my room, plugging my hearing aid into its charger. As I lay in my bed, the silence of the room was almost overpowering, as my thoughts turned to the looming interview in the morning.

I stood in the middle of Fort Gorges' expansive courtyard, braziers burning brightly all around me. Grief-stricken people huddled in small groups, some sobbing, while others stood or sat in silence.

A thick layer of blood coated the enormous altar stone, dripping down its sides and pooling onto the ground. Ghouls lurked nearby, snarling and smacking their lips as they feasted on the remains of the most recent victim.

I turned away, my stomach roiling.

VanWry stood at the altar, gripping the curved Persian sword in his hands. The blade was slick with blood, and a single ruby droplet fell to the ground with a soft plop. I watched in awe as it trickled down the blade.

VanWry stood dressed in black robes with magical symbols embroidered across them, and the hood pulled up to his forehead. He raised his hand and pointed toward the two young women. A much younger Julia Scalia, clinging tightly to her best friend, Katie Windell.

I moved forward, and I looked at my hands. Instead of my well-cut nails and caramel skin, the nails were dirty and the ends of my fingers were black.

I was one of the ghouls, a creature of the dark.

I walked next to another of my kind, whose face was puffy and distorted, and the pair of us seized Katie and tugged her away as Julia shouted, "No!"

We easily lifted her onto the stone and quickly ripped off her blouse and bra, which were filthy from her captivity. I felt powerful as we stripped her.

I clasped her tightly, my bloodied hand smearing crimson onto her porcelain skin. I leaned in close, my breath hot on her neck as I grazed my teeth over the throbbing vein. The smell of fear and blood filled my nose. I grabbed her head and yanked it back. She looked terrified, and I was ready to start my feast.

"Gremory, this stops now!"

I glanced up to find Digger perched atop the wall, my father appearing youthful and handsome alongside him.

Digger opened the large book, its pages illuminated by the moonlight like a magical charm. His powerful voice filled the air with unintelligible words, making me wince in pain as I stepped away from the woman on the altar. Suddenly, a flash of light erupted from the sword hilt in my father's hand. With a mighty leap, he came toward us, the blade ablaze.

He swung the fiery blade through the air, slicing through the ghouls that guarded their master. I looked back at the young woman lying on the altar; her pale skin illuminated in the moonlight. I felt a strong pang of hunger, a deep and primal urge to take a bite out of her.

My father moved through the crowd with the swiftness of a farmer harvesting wheat with a sickle. He wielded an incredible strength and power as he cut down his enemies with ease. His movements were graceful and precise like a dancer, and with the deadly skill of a ninja. I watched in awe, until I realized he was coming for me, a ghoul, ready to sever my head with the same ferocity as the others.

VanWry's blade glinted in the torchlight as he brought it up. My father's hand fell, and the weapon tumbled to the ground, extinguished.

I glanced over my shoulder just in time to see Julia assisting the young girl to her feet. My hunger was unrelenting, and I felt a desperate need to bite into living tissue.

I crouched down and picked up the severed hand, feeling its warm blood trickling down my arm as I ran from the scene. Unable to resist temptation's pull, as I ran, I brought the hand to my lips and plunged my teeth deep into the warm flesh.

I woke up with a jolt, my stomach heaving as I rushed to the bathroom. I retched violently, purging the contents of last night's meal.

I took a deep breath and splashed my face with cold water, attempting to quell the trembling in my body and compose myself.

I wasn't sure if I experienced a dream or a vision, but whatever it was, it explained why they couldn't reattach my father's lost hand. It wasn't a lack of skill from the doctor or a delay in getting to the hospital.

It was because the hand ended up in the gullet of an undead monstrosity.

At ten the following morning, I drove to a retail shop located in the area known as the 'Witchcraft District'. Initially, signage advertising this district was erected as a joke, with other parts of the city marked as 'historic districts'. However, the 'Witchcraft District' signs remained, as the local government believed it could be an interesting tourist attraction.

I pulled up to a store named *Awakened Spirit* and parked my car.

I had done my due diligence before visiting the shop, and I knew they offered a variety of services, from potions and crystals to aura-raising classes. What they didn't advertise was that the owners were founding members of the local Church of Satan.

Charlie Gillfeld and his wife managed the store, specializing in crystals and items associated with Satanism and the occult.

Facing the street were two picture windows, and a purple awning welcomed me to the store. I peered inside to discover an array of incense, ranging from brimstone to 'Love Spell Blend'. Boxes of rituals promised to balance my chakras and clear my energy. I was certain they were doing a booming business with tourists.

As I stepped inside, the beautiful aromas of oils and herbs immediately enveloped me as a small bell tinkled. I wandered through the shop, and passed tables displaying 'Affirmation Candles' and books, including titles such as Find Your Angel and Palmistry for Beginners. At the desk, a surly young blonde woman with tattoos covering both arms and multiple piercings on her face nodded at me.

I couldn't help but wonder what other parts she'd pierced.

"Good morning," I said. "I'm here to see Mr. Gillfeld."

She stared at me icily, as if my being there was the last thing she wanted. She muttered, "I'll get him."

Charlie Gillfeld stepped from the deep purple curtain and emerged into the light. He was an average height man, with a bit of a round belly and long, brown, braided hair and beard. He wore a black T-shirt emblazoned with an inverted five-pointed star and a goat face in the center — the Sigil of Baphomet, a renowned demon, and the emblem of choice for many adherents of the Church of Satan.

"Mr. Bennet?" he asked.

"Yes, Mr. Gillfeld. Thanks for meeting with me."

"I'm just glad we have someone interested in our story all the way from Philadelphia."

I shrugged. "Well, it is unusual, as is everything I've found about Thomas Neill since the fire."

He led me to a small private office.

"Now," he said as we walked, "you won't record me, right?"

"No, I just take notes."

"Good. Recording machines steal a part of your soul if you're not careful."

I nodded in agreement as he settled behind his desk and motioned for me to take a seat. I pulled out my notebook and pen from my pocket and asked, "Shall we start by discussing your background?"

"Sure," he said good-naturedly. "Just as long as you keep an open mind."

"Of course. You are the high priest of the Church of Satan, which you clearly affirmed is not based on devil worship."

He grinned. "Exactly. Satanism emphasizes the importance of individuality, autonomy, self-expression, and accomplishment. If you encountered a Satanist, you likely wouldn't be able to tell right away. You may observe that they're creative, smart, and maybe odd. But it's not a religion, it's a set of beliefs that helps one get the most out of life."

"However, you appear to enjoy dressing in black and wearing the Sigil of Baphomet."

He looked down at the logo on his tee-shirt. "It's cool that you recognize it. It's the Church's symbol, to let others know we are part of the group. Many people who see it just think it's a rock band they never heard of."

"Now you and your wife—"

"Yeah, Isis."

"Isis," I repeated. "You moved up here from Manhattan's Hell's Kitchen. I have to say it's interesting that you moved from Hell's Kitchen to Devil's Lake?"

"Isis and I had been involved with the Church for some time when we moved to Devil's Lake. It attracted us because of the low cost of housing in the city, despite its run-down condition. We found the name of the town particularly fitting. We purchased our house over a decade ago and the neighborhood has only improved since then."

I jotted things into my notebook, then with a deep sigh, I said, "Now to Thomas Neill and the Halloween House."

He became serious. "Yeah, you gotta understand. We thought we all knew Tommy real well — everyone thought he was a great guy."

"He was a member of the church, am I right?"

"Yes, but what happened does not reflect on the rest of us."

"I'm here to listen."

"That's good. some reporters want to lump us all in with... the stuff he did."

"If I'm following the story correctly, Neill moved up here twenty years ago?"

Charlie nodded. "The house had been a rooming house and was a real mess. The neighborhood wasn't very good when he bought the place. He'd have to use a screw gun to seal the door at night so that people wouldn't break in and rob him. He fixed it up in his own kind of aesthetic."

"What does that mean?"

"Tommy was an avid admirer of Halloween and took it to the extreme. You could find him crafting elaborate pumpkin figures in the yard. Some were jack-o'-lanterns made from twisted branches with fishhooks in place of a mouth. It was a creepy, yet wondrous sight."

"And Mr. Neill was a member of the Church with you?"

"Yeah, in fact, we held services in his living room until more of us moved up and we actually put the money together to get a building to hold services."

"Regarding the case, Devil's Lake had a reputation for missing transients over the last few years."

"Yeah, but we thought nothing of it. I mean, Tommy was doing stuff for homeless shelters in nearby towns. We thought it was a great idea, because it showed that the Church of Satan served the community as much as any other organization."

"Then, nine months ago, there was the murder of the homeless man near the lake."

"That was when the police started asking questions about homeless people that had disappeared."

"Now, I'm going to ask you something strange—"

"It's okay, I'm into strange," Charlie smiled at his own witticism.

I wanted to say, "I can see that," but I restrained myself. "A gravedigger came to Duivelsmeer to bury the homeless guy. Is that correct?"

He nodded. "Yeah, that was strange. I mean, this guy shows up in a big ol' truck and offers to bury the murder victim for free. Even stranger, people went to watch him dig the grave."

This surprised me. "Why?"

"Because of how he did it. He laid out this wooden form, the right length and width and all. Then, he used a pick-like thing with a flat blade—"

"A mattock?" I asked.

"What's that?"

"It's like a pickaxe, but the blades are flat in two different directions. I've had people tell me it's what a gravedigger uses to cut the sod."

"Seems like you know more about this than I do," Gillfeld replied with a shrug. "So they watched him do it, and damn, he had a grave dug in two hours. It amazed people that an old guy could do it that fast."

"Did you see the gravedigger after the burial?"

Charlie frowned in concentration. "He stayed in town for a few days, I think. Stayed at the Holiday Inn or something."

"And he left the day after the Halloween house burned down?"

He met my eyes. "Do you think he did it?"

"I'm more interested in what you think."

He leaned back in his chair. "We have a video of a guy all dressed up in a hazmat suit, who goes and pours two huge jugs of gasoline on the porch. I mean, the guy intentionally put gasoline at the front door and then went around and put gasoline at the back door and lit them both on fire. At first, we thought it was a hate crime, because Tommy was gay and active in the LGBTQ community. We all thought he died in that fire."

I jotted some notes on my pad. "During the cleanup, they went inside and found the bodies."

"It was part of the investigation. I mean, everyone knew Tommy was inside when the house burned. But then they found one body, and then another, and another. A lot of them had been, like, wrapped in plastic which had melted, and hid in walls and stuff. It wasn't until the medical guy looked at the remains and found out many of them had been dead for months, and even years."

"You had been in Neill's house. Did you detect any unpleasant smells or anything?"

Charlie shook his head. "No. I mean, he usually had incense burning and had a little altar all set up and stuff."

I went through my notes for a minute. "He had an altar that was dedicated to the demon Gremory? I mean, there was the demon's sigil on the altar and all?"

"I thought Tommy did the altar just to bust on people. Y'know, since he was a Satanist, he had to have an altar dedicated to some demon. I thought it was a gag."

"And then the police found the cell in the basement?"

Charlie grew quite serious. "Yeah, and that's where they found Tommy. Turns out he was dead before the fire started."

"And someone had... beheaded him?"

"The police didn't want people to know that, but that's what I heard." He shook his head. "Like right out of a horror movie, y'know?"

"How has it been for you and the other church members since this was all revealed?"

"Bad. I mean, the police started looking at everyone in the group like we knew what he did to those homeless guys, and took part in it. They got warrants to go through our homes and stuff."

"But you came through with flying colors?"

"Isis and I have achieved something incredible," he said, indignant. "We bought a dilapidated crack house and restored it and also built a business. But some people couldn't take it. Juniper Laurel was a gifted fashion designer and renowned drag artist, who had been in adult films. He had a large following on social media, but the police constantly harassed him. He finally left town because he couldn't take the pressure, and he felt like he wasn't safe anymore."

"I'm sorry to hear that. Did you lose business because of the investigation?"

"Some, but we do a lot online, because Isis and I custom blend all the stuff. You know, it's unique. We even sell it on Amazon."

"Do the police have any information on the arsonist?"

"They continue to claim it's still an active investigation, but I call it nonsense." He stopped briefly. "Could it be that gravedigger? It's peculiar. He arrives, performs a free burial, lingers for a week, and leaves when a fire takes out the property. Come on, that's highly suspicious."

# SIX

I cruised around Duivelsmeer that afternoon, struggling to comprehend the events that had taken place in the town. Had Digger been here? Was he the one who killed Neill and then set his house ablaze? This totally transformed my opinion of Digger as a force for good. It seemed more sensible to rip down a wall, uncover a corpse, and alert the authorities than to murder the man and burn the house — yet he seemed to have done so. And what about the altar to the demon, Gremory? That was the name Digger yelled at VanWry in Portland. What was the connection?

Driving out to Devil's Lake, I found the dirt roadway that led to it had been closed off by a chain-link fence. I recalled they did this due to numerous suicides over the years. Hoping to get a glimpse of the lake; I stepped out of my car. The sky was dark and dreary, like the onset of twilight, and it gave me the creeps as I made my way to the barrier.

Regardless of the fence that surrounded it, I found a large broken gate I could walk through with ease. Despite signs posted on trees claiming the police monitored the land and warning it was dangerous, I persisted.

In my research, I had seen a photo taken in the early 1900s. The image depicted a cluster of Victorian-clad figures standing in front of a magnificent, untouched lake. The beauty of the landscape was truly captivating.

This lake was a far cry from the vibrant spot it had once been. The murky water swallowed the light, the trees and shoreline cloaked in a darkness that seemed alive. The low whine of mosquitoes replaced the cheerful sound of birds, as if their song contained the sorrow of the dead. Even the sky was aware of the despair emanating from the lake, with heavy clouds obscuring the sun.

I was eager to get back to my car.

As I cautiously returned through the broken fence, I noticed a City of Duivelsmeer police car parked next to my Chevy Trax. Two officers were standing outside, examining the interior of my car through the windows.

As I approached, the male cop looked up at me. "This your car?"

"Yes, sir," I said as I approached, making sure my hands were out of my pockets and empty. The last thing I needed was to make a cop nervous. "I just went to see the lake."

The other cop was a tall, red-haired woman with a no-nonsense attitude. She wore sunglasses, which I found odd on such a murky day. "Didn't you see the signs? You're not supposed to enter the cordoned off area."

I stole a quick glance at the opening in the fence behind me, but I thought it best not to push my luck with a local police officer.

"Sorry, I'm a reporter working on a story about the town. If you'll allow me to reach into my pocket, I have my ID from the Philadelphia Examiner."

The woman folded her arms. "Okay, let's see it."

Her partner's hand hovered near the weapon at his hip, while I slowly withdrew my billfold containing my ID card from the newspaper and offered it to the woman.

The man relaxed and stepped closer to look over her shoulder as she opened it.

"Reporter, huh?" the man said, his jaw set. "We noticed you were talking to those freaks this morning."

"Excuse me?" I frowned. "Have you been following me?" I fought to keep the edge off my voice.

"A stranger comes into town, starts asking questions—" the woman said and shrugged. "We've been watching you."

"Yeah, we pay attention," the man finished.

"Mr. Bennet," she said, checking my name on the ID. "Can I please see your driver's license?"

Once again, I reached slowly into my pocket and pulled out my wallet.

"This license is from New Jersey," the male cop pointed out.

"Yes, that's my family's home address. The life of a reporter means a lot of moving around."

I was not pleased to be interrogated, and it infuriated me to discover that someone was tracking my movements. Even more disconcerting was that I hadn't noticed I was being tailed.

I would have to pay better attention.

"We're concerned about whatever story you might write," the lady cop said. "The last thing we need here is more bad publicity."

I exhaled heavily. "I understand. A serial killer was in your town, killing homeless people. That's not what you want all over the headlines."

"It's already been in headlines," the male cop grunted. "And every goddamn reporter tries to make the Police Department look like a bunch of incompetents."

"Officer, that is not my goal. I am actually trying to track down a man who was in town at the same time the house burned down. A gravedigger."

The male cop frowned. "You mean Mr. Hill? What does he have to do with this?"

"You know him?" I asked.

"He came by the day he arrived in town and gave us copies of his liability insurance and certification. I was working the front desk. Why are you interested in that guy?"

"I'm interested in everything about that case, officer," I said, trying to lie convincingly. "Again, I don't want to make the town look bad, and I especially don't want the police to look bad. I'm just trying to understand all I can, and I think that gravedigger might have some insights."

The man shook his head, but the woman took off her glasses, revealing a pair of stunning gray eyes. "If we get you the guy's address off his certificate, you'll leave?"

This was a tremendous breakthrough. I finally would have Digger's full name, and even better, I would get an address where I might find him. That had been my objective all along.

"I would, sure." I shrugged.

"Okay, but here's the deal," the male cop said. "No more trespassing where you don't belong, and no more interviews with the devil worshippers."

I resisted the urge to snap back at the cop, even though I was unhappy with them giving me orders and dictating to whom I could speak. I had already spoken to the person I intended to interview, and my curiosity about Devil's Lake was just a passing fancy. The female officer had the address for Digger, so I stayed quiet to get what I had come for — just like Poppa used to say, "There's no use making a fuss when you're getting what you want."

I met the officer's eyes. "Agreed."

The female officer offered an apology as she returned her sunglasses to her face. "I know it's not ideal, having to monitor you, but we have to make sure our town's not ruined because of this."

"Protect and serve," I said. "I get it. By the way, Charlie Gillfeld and his wife aren't any threat. I think they honestly didn't know what Neill was doing."

"Well, we're still not sure of that," the male officer replied. "I mean, the Church of Satan? And the guy had an altar in his house?"

The woman officer smirked. "I think he's more interested in selling his oils and candles than working for the Lord of the Undead."

I couldn't help but smile at this. "I have to agree."

"I'll find that address," the woman said. "You're staying at Rudy's place on Washington Street?"

"Yes," I said, surprised that they even knew the location of my lodging.

After being given back my driver's license and newspaper ID, I drove back into the heart of the city. I spent the rest of the day typing up my notes and studying all the information I had about Digger.

I was deeply unsettled by the possibility that Digger had burned down the house and beheaded the person inside. Though, how else could the police have learned of the multiple bodies in the walls and a prison in the basement?

I also wondered about the altar built to Gremory.

In Portland, VanWry had summoned an army of ghouls. But why ghouls — whose insatiable hunger for human flesh makes them difficult to control — instead of zombies? What dark forces were at work?

Digger had been a part of my life for years — stories of his heroism always came back to me. Six months ago, there was an actual sighting of him, as well as the fact that he may have been at Poppa's funeral.

As I typed, I tried to get my head around all of it.

An hour later, the male police officer knocked on the door downstairs. When I answered it, he handed me a photocopy of Digger's official license from the State of New York.

"I thought the woman would drop it off," I said.

"Anastasia? She was only helping me out a little today. It's actually her day off. She usually works overnights. Now you said you're gonna leave tomorrow?"

"Yes, in the morning."

"All right then," he said as he turned and walked away.

I read the certificate in my hands — Everett Hill.

I had a name.

I hoped it was the one he used.

Researching the listed address online, I soon discovered it to be the location of the Cemetery of the Blessed Sacrament in Airmont, New York — a Catholic burial ground.

I pondered the possibilities. Could Digger be part of the cemetery staff? It seemed plausible. He would have the perfect cover as a groundskeeper and gravedigger, and with the assistance of the Church, he would have access to information about a variety of cases that required his special talents.

I uncovered an interesting detail while exploring the map of Airmont, New York — the town was home to a Jewish cemetery, a Lutheran cemetery and the Catholic one. With the three in the area, Digger would have a very reliable source of income. Considering the speed with which Digger worked, he could keep quite busy indeed.

Online, I learned the cemetery was only an hour away. I looked up how to get there and saved the information to my phone.

I was on high alert after my altercation with the police earlier, carefully keeping my eyes peeled in case I was being followed as I made my way to dinner.

I drove to the far side of town and ate at a place called the Atlas Brewing Company.

I fixed my gaze around the room, regularly scanning for anyone I'd encountered earlier. As I glanced around, a woman approached my table. Her voluminous red tresses cascaded down her shoulders, and her elegant black dress hugged her curves.

"Mind if I join you?" she asked.

The distinct shade of grey eyes revealed her to be the cop from our encounter earlier that day.

"Please do," I said, standing to help with her chair.

"A gentlemen," she said with a smile. "Don't see many of those anymore."

"I try," I said as I settled back into my seat. "You certainly look different from this afternoon."

"You recognize me?"

"Your eyes are a very unique color."

"And yours are two different colors, which got my attention." She raised a finger as the server came by. "I'll have an After Dark," she told him. "I wanted to apologize for today, and I'm off duty now. I'm Anastasia."

"Josh. Reporters run into that sort of thing. I understand how an incident like this can become fodder for the press and a pain in the ass for the police."

The server arrived and presented Anastasia with a dark beer, complete with a foamy top.

"The press swept in and made it a big deal about the failures of the police. After that, they suggested the Police Chief and the Mayor should resign, and blah, blah, blah," she said and then sighed. "Once they got every drop of blood, they could from the story, they ran off, leaving a trail of damaged lives in their wake."

I nodded sympathetically. "I understand. That isn't my purpose at all."

"No, you're just looking for that gravedigger," she said and took a sip of her Porter. "Why?"

I shrugged. "He's turned up at several places I've been researching, so I figured it wouldn't hurt to talk with him."

My food arrived, and I asked Anastasia if she'd like anything.

"No, I'll eat later," she said with a smile. "That isn't really what I'm in the mood for."

"What are you in the mood for?"

She gazed at me, leaned forward, and said in a sultry voice, "I have a few things in mind."

I felt butterflies flap about in my stomach. Or was the tingle a bit lower? "You're sure your boyfriend won't mind?"

She chuckled. "What, the cop I was with this afternoon? We just work together. I have no boyfriend in this town. After all, I'm a cop and the locals find me intimidating." She glanced around the room. "To be blunt, no guy in this town has the balls to even approach me."

"I'm surprised."

This made her smile. "Oh, I get my fun where I can."

The server took my plate away, and I suggested getting another round of beers. She agreed and smiled knowingly. She glanced around the room to make sure no one was within earshot before leaning in. "You're staying at Rudy's place? The one with the tower room and the separate entrance?"

"Yes."

"Then let's finish our beers. You go back to Rudy's and leave the door unlocked. I'll come by and show you what I'm like when I really let my hair down. How does that sound?"

"It… um… sounds nice," I stammered.

"Good, you leave first, and I'll be behind you in five minutes."

I finished my beer and paid the bill, then hurried to my car. When I arrived at the Air BNB, I double-checked the door was open and dashed up the stairs. I tucked away my laptop and notes and hurried to make the bed.

Draping a small towel over the lamp, it faded the light to make the room dark enough to add a more intimate atmosphere for two people getting to know each other.

I settled into the armchair, anticipation coursing through me. After a few minutes, I heard the door down the stairs creak and soft footfalls as she came up the stairs.

I couldn't help feeling anxious. After all, I'm not exactly smooth interacting with women, and it had been a while since I had been with someone. My father's passing and my focus on finding Digger had sapped my libido.

But now, my desires were returning with newfound strength.

I left the door at the top of the stairs ajar, yet she still knocked.

"Come in," I croaked, annoyed that my voice broke like a kid.

Anastasia entered the room with a grin, barefoot and leaving her shoes by the door.

I stood up as she approached, and without a word, she kissed me. The taste of her was a combination of beer and woman, but there was also something else that I couldn't quite pinpoint, a flavor I was unfamiliar with.

"Oh yeah, I definitely want something dark," she said. She pulled her dress off over her head in one swift motion.

This was a woman who wasn't afraid to make her intentions clear.

Her body was firm and warm against mine. We were both barely dressed, and I felt the heat radiating off her skin. I discarded my shirt on the floor and pressed my lips against hers as we moved toward the bed. I felt her strength as she guided us there, and I was powerless to resist.

She pushed me down onto the bed and unclasped her bra, freeing her breasts. She grabbed my hands and pressed them against her chest. "Squeeze hard. I want it hard."

She straddled me and moved against me, making soft noises of pleasure as her lips met mine once more.

There was that peculiar flavor again. It was stale... and unpleasant... like a decaying tooth.

She moved away, lifting her hands to rest on top of mine, and the pressure I had been applying to her breasts ceased. "Is something wrong?" she asked.

"Your mouth has a funny taste," I said, groaning as she rubbed her pelvis against me again.

"Fine," she panted. "Then we won't kiss."

Her fingers went to my belt, and she tugged at it. Meanwhile, my palms were still resting on her breasts.

"Hard," she demanded through gritted teeth. "Squeeze them hard."

Most of my lovemaking technique was gentle, but I complied since she asked for it. It delighted her when I gripped her firmly, and her pleasure increased as she loosened my pants.

"That's it," she encouraged. She extracted herself from my grip, stood and removed my shoes. With a swift tug, she pulled my pants off my legs.

Then, with nothing more than our underwear separating us, she climbed on top of me again, and fastened my hands to her breasts. I kneaded and pinched as hard as I could, and she gasped and squealed. She rhythmically thrust her hips against me faster and faster.

She pulled my hands from her breasts and held them over my head with astounding strength. She raised her face — and I froze.

Her eyes were glowing.

They were no longer a soft grey, but shone with a bright, unholy purple hue.

The fear that filled me was overwhelming. It rooted me to the spot, unable to move, unable to think. She seemed to size me up, and I was certain that whatever she had planned, it would not be good.

My fears became realized as her tongue snaked out of her mouth, extending to almost a foot in length and forked. She leaned forward, and I recoiled as I felt the wet, slimy trail of her tongue run up my chest.

Suddenly, I had no desire for this woman — or whatever she was — at all. I remembered my self-defense training, but I was powerless, lying on the bed with her firm grip pinning my hands above my head and her body pressing down on me.

I did not know what to do.

I shivered in the darkness, the only light coming from the street outside. My forehead was slick with sweat and my heart thudded so loudly I was sure she could hear it. Towering above me, her face was almost indistinguishable in the dark, until my gaze fell on her piercing purple eyes. As they locked onto mine, I thought those eyes would be the last thing I ever saw.

"Get off him, monster," a voice thundered from the doorway.

The stimulating movement stopped, and her tongue snapped back to its place in her mouth. Her eyes, illuminated by that deep purple light, shifted to the door.

At the open door was a heavyset man with a broad frame. He had white hair pulled back in a tight ponytail, and a full beard cropped close to his face, which was weathered and lined with age. He wore what looked like a pair of suspenders connected to a thick belt with leather pockets on it, and he held up an unusual cross in his right hand.

Anastasia's expression darkened with fury. The woman who had sparkled with beauty during my meal was now a horrifying hag in her rage.

"Nekrotháftis," she spat.

"Digger?" I murmured, astounded that the very person I had been looking for was now right in front of me.

"I knew you were in town, and I know what you are," he said and raised the cross. "Vrykolakas."

With a cry of rage, she released me and leapt off the bed with the speed of a tiger. She lunged toward the window, but Digger was ready. He swiftly shifted the cross from his right to his left hand and hurled something that glinted in the light.

She reached the window and was struggling with the lock. The small object he'd thrown hit her shoulder and, with a hiss of burning flesh, embedded itself there.

The rectangular head of an old handmade nail stuck out of her back.

Anastasia let out a pained scream and dropped to her knees as this minor wound seemed to inflict unbearable pain. "It burns," she screamed and turned to face us. "It cannot be."

Digger reached into a pouch on his belt with his right hand, and in one swift motion, hurled another nail straight at her. It landed with a thud, piercing her chest just above her left breast. She gasped as the nail sunk into her skin with a sizzle.

"I have them, monster," Digger yelled. "Nails from the Isle of Lesbos, used to destroy your kind since ancient days."

He threw another nail and another, eliciting cries of agony and profanity from her with every impact.

He grabbed the handle of a hatchet that lay in a pocket against his back.

Anastasia was on her knees, struggling to remove the nails embedded in her body. She desperately clawed at them with her impressive strength, to no avail — the nails were stuck fast.

Digger grabbed her hair, lifting her face to meet his. "The bodies found in the Halloween House were missing their livers. Your feasting is over, bitch."

Her face contorted with fury, her teeth sharpened to points, and her deep purple eyes gleamed with a bright light within. Her fingers were like claws as she reached out for Digger.

With a single swing of the hatchet, the body dropped to the ground, still twitching, and Digger lifted the severed head.

I screamed and stumbled backward, pressing myself against the headboard. I expected a gush of blood to pour out, but to my shock, no liquid came from the severed neck. The purple light in its eyes extinguished and the detached body slumped to the ground, crumbling into ash. Digger dropped the severed head, only to watch it disintegrate into a mound of dust, along with the body.

Digger panted with exertion, bracing himself with his hands on his knees. After a moment of stunned silence, he stood upright and secured the hatchet in his waist pouch.

He glanced at the pile of dust. "You may end up with a cleaning fee because of this."

I looked at him, fighting the urge to vomit. "W-What was that?"

"A Vrykolakas," he muttered, "a Greek revenant. It's like a vampire, an undead creature that leaves its grave and travels around the world. They strangle people." He took a step closer to me, getting more stable on his legs. "If you'd banged her, she would've suffocated you during climax."

I looked down at the pile of particles on the floor, and then back at Digger. "But I saw her outside... in daylight."

Digger nodded. "They can roam around in the day, though they must stay out of bright sunlight," he began. "They have a taste for the human liver, heart, and blood. The Greek cross is their nemesis, as it weakens them and can even trap them in their coffins. To fight them, you need a special nail from the Island of Lesbos." He reached into his pouch and pulled out one of the ancient-looking nails as an example.

I met Digger's eyes. "You saved my life."

He shrugged. "I saw the bodies at Neill's house. I knew there was still a Vrykolakas in the area. I've been trying to track her down, not sure who she was. I had to wait for her to reveal herself."

"Wait," I exclaimed, rising from the bed as I comprehended his words. "You used me... as bait?"

He picked my pants up off the floor and threw them at me. "You better put on some clothes, Joshua."

"You know who I am?"

"I've been expecting you. Now, you need to get out of town and so do I, right now. Pack up, and I'll meet you outside, at your car."

He glanced down at the remains on the floor, his jaw set. He turned away, his feet swiftly carrying him down the stairs. I remained rooted to the spot, my body still shaking.

# PART TWO:

# LEARNING

# THE JOB

# SEVEN

I confronted him at his truck, the bitter taste of Anastasia's kiss still lingering in my mouth. "You were there, weren't you?" I said, throwing my bag into my car. "At my poppa's funeral?'"

He gazed at me, stone-faced. "Yes. Your father was one of the finest men I've ever known. I had to be there — to make sure."

I frowned. "Make sure of what?"

"The circumstances of your father's death left questions. The first one was whether he would… rise."

"Rise? You mean — rise from the dead?"

He nodded. "I had to be there to make sure he didn't." He slid his hand over the handle of the hatchet attached to his belt.

"Of course he didn't! He was my dad, not some kind of—" I waved my arm at the house, the carnage Digger just enacted still vivid in my mind. I fixed my eyes on the older man. "He told me stories. About you, about… creatures. Were they true?"

Digger didn't face me, but gazed out into the street. "True enough."

"My father told me what the two of you did," I said. "Though maybe not all the details. I mean, I didn't expect a monster lady to try to kill me."

He considered this, then shook his head. "Sometimes, that's what happens when people go looking for me."

"What, monsters eat them?"

"She'd been in this town for years," Digger said. "Thomas Neill was supplying her victims."

I paused. "You mean those homeless people he killed?"

Digger nodded. "Now that I know she was a police officer, I figure she covered for him. I came back here because I knew her guard would be down and she'd be too hungry to be cautious. Then I saw you were here—"

"So I was right," I growled. "You used me as bait."

"It was your own fault for looking for me to begin with," Digger spat. "She picked you because you were from out of town and you were supposed to leave. Besides, I didn't invite her up to your room, *you* did."

"She would've killed me."

Digger pointed at his head. "That's what happens when you think with your dick instead of your brain."

I wanted to argue, but he had a point.

He moved to the rear of the pickup, lowered the tailgate, and opened the door of the canopy. Hidden behind the tailgate was a raised platform, and he slid a drawer out that extended several feet. He filled it with multiple tool boxes of various sizes and had multiple compartments that held an array of different tools, devices, and odd trinkets. He pulled out one toolbox, opened it, and put the nails into a plastic jar he took from it.

"I need your help," I stated plainly.

Digger glared at me with suspicion. "With what?"

"Something killed my father, and I want you to help me track it down and kill it."

Digger spun a lid on the jar of handmade nails and returned it to the toolbox along with the Greek cross, then put it back where it belonged. He took off his belt with the pouches and placed the hatchet in a foam cutout space where it fit perfectly. Rolling up the belt, he put it in a space and pushed the drawer back in.

"Look, Joshua — you just saw what almost happened. I don't think you're cut out for this. You should just go home. I understand you're a journalist — go start a blog or something."

"That's why I need your help," I said and gestured at the house where I'd been staying. "You took out that *Vry* — whatever she was... with no problem at all. You know what to do, and I need to learn."

Digger said, "You think because you took a few self-defense classes in high school, you're ready to do what I do?

I paused. "How do you know about that?"

"I know a lot about you. Don't act so surprised." He closed the tailgate of his truck with a bang and peered down the empty street again. "You got lucky tonight, but I can't be your goddamn guardian angel. Go home, meet a girl, have a life."

"What? Why?"

He turned on me with fury in his eyes. "Because I've lost too many people doing this. Your father almost died that night in Portland years ago. I've had others work with me, and some of them ended up dead. Excuse me, if I don't want you to be one of them."

"I need to find what killed him," I shouted.

"Calm down! We have to get out of here. A policewoman has gone missing tonight, and there had to be someone who saw the two of you talking at that restaurant."

He was right. "You think they'll come looking for me?"

Digger shrugged. "Maybe nothing will come of it."

I nervously brushed at my sleeves, feeling a wave of revulsion wash over me as I wondered if I had gotten any of the crumbling ash remains of that creature on me. "What about the dust up in that room?"

"The sunlight in the morning should dissolve it the rest of the way. People forget when they meet a *Vrykolakas*, it's one of their defense mechanisms. As far as an investigation, they won't find a body, Joshua."

"Josh, call me Josh," I said, overcome with uncertainty. "I want your help to find out what killed him and take it down. I want to learn about my father's past and maybe even my mother. "

"That's a tall order."

"I thought you could tell me. That's the reason I went searching for you."

"Well, you found me," Digger said and headed for the front of the truck. "I'll tell you what I know, but I can't do it here." He moved to the driver's side door of his truck and opened it. "You were planning to go to Airmont from here, right? Ever since you got a copy of my certificate?"

"Yes," I grumbled, annoyed that he knew that as well.

"Okay. Go to that address. In the back of the cemetery is a road that leads to my place. I'll leave the gate open for you. But I still recommend you go back to New Jersey and forget you ever met me."

He got into the truck.

I spoke up. "I'll see you there."

He slammed the door without another word and drove away.

"Great," I muttered, getting into my car without looking back at the house. "I almost get eaten, and now I'm going to spend the night in a cemetery."

I departed shortly after Digger, but as I drove south on the New York Turnpike, I considered what had happened. The night was strange from the start. Something was off with Anastasia, but I couldn't put my finger on it. I'd experienced a one-night stand before, but this was different. I now realized that there were warning signs I missed all along.

Growing up, my poppa always told me to be careful with women. He said they could be a distraction for a young man that could easily derail my life. I think his warnings really resonated with me, because even as I approached my later twenties, I still hadn't been in a serious relationship.

I reluctantly acknowledged that Digger was right: the woman, or whatever she was, had chosen me as her next victim with no qualms. As a journalist visiting the town, she knew that I'd be leaving soon, making me easy prey.

Her femininity captivated me, but I couldn't help but ponder if there was something more to her that drew me to her so intensely.

Or I could have just been thinking with the wrong head, like Digger suggested.

I shuddered to think about what she would have done with me. She was incredibly powerful, and disposing of me wouldn't have been an issue for her. Devil's Lake came to mind as a place to leave my corpse and car. The thought of my body weighed down by rocks, slowly decaying at the bottom of that filthy body of water, made me feel sick.

After she'd eaten my liver and drained my blood, of course.

For years, she and Thomas Neill had carried out a chilling mission: killing the homeless. Neill left the gruesome evidence of their actions in the house, perhaps kept as trophies.

I swore to avenge my father, but the experience tonight only pointed out how incredibly unprepared I was for making good on my vow. Digger was right. I knew nothing about stopping evil creatures.

If I wanted to stay true to my vow, I needed to learn quickly.

I was getting sleepy when I pulled off the New York Turnpike and into the town of Airmont. There were diners and malls, all dark at this time of night. There was more open land the further I went from the secondary roads, and soon I saw the sign that announced:

**Blessed Sacrament Cemetery**
**Archdiocese of New York**
**Open Daily 9:00 to 4:30**

I slowly crept down the side road, my heart pounding as I drove into the graveyard at night. The only light came from my headlights, illuminating statues of Jesus and Mary and causing me to jump in surprise. I made out the dark brick chapel and the towering mausoleum, both of which seemed to come alive in the eerie darkness. Gripping the wheel, I cautiously drove on, my headlights creating a shifting silhouette out of the tombstones.

From the paved driveway, I gazed at the wrought iron fences winding between the graves. The headstones, carved intricately, shone like bones in the darkness. Tall trees loomed, their gnarled branches twisted up to the night sky, as if reaching for something.

Finally, the road ended in a cul-de-sac large enough to allow limousines to turn around with a small dirt road beyond it. A chain with a battered metal "No Trespassing" sign lay on the ground, and I drove over it and into a wooded area.

I only went a few hundred feet when a large two-story house seemed to appear out of the gloom. It wasn't ostentatious or made to look like a medieval castle or anything gothic. The construction was a combination of stone and brick, and the building looked like it could withstand a war.

I parked my car next to Digger's truck. It was an older model, likely around ten to twenty years old, but in great condition. It had an extended cab with a metal truck bed cap — sturdier than your typical fiberglass one — closed with a sturdy lock.

I stared up at the remarkable abode, just as lights illuminated the front, allowing me to see the path to the stairs.

Digger came out the front door. "So, you found the place."

"Whose house is this?" I asked. "Is it part of your job?"

"You could say that." He said. He held up a small remote control and pushed the button, causing a pair of tall metal gates to swing into place, closing off the road. When I looked back, I saw glimpses of a high, black metal fence that encircled the property.

"The fence is iron," Digger explained. "A lot of bad things can't stand the touch of cold iron."

"If you say so," I mumbled, too tired to demand an explanation.

"Get your suitcase and come on in. I'll set up the guest bedroom for you."

Inside the house, the dark wood and the elegance of the manor-style interior impressed me. The foyer was lit with a warm glow, and I noticed the fine, dark wood floor and the intricately designed ceilings. The house was an example of old-world charm meeting modern American luxury. I realized the entire structure was something truly special.

"I can't believe that they give a groundskeeper a place like this," I gushed.

"I didn't say it was because I was the groundskeeper. I just said it was part of the job. I own the place."

"What, the house?" I gaped.

"No, the cemetery."

"You own the cemetery?" I repeated in stunned disbelief.

He glanced over his shoulder at me, and for the first time since we met, he seemed amused. "I own all three cemeteries in town."

I stopped walking and stared at the man. "But... how... why?"

"I came to this area when it had a lot of open land and made some sound investments in real estate through corporations I created. Then I built the cemeteries and hired people to run them, since I knew I couldn't be here to oversee the details. Would you care for a drink? I know I could use one."

"Um... sure." Considering I'd almost had sex with a creature who wanted to eat my liver, I thought a drink would be necessary if I was to sleep tonight.

In fact, for several nights.

He guided me through the house. Everything was immaculate and in order. We walked past a living room that had an exquisite oriental carpet and a custom-built wall unit. We continued to a luxurious dining room, and into a beautiful kitchen, adorned with white-tiled flooring and a sleek backsplash behind the sink.

He led me to a glass double door just off the kitchen, which opened onto a large deck made of redwood. He flipped a switch and floodlights came on, illuminating a glass table with several comfortable-looking chairs.

He grabbed a cut-glass carafe filled with amber liquid and two large brandy snifters, and set them on the glass table. He went back inside and returned with a humidor, a cigar cutter, wooden matches, and an ashtray.

He opened the humidor and offered me a cigar.

"I'm not really a smoker," I said.

"I don't touch cigarettes myself," he explained. "But a fine cigar at the end of a long chase is a rare pleasure."

He pulled out a cigar, removed the band, and snipped the end with a cutter. He then set a snifter in front of me and filled it with a generous amount of cognac before pouring some into his own glass. Taking a seat across from me, he lit the cigar.

Raising my glass, I admired how the liquid glistened in the lamplight. Something told me there was something extraordinary about this cognac. The scent wafted to my nose and filled the room. Its inviting fragrance was divine, and I couldn't wait to take a sip.

I took a large gulp of my cognac, enjoying the warmth of the liquid as it made its way down my throat.

Digger puffed at his cigar and took a sip of his own glass. "You're wearing a hearing aid. It's because you have Waardenburg Syndrome, right?"

"You did research on me?"

"What I could. I felt an obligation to… keep track."

"Tell me."

"Alright. Hearing problems as a baby until they diagnosed you. Your father had a speech pathologist work with you, and from the way you speak, they did a great job. You were an above-average student, a college graduate, and you quit your job after your father died. You've been doing research about me and you've been to Connecticut and Portland to interview people."

I looked at him, about to snap out a quick retort, but he held up his hand to stop me.

"I have to keep track of anyone trying to find out about me. I have an entire network of... associates... who help."

"Why?" I demanded.

He inhaled deeply from his cigar; the smoke coiling around his head like a halo. "I'm in a very specialized line of work."

"Most people think you're just a gravedigger."

He turned to me, stone-faced. "Is that all you think I am?"

"No," I admitted. "You're a hell of a lot more."

He grinned at this. "Interesting choice of words."

"What exactly is your specialized line of work?"

He took another sip of the cognac before he spoke. "I dig a grave when there is a concern that whoever is going in it... might not stay there."

He squinted through the cigar smoke, gauging my reaction.

"What about Fort Gorges and Duivelsmeer..."

"Both cases were pretty far along by the time they contacted me. In Maine, the police were aware of the disappearances. It was when a ghoul rose from a tomb in front of witnesses that I got called."

"They called you?" I said, shocked. "What? Do you have an eight hundred number or something?"

He looked at the drift of cigar smoke. "There are ways to get in touch. I told you, I have people who look for situations for me."

I took another mouthful of my cognac. The alcohol had already taken effect, and I was feeling relaxed.

He released a satisfied breath, watching as smoke rings drifted up to the sky like lassos. He paused for a moment before continuing, "By the time I discovered what was going on in Maine and investigated—"

"Investigated?"

"You don't think we just stormed in, do you Josh? Maybe with guns blazing?"

"No, it's just the stories my father told—"

"If I know Ephraim, he probably just told you about confronting the monsters. But there were many times when your father and I spent weeks watching, observing, and learning what the situation was before we moved in."

He let out a heavy sigh and shook his head in disbelief. Taking a puff of his cigar, he muttered, "That night at Fort Gorges... what a clusterfuck that was."

I frowned. "What do you mean?"

"Ephraim and I finally found the abandoned place where that bastard VanWry kept those people... and the ghouls."

"The abandoned amusement park?"

"Yeah." As the cognac took effect, it seemed to free his memory, allowing him to recall the events vividly. "We were planning our attack, because if we just went in, the ghouls would kill the prisoners. We finally worked out a strategy, but the night we planned to bust them out, Van Wry moved them to that damned island."

"You didn't know that they were planning to take them there?"

"No. Once we figured out where they were going, we nicked a boat and followed. We notified the Coast Guard as well." He stared at his drink. "By the time we picked out a suitable place to launch an attack, VanWry had started killing people." He closed his eyes. "If only I'd gotten involved sooner, figured out his plans — your father would have never lost his hand."

"It was your fault?" I said.

"No, it was VanWry's fault," he said sharply, then calmed himself. "I have nothing but respect for your old man, Josh. He was the one who stopped the sacrifices, saved those people, and took on VanWry."

"And afterwards, he couldn't fight with just one hand, so he was no good to you," I accused.

Digger spoke with urgency. "Your father was a force to be reckoned with, even with only one hand. He was an incredible warrior and a real powerhouse." He leaned back in his chair and sighed. "I'm guessing you never got to witness him in action."

"Once," I said quietly, the memory bright in my mind. "When I was seven. He killed a creature. Part woman, part snake —and she could mimic other things."

"A Lamia,' Digger said, quietly.

This surprised me. "Yes, that's what he called it."

"How did he stop her?"

I pulled out the chamois bag and placed it on the table. "With this."

Digger put down the cigar and his glass and undid the strings. He pulled the golden handle out of the bag and turned it over in his hand. "The *Lahat Chereb.*"

"What?"

"It's Hebrew. An ancient artifact of unimaginable value that's called 'the flame of the whirling sword.' According to the legends, the angel Uriel guarded the gates of the Garden of Eden with this."

"An angel? You expect me to believe that?"

"A vampiric creature almost killed you tonight," he snorted. "So, yeah, I really don't have a problem believing in angels."

He carefully placed the item into its bag and passed it back to me. The effects of the cognac, combined with the horror of the decapitation and the extended journey, had left me feeling drained and lightheaded.

"You're tired. We'll talk in the morning, then I'll send you on your way." Digger rose and gulped down the last of his cognac.

I trailed behind him. We arrived in the entrance hall, and he effortlessly picked up my suitcase, marching up the staircase with ease.

He guided me to the second floor and pointed me to a room close to the staircase. At the foot of the bed sat a large chest, and Digger set my suitcase on top of it.

"You have your own bathroom, through there." He pointed at a closed door.

"Thanks," I replied, sure that I could fall asleep now.

He closed the door behind him.

I plopped down on the bed and pulled off my shoes, undressed to my underwear and grabbed my charging unit from my suitcase. I removed my hearing aid and plugged it in to the charger to get ready for the night.

I retrieved the golden sword hilt and held it in my hand. Now, I had a name for it as well. But why had I agreed to come here?

Could I convince him to help me find and track down the creature that killed my father?

I tossed and turned in the expansive bed, my mind racing as sleep gradually took over.

# EIGHT

I groggily opened my eyes, the light from the sun streaming in through the large windows of the bedroom.

As I threw off the sheets and blankets, a wave of soreness hit me — my body ached everywhere from my brief tussle with the undead Anastasia. I clearly had not been taking good care of my muscles.

Too many hours spent in a car or at a desk was my guess.

I inserted my hearing aid, then donned a pair of jeans and a T-shirt. My head pounded from the strong cognac Digger gave me the night before. Even so, I performed the stretches and techniques I had learned when I was a student of Aikido. These moves not only loosened my body but reminded me of defensive moves I could use in a potential altercation.

After being away from them for so long, it pleased me how easily the movements came back. It was like a comforting embrace, and I felt a sense of peace.

I made my way down the stairs, my head feeling clearer. As I entered the kitchen, I spied a single-cup coffeemaker and brewed myself a cup. Looking out the double glass doors, I saw Digger on the patio, typing away on a laptop, with a duffle bag at his feet.

Stepping out onto the patio, he glanced up, nodded at me, and returned to his work.

The sunshine was invigorating, providing a pleasant warmth as I sat down and sighed.

"Tired?" Digger asked, eyes still focused on the computer.

"Sore. I think you're right. I am definitely out of shape."

Digger gave me a once-over. "The Vrykolakas drains strength from its victims by taking away some of their life force — that's what happened when it kissed you. It makes the person it's hunting easier to kill."

I shook my head. "How the hell do you know this stuff?"

Digger shrugged without looking at me. "I've learned a lot over the years. Considering some things I've come up against, I had to educate myself." He indicated the duffle bag at his feet. "Look in there."

I carefully extracted a hefty book from the duffle. They crafted its cover from either wood or thick leather, and its pages were a deep brown, reminiscent of parchment.

"Is that…?" I asked.

Digger nodded. "My Grimoire, passed down to me long ago. I used it when I confronted VanWry in Portland all those years ago."

"Can I read it?"

I went to open the book, but Digger put his hand on top of it to stop me. "Wait," he said. "You can read it. It goes into depth about creatures, spells, and techniques." His fingers gently caressed the cover, almost lovingly. "But there are a few rules about it."

"It seems there are rules about everything."

"Pretty much. These are two simple ones. First, never read the book at night — only during daylight hours, got it?"

"Sure, I guess. And the second?"

"While reading it, do not say any of the words out loud."

I frowned. "That's it?"

"Take it seriously, Josh," he warned.

"All right, I agree," I said, giving in.

"Good. Now, I think I can help with your muscle soreness. Wait here."

He rose and made his way inside. I looked over the grassy yard to the landscape beyond. It was an amalgamation of trees, tall and imposing, and wild and untouched plants. A chorus of birdsongs filled the air, and the entire view was something to behold. Ferns grew in abundance around the house, giving it a wild and untouched look.

Like Digger himself.

He placed a glass of a strange green liquid in front of me. "It won't taste great, but it will give you strength and help you recover," he said.

I took a sip of the concoction and immediately noted the flavors of vegetables and herbs wash over my tongue. A bitter aftertaste lingered in my mouth.

"It's easier if you just chug it," Digger suggested, and then gulped his own glassful down.

I drained my glass, then took a sip of my coffee to rid myself of the taste and watched Digger type away on his laptop. His pale white beard almost glowed in the sunlight. He dressed in his usual jeans and work shirt, looking like a common laborer.

I now knew that was just an act.

He closed the laptop and reclined in his chair, grasping his coffee mug in both hands.

I spoke up. "Tell me, how did you meet my father?"

Digger turned his gaze toward me, contemplating for a lengthy moment. "I buried his father. Did Ephraim tell you anything regarding your grandparents?"

I shook my head. "Poppa always said his parents died before I was born."

Digger nodded. "That much is true. I take it he didn't tell you how they died."

"What do you mean?"

He sipped from his mug calmly. "Vampires killed them."

My jaw dropped. "What? But that's not — I mean it can't—"

He looked at me with a serious expression. "It wasn't normal in Plainfield, New Jersey, in the 1980s. But that was why I was there. I didn't just go to bury them. I was there to make sure they stayed buried."

I sat back as this washed over me. "But…how?"

"My research discovered that a group of vampires that went by the name of The Court Of Lazarus targeted your grandfather and grandmother. They slaughtered both of them in their sleep, and it was your father who found the bodies."

"He never told me," I said.

"At twenty-three, your father was wise beyond his years, and a powerful man. He saw the puncture marks on their necks and demanded an investigation. The coroner's report concluded that the cause of death was carbon monoxide poisoning. Your father knew the bodies lacked the deep red discoloration which is present with such poisoning."

"He knew that the coroner's report was bullshit?" I said.

Digger nodded. "But no one would listen to him, even though he went to everyone he could to get his concerns taken seriously."

I knew how doggedly my poppa could pursue something when he knew he was right. "How did you get involved?"

"I told you. My network of people was always looking for situations that needed my attention. I went there and offered to dig the graves, no charge. Who would turn that down?"

He had a point.

"They held the funeral service in the late afternoon, but I left the graves uncovered, so I could open the coffins and behead them when darkness fell, just in case."

"I thought you put a stake through a vampire's heart," I said.

"That can paralyze a vampire, but the only way to kill one is decapitation or exposure to sunlight. Well before twilight, your father showed up."

"What did you do?"

"Your father approached me with a look of desperation on his face, and uttered words that no one should ever say: 'Someone killed my parents, and I think it was vampires.' I told him what I was there to do and why. He stood back while I did it, looking like a man on the edge. When I was done, he joined me in filling in their graves."

I couldn't help but frown as I thought of my poppa, standing there silently as Digger hacked the heads off his parents. How was he able to remain so strong?

Digger went on. "We looked at each other after covering the graves, both of us dirty and tired, and he asked me, 'Are you going to find the folks that killed them?' I told him I was, and he said, 'Good, then I don't have to do it alone.' That was the beginning."

"Did you? I mean…find the people who did it?"

"We did, though I wouldn't call them people. They were not new vampires, which are more animal than human," Digger said, and he stared into the distance, lost in memory. "No, they could have left your grandparents alone. One vampire chose them because she coveted a necklace your grandmother wore out one night."

I gasped. "That was all?"

Digger fixed me with a determined stare. "Sometimes, that's all it takes. Ephraim and I investigated deserted structures in the vicinity, and we eventually found their lair — an abandoned religious 'home for the aged' in North Plainfield. After surveying the premises, we drew up our plan of attack."

"Did you go during the day?"

"It was tricky, as the roads to it were closed, and police patrolled them. But we got in more than once to scout the place out. The atmosphere was intimidating, but your father was a man possessed. He navigated the dilapidated corridors, unbothered by the musty smell of neglect and the looming shadows. We located the coffins, but left them undisturbed until we were ready to strike."

I frowned. "That was your strategy?"

"Yes. Once fully prepared, we raided the place one afternoon. We had all the tools: pry bars, stakes, wooden hammers, holy water, garlic, crucifixes, the works. We went through the rooms one by one, prying open the coffins and paralyzing the vampires with stakes before they could fight back. Then we beheaded them and returned the remains to their coffins. As we went deeper into the main building, down into the basement, we had to use lanterns to light our way—"

"Lanterns?" I questioned.

"Yes. You want something you can carry but put down easily. Also, a lantern projects light in all directions around you. The darkness of the basement was oppressive and eerie, dark enough that the vampires could come out of their coffins, and one did."

"What did you do?"

"It was what your father did. I was prying open a coffin when a vampire lunged at me. Its strength was immense, pinning my arms and dragging me close. It twisted my head so it could get at my neck. The smell of its putrid breath was overwhelming and its hands were icy cold against my skin. But before it sunk its teeth into me — wham! Your father hits it in the head with a pry bar. The thing fell back and the pair of us started beating it down, and Ephraim gets out his machete and brings it down on the creature's head, yelling, 'This is for my momma!'"

"Jesus," I whispered.

Digger sat back and took another sip from his mug. "That's pretty much what I said, too. We departed from that awful place, all the vampires slain. I turned to him and asked if he was interested in a job."

"And that's when you two started working together and traveling?"

"Pretty much."

I finally asked the question that had bothered me all my life. "When did he meet my momma?"

Digger stared at me, weighing his answer before he said. "How do you feel about New Orleans?"

This came out of left field and I didn't know how to respond. "In general, or are you asking about something specific?"

"I'll ask a different way. I have something to do in New Orleans. You might not be a warrior, but you might help."

"Really?"

He sighed. "If you're serious about finding what killed your father. Going with me would give you a chance to see what your father used to do. I could also tell you about your mother once we get there."

This intrigued me. I knew so little about my momma, and asking my poppa questions about her only made him depressed. If I was indeed intent upon catching the thing that killed Poppa, some practical knowledge would help. "You want to fly us down to New Orleans?"

He shook his head. "I can't. I need my truck. It's got all of my equipment."

I considered it. "That would take — I don't know — like, twenty hours to get there, and that's without breaks."

He grinned in a way that grated on my nerves. "I know a few shortcuts."

I exhaled heavily. "When would we leave?"

"Tomorrow."

I considered it. I had learned my father's stories were true, and that Digger knew how to kill such creatures. Add to that a chance to find out about my mother. Before I could stop myself, I said, "I guess so."

"Good, we can wash our clothes and pack up today. Bring anything you might need."

"Might need?" I repeated.

He grinned again. "Like the Lahat Chereb. Have you used it yet?"

"I-I don't know how it works," I admitted.

This surprised Digger. "Didn't your father tell you?"

I hung my head. "No, he just told my step-mom to give it to me."

Digger paused. "Step-mom? Ephraim got married?"

"Yes, to Lizzie, years ago," I said. "I thought you were keeping tabs on us."

Digger sighed. "Last I heard, she was just your housekeeper. I guess over the last few years, I let things fall through the cracks."

"I guess," I said.

"You know, we might face zombies."

I nodded and quickly rattled off, "Slow, stupid, but relentless. The only way to stop them is decapitation."

His eyebrows lifted. "Turns out you know a bit, after all."

I shrugged. "My poppa told me about the different kinds of undead."

"Pity he didn't say anything about a Vrykolakas."

"Did you two ever fight one when he worked with you?"

Digger scratched his beard. "I guess not. What weapons do you like? I have my axe and a 'Hunga-Munga' in my truck. You ever use one?"

"I've had self-defense training, some fencing, but I haven't worked a lot with weapons," I said, taken aback. "I'm a reporter, not a superhero."

"And you've never used the Lahat Chereb?" he asked.

I shook my head. "I saw my father use it one night. I also learned that it was the weapon my father used the night he lost his hand."

Digger met my eyes. "You might not be able to use it at all."

I found this made me angry. "What does that mean?"

Digger clenched his jaw tightly. "It's... special. Whoever has it must be spiritually prepared to use it. Your father and I spent days preparing ourselves before that night on the island."

"The one time I saw him use it," I explained. "He just mumbled a few words, and it worked. By the way, is it really made of gold?"

Digger looked away. "Yes. Gold is one of the most conductive metals there is, and it is one reason it's so powerful. Bring it out."

I got my computer bag and withdrew the small chamois bag. I pulled out the ancient sword handle, feeling the cold metal against my skin. I sensed a profound strength emanating from it and examined it intently. "Can I use this against zombies?"

He examined the shining item in my grasp. "It can fight any evil entity. But, since you're a beginner, it would be smarter to start with a knife."

"Can you teach me the words that activate it?"

He pointed at the book I held. "The words are in the Grimoire."

"Does that mean yes?"

"It means you should read that book, and we should pack to be ready to go, and then we need to make preparations," he announced as he stood.

"Laundry and stuff," I agreed. "What else?"

"Ritual baths, haircuts, and we have to clip our nails."

"Why?"

"So, a voodoo master won't be able to use them against us. Come on, let's go upstairs."

We went up to the second floor; me carrying the heavy Grimoire, and the chamois bag with the sword hilt. Once in my bedroom, Digger went into the bathroom off to the side, where he started water running to fill the tub.

"That's for me?" I asked, and he nodded. "What's involved with a ritual bath?"

He turned a knob on the large tub. "I'll add some oils and herbs, very specific. The barber and manicurist will arrive in about an hour."

"What's all this about haircuts and nails clipped?" I challenged, as steam filled the bathroom.

He looked at the water as it flowed into the tub. "We have to be careful when we're there. If an enemy can get ahold of a strand of your hair or a fingernail, they can make a voodoo doll and use it against you."

I raised my eyebrows. "You believe that?"

"I believe in taking precautions," he countered, as he headed for the door.

"In case of what?" I asked.

He just kept walking.

It exasperated me. I discussed zombies as if they were a reality, but when he brought up voodoo dolls, I was skeptical.

Uncertainty filled my mind. My vow at my father's grave led me to embark on this journey. Digger seemed to no longer want to send me home. It appeared instead that he wanted me to go with him. If I was to understand what my father went through, and how to fight these creatures, I had to walk in his footsteps.

And going with Digger was the only way to do that.

# NINE

T he ritual bath was quite pleasant. After Digger started his own tub, he returned, holding a tall bottle with a crystal stopper. Floating in an amber liquid were flakes of different herbs and roots.

He emptied some of the fragrant liquid into my bath, creating an exquisite aroma that filled the room.

"One half-hour, no less. I'll come wake you if you fall asleep."

"I won't fall asleep," I muttered.

I stepped into the steaming hot tub, and the heat immediately enveloped me, taking my breath away. I needed to go slowly to lower myself in, but when I did, all my aches and pains vanished as if into thin air.

I lay my head back and closed my eyes, inhaling the herbs and scented oil. I thought I had just closed my eyes for a minute when there was a pounding on the door.

"Time to get out of there, Mr Bennet," Digger yelled through the door.

"I am, I am," I shouted back. I wasn't wearing a watch, but the water had indeed cooled. Wrapping myself in a towel, I headed into the bedroom.

I changed into a fresh shirt and a pair of khakis, then flopped down on the bed, feeling energized. The drink and the bath left me feeling completely rejuvenated — all my muscle soreness had melted away.

I paged through the huge book, and it was quite comprehensive, split into three sections. The first section detailed different creatures, most of the malevolent variety, and the techniques used to combat them. Turning to the second part, it discussed divination techniques such as Tarot cards and runes, as well as how to use them. The third section consisted of incantations and spells, most of which were written in English, though some were in other languages such as Hebrew or Latin, which were transliterated for an English speaker. These pages listed spells for protection, spells to use against enemies, purification spells and more.

Then I turned a page to see:

### Lahat Chereb

The ancient text had the key to unlocking the legendary sword, written in Hebrew and transliterated into English.

I gazed at it, my heart longing to give it a go. I had promised Digger not to utter a single word out loud — and I had to keep my promise. With a deep breath, I placed the book on the bed with the chamois pouch and went off to search for him.

Digger was downstairs in a fresh pair of jeans and yet another work shirt. Was that the entirety of his wardrobe?

Digger was sitting on the back patio, basking in the sun's warmth and the brightness of the day. His fingers were busy, tapping away at the phone as he texted someone.

"Digger, I found the words for the *Lahat Chereb* in your book, but you told me not to speak any of the words of the book aloud."

Digger glanced over at me. "I think we can make an exception for that one. But I'm pleased you checked. It means you took me seriously."

"Who are you texting?" I asked as I drew near.

"I'm making sure that my people have all the duties covered in the cemeteries," he told me. "I have to be certain all funeral services have what they need, and that there are people in place for any urgent needs."

"Meaning... graves?" I asked.

He tapped on his phone. "That as well."

"Do any of your staff dig them by hand, like you?"

He smiled with pride. "One or two have the skills. But I set up this place so that a backhoe made more sense."

I frowned. "Then why do you dig them the way you do?"

His smile faded. "Because usually when I am involved, there's a reason the 'dearly departed' might not stay in the ground. I know techniques and rituals to counter an attempt to make them rise, and I stay there to make sure they don't."

The doorbell rang, and he walked past me into the house.

He had set up the two chairs with a brazier in between. Glowing charcoal, heated in the metal box, its color transitioning to a deep red.

Digger returned to the patio, accompanied by a short man with a really magnificent mustache and an Asian woman with a small smile.

"This is my guest, Joshua Bennet," he said to the pair. "Josh, this is Ahnjong and Aldo. They will act as our manicurist and barber today."

I nodded to the man and bowed to the lady, who returned the gesture. The woman looked me up and down, said something that I think was Korean, and headed into the kitchen.

Digger, with no hesitancy, spoke back to her, also in Korean, and then looked at me. "You should sit and remove your shoes and socks."

"I thought it was a manicure?" I protested.

"And pedicure. She's getting warm water for the soak." He turned to Aldo and spoke in rapid Italian.

Aldo's eyes lit up, and he placed a shoulder bag on the table and put out the equipment of his trade: scissors, electric razors, combs, and brushes. Aldo pulled out a barber's cape and draped it over Digger, fastening it at the neck.

I slipped off my shoes and socks, and Ahnjong placed a basin of warm water in front of me. She worked on my feet, clipping and shaping the nails.

She shook her head and said more in Korean.

Digger chuckled. "She says you take terrible care of your toenails."

I sighed. "You got me there."

She snipped my toenails and then tossed the clippings into the brazier, where they hissed and crackled as the flames consumed them. I looked up to see Aldo doing the same with Digger's hair. He cut away with precision, barely leaving any clippings on the deck, and most of them going straight into the fiery brazier.

Aldo and Ahnjong worked quickly, taking turns with their tasks. Aldo worked on my hair, giving me a well-shaped cut, while Ahnjong gave Digger a professional-looking manicure. The results were amazing — she buffed my nails to a glossy shine, and he made my hair look sharp and neat.

African-American hair can be tricky to style and manage, especially mine with its tight curls and stiffness. That's why so many black men turn to black barbers for help. Aldo made it look easy, like he had been cutting hair for every brother in the neighborhood for years.

Once they were gone, Digger swept up a few stray hairs and disposed of them in the brazier, where they smoldered and disappeared.

"I still don't understand this," I told him as the smoke blew around us.

"I'm not surprised."

"You speak Italian and Korean?"

"As well as seven other languages, including Latin. You wouldn't believe how handy that is with demons."

"Digger, I have to be honest. I don't know how much help I will be fighting zombies. I've done nothing like that in my entire life."

"Which is why I suggested you go home."

"What changed your mind?"

"A look in your eyes. At some point, you had to believe that your father's stories were more than just stories, didn't you?"

"Why do you say that?"

He grinned ironically. "Because if not, you wouldn't have come looking for me. But once we get to New Orleans, you and I are going to have to get you into better shape. In case we run into any *Vrykolakas*."

I looked at my feet. He had a point. "Look, I remember the exercises from the self-defense classes I had as a kid. I'll start doing them every morning."

"That's a start."

"I never expected to become a vampire-slayer or whatever you are."

"If you intend to avenge your father, you need to learn a lot of things."

"Do you know what kind of creature killed him?"

Digger stuck out his lips in thought. "I got a copy of the coroner's report."

I shook my head. "That guy! He thought my poppa got wounded and bled out, the blood going into the ground."

He made a snort of derision. "Right, as if that happens all the time. The problem is that I'm not familiar with a creature that leaves a circular wound like there was on Ephraim's neck."

"You saw the wound?" I said, surprised. "How? When?"

"Let's just say I have my ways. I don't know what could have done that, but maybe there's something in the Grimoire that I've forgotten."

"I'll go through it and see if I can figure it out. I also want to hear everything you know about my momma."

Digger nodded. "Let's get to New Orleans, first. Some of it is hard to explain. But I promise you, from this trip, you'll understand your father a lot better," Digger turned from me and added, "You might not like everything you discover. Get your things and we'll move out."

"Do you have a hotel booked?" I asked, grabbing my suitcase and my laptop bag.

Digger grabbed the duffle with the Grimoire, and the pair of us headed for the front door. "We won't need it."

"Look, Digger, I checked. It's twenty-one hours of driving, and I don't think I can stay in a car that long, let alone in your truck."

He grinned as we walked down the front steps and went to the pickup truck. He opened the passenger door and placed the duffle on my seat. "You'll find my truck very comfortable."

"I doubt it," I grumbled. "But even if we trade off the driving —"

He turned to me. "Put your bag in the back of the truck. We must keep the Grimoire up front with us. I need to check a few things, lock up, and we can go."

I opened the tailgate of his massive pickup truck and set my bag on top of the elevated platform that contained the pair of long drawers I had seen in Duivelsmeer. As I glanced inside, I noticed a stack of carefully arranged planks of wood and sheets of plywood. Various tools of different shapes and sizes caught my eye: shovels, picks, and a mattock. Each one seemed to be secured to the sides of the pickup bed. I couldn't help but wonder if they were useful tools or dangerous weapons. I reached in, unfastened the mattock held in place with leather straps and buckles, and hefted it in my hand.

This extraordinary tool was a two-in-one marvel — one side featured a hoe with a chopper edge for loosening dirt and pulling rocks, while the other boasted a sharp axe edge, ideal to cut through roots or, if need be, a zombie's head. They made the handle from hardwood, providing extra power for a full-force swing.

"Like it?" Digger asked as he came up behind me and threw another duffle into the back of the truck.

"What's the handle made of?" I asked as I swung the implement, feeling its balance.

"Ash wood. It's a tree sacred to the Druids and long associated with witch's brooms and magic wands."

I shook my head, returned the tool to the truck, and fastened it in place. "Everything has a story with you, doesn't it?"

"Most things have a story if you think about it. An old pair of comfortable shoes, a ratty bathrobe you don't want to throw away, a record player in an era of digital downloads — all of them with their own unique story." He walked up the stairs to the front door, which he secured with a key. "You ready? Let's move out!"

Confined with Digger in the front seats of his truck, after two tiresome hours on the road, it was getting to me.

I tried to pore over the meticulous creature section of the Grimoire, but his preference for country music made it difficult to focus. The first hour and a half was bearable, but then he began crooning along with the tunes, and I just couldn't handle it anymore.

Some people don't like Rock and Hip-Hop, but at least the singers can sing.

Digger could not.

He sang out of tune, forgetting the words, and his songs of loss were an unappealing cacophony of woe. I grimaced as he made the ditties about losing wives, girlfriends, trucks, and even the damn dog, worse with his discordant voice.

"Perhaps we can have some different music?" I finally suggested.

"Sorry, was I singing too loud?" Digger said.

"Yes." I grimaced. "And I'm trying to read. Silence would be better."

He reached for the dial on the radio and clicked it off.

We were journeying along Highway 80 West. My curiosity was mounting when we would turn onto a road heading south. It tempted me to pull out my phone and access the GPS, yet my companion appeared to have his route memorized.

While reading, I was surprised to discover vampiric creatures like the *Shtriga* from Albania, *Strigoi* from Romania, and even the *Chupacabra* from the American West. It fascinated me to learn about the techniques needed to stop these monsters, most of which required decapitation.

Digger was right about one thing, though; the seats in his truck were comfortable, and I slipped into a light doze.

"You like waffles?" Digger asked, and shoved me with his elbow to make sure I was awake.

"Hm?" I said, coming around. "Waffles? I guess."

"I'm going to take you to a place that does breakfast all day," he said cheerfully as he pulled us off on the exit for Belefonte, Pennsylvania. "It's called 'the Waffle Place,' and it's a great little restaurant I found in my travels."

We pulled onto a separated four-lane highway and headed south.

All I could see out the window was empty land. "Why did you travel here? There's nothing out here."

"Sure there is!" he grinned. "There's the Waffle Place."

He exited the busy four-lane highway, and the road narrowed to a two-lane country road, taking us into the heart of a quaint Pennsylvania town. Here, we found old-fashioned hardware stores, pizza places, real estate offices, and banks.

On one side of the street were large brick houses and well-designed Victorians, while a large cemetery occupied the other side. In that moment, I grasped how Digger could have been here in the past.

The houses grew smaller and closer together as we approached the center of town. Finally, Digger pulled into a lot across from a large house that was painted a terrible shade of aquamarine, and had a sign:

### The Waffle Place
### A Local Legend

As soon as we stepped through the door, the tantalizing aromas of food wafted through the air. My stomach grumbled in anticipation. They decorated the interior with maroon indoor/outdoor carpeting, except for the 'bar' area, which had white and black tiles on the floor.

We sat at a table with four wooden chairs made with green vinyl seats.

Digger grabbed the menu off the table.

I grumbled, "At the rate we're going, we won't be in Louisiana until next week."

Without looking up from the menu, Digger said, "I think we can do better than that."

Not too crowded, the waitress quickly arrived at the table. She was in her thirties and had bleached blonde hair. Despite her rushed makeup and chipped nail polish, she had a warmth that came from enjoying people's company.

"Hey fellas, whaddya want to drink?"

We placed our orders, with me settling on a Tuna Melt and Digger selecting a Big Banana Waffle accompanied by a side of bacon.

I waited until the woman walked away and said, "The Big Banana Waffle? What are you, five years old?"

Digger chuckled. "Actually, it has fresh bananas and berries, and I don't have to put syrup on it. It's just that the waffles here are so dang good."

When our food arrived, I found the tuna melt delicious, and Digger relished his large waffle covered with fruit.

I was anxious about our drive to Louisiana. I set out on this road trip with one goal in mind: to learn what my father went through and uncover the truth about my mother. But now, I wondered why I was here, facing what seemed like a never-ending truck ride. This was not what I had planned to do.

We got back into the truck, Digger in the driver's seat again. He looked at his watch and said, "Looks like we're right on time."

"For what?" I asked as he pulled out of the lot and back onto Main Street, heading north.

"I told you, I have some shortcuts."

"And this shortcut requires you to go north? Shouldn't we be heading south?"

He gave that damn impish grin again. "We will be."

I sat back and closed my eyes, exhaling heavily. I decided I had to get some rest so I could be ready for my turn at the wheel. "Let me know when you want me to drive."

We drove for about ten minutes, and the sound of thunder in the distance only agitated me. An impending summer storm would further delay our journey. I couldn't help but feel a little disappointed in Digger; the tales my father told built him up to be such a colossal figure. I decided no real person could ever live up to that image.

Then again, he had saved my life.

A brilliant flash of light shone through my closed eyelids and startled me awake. An explosive thunderclap followed, which shook the truck as if a bomb had gone off beneath it.

I jolted upright, my eyes wide open. We were still on a two-lane road, with tall trees lining either side. The sun was shining brightly, with no sign of a cloud in sight.

"What the Hell was that?"

Digger grinned. "Our shortcut. We're now about two hours from New Orleans."

"Yeah right."

He just kept that stupid grin on his face as he said, "Check your phone. You got a GPS on it, right?"

I had an overwhelming desire to ignore his foolishness, but I pulled my phone out of my pocket.

According to Google Maps, we were on Route 83 near a large body of water — with New Orleans in the bottom right corner.

I spoke into my phone. "What is my location right now?"

The female voice replied, "You are on route eighty-three in Franklin, Louisiana, in the United States."

I stared at the moving dot on my map. "That's not possible."

"I told you I knew a shortcut," Digger chuckled merrily.

"We just went halfway across the country," I said, shocked. "That's not possible."

Digger watched the road, that grin stuck on his face. "It's possible, but most folks don't know how to do it."

"But you do?"

"Since we're here, I guess so."

"But — but—" I sputtered, trying to think of a logical argument.

He glanced at me and grew serious. "Ley lines."

"What?"

"Ley lines," he repeated. "It's the Irish name for fairy paths. The same thing as *dragon lines* to the Chinese, or a *djinnway* to Arabs, *spirit lines* to the Incas, or *song lines* to the Australian Aborigines."

"I'm not following you," I said.

"Invisible, interconnecting magnetic lines of force are all over this planet. I encountered an elderly mystic who had devoted his life to understanding and exploring them. He showed me how to use the energy from the Ley lines to transport myself from one point to another."

"My father mentioned nothing like that."

He spoke solemnly. "I didn't learn about it until after we parted. People use them for geomancy and other forms of divination. Some say it elevates human evolution and awakens hidden powers, while others believe it can summon demons. But it sure has saved me time when I'm driving."

I shook my head, trying to get my mind around it. "But things don't just — just—"

"Disappear?" Digger snorted. "Haven't you heard of the Bermuda Triangle? There are other mysterious places where planes and ships have vanished, too. These places have Ley lines running through them, and you need to know where you're going before you enter the energy line. Otherwise, you could end up anywhere."

He shrugged slightly as he pulled the truck onto an entrance to Highway Ninety and headed east.

I still couldn't let it go. "You get on one of these Ley lines, and you end up on another one, in a different location?"

"Basically. I'm not sure if you actually teleport, or you just move so fast from one place to the other that it looks like teleportation, but it works."

I glanced at my phone and set the navigation system to New Orleans. The estimated time of arrival was less than two hours, allowing us to reach the city before nightfall.

Over the past two days, my perception of the universe had shifted unexpectedly. I can only imagine the emotions my father experienced when he was a young man working alongside Digger.

He turned on the radio and found another Country-Western station.

I sat back as we traveled down the highway and Digger started singing.

# TEN

At about five in the afternoon, we drove the quaint streets of New Orleans and into the French Quarter. I was unfamiliar with the area, having only heard stories about it from my father.

We pulled onto Bourbon Street, where tourists jammed the sidewalks. At night, they shut off traffic and people filled the street, looking for jazz or alcohol, usually both.

We stopped at the edge of the roadway and Digger's huge truck filled the narrow street.

"Wait here," he said.

Just next to us stood a tall Creole Townhouse made of brick, its entrance a wide carriageway with its green shutters flung wide open. Through the windows, we saw bottles of colored oils and crystals that sparkled in the light. A sign hung over the door:

**Marie Lee's VooDoo Shop**

**Genuine VooDoo Love Charms**

**Attract Money**

**Stop A Rival**

After a few moments, Digger emerged with a key. He opened the metal gate next to the shop and instructed me to help guide pedestrians as he pulled the truck into the parking space.

"Make sure you bring the book in with you," Digger said.

I slipped it into my computer bag with my laptop. It barely fit.

"And when our host gives you a bedroom, hide it in the room."

"Hide it?" I said, frowning. "Why?"

"Because you can't be too careful." Digger said as we came out to the street, and he locked the fence behind us.

As we stepped into the VooDoo shop, the smell of aromatic oils and burning candles filled the air.

Digger smiled when an African-American woman emerged from behind the counter. She was slender and middle-aged, her hair hidden by a turban. Smiles had etched lines into her face, and a loose caftan hung from her body. Jangling bangles adorned her wrists, and she tipped her long fingers with ruby-red nails.

Showing his respect, Digger leaned forward and kissed both her cheeks in the French style.

As I walked in, her gaze fixed on me and I couldn't help but feel uneasy.

Digger spoke. "Marie, this is Joshua Bennet, the young man I told you about."

She whispered with a Creole accent, "So, this is him?" She glanced at Digger, then back at me and talked louder. "Oh, you are the spittin' image of your father."

Unexpectedly, she pulled me into a hug.

"Don't scare the man, Marie," Digger chuckled.

"You knew my father?" I asked the woman as she finally let me go.It surprised me when I noticed her eyes were wet.

"Oh, I could tell you stories," she said with a sad smile. "I knew your father quite well."

I felt heat rise in my face as a wave of embarrassment rushed through me.

"Digger told me that your father... passed," she mumbled.

"Yes," I said. "He died months ago."

She nodded wistfully. "I was afraid he would come to a terrible end."

I lifted my eyebrows at this.

She walked to the shop's glass door and flipped the closed sign, locking it shut with two locks.

"Come, we must talk," she said. "Do you want tea?"

"Only if it's your tea, Marie," Digger said.

She smiled as she led us through a doorway draped with curtains, into a room full of shelves stacked with boxes. We passed through another curtain and into a kitchen, with a table and four chairs.

"Sit, sit," she said, filling a kettle with water from a nearby sink and wiping her face with a small towel. "I am so glad you came so quickly, Digger."

"It sounded important, Marie," Digger said, sitting at the table. Worn blue vinyl covered the chairs, and I sat opposite my companion.

Marie was busy preparing a teapot as I watched. "There are some who might not listen to a crazy voodoo lady."

Exactly what I was thinking.

"Marie, when you call — I take it seriously," Digger insisted. "You are one of the sanest people I know."

As the kettle heated, Marie put out saucers and teacups in front of each of us. "Then you have to understand — someone is making zombies."

"Start at the beginning, Marie," Digger said.

"About a year ago, a man came from Haiti, a houngan—"

Digger glanced at me. "A voodoo high priest." His eyes moved back to Marie. "Was he any good?"

"Good is not a word to use on that man," Marie spat. "He called himself Moonwa."

Digger made a chuffing sound of disgust. "He referred to himself as the 'dark man'?"

"Wait… what?" I asked.

"Moun nwa means 'dark man' in Creole," Marie explained. "He was strong with the loas, the Gods of voodoo. He built a hounfò, a temple here in town, and drew in people. It was odd, because he attracted followers so quickly. It was as if he had help…"

"You think he's the one making zombies?" Digger asked.

"Yes, and no," Marie demurred.

"What does that mean?" I grumbled in exasperation.

Digger glanced at me sternly, then silently motioned for me to be quiet by pressing a finger to his lips.

Marie smiled. "Although he gained strength and followers, he died suddenly."

"Were other practitioners worried about what he was doing?" Digger asked.

Her smile was that of a cat after it has eaten the canary. "Perhaps. Who knows what can end up in a man's drink if he is not careful?"

I peered down at my empty teacup and felt uneasy.

"His death wasn't the end, I gather?" Digger asked.

"No. A young woman — whom I have known since she was a child—went to his hounfò and spoke to his followers. Soon, the congregation was following her commands."

Digger frowned. "You think Moonwa has possessed her?"

"That is what you call it. In Haitian voodoo, they know it as 'mounting the horse.' This often happens when a congregate allows the loas to take control. To be possessed by the loa is a great honor. However, I think Moonwa himself possesses this young woman, without the blessing of a loa."

"So let me get this straight," I said, getting yet another dark look from Digger. "You're saying a dead guy possessed this woman?"

"He made her into his chual," Digger explained. "It means that her will is gone and only his will is done."

"I believe Moonwa is acting through her to create zombies," Marie intoned. "To call down vengeance upon those of us who stopped him in his mortal form."

"This complicates things," Digger sighed.

"How so?" I asked.

The steam rose from the kettle as Marie got up from her seat. She poured the boiling water into the teapot, then set it in the center of the table on a trivet.

Digger broke the silence with a startling observation. "A demonic possession is easier, because for the demon to use the person's body, the possessed person agrees to it."

I shook my head. "How does that make it easier?"

"You don't see?" Marie asked. "When you allow a demon to possess you, it corrupts your soul. There is no longer any good in you."

"For that reason," Digger chimed in, "I would have no trouble killing someone possessed by a demon."

"But this possession is different," Marie added.

Digger nodded. "The girl is an innocent. She did not agree to the possession, Moonwa forced it upon her."

I nodded. "You want to free her without hurting her?"

"Exactly," Marie said and glanced at Digger. "He is quick."

"He grew up hearing his father's stories."

"Ah! I hope he learned much from his father's mistakes." Marie looked over at me apologetically. "Forgive me. I mean no disrespect for your father. When I knew him, he was headstrong, and thought he knew more than he did." She looked back at Digger. "Fortunately, I got him to where he was willing to learn."

"You offered things I never could, Marie," Digger said as he poured himself a cup of tea.

Marie laughed, and her laughter had a sweet tone to it. "That is true."

Digger filled two cups with tea and grabbed the sugar bowl and cream pitcher from the cabinet and fridge, respectively. His familiarity with the kitchen surprised me.

"What do we do?" I asked, as I added cream to the tea. "Do you have something to push this ghost — or whatever it is — out of her?"

Digger put a spoonful of sugar in his tea and stirred it slowly, his eyes focused on the cup. "It requires an exorcism. But first, we must stop the creation of more zombies."

"How?" I asked.

"We observe."

I frowned. "That's it? Observe?"

"We will confront the spirit, but first we must stop the creation of any more zombies, and eliminate any already created. As long as there is an army of the undead to protect the physical form he is inhabiting, we cannot push him out of the possessed woman."

After enjoying a cup of the exotic tea blend, Marie guided us up to the third floor of the building. Here, two bedrooms were ready for us. I lugged my baggage into the room and carefully concealed the Grimoire beneath the mattress, though I had doubts about the security of this hiding spot.

I returned to the kitchen, bringing my laptop, and I found Digger had the local newspaper, the Times-Picayune, spread out in front of him.

I glanced over at Digger as he flipped through the pages, a pair of round glasses perched atop his nose. "What are you searching for?" I inquired.

"I'm reading the obituaries," Digger said, and then chuckled. "I'm pleased to tell you I'm not listed in it."

"How do the obituaries help?"

He kept looking at the paper. "Someone is making zombies. What do you need to do that?"

"Dead bodies, I guess."

"Right, but you don't want one that's too old, or anyone too well-known, or you're going to attract attention when people see a congressman or celebrity lumbering mindlessly about."

"I never thought there were criteria for picking someone to make into a zombie."

"Of course there are! Another choice is the physical body. Zombies are strong, but not superhuman, like ghouls. A zombie is stronger than a human, but you don't want to pick a person with weak bones or a frail physique. You want to pick someone fairly hearty, maybe who died in an accident."

"You're checking on recent deaths that would reflect those attributes?"

"Got it. The obituaries list the age of the deceased, and sometimes what they died of. But more important, the time of the funeral, and where the burial will take place."

"I guess that would make it easier to dig him up," I offered.

"They place people in above-ground tombs in this town, Josh, because of flooding," Digger replied, looking up at me above the glasses. "It's why it's such an ideal place to make zombies. You don't have to dig them up at all." He returned to the paper but kept speaking. "Except for the Jewish cemeteries. That tradition is a ground burial, so each grave has raised concrete walls and they elevate the dirt to compensate for flooding. But I'm focusing on above-ground tombs."

That made sense. I didn't know what it took to turn a corpse into a zombie, but why exhaust yourself digging them up if you didn't have to?

"I found two likely selections," Digger said. "You and I are going to observe those burial locations tonight."

"What if this girl... um... the bad guy, shows up to make a zombie?"

"Then we stop him, any way we can."

# ELEVEN

D igger wisely moved the truck six blocks away to Esplanade Street, which was much wider and he could park the vehicle on the side of the road. That way, we'd have access to it and be able to walk down Bourbon Street in the opposite direction of the bars and the revelers.

He advised I take a nap and went to his room.

I attempted to drift off to sleep, yet my eyes were open, and the sight of the ceiling fan spinning overhead transfixed me.

I was getting ready to go on a mission with Digger, like my poppa talked about.

The past few days had been life-threatening. I hadn't expected the attack of the Vrykolakas, and I was unprepared when it happened. But now, I would soon head to a graveyard to confront an evil voodoo master and zombies. The mission seemed almost impossible. I lay in bed, too wound up to sleep, as I contemplated the outcomes of this endeavor.

I finally uncovered the Grimoire and resumed my reading, this time focused on zombies. Various forms and names were revealed, such as *Nachzehrer* from Germany, which drains the life force from their own kin, *Gjenganger* from Norway, which are the dead that are searching for their murderer, and even *Draugr* from Scandinavian folklore, which are reanimated corpses of Vikings.

I felt overwhelmed looking through the pages that detailed the various creatures and their capabilities. I wondered how I was ever going to remember all this information and discern the nuances between them. Was this even necessary?

Finally, I turned to the page with the blessing to activate the *Lahat Chereb*, and carefully wrote it in my notebook. I mustered the courage to retrieve the golden hilt. Digger had cautioned me on the importance of spiritual preparation to wield it correctly. Even so, I felt adequately equipped.

Grasping the relic tightly, I recited the incantation with conviction. As I uttered the last syllable, I lifted my gaze. I expected the incandescent sword to materialize as my words reverberated through the room.

Nothing.

I added an "Amen."

Still nothing.

I began again, slowly speaking the words, taking my time to savor each syllable, before finishing with an Amen. My gaze remained fixed upon the shining golden hilt of the sword.

After my fifth attempt, I just put it back into the chamois bag, unsure what this meant.

I also put the book away as the sun was setting.

At about eight PM, Digger knocked on my door and announced, "Dinner."

I returned to the kitchen downstairs, where Marie had cooked a large pot of something. She doled out generous servings for us both, and we had strong coffee to go with it.

"What is it?" I spoke up.

Digger laughed. "Don't you know *Jambalaya* when you see it?"

"In New Jersey, we just call it stew," I offered with suspicion. "What's in it?"

"What isn't?" Marie said, also laughing. She counted off on her fingers. "Rice, sausage, shrimp, onion, celery, okra, carrots, any old thing we have to put in it."

"It's not too spicy for the beginner, is it Marie?" Digger asked.

"It will be fine. I took it down a notch," she assured him.

I picked up the coffee and noticed it had a funny smell. "What's in the coffee?"

"Chicory, Josh." Digger smiled. "It's how people drink coffee down here. It's strong, but I think you'll like it."

I took a sip of the coffee, and the robustness of the brew was obvious. There was an added hint of the herb that was unusual, yet not unpleasant.

I hesitantly took a bite of the *Jambalaya*. The spice was present, but not overwhelming, and the combination of the various flavors blended perfectly.

I savored the taste and ate with gusto, suddenly aware of just how hungry I was.

Marie had served herself, and was eating delicately. She glanced at Digger and said, "I put a few extra herbs in the food to help you tonight."

Digger smiled as he ate. "You're the best, Marie."

"You must free me of this problem. The last thing N'Orleans needs right now is trouble like this."

"No one needs trouble like this," I said.

"I wish I could get out ahead of anything coming our way," Digger said.

Marie nodded. "I could use the tarot cards. Read your fortune."

Digger shook his head. "Not tonight. I think I only want you to read my fortune when the sun is shining." He met her eyes with a very serious look. "Clem asked me to visit. He said it wasn't an emergency, but I have to go to him as soon as I can."

"How is Clem?" Marie smiled. "I haven't seen him in so long."

"He's doing well, and so far, he's kept his community together."

"He has a very big heart, that fellow," Marie murmured.

We ate without speaking, the silence between us heavy and full of unspoken words.

I had no idea who Clem was, so I kept my thoughts to myself. My mind was racing with all the tales my poppa used to tell me as I prepared myself for whatever the night might bring.

I hoped I had adequately prepared myself.

At eleven, Digger knocked on my door. "Are you ready to visit the Cities of the Dead?"

I opened the door to see Digger dressed in black pants with that green Peacoat and a wrinkled camouflage 'Boonie' style hat on his head.

I was wearing a long-sleeve black T-shirt and black pants. "Cities of the Dead?"

"That's what the cemeteries are called here."

I nodded. "Because they're all above ground." I looked Digger over. "You don't look like you can be very sneaky with that coat on."

He opened the thin jacket to reveal his thick belt with the leather pouches that could hold different weapons.

"Okay I get it now. We need to go in armed."

"I'm planning on reconnaissance. But we need to be ready for a fight. Can you handle a knife?"

"A knife? I guess," I replied.

We exited the townhouse through the side door, and Digger brought the key to unlock the wrought-iron gate. We were a distance from Canal Street and its bustling nightlife. Only a few people were strolling the sidewalks and chatting amongst themselves.

We made our way to the truck on Esplanade. As Digger gunned the engine, he said, "We're lucky, the two cemeteries we're watching tonight are right across from each other."

"How do we communicate?" I asked.

"We'll text with our phones on vibrate. Let me give you my number."

He spoke the numbers quickly as the truck cruised through the shadows of the night. I entered them into my phone.

"Do you need me to give you my number?"

"I already have it, Josh."

His actions took me aback. How did he get my phone number if I had never given it to him? This was yet another thing I needed to ask him for clarification.

We followed Esplanade Avenue until we reached Interstate Ten, looming on an elevated road high above us. Turning onto North Claiborne Avenue, we headed up Canal Street. Tracks for the streetcars that ran through town divided the four-lane road, though only one streetcar was in use at this late hour. As we drove by, the bright gas stations, tall glass office buildings, and bars lit the night up, with the sound of jazz spilling out into the streets.

As we drove under the looming oaks, they appeared to glare down at us, as if they would lash out at us for daring to pass. Then, when a lavender building came into view on our right, Digger steered the car onto North Anthony Street and pulled up to the curb.

We got out of the truck and Digger opened the tailgate and began loading supplies into the pouches on his belt. "We'll be walking from here," he declared. "What's your religion?"

"Agnostic."

He stopped and stared at me. "Fine time to learn that. I'm shocked a son of Ephraim Bennet would be a freakin' Agnostic."

I shrugged. "Okay, Christian I guess."

He shook his head and pulled out a crucifix on a chain. "Since you'll be dealing with Haitian voodoo, a Catholic symbol would be best. Put it on."

He handed me the crucifix, and I put it over my head.

"Might not work if you don't have faith in it," he muttered.

"I'll... um... do my best?"

"Well, that's reassuring," he grumbled, his voice dripping with sarcasm.

He handed me a short knife in a sheath with a heavy clip. It was a small blade only about six inches long that came to a wicked point. Digger explained how to put it in my boot, using the clip to secure it to the inside of my left leg, as my right was my dominant hand. He said I could retrieve it quickly if I needed it. My pants leg pulled down over the hilt, completely hiding it.

"Remember," he said, "we are just observing." He pulled out the small hatchet that had saved my life a few days prior. Turning it so that the handle was at the small of his back, the axe head tucked neatly away into its pouch. He then grabbed an empty shoulder bag and pulled out a large knife, roughly the size of a machete. It had a curved iron blade, like a crescent moon, with a long pointed blade at the bottom of the curve. A second sharpened blade jutted out as a crossbar above the wooden handle.

Hanging it from a strap on his belt, he made sure he hid it beneath his long coat.

"What on earth is that?" I asked.

"It's a Hunga-Munga," he said. "A traditional African weapon and very effective for this kind of work."

"A lot of weapons for observation," I said with raised eyebrows.

He shrugged. "Okay, you're the one observing. If you see someone wandering around, you text me. Now let me get you to a place where you can watch the tomb."

"You know which tomb it is?"

"It should be obvious once we get to the location."

We walked to Canal Street and made a right, just two guys walking around, trying not to draw attention to ourselves. His peacoat concealed the items on his belt, and the bag he carried appeared totally innocuous.

A large insect scuttled across my path, startling me. I moved aside, ensuring I didn't accidentally step on it.

"What the hell was that?" I hissed.

"Just a bug," Digger said, annoyed that it bothered me.

"Just a bug?" I repeated. "It was a cockroach the size of a bird!"

"The locals call them Toe-Biters," Digger assured. "The streetlights attract them. They can't hurt you."

We continued our walk, but the large bugs kept rushing out of the grass on both sides of the sidewalk. With every step, we would hear a sickening crunch as we stepped on them.

We left a path of broken insect shells behind us, their insides oozing out in thick, black goo.

I walked alongside Digger, trying my best to avoid the small and scurrying creatures beneath our feet. Despite my efforts, I stepped on some of them and felt disgusted as I heard the crunch of their shells. Meanwhile, Digger continued on without a second glance, seemingly unbothered by the destruction in his wake.

We strolled up the street lined with office buildings, and as we drew closer, I understood why Digger had called the cemeteries "The Cities of the Dead". The tombs and mausoleums were short little buildings packed close, leaning at odd angles, and ranging from plain to lavish to eccentric. Jutting crosses and statues cast contrasting shadows from the streetlights on the roadway. The rows of tombs resembled a vast network of streets on both sides of the spacious four-lane road, enclosed by ornate wrought-iron fences.

It went on and on, as far as I could see. At the end of the block, some quarter mile away, Canal Street ended at another graveyard, with the peak of a church steeple visible in the distance.

I stopped walking, and my mouth fell open. "How far does this go on?"

"It's a hundred and fifty acres, so, a ways," Digger said. "New Orleans is one of the oldest towns in America. They've been burying people for a long time."

We arrived at a gate made of intricately curved iron that was secured with a padlock over a box of metal.

I snickered at this. "They lock the cemetery. Are they afraid people will break in?"

Digger handed me a small flashlight and instructed me to shine it on the lock. He then pulled out a set of picks and worked on it. "Vandals get in, but the real reason cemeteries have fences is to prevent what's inside from getting out."

I frowned. "You're kidding. I thought it was to keep kids from doing graffiti or something."

"Have you ever wondered why they surround cemeteries with wrought iron fences? Like I told you at my house, the undead have a problem with iron."

He took the padlock off with a flick of his wrist and removed the chain, then opened the small box. He released the latch, opening the gate, and I handed him the flashlight.

"Keep it," he said, stepping in. "You might need it, and I have another. But don't use it unless you have to."

He grabbed a second flashlight and used it to ensure the chain and lock remained unfastened, but appeared as they had when we arrived.

"Go out through this gate and secure it on your way out."

"I'll try," I said, and found my mouth was dry.

"Make sure you do. There may be more things in this cemetery than just zombies."

I had no clue what he was talking about. We walked forward; the streetlights providing scant illumination. In the distance, I saw the lights from other roads, but on the pathways between the tombs it was nearly pitch black.

Digger was familiar with these trails, as if he had memorized them. He curved his way around two tombs and halted to signal me to follow him down another path.

We were standing across from a tomb with an open doorway, the entrance not sealed by bricks and mortar like the others. A pile of bricks lay in neat rows against the side of the structure.

He spoke in a hushed voice. "That's the place where they put the man today. They won't seal it up with the bricks and mortar until tomorrow."

I stepped closer to the tomb and noticed a small round hole in the ground in the pathway where I stood. I looked inside and saw shelves lined with coffins. "How did they ever fit him in there? I mean, wasn't it full already?"

"It was. They took the oldest coffin off its shelf, separated the remains, and put them back into the tomb, probably pushed to the rear of the vault, or in the bottom."

I gasped. "Is that... appropriate?"

Digger shrugged. "They've been doing it that way for hundreds of years. Now I gotta get to my location, and it's getting late. I'll text you once I'm in position. You text me if you see anything."

As he walked away, I kept my gaze on him until he was out of sight. I moved between two burial chambers and back onto a path further away, out of sight. I sat on the steps of another crypt, blending into the shadows and making myself a less noticeable target. I still had a clear view of the open tomb.

Since it was early summer, it was warm, but not too hot.

I shifted uneasily on the hard stone beneath me as I glanced at my watch. Almost midnight — the perfect time for a grave robber to do their work. Uncomfortable or not, I had to see what was going on, in case our zombie maker showed up.

I was at a loss about how I could help Digger if our villain arrived at his location. I had no way of tracking him down.

Then again, I doubted Digger needed my help.

He had an array of items tucked away in the pouches of his special belt. Add to that the Hunga-Munga and his hatchet, which he skillfully wielded to defeat Anastasia. He only equipped me with a crucifix and a small knife tucked away in my boot, and I was unsure of how to use either.

As I made myself comfortable, the melodic sound of crickets surrounded me. My gratitude for opting to wear boots rather than shoes grew as I realized those enormous cockroaches might lurk in the shadows. A surge of unease overcame me as I considered the number of the insects I had unwittingly crushed underfoot. Were there more scurrying about and having a raucous gathering in the sepulchers, unbeknownst to me?

My heart skipped a beat, and I jumped at a sudden vibration from my phone. I opened it and the brightness of the screen was almost too much to handle. I adjusted the settings to the darkest view and read the text from Digger:

I am at my location, not far.

Text me if you see anything.

I sent a quick reply to let him know I got the message. Digger worked hard to pick out just the right locations, but what if he was wrong? If the zombie maker went somewhere else, we wouldn't have a clue.

I wished I had brought a coat with me as I settled in for a long night. The hard stone step was already making my backside sore.

The crickets fell silent.

I stayed in the shadows as I noticed a light coming down the paths of the graveyard. It was still a ways away, but I could tell it was unsteady, like a fire rather than a flashlight. My phone in hand, I texted Digger:

Something is happening here.

I heard people coming closer, but their footsteps were strange — it was as if they were shuffling instead of taking normal strides.

As the bright light approached, I pulled further back into the darkness, keeping my eyes trained on the figure at the front. At the head of the line was a black man in a white shirt and pants, carrying an eight-foot pole.

Why did they need a pole?

They walked along the dark path, the first man leading the way and a shorter man following close behind, holding a lantern with a burning wick. The lantern illuminated his face, which was bloated and pale. His limbs were twisted and distorted, and his hands bore flesh that was blackened and peeling away. His jaw was missing, the flesh torn at the cheeks and the upper teeth exposed in a hideous, permanent grimace.

I sucked in a breath and shuddered as I realized the other men with the black man were — zombies.

The first man set the long pole directly into the round hole I saw earlier. The group of men dressed in dark clothing shambled around the pole in a circle.

A white-haired man's sickly pallor and decaying skin marked his grotesque transformation. He stepped up to the man in charge, offering him a sizable sword. He took the sword from the mindless servant, unsheathed it, and swung it around with practiced ease.

Great. Armed only with a six-inch knife, while this guy was waving around a three-foot sword.

The man in white returned the blade to the decaying white man, who held it motionless. Taking a basin filled with a bright powder, the man in the white shirt drew lines on the ground.

My heart raced as I observed the zombies in dark clothing. Motionless, their expressions blank, each one in a different state of decay. I counted eight of them, and I knew if they saw me, they would attack in an instant.

I got behind the tomb and texted Digger a second time:
Hurry,
they're zombies and one guy is doing stuff.

The eight undead things stood in frozen silence. The man in the white shirt continued to pour the powder from one hand to create intricate designs on the ground around the pole.

Marie said the spirit of the dead conjurer had possessed a woman, yet the person drawing the symbols was obviously a man. Why was he drawing symbols? Then, in the faint light of a flickering lantern, I saw a figure in a white dress draw near.

My breath caught in my throat as a woman approached. She was breathtakingly gorgeous, more beautiful than any other woman I had ever seen. She possessed caramel skin that was luminous, and her hair was a wild tangle framing her face. Her body was voluptuous, with a full chest and perfectly curved hips. Even more enchanting was her face, with a delicate nose and lush lips — it felt as if every dream I ever had of an ideal woman had come to life.

"*Tounen,*" she said. It sounded like a variation of French.

Haitian Creole, maybe?

That made sense. What language would a Haitian voodoo high priest use?

Her words had an immediate effect on the zombies, who stepped back, including the man in white. He had drawn the intricate symbols in a matter of moments, his hand moving so quickly that it seemed he must have done this hundreds of times before. Even in the dim light from the lantern, the bright white powder stood out, a pattern of lines on the ground.

The woman raised a large rattle made from a brown gourd. Encircling the gourd was a thick rope covered with colorful beads. A thin string secured a silver bell with a black top to the base.

With a steady rhythm, she shook it.

The white-clad man whipped off his shirt and tossed it aside. He moved gracefully around the intricate designs, avoiding smearing the symbols. Taking the sword from one zombie, he unsheathed it and swung it wildly through the air, as if battling an invisible foe.

The man danced about, waving the sword with ease. He may have lacked the skills I mastered in my fencing classes years earlier, but I really did not want to go up against him with my tiny knife.

I glanced around, wishing Digger would get here, and then the sound of the rattle stopped.

The man's body glistened with sweat as he grabbed the scabbard from the zombie's grasp and belted it around his waist. He then slid the sword into the scabbard.

The woman gave the rattle to one of the undead before slipping off her shoes and reaching to the front of her dress to unbutton it.

She had all of my attention.

The man, only in white pants now, the sword at his waist barely grazing the ground. He gently grasped the straps of her dress and I watched as it slid off her shoulders.

I almost moaned when she removed the garment. She stood in the soft light, completely naked and utterly stunning, the most gorgeous creature I had ever seen. The man in white pants handed the dress to the zombie with the rattle, taking the gourd and shaking it himself.

The woman stood in the center of the patterns etched into the ground, her body bare. She moved in a sultry, circular dance, her hands gliding over her curves as if in invitation to the spirits. Her eyes were closed and her head thrown back in pleasure as she tantalized the night air.

I found myself entranced, totally enraptured by the scene before me. This was an experience unlike anything I ever encountered before, a truly sensuous and primal moment.

"Good, we still have time," a voice whispered in my ear.

I almost cried out in shock. I was so intent on the woman that I hadn't noticed Digger's approach. My heart was racing as I fought to calm down.

"The guy with the white pants has a sword," I hissed.

He grunted quietly. "They always do."

The woman came to a standstill, held up her hand, which caused the rattle to cease.

She looked out into the darkness around her and said, *"Yap gade nou!"*

Digger rose to his feet. "They know we're here. Watch my back."

My heart raced as I followed Digger, who had drawn the Hunga-Munga blade from his belt. He kept the weapon concealed beneath his pea coat as we ventured past the tombs.

The woman, whose face had looked so beautiful, was now twisted in rage. *"Tonbo!"*

"Glad you recognize me, Houngan," Digger said with a sly smile. "No need for introductions, then. I have taken responsibility for the man you wish to turn into a zombie, and he will remain in his tomb. Are you going to leave quietly, or do we have to do this the hard way?"

The man with the sword drew it slowly from its scabbard, the menacing glint of the blade unmistakable.

"I guess that means the hard way," Digger said, raising the Hunga-Munga just as the man swung his sword right at Digger's head.

Digger gripped the multi-blade weapon in both hands and thrust it forward. This move jammed the sword between the curved sickle blade with the shorter, pointed blade of the weapon. The man attempted to free the sword, but Digger just used the blades as leverage to yank the sword out of his hands. Digger spun around, striking the man in the face with the hilt of the weapon. The man went down, unconscious, and Digger twisted the Hunga-Munga to let the sword fall free.

Using this as a distraction, the woman shouted, *"Touye li!"* She snatched the rattle and her clothes and sprinted away.

"Follow the girl," Digger yelled over his shoulder at me as the men in black moved toward him menacingly. He brandished the Hunga-Munga and with a single, sweeping motion of its blade, severed the head from his nearest assailant. The head flew through the air and tumbled end over end to land at my feet with a wet thud. I stifled a wave of nausea, as I stared at the man with the missing jaw, gazing up at me with its hideous smile of rotted flesh.

Digger glared at me. "Chase the girl, damn it! Stop her, tackle her, bind her, but do something."

I swallowed my rising gorge and took off in the woman's direction, as Digger stabbed another zombie with the weapon's pointed blade. He easily decapitated it with the sound of steel passing through bone and dead flesh.

She was ahead of me, running naked in the pale moonlight. Her white dress flowed over one arm, the shivering burr of the rattle accompanying her strides. She ran with abandon through the tombs and crypts, but I was catching up.

She tried to hide from me as I drew closer. I was unsure what I would do when I finally caught up with her. Would I try to pin her down and threaten her with my knife until Digger arrived?

Then again, he was fighting eight zombies — well — he'd brought it down to six already...

As I rounded the bend, there she stood in the center of the path. She clutched her dress in one hand, the rattle in the other, her breath coming in short, labored bursts. The moonlight highlighted her glistening skin, and I couldn't help but marvel at her beauty.

I came to a full stop and looked at her, panting myself.

"You do not wish to hurt me," she said with a slight accent.

"No, I don't," I gasped. "But you have to come with me."

Her smile became seductive. "What do you want to do to me?"

She stepped toward me, and I took a step backward. Could this woman really be under the power of a *houngan*? If so, I knew little about voodoo and was afraid of what she might do to my mind if I let her get too close.

She halted and fixed me with her mocking smile and purred, "I can tell you want to touch me."

I pulled the knife from my boot, brandishing it in a basic defensive stance I'd learned in fencing class. "Lady, you're coming with me," I stated, trying to sound fierce.

Her features reflected anger, her eyebrows knitted together. "You threaten me with a *beni lam*? How dare you!"

She motioned to me and the next thing I knew; I was flying backwards. It felt like a professional boxer had punched me in the stomach as I tumbled to the ground. I struggled to sit up, pain pulsing throughout my body, only to see her grinning at me with an evil sneer.

"I know what you fear, *amatè*," she crooned and shook the rattle. *"Pinèz atak."*

A vast black wave surged toward us at incredible speed — thousands upon thousands of monstrous cockroaches. They surged around her feet without making contact, like water rushing around a rock in a stream.

I stood up, the small blade shaking in my hand. She referred to it with a special name, and I felt certain that if I stabbed her with it, the bugs would go away.I looked at that beautiful face — even with her so angry and twisted with hate, I could no more stab her than I could vandalize the Mona Lisa.

It rooted me in terror as the giant bugs moved as a seething, writhing mass. They crept toward me with their eerie, synchronized movement. The enormous cockroaches swarmed around me. As the first few reached me, I frantically stomped on them and swatted them away. I knocked a few off, but others clung to my hands and bit into my flesh.

They crawled up my legs, their little teeth biting through my denim jeans. They moved up my legs and arms, into my hair and over my face. I screamed and fought, but the bugs were relentless. They bit through my clothes as I thrashed and flailed helplessly in their midst.

My heart was going to explode. Panicked and frantic, I tried to run. Every step seemed to attract even more of the insects, as they crawled out from behind tombs and crevices in the ground. The festering mass of creatures quickly covered me from head to toe and their size made them impossible to shake off.

They wriggled and crawled into my mouth, nose, ears, and burrowed into my clothes. They forced me to close my eyes to prevent them from blinding me. I screamed, but I felt them inside my mouth. The monsters blocked my nostrils and I couldn't breathe. Every inch of my body felt the sting of their bites as they continued to attack.

*"Pinèz ale!"* a male voice shattered the night. "Begone!"

The creatures leapt off me, crawling out of my nostrils and dropping from my hair. Greedily, I sucked in air and hastily pushed the disgusting things off me. I stumbled to the steps of a nearby tomb. Dirt covered my clothes and rips and tears covered my shirt in hundreds of places.

"I take it she got away?" Digger panted, collapsing on the steps next to me.

I looked over at him. I wasn't sure because of the light, but he looked paler than he did before. He was breathing hard, and holding the Hunga-Munga, dark liquid dripping off it.

I was breathing hard as well, and still had the taste of bugs in my mouth, which I tried to spit away without vomiting. "How did you get the things off me?"

He shrugged, sucking in deep breaths. "I used a counter-spell."

"You don't look good." I said, fighting to ignore the burning of hundreds of cockroach bites.

"Let's see you behead eight zombies, and run all the way over here, and see how you do," he huffed. He looked out at the dark tombs all around us. "I need your help. Her servant is unconscious. We need to carry him to the truck."

"What about the others?"

"They're dead," he said and straightened his back. "Well, they were already dead, now they ain't moving."

"Are you up to this?" I asked as I pulled off one of my boots and a dozen bugs fell out, some of them crushed. "What are we going to do with that guy? Interrogate him?"

Digger shook his head wearily. "More or less, but he'll be useful. Marie has ways to get the information we need."

I pulled off the other boot and dumped another dozen bugs onto the ground.

# TWELVE

I stared at the man lying on the ground, the one who had drawn the mysterious symbols. I held his majestic sword, though the scabbard still hung around his waist. Digger walked off unsteadily, looking like an old man, to move the truck closer. This left me alone with our prisoner and the decapitated zombies. The dim light of the lantern shone as their lifeless eyes stared up at me. I could have sworn one of them even winked, but I hoped it was a trick of the light.

Finally, Digger returned. He removed the belt and scabbard from the unconscious man, and I strapped it to my waist. While holding a lantern in one hand, I assisted Digger in dragging the captive down the path. His sliding feet echoed on the cobblestones, similar to the scuttling of those awful insects or the shuffling of undead zombie's feet. I stumbled a few times, constantly glancing back in terror. I was afraid that a pack of decapitated corpses with pallid fingers would reach out to grab me, or a tidal wave of bugs prepared to wash over me.

We maneuvered the unconscious man into the back seat of the pickup truck and drove off. I scratched incessantly at the bites covering my skin. The bumps had become raised and were incredibly itchy, driving me insane.

"What about the bodies?" I finally inquired.

Digger frowned. "You mean the zombies?"

"Yes. We left... well, you left... eight beheaded bodies lying out there in the open. Won't that get the police involved?"

"Probably."

I scratched several bites on my scalp. "Won't they want to know who murdered them? They might come looking for us."

"I doubt it," he said simply.

"Why's that?"

"Because once the bodies get to the Medical Examiner, he'll find that they've been dead for some time. The police will conclude that someone opened several tombs. Then, left the decapitated bodies of the residents out after desecrating them. That lowers the charges from capital murder to a high misdemeanor."

The man in the seat behind me groaned and raised his head. Stopping at a traffic light, Digger turned and gave him a sharp blow to the temple and he fell back, unconscious again.

"Was that necessary?" I argued.

"Eight beheaded zombies and you're worried about me clocking a guy?" Digger complained. "Look, we need him to be out until we can secure him. Voodoo priests can be strong. If this one really is a *bokor*, he might have some tricks like the little lady with the bugs. Do you want more of that?"

"No." I shuddered at the thought of the vile creatures crawling all over me again. I rolled down the window and spat out a crunchy piece that could have been a bit of a leg or an antenna.

It was the dead of night as we drove up Bourbon Street, the only sound being the squeaking of the gate as I opened it. Digger pulled the truck in next to Marie's store and shut off the engine.

With the gate secured, we carried the man through the side door and into the small kitchen in the back of the shop, where Marie was waiting, despite the late hour. She guided us down a hall past the kitchen to a room that had a voodoo shrine set up on a large table.

A shiny black cloth covered the table, the top adorned with statues and dolls of the Virgin Mary, and a black woman wearing a headscarf. Around the table lay an array of colorful beads in a variety of sizes, a small incense burner, and tall vases of fresh flowers. Illuminating the scene were multiple candles encased in glass tubes, which were etched with symbols.

I pointed at the designs on the glass tubes. "Those were the same symbols that this guy was drawing on the ground.

"They are called *veves*," Marie explained. "It is what is used to ask the help of the *loas*."

In the center of the room were four chairs, three of them positioned to face the shrine. Marie placed the fourth in front of a laden table, facing outward. It had solid wooden armrests, and Marie instructed us to bind the man's hands to them using the black cord she provided.

As Digger and I tied him up, Marie noticed my continual scratching. She took my face in her hands and raised my head, inspecting the tiny bumps covering my skin. "What happened to you?"

"Um… bugs," I mumbled.

She nodded. "I have a salve for that. It looks like they wanted to make you their dinner."

I nodded silently. If it wasn't for Digger's timely arrival, would a pile of bones be all that was left of me?

We restrained the man and then Digger and I sat on either side of him while Marie took the seat in front. She placed a cold cloth on his forehead and raised an ammonia inhalant to his nose, causing him to cough and regain consciousness.

She pulled away, preventing him from biting or spitting on her as he lifted his head and surveyed us and the room.

"Welcome back, sunshine," Digger said dryly.

The man's gaze darted around frantically until his eyes finally settled on me and then Digger. "You!"

"That's right, me. They call me Digger. I'd like to have a little chat with you."

The man glanced down at his arms bound tightly and looked behind him to find the table with numerous flickering candles. His eyes widened in surprise. Then he faced the three of us. "You must release me."

The man spoke with a thick accent, and though he tried to sound authoritative, it was clear he wasn't in control.

"Or what?" Digger challenged. "You'll call the police? Maybe lodge a formal complaint after we picked you up in a cemetery with a sword and eight beheaded bodies?"

Marie glared at him. "You have used the *loas* to do dark, terrible red magic."

I never encountered the phrase 'red magic' before, but I was sure Marie had an expert knowledge of it.

She lifted a tiny container with a cork stopper from the table and doused the man's head with its contents.

He writhed and struggled under the thick liquid dribbling over him.

"What is that?" I murmured to Digger.

"Holy oil," Digger said with a glance at me.

She put down the oil and ran her hands through the man's hair. "I present the *lave tèt* upon you to purify this shell and bring forth your *gwo bonanj*."

"Nooo!" the man cried, his eyes closed and his body writhing.

Marie stopped moving her hands and held them on his head, her fingers wrapped in the tight curl of his hair. "We must release these bad things in your head and let another control you."

Marie reached for the rattle made from a gourd, similar to the one used by the woman in the graveyard. She carefully cradled the man's head in one hand while shaking the rattle above him and murmuring an incantation.

The prisoner thrashed and attempted to free himself, to no avail.

Finally, Marie put down the rattle and sat back down, still shaking it gently in a soothing rhythm. The prisoner stopped struggling and slumped forward, his head bowed and eyes closed.

Marie whispered, "Papa Legba, can you visit with us?"

The man's eyes suddenly opened — his eyes were completely red with no pupils. I almost toppled backward onto the floor in surprise.

A grin appeared on the man's face, and he spoke in a gravelly voice. "What you be wanting from me, daughter?"

I reluctantly turned my head, my body tensing as I avoided the sight of his piercing red eyes. They seemed to bore right into me, as if he could see every thought in my mind. I felt exposed under his gaze.

The red eyes moved to Digger. "I see the *Tonbo* is here. Been a long time, Digger."

Digger bowed his head. "An honor, as always, Papa Legba."

"Now this is a man who knows how to show respect for the old ways," he said and threw back his head with a laugh.

Marie spoke up. "May I burn an offering for you, Papa?"

He nodded, and Marie reached for a small earthenware dish. Inside was a mysterious dark liquid accompanied by brown leaves. She lit a match from the nearby candle and brought it close to the bowl, setting the mixture alight with a small blue flame.

"Is that rum and cigar?" he asked, and Marie waved the dish under his chin so the smoke rose into his face. He took a deep inhale of the smoke and sighed. "Yes, and a good cigar, too. You do know what I like, daughter."

She nodded and carefully placed the dish on a trivet on the altar. The dish's contents began to smolder, and the aromas of burning tobacco and rum filled the room.

The prisoner's red eyes shifted to me. I looked away, not wanting to make any contact.

"This one is new, *Tonbo*?"

"Yes, Papa Legba. His father worked with me in the past."

"And taken by dark forces," he said, and faced Marie. "Why have you called me through this..." he looked down at his body, his lips curled in disdain "...inadequate vessel, eh?"

Marie bowed her head again. "We meant no disrespect, Papa. But this man has many dangerous secrets. He has been working with a *houngan* who is raising up zombies."

"I see. Yes, this one fancies himself a *bokor*," he said and then laughed again. "But the woman, a powerful *houngan* possesses her with his spirit. You must free the woman or it will crush her soul."

"What of this one, Papa?" Digger stated. "He has helped her."

"I see, yes. But he does it only for money, and to be seen with the powerful one. Greed curses him."

"We need to find the woman, Papa," Digger said. "What can I do to find her, to stop the evil creature inside her?"

The man smiled broadly again. "I can see her. In the daylight, she hides near the water. In the park named for the moon, in a building that tells her she is beautiful."

Digger nodded, though I had no comprehension of what was being said. It was as if he were speaking a completely unfamiliar language.

"What shall we do with this one?" Marie asked, gesturing at the man tied to the chair.

The man smiled. "You need do nothing, his actions have offended the *loas*. He has sealed his fate."

He spoke with such menace that it filled me with dread.

"Papa Legba, I ask your permission to free this woman and remove the possessing spirit," Digger said. "I do not wish to offend the *loas* or you."

"Ah, *Tonbo*, I have missed talking to you," the man exulted. "I have looked into the dark soul that possesses the woman who was once our servant. He no longer does things the right way. You may free her, the *loas* give their blessing."

"Thank you, Papa Legba," Digger said.

"I must warn you, Tonbo. Something hidden is reaching out, and it's coming for you. Something ancient and strong."

Digger nodded.

He turned to face me with those awful eyes. "And you as well." The man threw his head back with a choking sound, and the body shuddered. When he raised his head, he looked exhausted, but his eyes were normal again.

"Untie him, and put him out front," Marie said. "He is no longer our problem."

Digger and I untied the ropes that were restraining him and the man did not struggle. The spirit that possessed him had sapped all his energy. We positioned ourselves on either side of him and led him out of the house with unsteady steps.

Out on the street, we let him go and headed back inside, but the man spoke. "Wait, you can't just leave me here. The *loas* are angry with me."

Digger looked at him. "You were the one who used their blessings for darkness. You picked your own fate."

"What can I do?" he asked and tears were in his eyes.

"Get to a church. That's your only chance," Digger said. "It's what I would do."

He closed the door.

"Is that wise to just let him go like that?" I asked, as Digger walked back to the kitchen. "What if he goes to the police, tells them we kidnapped him, turns us in?"

"Who would believe him?" Digger said. "Besides, Papa Legba, who communicates between humans and *loas*, possessed his body. Papa was inside of him and could see into his soul. How the *loas* judge him is in their hands."

"Why did he call you *Tonbo*? That girl in the cemetery, she called you that as well."

Digger shrugged. "It's just Creole for gravedigger."

Marie grabbed my arm and held a small jar in her hand. "I have that salve for you. We'd best put it on if we don't want you to become infected."

She ordered me to take off my shirt. When I hesitated, she said, "Come on young man, you ain't got nothing I haven't seen."

I slipped the tattered shirt over my head, the fabric full of holes. Delicately, I removed the crucifix and chain from around my neck and placed it atop the ruined garment.

"The pants too," she said. "We got to make sure there aren't any of those damn bugs on you."

I peeled off my boots, socks, and trousers, and a flurry of dead bugs fell out onto the floor. I shivered in disgust, feeling the hundreds of swollen bites all over my body.

The scent of the salve was pungent and unpleasant, but I would do anything to stop the relentless itching. I rubbed it onto my chest as Marie knelt behind me, gently applying it to my legs.

I looked over my shoulder and said, "No, Marie, you shouldn't do that. It's disrespectful to ask you to kneel like that."

She smiled up at me. "Your father taught you to be respectful of women. That is good." She gazed into my eyes. "But what will you do? You cannot reach your own back and you need my help. I'm not subservient, I'm simply helping apply the ointment on the areas you cannot reach."

She applied the ointment to my back, and the relief was instantaneous. I followed suit with my chest and arms, feeling the bumps disappear beneath my fingers. I was grateful that I wasn't able to glimpse myself in the mirror — I'm sure I wasn't a pretty sight.

She stood behind me, kneading the balm into my back while I applied it to my face and worked it through my hair. Finally, she handed me the jar. "You'll have to do the last part yourself, upstairs in your room."

I felt a rush of embarrassment and was thankful to have an excuse to get out of there.

"Wait about fifteen minutes for it to soak in, then take a shower. Very hot water. Then, right to bed with you," she said, sounding maternal.

I trudged towards the stairs in my briefs, and walked by Digger, who took one look at me and asked, "How do you feel?"

"Less itchy, why?"

"You just made it through your first trial by fire," he said and smiled. "And you're not dead."

He left the room, chuckling to himself.

"Are you gonna sleep the day away?"

I opened my eyes to find Digger standing in the sunlit doorway. I was about to say something unkind, but the sight of two mugs in his hands stopped me in my tracks.

"Is that coffee?" I muttered.

He held out a mug for me, and I took it gratefully and sipped it.

"The bites keep you awake?" Digger asked, returning to the doorway.

I shook my head. "No, but I kept seeing those damn bugs rush at me every time I closed my eyes."

Digger nodded. "Yeah, I can understand that. One time I went up against this one guy who controlled rats and made them attack. I had nightmares about that for weeks."

I gritted my teeth thinking about it, trying to not let my mind imagine it.

"Sorry. As the French would say, *Ce n'est pas le moment.*"

High school French was a long time ago, but I knew that phrase meant: "This is not the moment."

"*Mais, oui,*" I responded and sipped more of the coffee, feeling my energy return as the steamy liquid warmed me up. The addition of chicory made the dark brew rich and flavorful, and I was soon used to the unique taste.

I couldn't believe it when I looked at my arms and saw that the bumps were much smaller and weren't itchy. I was so relieved that Marie's potion had worked!

"Get dressed," Digger said. "You need some breakfast and we need to make a plan."

He left the room; the door closing behind him. I got dressed, pulling on my jeans and a dress shirt. I grabbed the crucifix and put it on at the last minute. I went into the kitchen, where he was waiting.

Marie was out in the shop's front serving customers and it surprised me it was past eleven AM.

Digger served up eggs and grits, biscuits and sausage gravy, and I had a helping of it all. Although I was from New Jersey, my father was a fan of grits, biscuits and gravy, and the taste of them here in "The Big Easy" was even better.

"Marie made the biscuits and gravy," Digger said after a sip of coffee.

"She's quite a cook."

Digger nodded. "Damn straight. If I had any sense, I would've married that woman, but she always liked your dad better." He sighed.

"Um... my Dad didn't... I mean, with Marie... after he was married?"

Digger looked shocked. "How could you think that of your father?"

"I don't! I'm just not sure of the timeline... that's all."

"After he met your mother, that was it. It surprised me when you told me he remarried."

"Lizzie is a great lady. She tried very hard to be a momma to me, as best as she could."

Digger nodded. "It's hard to be alone."

"You never married?"

He sighed again and took a forkful of eggs before he answered. "Couldn't. Too many bad people on my tail. And I kept going into dangerous situations like a damn jackass."

His gaze drifted up toward the ceiling as he searched for the right words. A sadness washed over his face as he spoke. "Throughout my life, I had people who helped me: Marie, your father, and others. Some stayed with me for a while, while it scared others off. A couple of guys ended up dead. Your father was always my favorite companion, and it crushed me when he left. I knew he had to go back to New Jersey, but I missed him."

"What was so special about my father?" I asked.

He sipped his coffee and grinned. "He had a gift, a second sense that would pop up when he needed it. Plus, he was a born warrior. I didn't know how he could give it all up. However, he devoted himself to you, and made it his mission to give you a normal life."

"He did... most of the time. Creatures attacked our house when I was seven."

Digger nodded. "So you told me. Something was trying to get you."

"Me? Why would something want to get me?"

"The monster that attacked you at your home, you told me was called a Lamia. She is an ancient demonic creature that kills children. She's native to Greece, and someone went to a lot of trouble to get her to New Jersey."

"There's nothing special about me," I told him. "I mean, Poppa always told me I could do anything, be anything, if I worked for it. But there were nights out by the fire pit..." I paused and looked at my coffee mug. "Those nights he'd sip Wild Turkey out of a bottle and tell me the scariest stories I'd ever heard. And he'd talk about you, and I used to think you were like Santa Claus or the Easter Bunny, some kind of mythical being that could piss thunder and shit lightning."

This made Digger chuckle. "Sounds painful."

"Most of the time, my poppa was just that, my poppa. A polite wave to the neighbors, a smile to his employees at the Alpha Oil Company, a kiss to Lizzie on his way to work. But on some nights, there was a darkness in him, and he couldn't get past it. That man was a stranger to me."

Digger slathered a biscuit with gravy and took a bite. "Now you know why I didn't marry. I've seen everything your father did... and worse. I wouldn't want to burden a family with it." He stood up at the table. "Now finish up. We got a *houngan* to exorcise."

I rose from the table and helped Digger put things away.

We stepped out of the side door and he got to work, strapping on the bulky belt with its many pouches. Lowering the tailgate, he pulled out one of those long drawers that were built into the truck. In it, there was a plastic toolbox, which he pulled out and opened. Nestled inside, dozens of bottles sat in a cushioning material. He took a few out and placed them carefully into the pouches.

He added other things: a large piece of chalk and a plastic water bottle filled with pink powder. Finally, he picked up the hatchet, slipped the head into its pouch with the handle up his back.

"The woman last night called my little knife a benny — something."

Digger nodded. "Probably a *beni lam*. That means a 'blessed blade.'"

"Somehow I knew that if I stabbed her with it, the bugs would have gone away."

Digger gazed at me. "But you didn't."

"I… couldn't. She wasn't doing it, it was something controlling her. She's a captive."

Digger handed me a leather belt with a single pouch from the cab of the truck. "This one should fit," he said.

I pulled it around my waist and Digger said. "That's the thing about takin' away someone's free will. You take away everything they ever were and everything they could ever be. And that's wrong. Go put the *Lahat Chereb* in that pouch."

"I haven't been able to make it work—"

"Think of it as a lucky charm. Bring it. I'll give you the boot knife, too."

I ascended the stairs to my room and retrieved the ancient gold hilt. I ran my fingers along its smooth surface, wondering how many centuries it had been around. How many people had held it in its long history?

I tucked the hilt of the sword into my belt pouch, then returned to the truck. Digger handed me the small knife, which I placed in my boot.

I looked up at him as doubt filled my mind. "Digger, you fight these things like it's nothing. What if I'm... not good enough?"

Digger smiled. "What you just said gives me hope. If you said, 'I can do it,' with no doubts, that would make me nervous. It's our doubts that make us honest and human. What you do need is a little more faith."

"What if I fail you?"

"Then I'd better have enough faith for both of us."

# THIRTEEN

We walked down Bourbon Street to Esplanade Avenue and headed toward the river. Digger insisted that was where we needed to go, we had no choice but to walk.

"You know where we're going? You understood what Papa whats-his-name said?"

"Papa Legba. He's the one who communicates between mortals and the voodoo gods, so make sure you know his name."

"I don't think I'm ever going to be involved with voodoo," I demurred.

"Josh, knowledge is power and you never know what you'll need. Showing respect to other belief systems is more than just a courtesy, it can save your ass."

We continued walking as I mulled this over. We headed left onto North Peters Street and into what appeared to be the warehouse district.

"You promised to tell me about my momma," I said.

Digger didn't even slow down. "I will, but it has to be at the right time."

"When will that be?"

"Soon, I promise." Digger pointed at the streets. "Katrina seriously damaged this entire area, back in Oh-five. Since then, they rebuilt it and added Crescent Park."

"So that's what was meant by a park named for the moon?"

"That's what I figure."

"What about the building that tells her she's beautiful? What does that mean?"

"I have a hunch. We'll just have to see if it pans out."

I shook my head. "Oh good, you have a hunch."

He flashed his mocking grin, and I trailed behind him, feeling defeated.

We came across a massive building, roofed and populated with an expansive open-air marketplace that spanned an entire city block. Vendors had their tables set up and were offering a variety of items, from straw baskets to handcrafted jewelry.

Across the street stood a seawall, with red letters that were taller than I, and read: CRESCENT PARK.

"Not much of a park," I noted as we walked past benches and a few scraggly bushes.

"We need to get to the open space," Digger suggested, and pointed ahead of us.

Perched next to the huge seawall, a massive rectangular concrete tower rose. They built it with large glass windows and an elevator inside, the machinery on top. Beside it stood a substantial metal scaffolding of stairs, allowing pedestrians to ascend and traverse the seawall.

"Can we take the elevator?" I asked, looking at the steps, which went up five flights to the crossover bridge.

"The stairs are always a better choice. Who wants to be stuck in a metal box when you're fighting something bad?"

And so we climbed the metal stairs. As we descended the stairs on the other side, we stepped onto a large concrete area covered overhead by a metal roof. It resembled nothing more than an airport hangar.

"Is this... the park?"

"Pretty much," Digger said. "It's more a concept of a park than actual greenery. Let's keep moving. We're not there yet."

We exited the building and began walking along the expansive concrete pathway. The mighty Mississippi River was to our right and ahead of us, the majestic Crescent City Bridge sparkled in the distance.

We finally reached a closed chain-link fence that blocked our path.

"I guess that's it," I said.

Digger pointed. "Look over there."

My gaze trailed after his pointing finger to a five-story red brick edifice. I spotted the words "YOU ARE BEAUTIFUL" in white lettering painted on its side.

I surveyed the space between us and the building, and there were formidable barriers. An eight-foot chain-link fence, a train with a mix of box cars and cylindrical black tank cars. Past that was the sea wall, though it was much shorter in this section.

"You have got to be shitting me," I said. "You expect us to get to that building? We could've just driven there."

"I wasn't sure where it was, and you only see the lettering from this side."

I shook my head. "There is no way in Hell we can get to it."

I felt a wave of unease wash over me as Digger grinned once more. "Follow me."

He hopped onto a nearby park bench, leapt over the rail of a metal fence, and swung himself down to the ground below.

"Get my freakin' neck broken," I muttered, but followed suit. When I grabbed onto the edge of the elevated sidewalk and hung by my hands, the drop to the ground was not too bad.

Digger pointed to the eight-foot-tall fence. "There's a break in it over there," he said. "Two problems solved at once."

Digger let out a gleeful laugh and climbed a ladder affixed to the side of the tank car. I did not know how this would help us circumvent the other impediments, but I went along with it, anyway.

Once I arrived at the top, I grunted in disgust. "This will be great practice for my cat burglar career."

He climbed up onto the top of the wall. He then lowered himself down with his hands and disappeared. I followed suit, and soon enough, I was safely back on the ground, shocked and surprised that we had made it.

We looked up at the building. Several of the windows were missing, and the place had an unused look.

"What is this place?" I asked.

"Abandoned warehouse. Great hideout for a voodoo sorcerer."

"Yeah, and the creepy factor is an added bonus."

Digger guided us up a trio of worn concrete steps to the entrance. A heavy sheet of metal with rusted hinges was all that separated us from the other side. In place of a doorknob was a hole with a hefty chain connected to the doorframe. Digger yanked the chain through the opening, finally revealing a closed padlock.

The sunlight made visibility easy, and he worked a piece of bent wire into the lock, opening it in seconds. We stepped in, and he draped the chain through the entrance and placed the lock on the floor.

In the hallway's darkness, our eyes slowly adjusted to the dim light coming through the few remaining grimy windows. Sturdy wooden planks made up the flooring littered with dirt and debris. Our surroundings were quiet and gloomy, in stark contrast to the bright sunshine and traffic noises outside.

The hallway opened up to a larger space. Faint rustling noises filled the air, producing an eerie sound. Digger halted in his tracks. "Rats, dammit," he muttered through clenched teeth.

It was the first time I ever saw fear in his eyes.

The pungent aroma of rotted wood and mold hung in the air as we approached the open staircase, but I soon detected a sweeter scent — something inviting.

"Is that incense?" I hissed.

Digger nodded. "The houngan knows the loas are not happy with what he has done. He is trying to win them over."

"Do you think he... she... can?"

Digger jutted out his chin. "The loas can be fickle. That's why we have to get involved. Papa Legba gave us permission to cast out the spirit, but it won't be easy."

He trudged up the stairs, and I followed closely behind, my eyes glued to the ground in search of any signs of movement.

Suddenly, a large rat skittered across the floor, darting from one dark corner to the next, making me jump.

As we ascended the staircase, the aroma of incense became more intense. Arriving on the second floor, we found ourselves in a single, dark room. The only thing breaking up the space were the metal support beams that ran throughout, instead of walls.

Digger reached under his jacket and freed the hatchet. We crept up the next set of stairs.

"Are you sure she's here?" I whispered.

He nodded tersely and began ascending the steps, wielding his hatchet. When he reached the topmost step, two sinister figures lurched out of the darkness. Their slow, staggering steps echoed off the brick walls.

Last night, in the darkness, I hadn't been able to make out all the features of our opponents. With a window slightly illuminating the room, I could observe them as they shambled forward. Their rotting flesh hung from their bones as their gaping mouths exposed yellow teeth, a milky film gleaming over lifeless eyes.

"Stay back!" Digger raised his axe, beads of sweat trickled down his forehead. The stench of rotting flesh became overwhelming, and he shuddered at the sight of the half-decomposed corpse lurching toward him. With a fierce cry, he swung the axe, its sharp edge cleaving through bones and sinew. The zombie's head rolled off its body and tumbled down the steps. I leapt out of the way to avoid it. Not a single drop of blood spilled from the head as it rolled past me.

The other zombie, its pale skin missing from most of its face, grabbed his arm that held the hatchet. With a strength that seemed to defy nature, it hurled him across the room, Digger's cries of agony ringing out as he disappeared into the shadows.

I yanked the knife from my boot and sprinted up the stairs at the undead thing. The stench was unbearable, rotten flesh mixed with dirt and sweat. With only my instincts guiding me, I thrust the blade deep into the zombie's chest. As I did, flames burst out around the blade, and I jumped back. The decaying hands of the creature fumbled for the hilt, attempting to extract the blade as it smoked and burned its rotting flesh.

A hissing sound filled the air as the creature convulsed, retreated backwards, the knife lodged in its chest. Smoke oozed from the spot, and the creature gurgled noisily as it stumbled away.

Digger was up, axe held firmly in his grip, but moving with an obvious limp. With a powerful swing of both arms, he sent the decaying head flying as the body below it convulsed, and with one more spasm, it finally crashed to the ground.

He yanked the knife free from the corpse's chest, offering me the hilt.

"Are you all right?" I worried, with a glance at his leg.

"Still think we're in the wrong place?" Digger asked, his breathing labored.

I shook my head.

"Nice reaction time, jumping up the stairs and using the knife."

"Why did it burn him?"

"It's a blessed blade, blessed by a bishop," Digger explained, catching a slight rasp in his breath. "It disrupts the energy that animates those things." He looked up at the ceiling. "There are going to be more."

"How many?"

"Don't know. But we reduced their numbers last night," he said and met my eyes. "Let's move."

As Digger and I made our way up to the third floor, we both maintained a vigilant state. Moving ahead with caution, our eyes darted around to evaluate every doorway as we passed. Cautious steps led us toward another set of stairs as our footsteps echoed from the dark walls.

At the bottom of the next flight of stairs was another one of them — a pale, gaunt woman in a tattered white dress. Her nose was completely gone, leaving only a gaping hole in the center of her face. But it was the lifeless, decaying look in her eyes that was the most disturbing for me.

Digger cautiously checked our surroundings, making sure we weren't being led into a trap, with the woman acting as a decoy.

"She's not attacking," I said.

"I'm aware of that," Digger said, and checked the hallway again to make sure there wasn't another zombie nearby. "Head up the stairs."

I stepped in front of Digger and slowly ascended the next staircase.

With a gurgled snarl, the woman lunged at Digger. He swung the axe, smashing the woman against the wall. Her head rolled away, the mouth still moving for a few moments as her body slumped lifelessly to the ground. The force of the strike had embedded the hatchet into the wall.

Grunting with effort, Digger yanked the hatchet free and headed up the stairs, taking the lead once more.

A smoky haze and a heady mix of fragrances greeted us at the top of the stairs. The smell included fresh flowers, perfumed oils, and herbs blended together. It masked the musty odor of mildew and putrefaction that filled the decrepit building.

I held my breath, gripping my small knife as I watched Digger reach the top of the steps. He cautiously peered into the smoky haze, only to duck back down and take several steps back. I braced myself, expecting an attack to emerge from the fog.

"Anything?"

"Nothing at the top of the stairs," he said. "Our adversary has one heck of a voodoo altar set up."

I nodded. It would make sense that she would.

"Time to face the music," Digger said. "You ready?"

"No," I replied.

"That's the right answer. Let's go."

Digger led the way, taking the steps two at a time. I followed closely behind, trying to keep up. Together, we reached the top.

At the back of the room, an imposing voodoo altar stood tall. It was a large table, adorned with intricately carved statues of Catholic saints and ancient deities, crafted from wood and stone. Floral arrangements of fresh flowers, strings of pearls and beads, and a glimmer of gold and diamonds. On the floor to the side of the table, a small brazier, similar to the one Digger had used to incinerate our hair and fingernails, smoldered with herbs and leaves.

A second smaller altar table was in front of the extravagantly decorated one. This table was empty with a white cloth covering it, that had a large brown-red stain on it. An array of knives, each smeared with dried blood, lay atop it.

The woman I encountered the night before was now standing before the smaller altar. She appeared tranquil and her expression gave the impression that she was expecting us.

A smile curled on her lips. "Tonbo, what took you so long?"

Digger looked around the room, unsure if something would attack through the mist. "We had to deal with some of your servants. What happened to your little helper?"

"He is dead," she said, and her smile grew wider. "Which is convenient for me."

Something emerged from the mist and smashed into Digger, throwing him off his feet. I turned to see that it was the man we had captured the night before.

He was barely recognizable.

His once vibrant dark skin was now paler and his body sported multiple wounds. The most conspicuous wound was a long gash across his chest, a result of multiple knife cuts. His eyes were bloodshot, as though he hadn't slept in days. It was clear he was no longer alive.

She made him into a zombie and he would never sleep again.

I braced myself as he spun around, his dead eyes fixed on me. He lunged at me, and I readied my knife, my heart pounding in my chest. Sweat beaded on my forehead and my hands were slick.

As he came toward me, I jumped to the side and used his momentum to my advantage, driving my knife deep into his back.

A hiss of smoke and flames rose from the wound, and he clawed the air, desperately attempting to remove the blade, but it was too far down his spine for him to reach.

He stumbled about and I pulled Digger to his feet. He seemed undamaged from the attack.

"Is that the best you have, houngan?" he bellowed at her. "'Cause it ain't much."

She gazed at the flailing zombie with no emotion on her face. She watched it as if it were an insect pinned to a board. "No, that is nothing. I know what you fear, Tonbo. Both you and your helper."

She stepped into a circle of white powder on the floor. Digger took one look at the circle, muttered, "Oh shit," and handed me his axe.

I gazed at him, confused.

"Cover me," Digger yelled, and fell to his knees. "I got something I need to do."

I watched in awe as he knelt on the floor and pulled a stick of chalk from a pouch. He drew a line, a gentle curve that slowly grew longer and wider. I stayed close, my eyes fixed on his work as he filled the planks with white marks.

We heard a strange noise echoing throughout the building — a chittering sound. We could also hear the faint tapping of tiny little claws on the wooden floor, steadily climbing the stairs.

"What is that?" I shouted.

"Focus," Digger growled through gritted teeth.

Cold air washed over me as something appeared from the stairs. It was man-sized and had a slow, shambling gait — another zombie. Digger kept on drawing, and I realized what he was doing. He was forming a large circle on the floor, one big enough to fit the voodoo woman, her own circle, and us inside.

The woman shouted, "Stop that!" She raised her hands, yet remained within her own circle.

I turned to the oncoming zombie. Its face was a mess of decaying flesh, with bits of skin and muscle hanging off in chunks. It had glazed over milky eyes, the nose hung in shreds from the bone beneath. On his head were tufts of hair, and the hands hanging out of the remnants of a three-piece suit were skeletal, with long, jagged nails.

With a yell, I swung the axe with all the power I had. I didn't get the angle right, and instead of immediately slicing the creature's throat, I struck it in the middle of its cranium. The blade plunged deep into its head, halting the creature's advance, but when I tried to remove the axe, it was stuck fast.

The undead creature stretched its arm up, desperately attempting to remove the axe. Despite its superior strength, it couldn't find the right angle to pry it away.

"That's a fuckin' fine kettle of fish," Digger bellowed. "Get in the circle, without touching the line!"

I stepped across Digger's bold line of chalk as the two zombies clumsily attempted to dislodge the weapons embedded in their bodies.

The woman unleashed an onslaught of expletives at Digger, yet she made no move to physically strike out at either of us. She was unwilling to step outside of her own protective circle.

Digger pulled out the bottle of pink powder and sprinkled it over the chalk circle, careful to create an unbroken barrier on top of the chalk. His gaze was intense with determination to accomplish his task — yet I detected fear in his eyes.

If Digger was feeling fear, it was not a good sign.

"You are too late, Tonbo," the woman shrieked. "My pets are coming to kill you."

She was only a few feet away from us in her circle in the middle of our larger circle. Again I heard the chittering much closer and a new sound — the sound of tiny legs scratching against the wooden floor. I stood frozen in fear at the sound of the insects, those terrible, awful bugs.

"Hurry," I squealed as Digger finished the coating of powder on the circle. He stood up straight and said strange words in a deep voice.

"No!" the woman spat. "You will all die!"

Digger grabbed another bottle that contained a clear liquid from one of his pouches. He carefully trailed the liquid around the circle as he walked, steadily pouring it, his lips moving as he did.

The woman was clearly impacted by something, and she sank to her knees inside her circle, her features twisted in anguish.

In the dim light, I could see hundreds of beady eyes glinting with malevolent intelligence. The room suddenly became alive with the chittering of thousands of rats. Their writhing bodies moved up the stairs and into the room, and they spread out to fill the space. It was as if the floor itself suddenly became a moving mass of dark, slick, furry bodies. The sound of their claws against the wooden floor was like a death march, and their squeaks filled the air with an ominous feeling of dread.

At the same time, millions of the giant cockroaches or water bugs flooded into the room like an invading army, filling every crevice. Squirming insects were in every space on the ground while their repelling scent and continuous clicking made my skin crawl with disgust and fear.

I watched in horror as the rats moved closer, their black eyes gleaming in the candlelight and their noses twitching. With their sharp teeth bared, they stopped at the edge of our circle, unable to cross the barrier Digger had created.

The bugs came pouring out of the darkness to swarm over the pair of unsuspecting zombies. They crawled over them in a frenzied mass, biting them with their sharp mandibles. In seconds, the sheer numbers of the attacking pests engulfed the zombies. The once human figures were now a writhing mass of tiny black bodies, who didn't discriminate between fresh and decayed flesh.

The two zombies both stumbled and fell, overwhelmed by the vast number of bugs that attacked them. The man who had been their captive let out a gurgling sound as he hit the ground, his body quickly becoming a feast for the swarm.

I stared in shock as the rodents seethed outside our ring of protection, their beady eyes glinting in the darkness. The rats were hungrily drooling and snapping their jaws, and even the bugs were not safe from their vicious appetites. One rat grabbed a bug and crunched it between its teeth, devouring it in an instant. I watched, horrified, as the creatures encircled us, unable to cross the line of safety created by Digger's circle.

"What did you put on that circle?" I demanded.

Digger glanced fearfully at the rats, mirroring my terror of the savage insects.

"The Pope blessed the chalk I used. That reddish powder was a combination of herbs that burn away evil."

"And the liquid?"

"Holy water," he said, watching the movement of the vermin. "I figured we needed it."

We turned to see the woman still down on her knees. She raised her head and glared at us. "I will kill you, Tonbo."

Digger's jaw grew tight as he spoke. "I doubt it. You locked yourself into a circle so you could unleash the things we feared upon us. Don't blame me if I just turned it around on you."

Digger pulled another bottle of the clear liquid from a pouch and poured it on the inner circle around the woman. He spoke under his breath. "Sancte Michael Archangele, defende nos in proelio…"

The woman screamed and reached out for Digger, but an invisible force wouldn't allow her to reach beyond the confines of her own circle.

Digger grasped the bottle and gave it a shake, sending a sprinkle of holy water flying. The droplets pelted her face, eliciting a hiss upon contact with her skin. She stumbled backward as smoke flew from where the holy water landed. She sank back to her knees with a pained shriek.

Digger took a deep breath and pulled out a folded purple cloth from his pouch. The rats flocking outside of our circle were now being joined by the repulsive water bugs, their scurrying bodies searching for any opening to get to us.

Looking past the squirming swarms of insects and rodents, I noticed the piles of bones arranged as two human skeletons. One had an axe wedged firmly in the skull. The other pile was much lighter, with traces of fresh blood and bits of flesh still clinging to the bones, and a small knife embedded in its spine.

Digger unrolled the deep purple fabric, revealing a Priest's Stole, which he kissed before placing it over his head. In his hand he held a six-inch crucifix he had carefully wrapped in the fabric. Taking a vial of holy water, he touched it to the four points of the crucifix before making the sign of the cross on himself. He then retrieved a small book, kissing it before placing a drop of the holy water on the cover.

"You're Catholic?" I asked.

"Not completely," Digger said and held out the bottle of holy water. "Here, cross yourself."

"You know I'm not Catholic."

He indicated the hordes of hungry rats and bugs scurrying over each other, fighting to reach us. "Why risk it?"

I dipped my fingers in the water and made the motion, my heart pounding. The insistent rustling of the ravenous creatures just outside of the circle drowned the sound of our own ragged breathing.

Digger turned to the woman in the circle. The spots on her face where the holy water landed were red, but the smoke had faded away.

"Foul spirit, I call you out," Digger bellowed as he held up the crucifix. "Moonwa, you must leave this child."

He flicked the bottle and more holy water struck her, making her scream again.

"In nómine Pátris, et Fílii, et Spirítus Sancti. Amen..." he began.

Digger read from his Latin prayerbook, flicking holy water at intervals and speaking in the ancient tongue. He chanted for almost ten minutes and I knew this was the ritual of exorcism. As the words escaped his lips, the creatures outside the circle became disoriented, bumping into one another as if inebriated. Some bugs seemed to merely vanish, crawling into cracks in the wall and floor. The rodents frantically clawed at their fur and finally scurried off to the darkest reaches of the room.

Digger raised his voice to a yell. "Per Chrístum Dóminum nóstrum. Ámen." He stepped into her circle and held the top of the crucifix against her forehead. She let out a shriek and swung her arms, scratching her nails across Digger's face. Immediately, she weakened and fell to the ground. Digger stepped back, his face now dripping blood from the wounds.

The only occupants remaining in the room were Digger and I, the lone woman, and the skeletal remains of the two zombies.

Digger erased a portion of the inner circle with his foot. He then moved to the outer circle and repeated the same process. I could only assume his intention was to disrupt whatever supernatural force powered them.

He approached the larger skeleton, planting his foot on the spine and gripping the hatchet handle tightly, pulling it free. With a powerful swing, he severed the top of the spine, causing the skull to roll free.

It came to a standstill at my feet. I met his eyes. "Was that really necessary?"

"We want to make sure the skeleton doesn't reanimate."

"It can do that?"

He shrugged nonchalantly and shifted his focus to the other skeleton. "At the end of the day, it's just a zombie missing its flesh."

He pulled the knife out of the spine and offered it to me. I returned it to my boot, just as one bony hand reached out and clutched Digger's ankle in a weak grip.

I gasped.

Digger stared down at the skeletal hand clamped around his ankle. "See? He still has a little energy left in him. Probably because he was a bokor turned into a zombie."

He swung the axe, and the skull flew off and rolled to the other end of the room. The remaining pile of bones collapsed, releasing Digger's leg.

We turned to see the young woman was standing. Her dark skin, free of the burn marks left by the holy water, glowed in the sun, accentuating her delicate features. She glanced downward and slowly stepped over the circles drawn on the ground before coming toward us with an expression of wonder.

"Pardon me, gentlemen," she said with her slight accent. "I am not sure — where I am."

I smiled. "What's your name?"

"My name is Widelene, but everyone calls me Willow."

I swallowed hard. Her very presence mesmerized me. "I'm Josh, and this is… um… Digger."

"How do you feel?" Digger asked, looking into each of her eyes intently.

"Light-headed," she replied. "Like I have been sleepwalking."

Digger nodded. "Come with us, and we'll get you some food and a place to rest."

She smiled, and my heart melted. "That would be very nice."

# FOURTEEN

D igger held a handkerchief to his wounded face as he guided us through the bustling streets of New Orleans. I kept close step with Willow, now that I had a name for her instead of simply referring to her as 'the possessed girl.'

Willow seemed unfamiliar with her surroundings, as though she hadn't seen the city or felt the warmth of the sun in a long time.

I wondered just how long she had been controlled by the dead *houngan*. I also wondered about the way she had teased me in the cemetery, shifting from temptress to attacker so easily.

Willow occasionally asked questions, but Digger would only reply curtly, telling her to wait until we were safe.

We finally arrived at Marie's place. We went in through the side door and into the kitchen, where Digger began preparing tea. I asked him if I should make something to eat for Willow.

"After tea," he snapped.

I returned to the table and sat next to Willow. "What's the last thing you remember?"

"Ah," she said. "I was at the *Cafe du Monde* having coffee and *beignets*."

She was discussing the famous Mississippi River cafe that served chicory coffee and French doughnuts.

"Evans — a man I know — came up to me." She leaned over the table as if to impart a secret. "They say he is a *bokor*."

"Can you describe him?" I asked.

She took a moment to reflect. "Skinny, about my height, and he likes to wear white clothes all the time."

Digger and I exchanged a knowing look. The description sounded like our prisoner who ended up as the dead skeleton, in the old warehouse.

"Go on," Digger encouraged, facing the stove.

"He told me his teacher was dying, and that he needed my help. I told him I was no doctor, but he pleaded with me, telling me that his teacher insisted only I could help him."

"Keep going," I urged, as Digger poured boiling water over the tea.

She frowned. "I followed Evans to that warehouse where you found me. It was just as it was today, with that huge altar. But on the front table was a man lying there. He was in great pain — he spoke to me in my head."

"In your mind?" I asked. "Had that ever happened to you before?"

She brightened at this. "Oh yes, I've heard voices my entire life, but this was different. I looked in his hand, and he was holding a doll dressed like me."

"A voodoo doll?" I suggested.

"Yes, with a lock of my hair, I don't know where he got it," she explained. "The next thing I know — I was standing there with you. The man on the table was gone, and the room was empty except for those skeletons."

"We saw no sign of the voodoo doll," Digger said. "That worries me."

"Wasn't it where you found me?"

"No," I said.

"I take it you are a virgin?" Digger pressed, setting filled teacups in front of us.

Shocked, I blurted, "Digger!"

She lowered her eyes to the table and her cheeks colored a slight reddish hue on her caramel skin. "I am... yes."

Digger sat at the table, his cup in front of him. "What was the date when you met Evans? Do you remember?"

She named the date. It was three months ago.

Digger nodded. "We should drink our tea."

I took a mouthful, and it tasted terrible. I almost spat it out, but forced myself to swallow it. It made me feel hot and like my throat was closing. I coughed and gasped. "What is this?"

Digger had his sights set on the woman sipping tea without batting an eye. After seeing her do so, he took a large gulp himself and then presented me with the sugar bowl. "It's a blend of dill, lavender, and parsley."

"I'll pass," I said. The idea of drinking more of it was revolting.

"It cleanses the spirit," Digger announced.

"No, thanks," I attempted.

He spoke through gritted teeth, "Drink it." It was clear he meant business.

I added several teaspoons of sugar, and even then, it was barely tolerable.

As I forced down the tea, Marie stepped into the room.

"*Madmwazèl,*" Willow said, and rose to give Marie kisses on both cheeks. "It is so good to see you."

"Your auntie has been anxious about you," Marie told her, then turned to Digger. "Did she drink the tea?

Digger nodded and smiled. "She did. Though Josh had a bit of a struggle with it."

Marie noticed the wounds on Digger's face. "Oh my! You have not come away undamaged. Let me get something for that."

Marie left the room, and Digger held the handkerchief to the scratches on his face.

Willow looked at Digger sadly. "Did I do that to you?"

"Yes. Drink the tea," Digger ordered.

"I like it," Willow said, taking a sip.

I gave him a dirty look and forced down another sip myself.

Marie returned with a kit and tended to Digger's wounds. Gently, she applied a gauze pad to the scratches as Digger winced.

"Big, muscular man beheads zombies, but can't take a little antiseptic?" Marie scoffed.

Willow spoke up. "*Madmwazèl,* these men say I have been gone three months? Is that the truth?"

"I am afraid it is," Marie said.

"That man with the Voodoo doll was a *houngan*," Digger said. "He possessed your body with his spirit and used you to do dark magic."

"What does her being a virgin have to do with it?" I inquired, since Digger had made a point of asking.

It was Marie who answered. "That makes her a pure vessel for the spirit to possess her. If she were not, he would not have been able to invade her mind."

"I must go to my auntie," Willow said, rising from the table.

"No, child," Marie soothed. "You must eat. I will bring your auntie to you later, after you have rested."

"You can't be out on the streets alone," Digger said. "Moonwa convinced his followers that you were his replacement — he may have left them instructions that put you in danger."

"What would you like to eat, my dear?" Marie said.

"Eggs, grits and toast if you have them," Willow said.

"Let me," I offered, wanting to do something, anything, to make this woman feel better.

"That's a good idea, Josh," Digger said. "Marie, can I talk to you in the shop?"

Marie and Digger stepped away from the kitchen as I prepared the grits, combining them with water in a pot. I wasn't particularly skilled in the kitchen, but I could whip up a batch of grits and eggs without breaking a sweat.

As Willow and I chatted, I almost burned the toast because of my lack of attention to the cooking. I was far more interested in talking to her.

"I grew up in Haiti, very poor. All of us, adults and children, had to work every day to make enough money for our family to eat," she told me. "I was lucky — at least I had a family, and my mother taught me to read in Creole and English."

"Where are your parents now?" I asked.

"Both dead — but again, I got lucky. My auntie brought me and my sister here to New Orleans years ago. I am grateful she did, or my sister and I would have lived on the streets."

I nodded in agreement. Her words sounded incredibly bleak, but she told the story as if it were just a casual anecdote.

"My sister is married now, with two babies."

"How old were you when you came to the United States?"

"Thirteen," she revealed. "I am twenty-three now."

She ate, and we talked. She told me about Haiti and New Orleans, and how she had what her auntie called, 'the sight.'

From a young age, she could communicate with spirits, both seen and unseen. As she finished her dinner, a deep yawn escaped her lips.

"I'm sorry," she said. "That was rude."

"Not at all," I said.

Marie came back and led Willow up to one of the guest bedrooms so she could get some rest.

The room seemed to grow darker when Willow left.

Digger came in, watching me clean up. The scratches on his face had scabbed over. "Look at that. You're practically housebroken."

I couldn't help but smile as Willow filled my heart with joy. Nothing could dampen my mood now.

"Sorry about the tea," Digger said. "I had to make sure that Moonwa wasn't tricking us. That we really cast him out."

"The tea was to poison him, if the exorcism had been unsuccessful?"

"No, he wouldn't have been able to drink it. Since the girl did, I believe she's free."

"We don't have to call her, the girl, anymore. Her name is Willow. Is Moonwa's spirit gone, then?"

"I'm not sure he didn't have another vessel, but his awareness might linger for a while. We're hitting the road again tomorrow."

I turned to Digger, suddenly crestfallen. "What? Why?"

"A friend of mine needs our help in Texas. We can drive over in less than five hours."

I was very disappointed. I just met Willow, and now I would have to leave her. "Okay."

"Willow needs to come with us."

"Really?" I exclaimed, and then tried to act casual. "I mean, you think she should?"

"She's not safe in New Orleans right now, as Moonwa's followers will search for her. Marie agreed that taking a trip with us will protect her until we're sure the spirit can no longer claim her."

I nodded sagely. "That makes sense."

"I'm glad you agree, because I want you to convince her to come with us."

I could not suppress my smile. "That will be my pleasure."

As night fell, I knocked on Willow's door.

"Come in, please," she said, and I opened the door a crack.

"It's Josh. Are you decent?"

She propped herself up in bed and flicked on the lamp that was perched on the bedside table. Her nightgown, which was borrowed from Marie, covered her every curve with a silky smoothness. Even so, she pulled the bedsheet up to her neck. "Yes, please come in."

I stepped into the room, leaving the door open. I stood at the foot of her bed. "Your auntie will arrive in about a half-hour."

She smiled at me. "I should get dressed."

Smiling broadly, we stood together before I cleared my throat and spoke up. "Um… we're going to be leaving tomorrow."

Her smile fell away. "Really? So soon? Where will you go?"

"To Texas. To someone who needs our help."

She tilted her head to the side; her gaze fixed on me. "Is that what you and your friend do? Go around helping people?"

I thought it over. I mean, this was my first time going anywhere with Digger. Until a week ago, I wasn't even completely sure he existed.

"Yes, I guess it is."

Eyes downcast, she said, "I will miss you."

"Digger would like you to come with us."

Her smile reappeared. "May I?"

"Yes," I said, and cleared my throat to cover for the goofy smile I was sure was on my face. "In fact, Digger thinks it would be a good idea for you to get out of New Orleans for a little while, just to be safe."

"You will be there as well?" Willow asked.

"Me?" I replied and stood a little straighter. "Yeah, I'm his right-hand man."

She looked thrilled. "That is wonderful."

"Yes, it is," I said, fighting the urge to hug her. "I'll — uh — see you in the kitchen."

With trepidation, I made my way down the staircase, exhilarated by the prospect of not having to bid farewell to Willow. My longing for her consumed me. I also felt a certain unease over her virginity. I had never been with a novice before, and I resolved to be cautious and take any next steps slowly. The last thing I wanted was to make her feel pressured into doing anything she wasn't ready for.

As I stood by the kitchen, I heard faint murmurs coming through the closed door of the adjoining room. I could discern the familiar voices of Marie and Digger, but the words were indistinct.

I tiptoed to the door and cranked up the volume on my hearing aid, straining to catch what was being said on the other side.

I could hear Digger's gruff baritone. "He keeps asking! You have to tell him."

"I...I cannot. Ephraim and I agreed on our story. It was the only thing we could do. You told me how a Lamia was sent to capture him as a child—"

"To kill him," Digger interrupted. "A Lamia is only used when a child is to be slain."

"How can I expose him to this now? You told me yourself, he does not know even how to use the *Lahat Chereb*—"

"He lost his father. He should know that his mother is still alive."

I barged through the door, startling them with my abrupt entrance.

"My mother is alive?" I demanded, breathing hard. "Why didn't you tell me?"

Digger and Marie locked eyes, neither saying a word.

Marie let out a heavy sigh and slowly lowered her head. "Because, Josh, I'm your mother."

# FIFTEEN

I stared at Marie. "There's no way that can be true. My mother died in childbirth!" Digger rose, and I felt a wave of anger wash over me. "Where do you think you're going?"

"I'm going to have some coffee," he said, not reacting to my anger. "I think you two need to talk."

He quietly shut the door. Marie sat still, my gaze fixed on her.

She tapped the top of the table and said, "Come, sit. There are things you should know."

Even while my breathing was still ragged and anger consumed me, it was impossible not to acknowledge Marie's kindness towards me since my arrival. Though I was seething inside, I forced myself to remain standing and kept my lips firmly pressed together.

She cleared her throat. "I am so sorry, but it was necessary."

"You're not my mother," I stated coldly.

She raised her chin. "Did you ever see a photo of her?"

I had never seen a picture of my mother. Whenever I posed the question to Poppa, he replied he had "gotten rid of them," and that it was "too painful to have a photo" of his late wife. I had accepted his explanation without further inquiry.

I spoke through gritted teeth. "So what happened? Next, are you going to tell me my father stole me?"

"Please sit, and I will tell you what I can."

I yanked the chair back, my expression hard, but I sat.

She looked at her hands for a moment, then met my eyes. "After that battle in Portland, where your father lost his hand, he went through a rough time. First, he was in the hospital in Portland for more than a month, then he came here to New Orleans. He was on pain-killers and fighting depression. After all, he almost died. At the end of February, I found out I was pregnant. As the pregnancy went along, things got better. He healed, and learned to work with a prosthetic hand, and got off the medicine."

"He never told me any of that."

"There was more he didn't tell you. You were born on October 29th which I am sure you know, at Tulane Medical Center. But on the 31st, Halloween, that was the first time they tried to steal you."

My head shot up. "Steal me? Someone tried to steal me? Why?"

"We weren't sure. Some woman claimed you were hers and tried to remove you from the hospital, but a nurse stopped her. Both your father and I thought she was just some mentally deranged woman. It was worse months later."

"How could it get worse?" I asked.

"We were living here, in this house. When you were only six months old, zombies came."

"Zombies?" I said as sweat prickled under my arms. "On Bourbon Street?"

She nodded somberly. "Thank goodness Digger was visiting to check on Ephraim and meet you. It was spring, so we had the windows open a little. In the middle of the night, we were all upstairs sleeping when we heard banging. Digger and your father headed downstairs to investigate, tellin' me to wait upstairs. I tol' them the Hell with that and went down with them. The front door was being broken into by two zombies, and we look out in the street and there were a dozen of the things out there. Digger dealt with the two at the door with his axe and Ephraim used the *Lahat Chereb*, stepping outside and swinging it with one hand. That's when I heard you cry."

"Me? What was wrong with me?"

"They were trying to steal you again," she said, a fierce gleam in her eye.

"What did you do?"

"What any mother would do," she said, her jaw tight. "I ran up those stairs two at a time, and went into your room, and there was someone... some *thing* in your room."

"What was it?" I asked.

She dropped her gaze to the floor. "I never got a good look at what it was, but I saw a female figure. The window was wide open, with the screen torn off. I screamed, and it leapt out of the window. I rushed over to the edge to see where it had gone, but all I saw down on the street were Digger and your father fighting the zombies."

"So it... flew away?"

She shook her head. "I do not know, but I stayed by your crib that night, not sleeping. In the morning, I came downstairs to see Digger and your father putting on a new door. The zombies, and what remained of them, were gone and the men looked like they had not slept. It was then I prayed to the *loas* to help me read the cards."

"A card reading?" I repeated. "You decided what to do from tarot cards?"

She lifted her chin in defiance. "I am very good with them, Josh. What it revealed to me scared me more. We had to learn more, so Digger and I did the ritual in which your father channeled Papa Legba. It was he who told us that a great power sought you, and you would not be safe growing up in New Orleans." She lowered her head, and a single tear crept down her face. "I did the hardest thing I ever did. I had to let you go."

My jaw dropped. "This makes no sense. You could've come with us. We could have all lived in New Jersey as a family."

"No, Josh. Papa Legba said that the dark forces were tracking you through me. As long as you were near me, you would not survive to manhood. Don't you think I checked with the cards over and over? The only way you could grow up in safety was far away from me."

Tears streaming down her face, she rose from her seat and I stood to embrace her as she wept. The emotional storm eventually passed, and I found a box of tissues. Though my anger had not subsided, I felt sympathy for her plight. This had been a hard decision for her to make, and I had no choice but to accept it.

I couldn't hate this woman. She was my mother.

"It's just… just," I stammered.

"I know," she said through her tears. "I lost my baby and now he comes to my door a big, strong man who looks so much like his father, who I also lost that day."

I finally took a deep breath, trying to speak. I had imagined this moment a million times and now I couldn't believe my mother was standing before me. Tears streamed down my face as I fought to find the words, to express all the years of longing and hope.

"Digger wanted me to tell you before you leave for Texas," she said, looking up at me.

All I could do was nod silently in response.

"Now go, get ready for us to go meet Willow's auntie," she said. "And try to forgive your mother, who loves you more than life itself."

I walked out to the door, and with a glance back at Marie, went into the kitchen. Digger sat at the kitchen table, drinking coffee.

"Is Willow coming with us?" he asked.

I looked at him, feeling as if I was not part of my body. "Willow will travel with us," I said, trying to be angry at the old man, but too drained to do it. "You knew all along."

He stared at his coffee cup. "I did, but it wasn't my place to tell you." He raised his head. "I noticed you didn't use the *Lahat Chereb* today." He pointed. "You're still wearing it."

Leave it to Digger to change subjects.

My hand went to the pouch on my belt. I had forgotten about the sword hilt and the pouch the entire time. "Like you said, it's my lucky charm."

He nodded. "In ancient days, people would carry an artifact to ward off evil. Of course, a righteous man can activate it just by wanting to do a noble deed."

"You used it at Fort Gorges."

Digger smiled sadly and looked at the floor. "I never said I was a righteous man."

"And you proved that by not telling me." My jaw grew tight.

He glared at me. "Maybe. But the truth is, your mother and father were willing to sacrifice anything to protect you."

I felt my temper soar. "And leave my father and me alone? Telling me my mother died?"

"If he didn't tell you that, you would have spent your entire youth yearning to meet her, to be in her presence," Digger said. "You have no idea how it tortured your father to lie to you."

I was so angry I couldn't respond. I stormed up the stairs and almost collided with Willow. She looked even more stunning than when I'd seen her before. Her face was glowing from the meal and nap she'd taken.

"Is my auntie here yet?"

I was trying to get myself under control. "Not yet. You're going to meet her at a restaurant."

She frowned. "Aren't you coming?"

I looked at the floor, trying to calm down. "I'm not really interested in going out to dinner."

"Oh, but you must come," she said and smiled at me. "You saved me, and I know my auntie will want to meet you."

I shook my head, still staring at the floor. "I wouldn't be much good."

She drew closer. "Please?"

Our gazes locked, and I could feel the desperation in her eyes. She was begging me to come, to be there for her.

I sighed. "All right."

"Good, let me get my shoes, and I'll be ready."

I stood there, still trying to make sense of my emotions, yet I had agreed to dinner as if my entire world hadn't just been turned upside down.

She returned, wearing her shoes, and took my arm to guide me downstairs.

As we came into the kitchen, Marie came into the room. "The shop is closed, and we must meet Lovelie for dinner. I will pay — will that settle us, Digger?"

"More than adequately, Marie. Besides, I would never ask you to pay for my services."

"That is a bad way of doing business," she chided him. "I'll wait at the front door for Willow's aunt." She gestured to Willow, and the pair of them headed out for the front of the shop.

I was still seething with rage towards Digger, so I finally voiced what I had been waiting to say. "You ask for money for your services, then?"

Digger looked surprised. "Do I look like a charity?"

"I thought you did it... to help..."

"I do! But I have a unique set of skills. How do you think I bought three cemeteries and built that house I live in?"

"I didn't think about it."

"How about your father? Where do you think he got the money to buy that oil company and take care of you? That came from his cut of the jobs we did together."

The entire situation became clear to me. "You and my father were nothing more than mercenaries?"

"Your father and I took enormous risks, and my clients don't have to hire me if they don't want to." He rose from his chair. "Folks like Marie exchange their services for mine. Who do you think mixed up that powder or got the holy water I used on the circle in the warehouse? Marie did. That's how it works, Josh. Now come on, we're going to dinner."

I wanted to reply, but at that moment, I was too tired and confused to fight.

In a short time, we were sitting in Cafe Amelie — Marie, Digger, Willow, myself, and Willow's aunt, Lovelie, who referred to Willow by her full name, "Widelene."

Her aunt hugged her upon being reunited, and was very charming to Marie and me, though she looked at Digger with suspicion.

Marie explained that a *houngan* had possessed Willow as if this were a common occurrence. In Marie's world or in New Orleans, it might have been.

Digger and I remained quiet. I didn't wish to speak. I was still processing what I had found out that evening, so I thought it best to let the others do the talking.

Finally, as we were finishing the meal, Lovelie addressed her concerns. "I understand you want to take my little girl away." She took Willow's hand.

"It's not like that, Auntie," Willow argued. Her Haitian accent had become much more pronounced since she sat down with her aunt.

Digger spoke calmly and quietly. "We believe it would be safer. Moonwa had many followers, and they knew of his possession of your niece. They might attempt to use her again."

"The dark man," Lovelie spat. "That I understand. My concern is my niece traveling alone with two men."

Digger nodded. "Our interest is only in her safety. She has told us she can speak to spirits. Her presence could help us."

Lovelie waved her hand dismissively. "She has spoken to the spirits since she was a child. My fear is what will happen at night —" She looked at me with misgivings. "—when a young man is near a beautiful girl."

Every eye was on me, and Willow appeared annoyed at her aunt's outspoken statement.

"Ma'am, I... have nothing but respect for your niece," I finally said.

Fortunately, it was Willow who saved the day. "Auntie, I am meant to do this. I can help them, as they helped me. How could I do less?"

Lovelie nodded, but her jaw was tight. "I did as Marie asked and brought your clothes in a suitcase." She glared at Digger and me. "But I expect these two to behave like honorable men."

Digger just nodded.

I knew they could trust Digger as an escort to Willow — but I no longer believed he was an honorable man.

# SIXTEEN

I didn't sleep well that night. My mind raced with thoughts of Marie and Willow and the vermin lurking beyond the perimeter of Digger's enchanted circle. I was jolted awake repeatedly, each time instinctively reaching for the pouch that held the Lahat Chereb and my notebook with the words needed to unleash its power.

I wanted to give it a shot, but I ultimately stayed in bed and worked to drift off to sleep again.

In the morning, I encountered Willow just as she left the steaming bathroom, her body covered only by a towel, her shoulders exposed and her feet bare. It rendered me speechless.

"H-hi," was all I could manage. She had bags under her eyes. "How did you sleep?"

"Not well," she said, and forced a small smile. "I kept having dreams."

"Not bad ones, I hope."

"Some bad… some good," she opened the door to her room. "You…were in… some of them."

"The bad ones or the good ones?"

She smiled. "Best not to say." And with that, she went into her room and closed the door.

I had it bad for her.

I made my way down to the kitchen for breakfast, where I found Digger already enjoying a meal. Filling my mug with the rich aroma of the chicory coffee, I took a sip. I certainly would miss its flavor once we departed Louisiana.

I took a moment and with coffee mug in hand, walked out to the front, into the shop, where Marie finished serving an early customer.

She escorted him to the door with his purchase, smiling and talking until he'd gone out and she shut the door. She turned to face me. "You look so much like your father standing there."

I nodded. "Many people say that I look like him. I've heard it all my life."

She forced a smile. "Are you going to help Digger in Texas?"

"I guess," I said, trying to sound noncommittal.

"You should. He needs your help, although he will not say so. He is not a young man, though he still thinks he is."

Sighing, I said, "I don't like leaving like this, knowing so little about you and Poppa. I mean, he got married to Lizzie. Was he a bigamist?"

She turned away. "The truth is Ephraim and I never married."

I was stunned yet again. "I never knew. The way Poppa spoke of you—"

"We planned to marry," she said, straightening several bottles on a shelf to avoid looking at me. "We adored each other and even made plans. But your father was in recovery, and then I was pregnant, and things just happened. Then you were born, and we had to adjust to that. Then the night the zombies attacked, we found out the prediction and knew we could never marry, and could not even be together." She finally raised her eyes to mine. "Josh, letting you go broke my heart. But the choice I made, that Ephraim and I made, saved you and allowed you to grow into a man."

She took my free hand. "We will talk about all of this, and you can yell at me because your father lied if you need to. I still love you and I am proud of the man you are."

Glancing in the curtain's direction, I plucked up my courage and said, "I will come back. I want to get to know you."

She smiled, and a tear slipped down her cheek. "I will see you soon, I promise."

Embracing her tightly, she sobbed in my embrace and I sensed an innate sense of comfort that I yearned for. When the tears subsided, she reached up and grazed my cheek.

"Now go fight those bad things."

Unable to speak, I returned to the kitchen, and took in the sight of Willow descending the stairs. She wore a pair of jeans and a simple shirt, a suitcase in one hand. She also carried a thick cylindrical wooden rod, like a dowel, measuring about three feet long with tape near both ends.

I pointed at the odd stick. "What is that?"

She smiled at me. "My weapon. It is good *pois* wood. Auntie was kind enough to bring it, and Digger said it would be wise to have it." She placed the bag by the door and helped herself to coffee and grits and sat. "I'm excited. I have never been to Texas before."

I still gazed at the wooden dowel. "That's a weapon? What could you do with that? It's just a stick."

She looked at me with an amused expression on her face.

Digger chuckled.

"What?" I said.

Digger spoke up. "Her father trained Willow in Kalenda, an African-Caribbean form of martial arts."

I frowned at her. "Really?"

"Yes," Willow said. "If I had my stick the day the man took me to that warehouse, things would have gone very different." She rose and moved to the wooden implement, picked it up and held it out, her hands near the tape on the ends. "With a stick like this, I kept my sister and I safe after the death of our parents." She looked me over from head to toe. "You know, for a hero, you know little."

"It's not his fault," Digger grunted. "He went to college."

"How does it work?" I asked.

Willow all but fell into a fighting stance, her legs wide apart and bouncing on her toes. Then, in one quick movement, she spun, turned, and was behind me, with her stick held tight against my throat.

She had moved so quickly; I was caught completely by surprise. "I surrender," I croaked, putting my hands up.

"Please don't hurt him," Digger said. "We need as many people as we can for the job."

Willow released me and let the stick drop to her side. She walked over and put it with her luggage. "I will have to practice. I am rusty."

"Rusty?" I marveled. "You moved like a blur."

"Willow has several skills that will help us," Digger announced.

"Really? What else can you do?" I asked, rubbing my throat. I was thankful she didn't give me a more painful demonstration. Why was I repeatedly drawn to women who could kick my ass?

"I can talk to the spirits," Willow said. "I know many different oils, powders, and incense used to make magic."

Digger looked sideways at me. "Sounds like you're more useful than my current companion."

I overlooked the remark.

Digger got up from the table. "Willow, I know you can handle yourself, but if we're in a situation and I tell you to stay where you are, will you do it?"

"I will," she said.

He didn't even look over at me. "Same for you, Josh."

I nodded in response.

"Okay, finish eating and we'll hit the road."

Willow and I kept making eye contact and smiling as we ate in silence.

Digger wasn't planning for any kind of magic on our journey — just the open road, highways, and the thrill of crossing from one state to another. Our trip started off with an awe-inspiring view of the Mississippi River, thanks to Interstate 10. No shortcuts, no Ley lines — just a classic American road trip.

As Digger drove and I rode shotgun, Willow peppered Digger with questions about our destination and purpose.

"We have to see a man about a problem he's having," Digger exclaimed. "Simple as that."

"What kind of problem?" she asked.

Digger sighed. "It's a problem with the undead."

"But what kind?" Willow gushed. "Zombies, maybe?"

"Vampires," Digger said plainly.

Willow sat back, considering this. "That is a dangerous situation."

I finally spoke up. "What is it? A problem like what happened to my grandparents?"

"It's not as easy as that, which is why I didn't talk too much about it. Somebody is creating new vampires. The problem with new vampires is that their need for blood is overwhelming, and they cannot control themselves. They become killing machines, driven by nothing but the desire to feed. If a vampire can get past the initial phase, if they have a mentor, someone to guide them and help them control their hunger, they can survive."

"My Poppa always said that vampires were not at all like Dracula," I said, facing the road ahead of us.

"You ever read the original book?"

"Um… no," I admitted.

"Well, you should. Bram Stoker knew a lot about vampires."

We drove on in silence.

Hours later, we pulled into the lot for *The Stage Coach Inn: East Texas' Nicest Place* at about four in the afternoon. It was an open-air motel with two stories of stairs and doors all facing the lot. Digger went to the office to grab our room keys while I lingered by the truck with Willow.

"Is this your first time in Texas?" she asked.

"Yes, I live in New Jersey."

"New Jersey? I have never been there either. Just Haiti and New Orleans," she confessed.

"It must be hard for you, after the things that happened to you, losing your parents and everything."

"Yes,'" she said, staring out at the wide-open country around the motel. "It was a battle for survival when I was young."

"Your stick-fighting helped?"

"I was grateful my father taught me the skills before he died. After that, moving to America, living in New Orleans, it was very different."

"Culture shock, I'm sure."

She nodded. "Here in America, I became very introverted. Growing up, I had few friends, and no boyfriends."

"I'm shocked at that," I said. "To be honest, I never met a girl as attractive as you."

She glanced over at me. "Do you think so?"

"I do."

With her free hand, she touched my ear. "What is this in your ear? Is it a hearing aid?"

I nodded. "I'm partially deaf."

She pulled her hand back. "Is it easily broken?"

I chuckled. "No, they're pretty sturdy. I put it in a charger at night."

She frowned at this. "And when you do, you cannot hear?"

"Not much. But I read lips really well."

She smiled, delighted by the idea. "Show me."

"Okay," I told her, stepping back several paces. "Now look at me, and whisper something."

She watched me dubiously, then faced me and whispered.

I stepped close to her. "You said, this is something you would like to learn."

She smiled again. "Very impressive."

"If you two are finished with your proclamations of love," Digger said in his booming voice. "Get your luggage to your rooms. We have to get ready for work."

I wanted to complain to him for ruining the moment, but what would be the point?

Digger gave us each a key card, then drew close to me and muttered. "I'll be in the room between both of yours, so don't get any ideas."

I ignored this. "What do you mean, get ready for work? What are we doing?"

Digger looked at me with surprise. "Digging a grave, of course."

I entered my room and began rummaging through my wardrobe to find a pair of jeans and a plaid flannel work shirt. Boots I already had, but I knew I would need to get a proper pair of work boots down the line. I had only intended to find Digger to get information about what killed my father. Now here I was, helping him dig a grave. I had gone from being a mere bystander to being part of the events. How did that happen?

We all gathered out front at the truck, Digger dressed for the occasion in his peacoat and floppy hat. Given the scorching Texas sun, it wasn't such a bad idea after all. Willow had on a long sleeve shirt and her jeans and carrying her fighting stick. She headed back to her bench seat behind us.

We drove into the center of the small town as a sign greeted us:

**Welcome to Warren Rock**

**Wide Open Spaces**

As we drove through the town, I noticed an auto parts store, a hardware store, and mostly single-story houses. There were dollar stores and large churches — it seemed impossible that vampires could be attacking such an ordinary place.

After leaving the multi-lane highway, we drove down a narrow paved road, branching off into dirt paths. Wooden fences lined the sides of the road, and beyond them were horses and cows grazing in the fields.

To our right, as we drew closer, a small cemetery lay hidden behind a chain-link fence.

Digger drove up to the graveyard where an American flag proudly flew from a tall pole in the center of the grounds.

Digger silently exited the truck, making his way to open the tailgate. I glanced back, catching sight of Willow's concerned expression.

"What's wrong?"

"This place has spirits that are unhappy. Someone sent them to their graves before their time."

"How do you know?" I asked.

"I sense their torment."

"Will you be okay?"

Her hand went to her head. "I want to learn what they are trying to tell me."

Carrying two eight-foot-long wooden planks, Digger made his way past several gravestones before laying them down on an empty patch of ground. He crouched and ran his hand through the grass, revealing a small metal circle. Pulling a piece of paper out of his pocket, he carefully unfolded it, examining and comparing it to the ground in front of him.

"What's that?" I asked.

"A map of the plots in this cemetery," Digger explained. "I'm double-checking the plot number. We don't want to go digging in the wrong spot."

"How do you know where to dig?" I asked.

"The shiny metal disk in the southwest corner of the lot is a stainless steel marker with a lot number. In the past, these would have been clay markers with a stamped number. However, modern technology means metal detectors can locate the markers should the grass grow over it."

"And you have one of those in your truck, I'm sure."

"Absolutely. Each lot has four plots, each measuring two-and-a-half feet in width by eight feet. Of course, if a special coffin is being used, in which case they have to let me know ahead of time. If there are any discrepancies, I would have to dig out the hole on site, which is not ideal in front of grieving family and friends. It's important to ensure that everything is correct during such a sensitive time." He turned to me. "Help me carry some tools over, will ya?"

Digger gave me a pair of work gloves and then passed me two pieces of wood, a shovel with a flat, square blade, and a half-moon shaped edging tool. He picked up a mattock, a pick, and another shovel for himself.

We returned to the gravesite and dumped the tools. "We'll want to take the sod off first."

He handed me the edging tool and grabbed a flat square shovel. Together, we worked our way down the sides of the frame, cutting away the grass and digging into the dirt. It was hard labor, and the heat of the day was making me sweat.

Willow stood beside a tree, her eyes following us as we toiled.

After we cut lines into the grass around the frame, Digger disconnected the pieces and set the frame open at each corner. He used the flat shovel to cut a rectangle of sod, then pried it up, and dug under it to release it from the ground.

He called over to Willow. "Hey girlie, everyone works here."

She shook her head as if coming out of a dream and ran over. "Of course. What can I do?"

"We'll rip up the sod. If you could pile it right there, it would be a big help." He pointed a few feet away. "Get gloves from my truck."

We soon got into a rhythm. I cut the sod, Digger pulled it up, and Willow stacked the rectangles into neat rows, one on top of another.

Digger and I started at opposite ends of the grave, each of us gripping a spade tightly. I moved slowly and steadily, but Digger was like a machine, shoveling dirt at an incredible speed. Before I had gone two feet from the edge of the grave, he reached me. As we dug deeper, the soil changed from dark loam to red clay.

Digger smiled. "Red clay is good, doesn't need boards to support the sides unless we hit an underground stream."

"What happens then?" I asked, breathing hard.

"We board up the sides and stick a pump down there until the funeral. Last thing we want is the coffin floating up after they lower it in."

"Has that ever happened?" Willow asked.

"Sometimes. Almost anything that can go wrong has gone wrong for me at one time or another. I've experienced the unfortunate incident of a coffin strap breaking and dropping the coffin in the grave right in front of everyone. Another time, the webs snapped, and the coffin dropped, causing the lid to pop open, and the poor woman fell out."

"What did you do?" I asked.

Digger leaned on his shovel. "Made sure I didn't crack a smile. Let me tell you, that time it wasn't easy."

We started digging again, and I tried to go faster, but I couldn't match Digger's speed. I wiped the sweat from my brow as I looked at our open hole, my muscles aching from the backbreaking work. I could see why people used a backhoe instead of manually shoveling the dirt out.

It embarrassed me that Digger was moving so much faster than I was, but I did my part as rapidly as I was able. In about an hour, we were over two feet down. After another hour, we reached the requisite four-and-a-half feet.

Even though I'm about six feet tall, I struggled to get myself out of the hole. I offered Digger a hand, and he was heavier than I expected as he climbed up the side.

"Most men would have taken five hours to dig that," Digger noted. "Two hours for a beginner isn't bad."

I was panting and my muscles felt like lead. "You did all the work. I barely moved half of the dirt you did. How do you do that?"

Digger shrugged. "I learned some shoveling techniques that come in handy. The rest is just practice, Josh."

"I think both of you did a good job," Willow said.

Digger smiled at her. Then we all headed to the truck. "I've got the boards to cover the hole and an extra tarpaulin to cover the dirt in case it rains."

"When is the funeral?"

"Tomorrow," Digger answered, opening the tailgate and handing Willow the folded tarpaulin. "Just a single burial, which is better than a multiple."

"What do they do with a multiple burial?"

"If you have two caskets going into one grave, you dig down at least eight feet," Digger said, handing me a long plank of wood. "Occasionally, I get a location where you have to bury down twelve feet, at which point, you're so deep in the ground, you feel you need a miner's helmet and a caged canary. Climbing twelve feet down into a narrow grave is a daunting task. It requires a ladder and a bucket and pulley to transport dirt out. Those brave enough to take on that challenge will find the experience unnerving."

Digger and I both lugged several planks, each at least nine feet, to the open grave. Digger used them to bridge the gap over the pit and I assisted Willow in spreading out the second tarpaulin to cover the pile of soil.

We were all covered in dirt and grime, and sweat stains formed under my arms on my shirt.

Digger dusted himself off and looked at the pair of us. "Let's head back to the hotel, get cleaned up, and I'll take the pair of you out to dinner. Then we have to meet our client."

Exhausted but without a word, the three of us climbed back into the truck. Digger drove us out to the street, while I took one last look back and securely closed the gate behind us.

I was famished as the clock struck seven, so I showered and the three of us headed out to a nearby barbecue joint.

At first glance, it wasn't much to look at — plain plastic tables and chairs with a laminated menu. On the plus side, the barbecue was amazing and well worth the visit.

For once, Digger wasn't in any kind of hurry. I found it odd, since he said we were meeting the client later. After we ate, I checked my watch, and it was past eight-thirty, and an eerie darkness filled the twilight sky.

"When are we meeting the client?" I asked.

"After dark — about nine o'clock this time of year," Digger explained.

"Are we dressed well enough?" I said. Digger had told us to dress casually for the restaurant.

Digger smiled. "When was the last time you saw me in a suit?"

"Um… never."

"Then we're fine. But, Willow, I want you to be very aware of what's going on around you at all times while we're there. Got it?"

She nodded in agreement. "Should I bring my fighting stick? I have it in your truck."

"No, someone might misinterpret you carrying a wooden weapon."

"Why does she need to be careful?" I asked.

"We should be on our guard, anyway," Digger stated plainly. "We freed Willow from a powerful cult. They might not want to let her go so easy."

As the night sky enveloped us, we were back in the truck, barreling down the streets. No hills or mountains were in sight, the trees were the only thing breaking the horizon, and the moon slowly rising above them. We continued our journey, the darkness of night surrounding us.

We turned onto another two-lane road, and after another ten minutes, a large illuminated sign greeted us:

**The Warren Rock Ranch**

**Cattle Ranch and Abattoir**

**Finest beef you'll ever have**

"What's an abattoir?" Willow asked.

"That's a fancy name for a slaughterhouse," I explained as Digger started down the long driveway. There were several large barns on both the left and right of the roadway as we headed up to a large house in the distance.

Illumination in the outbuildings indicated people were still working. I wondered what tasks the night shift would be engaged with.

As we drove up, we noticed two large bunkhouses and a foreman's cabin, hinting at the size of the workforce. Finally, we arrived at the main house.

The house was only two stories, but it was quite large and made of stone. Steel beams supported a canopy over the front door, and Digger pulled right under it.

The door was daunting, crafted of one solid slab of oak. Digger turned off the headlights before stepping out. When he reached the door, it opened in one smooth movement.

The lights from inside the house silhouetted the person in the doorway.

Digger politely said, "Everett Hill to see Clem."

The woman's compact frame was accentuated by a blue pantsuit, and large glasses were on her face. Her fair complexion contrasted strikingly with her deep mahogany hair. Her gaze was unwavering and dismissive as she spoke. "They did not inform me of any visitors expected this evening."

A booming voice spoke out. "Well, I'll be damned if it ain't Digger hisself. How are ya, boy?"

Strolling down the wide hallway was a sturdy man wearing an enormous cowboy hat. He was tall and muscular, with dark hair and a handlebar mustache. His skin was just as pale and flawless as the woman's.

As Willow and I entered the house, the man embraced Digger in a warm hug.

"Sorry, Clem. I didn't know we were expecting guests," the woman said, stepping back a few feet.

He released Digger and turned to the woman. "Relax Claire, this is more of a social call. Why don't you head back to the office and we can clear up that paperwork in about an hour, all right?"

She reluctantly nodded in agreement, her expression conveying her displeasure. Turning her back, Claire strode away, her conflicted emotions trailing in her wake.

He looked at the three of us with delight. "You brought some help, did ya? Y'all come on inside."

I did not know what to expect, but it definitely wasn't this 'good ol' boy.' Was he the one who contracted Digger to pursue vampires?

The inside of the house was even more impressive than the outside. The front entranceway was large enough that Digger could have just driven his truck down it. There was fine wood and short stone walls, and a beautiful red and gold oriental carpet on the floor. A pair of decorative shrubs were at the end of the hall and the ceiling was a good twenty feet above us. Willow took a few steps in circles to revel in the open space. Past the hallway, the room opened up, with a full bar on one side and a living area near the opposite wall.

"Y'all want anything? We got a fully stocked bar."

"I'll have a beer. How about you, Josh? Willow?"

We both requested water, and Clem gestured for us to sit on the sofas.

Willow headed right to a chair, and I saw our client grab Digger's arm as they headed to the bar. He spoke in a low voice, but I could read his lips. "Was it a good idea to bring her here?"

Digger spoke quietly as well, but I could see his mouth and followed the conversation. "I figured you and your staff could control themselves. Looked like your assistant wasn't happy we're here."

"Claire likes to be kept in the loop, but I couldn't do that this time," the man said as he picked up two bottles of water. "I made sure only me and Serenity knew you were comin'."

I accepted the bottles of water and handed one to Willow as a tall woman entered the room. Her long, chestnut brown hair cascaded down her back, framing her heart-shaped face perfectly. Her emerald green eyes were wide and full of life, and her lips were a soft pink. She wore a simple, yet elegant, off-white dress, with a navy blue sash tied around her waist. Her features were delicate, with the same porcelain complexion as our host, yet she appeared to be much younger than him. She said, "Clem, I see you've offered our guests something to drink."

"I did, dahrlin'," he told her. "Folks, this here is Serenity, my wife and my partner in all things."

Serenity gazed over at Willow and her eyes seemed to sparkle. "An innocent, here?" She glanced at Digger. "Was that wise?"

"It was necessary, Missus," Digger said. "A voodoo cult is pursuing her."

"The lesser of two evils, I suppose," the woman said with a shrug. "What is your name, child?"

Willow stood up and said, "People call me Willow, ma'am."

"It suits you," she said, her eyes running up and down Willow's body. She turned away suddenly, breaking the spell. "I'm being rude. Digger, come give me a hug, for old time's sake."

Digger approached the woman, who was almost as tall as he was, and embraced her warmly.

"Thank you for coming," she said as they parted, and she looked over at me with a puzzled expression. "Is that Ephraim Bennet?"

"That's Ephraim's son, Josh," Digger disclosed. "He's assisting me."

"I thought he looked familiar," Clem said, with a smile that curled up his mustache. "You look a lot like your father, 'cept for that one blue eye ya got."

"That's what people tell me," I said.

"Well, tell you what, y'all sit. For the newcomers, I'm Clem Reins, the owner of this place. We offer the finest beef in all of Texas and I have to tell you, we take a lotta pride in that."

"What makes your beef so special?" I asked.

"Well, young man, I'll tell ya. We raise a select breed of Japanese cattle called Wagyu, which is known for its flavor and marblin'. Y'all heard of Kobe Beef, right?"

"Sure," I answered.

"Well, that's Wagyu cattle, and the name for Kobe came from the capital city in China."

Serenity smiled and took up the story. "We treat our cattle extremely well. They lead pampered lives and we attend to their every need."

"Even when we kill 'em, it's a peaceful process," Clem explained. "Our unique technique actually adds to the flavor of the meat."

He and Serenity exchanged glances and gave each other an affirmative nod.

"What technique do you use that would be peaceful?" I asked.

"Sucking out their blood, of course," Serenity said.

I gasped in surprise, sending a spray of water out of my mouth.

"I am afraid my young friends here are not fully aware of your situation," Digger said, and rose. "As you know, I play things close to the vest."

This made Clem laugh. "Of course. You're the best dang secret-keeper in the world. You could torture this man and he wouldn't give you so much as his grandma's phone number."

Serenity gazed at us with her remarkable eyes. "Allow me to explain. Everyone who works the night shift here at the ranch — we're all vampires."

# SEVENTEEN

Willow and I gaped at the statuesque woman. Digger, Clem, and Serenity, however, were unaffected by her words.

I caught my breath. "Vampires? But I thought — we were here to—"

"Fight vampires?" Digger said, completing my sentence. "That's correct. Clem and Serenity hired us to stop someone who is creating rogue vampires."

"I think we should explain things to the young people," Serenity said with a casual smile.

Clem nodded. "Y'see, we got ourselves a good thing goin' here. We started this ranch with the purpose of helping our community."

I stammered. "B-but your community — I mean — do they attack people?"

"Some of them did," Serenity sighed. "But the point of the ranch was to create a food supply that didn't harm any humans. We raise the cattle and treat them very well. When it comes time for them to go to market... we feed."

"It's also humane, because the critters just get jabbed one quick time," Clem explained. "And then the venom in our bite makes 'em feel good."

"And one cow can feed many of us," Serenity added, "and we store any excess blood."

"Got ourselves the best dang blood bank you ever saw. Not to mention, the anticoagulant in our venom tenderizes the meat in ways you can only imagine," Clem stated proudly.

Digger spoke up. "The Reins and their staff have found a way to feed their hunger yet have a thriving business as an active part of the community."

"Damn straight," Clem added. "We also hire people who work here during the day, taking care of the cattle. Only a few of them know our secret, and they help us keep going."

"Why do you have a problem with other vampires?" I wondered.

Clem stood. "Someone is out there making new vampires, young man. Every one here at the ranch is at least a hundred years old. All of us just want a peaceful life, where we can live and not worry about leavin' a trail of dead folks, or being shunned by humans. Y'see, new vampires are out of control, they're wild. They are so overwhelmed by their hunger, there ain't no way to reason with 'em. We've stopped two new vampires in the last two months. We tried to help 'em, but we couldn't and one of my boys got hurt taking one of 'em down. Took him two weeks to recover, and we heal damn fast."

"Those two new vampires killed a young woman before we put them down," Serenity said and shook her head. "There is a risk, if this keeps happening, then our neighbors will become suspicious, even of those of us who have been living in this area for many years."

"Thass right." Clem pulled off his hat, revealing a full head of bushy hair. "The last thing any of us want is trouble, or worse, people investigating. We need to stop any more new vampires from rising, and find who's creating 'em."

"How does a person get turned into a vampire?" I interjected.

Clem glanced sidelong at Digger. "You ain't told this one very much, have you?"

"He's studying, but I thought it would be best to hear from the source," Digger said.

Clem nodded. "It takes a vampire to make a vampire. When a vampire attacks a person and sucks their blood, they usually just die. But if the vampire feeds the human some of his own blood —"

"Or hers," Serenity insisted.

"Yeah. They convert them. This process takes a couple of nights, the vampire feeding on the human and then feeding the human. The last part is that the human dies and then rises as a new vampire."

"A hungry new vampire," Serenity stressed. "Overwhelmed by the desire to feed, basically little more than a wild animal."

Digger looked at Willow and I. "You see the problem? We have to stop any new vampires, and find the creator and remove him, so he can't make any more. Got it?"

"The most recent death was our mayor," Clem confided. "He's the one being buried tomorrow."

"We have... an associate... who works the night shift at the morgue. He let us know that Mayor Perkins had the marks on his neck, and blood in his mouth from taking the vampire's blood in return."

"Won't he rise tonight? Before the funeral?" I wondered.

"The process takes a day or two once the victim has died," Digger clarified. "They'll bury him tomorrow, and he should rise tomorrow night."

"The vampire who created him will be there to see him rise," Clem said.

"Why is that?" Willow asked.

"A new creation draws its creator to themselves when they rise for the first time," Serenity said.

Digger nodded. "They can't help themselves. Whoever it is, they will be nearby." He looked at our hosts. "We have to stop him, whoever he is."

"My fear is that they targeted the mayor on purpose," Clem said. "People will recognize him and know he's dead. That will bring a lot of attention if anyone sees him."

"Which would put our safety and secrecy in danger," Serenity worried.

Digger returned his attention to the Reins. "You were right to call me in. If someone is making vampires and abandoning them, it puts your ranch in danger, as well as everyone in this town. I'll take care of this and find out who's behind it."

"Digger, we'd be right grateful if you did," Clem said. "We got a good thing going here, as well as a profitable business."

"I've had your steaks," Digger said with a smile. "It would be a shame to not have them on the market."

We drove back to the hotel, my mind completely in shock. Could it be true that two ranchers were actually vampires? And they had other vampires working on their ranch? It was all so unbelievable.

As we drove, I asked Digger a question. "Should we go to the morgue, check for the bite marks on the mayor?"

"Nope. I trust Clem's people. But it seems like they picked the wrong person to convert."

"What do you mean?" I asked.

"Well, if I were a vampire, and I wanted to take over a town, I'd pick someone like the town drunk to start. I keep him under wraps and then have him show up out of the blue, no one the wiser that I'd turned him. Going for a target who everyone knows is dead and anyone can recognize seems like a poor choice."

Willow spoke up from the back seat of the car. "Maybe they were counting on the shock value." She had been relatively quiet during the entire ride, and her comment took me by surprise.

"Shock value?" Digger repeated.

"Yes, they bury him in a big public display and everyone knows he's dead," Willow mused. "Then when he attacks his first victim, the person is too shocked to flee."

"Is that what happened when you saw Moonwa?" I asked and then cursed myself for bringing up something that was probably a painful situation for her.

She didn't take offense and took a moment before replying. "I think so. When I saw the altar and the voodoo doll with my likeness in the man's hand, it so surprised me I let down my guard. It allowed that man to possess my body."

"Marie has people looking for that doll, Willow," Digger said. "It's only a matter of time. But your insight is helpful. If the reason the vampire took the mayor was the shock value, then the creator is trying to scare the people of the town. He doesn't want to sneak into town, he wants to stomp right in."

I turned around to see Willow, and she was sitting straight up, her gaze fixed and intense.

"Willow, what is it?" I asked.

"Stop the truck!" she commanded.

Digger hit the brake, bringing the vehicle to a stop on the side of the road. We both turned to face her.

She closed her eyes, shook her head, and then looked at each of us. "They are coming for me."

"What?" I blurted.

Digger faced front and looked at Willow in his rear-view mirror. "Where, when?"

"At the hotel. Several men, I am not sure how many."

Digger moved to the back of the tailgate.

I turned to Willow. "How do you know this?"

Willow shrugged. "The spirits talk to me. They are warning me."

"Wait here," I told her and moved out of the truck to join Digger.

He switched on a battery-powered lamp and placed it atop the open tailgate. He buckled on his belt with all the various pouches. Sliding out both drawers in the back of the truck, he pulled items from various toolboxes and compartments, loading the leather pouches.

"There will be at least four of them," he muttered.

"How do you know that?"

"It's the Voodoo number for covering all the angles. It's also the mystical number for the crossroads, which is an important voodoo *veve*."

"No axe?" I said as he passed his hand over the hatchet.

He glared at me. "These are people, not zombies."

"What should I carry? The *Lahat Chereb*?"

He met my eyes. "Any luck getting it to light?"

I hung my head. "I… I haven't been able to."

"I'm going to use a wooden staff. It's a good defensive weapon, and I had a wood carver cover it in *veves*," Digger said. "You have hand-to-hand training, right?"

I glanced at Willow in the truck and then back at Digger. "Digger, that was back in high school."

Digger shook his head. "Let's cover all the bases." He reached into a toolbox that was unfamiliar to me and produced what looked like two black plastic guns.

"Are those — Tasers?" I asked.

"Yup," Digger said. "Let me run down how they work."

I quickly gained a basic understanding of the weapons, and Digger handed me two leather pouches and a belt. I slid the pouches on the belt and strapped it on, placing a Taser in each one.

Digger secured a long pouch to his belt which held three solid metal knives. He also grabbed a six-foot-long pole of wood, which was adorned with line-drawing symbols similar to the ones the man in white had drawn in the graveyard.

I looked at the implements and asked, "Do you have everything in this truck of yours?"

"Most things. That's why I need to bring the truck," he said, and reached in to retrieve the small blessed blade I had used in New Orleans. "Here, you know what to do with this."

As I slid the sheath into my boot, he carried the wooden staff to the front, opened the door, and carefully handed it back to Willow.

I looked at her. "I have a pair of stun guns. You should take one."

"I am used to my fighting stick," Willow said. "Even though it has been a while since I handled it."

Digger started the truck and pulled it back onto the road. As we pulled into the hotel parking lot, we all grew tense, our eyes darting around in search of any potential danger.

Digger warned, "Be alert. There are four of them, and they want to surprise us. When you face someone, prepare for an unexpected attack from your rear."

A mysterious figure loomed outside the door to Willow's hotel room — a tall black man, carrying a three-foot staff similar to the one Digger had given her.

Digger cut the headlights. "One at twelve o'clock. There will be one at three, one at six and one at nine." He cautiously opened the door and stepped out, and Willow handed him his pole. Digger's gaze was fixed on the stranger.

I stepped out on the far side of the vehicle and Willow stepped out to stand in front of Digger.

The man stayed out of the light, not moving, but he gazed at Willow in a way I didn't like. *"Ou menm, tifi.* Girl, you come with me."

Willow said, "I will not."

Digger added, "Leave us. *Ale avèk ou."*

My Taser in hand, I kept my gaze locked on the man in front of the hotel room, while my peripheral vision scanned the shadowy corners to my right.

With a yell from Digger's left, a man ran toward him with a machete raised above his head. Digger reacted with a low swing, clocking his machete-wielding attacker with a blow that knocked his feet out from under him. The man dropped to the ground.

On pure instinct and luck, I whirled around and saw another man sprinting towards me with a machete aloft. With no hesitation, I fired my weapon and two prongs shot out, connecting with his body. His eyes widened in shock as the current surged through his veins, and his muscles locked up and the machete dropped from his hand as he went down.

I looked up and saw the first man moving toward Willow, brandishing his short stick like a baseball bat. Willow stepped forward, her stance wide, doing that bouncing movement she had demonstrated back in New Orleans. Wielding her stick with both hands, she effortlessly blocked the man's blow. With a swift motion, she swung her stick with her left hand, striking him in the chest. She switched it to her right hand and struck him again. The man staggered back from the force of the blows.

I dropped the first stun gun and pulled the second one, glancing left and right to locate the fourth assailant. As Willow battled the man with the stick and Digger took on his foe, I went to my fallen attacker and kicked the machete out of his reach.

Locked in a fierce battle, their sticks clashing as they moved from side to side. Willow and the man moved in an intricate dance. She tried to strike, but he blocked her attempt and they stepped away from each other, circling warily.

"Josh," Digger yelled.

I whirled around and saw the fourth man emerge from the shadows. He held a gun pointed straight at me.

I leapt behind the tailgate of the truck and tried to fire my weapon at the attacker, but he was too far away and the prongs clattered uselessly to the ground. He grinned menacingly and advanced closer; the gun trained on me, moving in to get a clear shot.

His expression changed to shock and surprise as he was struck in the shoulder by an object. Unbelieving, he looked down to find the hilt of a knife embedded in his arm. Letting out a cry, I rushed forward and using a spin-kick I had learned years ago, jumped and kicked him in the head. He went down and I reached past him to grab the pistol from the ground.

He immediately pummeled me, his fists hammering, but the pain from the knife lodged in his shoulder seemed to weaken the blows.I was running on pure adrenaline and I took the cold, hard metal pistol and smacked him on the side of his head, knocking him unconscious.

I fell on top of him, then rolled over and stumbled to my feet to raise the pistol at the man fighting Willow. This surprised him, and before he could react, Willow landed a powerful blow to his head, sending him down to his knees.

Even on his knees, he swung his own stick and swept Willow's feet out from under her so that she crashed to the ground. Digger had defeated his attacker, and he moved close enough to swing his staff and knocked the remaining adversary to the ground, unconscious.

Both Digger and I were panting with exertion. I handed him the gun and rushed over to Willow. I knelt down and cradled her in my arms, lifting her up and taking her back to my room. Unlocking the door, I brought her inside, just as the flashing blue and red lights of a police car outside told me that someone had called the authorities. Digger knew where I was if the cops wanted to speak with me.

I lay Willow on my bed and hurried to the bathroom to get a cold washcloth. When I returned and placed it against her forehead, she moaned and began to wake up. I assured her that she was safe, saying, "It's Josh, you're in my room."

She opened her eyes and muttered, "I guess I'm a little out of practice."

"Are you kidding?" I told her, a smile on my face. "You were magnificent out there. I could kiss you!"

I felt a wave of heat wash over me as I realized what I just said. Was that really me talking?

"That is a good idea," she said and raised her head to put her lips to mine.

I felt an electric spark course through me, from my lips to my toes, as I passionately kissed back. Voices and a knock on the door suddenly interrupted us.

I opened the door to meet with a tall, muscular Texas State Trooper. His uniform was a deep brown with blue epaulettes, and he wore a matching cowboy hat. His air was that of authority and seriousness. "Evening, sir. I understand you and a young lady were involved in an altercation?"

"Yes, sir."

He glanced over to see Willow lying on the bed. "Does the young woman need medical attention?"

Willow sat up and let her legs hang over the bed. "No, officer, I am all right. I do not need a doctor."

The man nodded and returned his attention to me. "May I ask you to step outside?"

I did so. Even though he'd asked it as a question, I really didn't see that there was any way I could refuse.

Digger was conversing with a trooper while two other men and two state trooper vehicles stood nearby. They had handcuffed the four attackers who were sitting on the ground near the police cars. One of them had a hastily applied bandage on the knife wound in his shoulder.

"Do you know these men?" my trooper asked, blocking me from being able to glance over to Digger.

"I know the man over there, Everett Hill," I admitted, pointing at Digger. "Never saw the other men before."

"Any idea why they would attack you?"

"I believe they were attempting to kidnap my girl," I said.

"Your girl?" he repeated.

I questioned why I uttered those words instead of her name. But in my heart, I felt she was 'my girl,' or at least my responsibility.

"Yes, sir," I conceded.

"You stay out here. I am going to go in and talk to the lady, all right?"

I nodded slightly in acknowledgement as he walked past me and into the room. I stayed close to the window, peeking in to watch as he spoke to her.

I now had a clear view of Digger and the trooper he was speaking to. With my ability to read lips, I could make out their conversation. Digger was describing the events of the attack, gesturing toward the weapons and each individual involved.

I cautiously peered into the room and although I couldn't hear the conversation, I easily deciphered what was being said. The trooper was asking typical questions, such as "who were these men?" and "how do you know them?"

An ambulance arrived and two EMTs stepped out. A third trooper directed them to the injured man. The EMTs examined his shoulder wound, carefully unwrapping it and quickly determining the extent of the injury.

Peering into the room, I noticed Willow's responses were straightforward and lacking embellishment. This was a wise decision. Witnesses often provide too much detail which can draw unwanted attention from law enforcement.

Soon, the trooper finished and came out. "Were you the one who used the Taser?"

"Yes, sir. Is there a problem with that?"

He grinned. "Not in Texas."

The troopers departed, and they removed our attackers from the scene. The troopers took away three of them in two police cars and the last one went in an ambulance, escorted by another trooper.

Digger handed me the stun gun. He had reloaded it, ready for use.

I glanced at the pouch with the knives attached to his belt. "You're a knife-thrower as well?"

"Studied with a guy up in New York, a world champion," Digger said. "These are silver. They come in real handy with werewolves."

"Werewolves," I said, my mouth dry. "There are werewolves?"

Digger nodded.

I went on. "Do you think those men were from the cult?"

"I have to believe they were trying to get their vessel back."

"That's a terrible thing to call Willow," I snapped.

"It's how they see her," Digger said. "To them, she's not a person, but something to be used. I'm just wondering how they tracked us all the way from New Orleans, and if there could be more on the way."

I pondered that, and it filled me with apprehension.

Digger gave me a peculiar grin and warned, "Be sure to keep an eye on Willow." He headed for his room without a look back.

I walked into my bedroom and saw that Willow had returned to her spot on my bed.

She sat up as I entered. "May I stay here? I don't wish to be alone."

I remembered the warmth of her kiss from before, and I felt the heat spreading through my body. "Sure, I'll... um... take the chair. Do you need anything from your room?"

"No, I'm fine. I'll just sleep in these clothes."

"Good idea. I'll do the same."

She went into the bathroom as I took the boot knife off and put it on the dresser, kicked off my shoes and tried to see how I could get comfortable on the chair. She came out, wiping her face with a towel. "I used your toothbrush. I hope you don't mind."

"Um...no... we kissed and all," I said, my embarrassment rising. I went into the bathroom and splashed some cold water on my face, trying to cool off.

I entered the room, and she was in bed. This helped to quell my desire. Taking out my hearing aid, I placed it in the charger, reducing the sound in the room. Now I could no longer detect her breathing.

I grabbed a blanket from the closet and made my way to the chair. I flicked off the light switch and settled down, wrapping the blanket around me. "Good night," I murmured.

She probably responded, but I couldn't hear her. I shut my eyes tightly in an effort to drift off to sleep, but it was a futile attempt.

Willow's warmth preoccupied my mind and her velvet lips kept me awake. The cheap furniture made it impossible to settle into a comfortable position.

A tap on my shoulder startled me. When I opened my eyes, I was face to face with Willow, her lips forming the words, "Were you sleeping?" The dim lighting of the room had allowed my eyes to adjust, and I could now make out her features.

"Not at all," I told her.

Her hand softly ran through my hair as our lips locked once more. I felt every sensation in my body as I embraced her. She moved against me, and I felt the warmth between us. Our kiss deepened as it ignited our passion. The taste of her was like no other. I felt a thrill as I held her close.

I felt her hand move to the most intimate part of me. Every nerve in my body came alive, almost like being struck by lightning. Her caress was so sensuous that it completely overwhelmed me.

I moved my hand lower on her, but she gently pushed it away. She then took both of my hands and placed them on the armrests of the chair. Gazing up at me, she unzipped my pants and pulled them down. "I want to show my appreciation," she said softly. "Let me do this for you."

Then, she used those lips in ways that I will never forget as long as I live.

She pulled moans from me as she worked her magic. When she finished, she slowly rose from the chair and declared, "That is enough for tonight."

She returned to the bed, and she left me feeling in awe of what had just happened.

I drifted off into a blissful slumber.

# EIGHTEEN

T he next morning, my muscles were sore from the previous day of digging and the fighting with the voodoo cultists. I also felt invigorated from my encounter with Willow and my head swam with the possibilities before us.

The bed was empty. Willow was gone.

At first, it surprised me, but then I decided she must have just returned to her room.

Still feeling uneasy, I took a quick shower, which loosened my muscles and brought me fully awake.

I dressed and inserted my hearing aids by the time there was a knock on the door. I opened it to find Digger.

He stepped in without even a "Good morning," and looked around the room, his mouth twisted into a teasing smile. "I'm surprised that you're alone."

Playing dumb, I said, "I don't know what you mean."

"Come on Josh, I wasn't born last night," he beamed. "The way you two were mooning after each other. I figured it would happen. I just didn't expect it this soon."

I rubbed the back of my neck, hoping to avoid answering.

"Where is she?"

I couldn't deny it any longer, and then again, why should I? "I don't know. She was here when we fell asleep and gone when I woke up."

Digger's smile fell from his face, replaced by a look of concern. "Do you know when she left?"

"No, I was asleep—"

Digger moved fast for an older man, stepped out of my room and knocked on the door just past his. "Willow? It's Digger, you in there?"

He pulled out several keycards, and put one in the door, and it opened.

I followed him into Willow's room. "You had an extra key for us? Do you know how creepy that is?"

"Says the man who would have had his liver eaten if I hadn't barged in to his room in Duivelsmeer."

He moved to the suitcase and threw it open. All of Willow's possessions were there.

"Maybe she went for coffee?" I said.

Digger looked up at the ceiling. "Five, the voodoo number for domination. Shit! Why didn't I see it?"

"What are you talking about?"

"There was another cultist. Probably equipped with that voodoo doll we never found to control her." He turned to me, eyes ablaze. "Is she still a virgin?"

"Yes. We... um... she did... other things... last night."

"I don't need a scorecard, Josh." This made him pause. "The problem is, if she's still a virgin, Moonwa can still possess her if his spirit hasn't moved on."

Frantically, I exclaimed, "Wasn't the exorcism supposed to handle that?"

Digger shook his head. "I need a seer. Let me call Marie. I have an idea — if they didn't get too far."

He headed back into his room. I assumed he was calling Marie, and I headed back to my own.

I found her fighting stick and headed to Digger's room with it. "Will this help? She was fighting with it."

Digger nodded, as I handed it to him. "Go get a weapon."

As he got on the phone, I went back to my room to get the belt with the two pouches. I put the Lahat Chereb in one pouch, the Taser in the other, and the blessed blade in my boot. I then headed out to the truck to wait.

"Okay, let me know," he said on the phone, as he approached the truck, ending the call. He unlocked the tailgate, pulled out the drawer and opened a built-in box. He removed a leather-bound tube that was about twelve inches long, and a rifle with an impressive scope from under a blanket.

"Lock 'er up," he told me.

I closed the tailgate and made sure it was secure. "Is that gun necessary?"

"Only if we want to stop them," Digger said, as he checked the weapon to make sure it was loaded and then pointed his finger to an area in the back of the motel. "We need to go over there."

"Isn't getting into the truck and going after them a better choice?" I said. "We don't even know for sure if they took her."

We moved behind the motel and were now out of sight from the highway.

"Do you believe that she'd run off on you after last night?"

I paused. "I hope not."

His phone made a sound, and he opened a map image on the screen. "Good ol' Marie. She is good at what she does."

I looked at the map. "How far do you think they've gone?"

"They are about two hours away. Whoever got her is taking her by back roads to avoid pursuit, and the Ley lines."

"Let's get back to the truck and get going," I pleaded.

Digger took one more look about and then put his phone away. He handed me the rifle, which I hung over my shoulder.

"Take my arm and whatever you do, do not let go."

"What are you doing?"

Now that he had both hands free, he pulled the tube from his pocket and opened it. A small scroll fell into his hands, made of parchment and ancient. "You got a good grip there, Joshua?"

"Yes, but I don't know why," I said firmly, locking my arm with his.

He put the tube back into the pocket. The small scroll had shiny ends on it, and from that close range, I would swear they were gold. There were a series of lines with Hebrew lettering across it.

"Don't look at the scroll," he demanded. "Avert your eyes. In fact, close them."

I did as he asked. "We should go after them, if you know where they are."

"That's the idea," Digger agreed as he intoned words in a foreign tongue.

A blast of air yanked Digger so hard, I almost lost my grasp on him and it blew against my face like a wind tunnel. I tightened my grip and held on to him and the rifle for dear life.

"You can let go, now," Digger said, and I opened my eyes. The motel, the parking lot, and the nearby busy highway had disappeared. Instead, we were on the shoulder of a two-lane road with trees on both sides, and a babbling brook nearby.

I looked around as Digger rolled up the scroll and returned it to its leather container. I fell to my knees and vomited all over the sandy side of the road. Digger grabbed the gun from me as I collapsed.

Digger stood over me. "That happens the first time. Fortunately, we only use that in extreme emergencies."

He pulled a small bottle of water from a pouch and handed it to me. I took it gratefully.

"What just happened?" I groaned. "How did we get here?"

"Kefitzat HaDerekh," Digger said, as I drank the water. "It means 'jumping the path,' or 'contraction of the road.' Jewish holy men, called Baalei shem, found what they called, 'the secret names of God,' which allowed them the ability to get places much faster."

"Did we just teleport?" I asked, feeling barely strong enough to get up off my knees.

He looked both ways on the roadway. "We're here, ain't we? Now, we've got about five minutes until the cultist arrives with your girlfriend. I noticed you brought the Lahat Chereb. Can you make it work? It might help."

I nodded. Was Willow now my girlfriend?

I pulled out the hilt of the Lahat Chereb. Closing my eyes, I tried to think how I could be a righteous man. I was trying to save the woman I loved. What could be more righteous than that?

I pulled out my notebook and read the words with as much passion as I could.

I got through the entire prayer and then held the hilt aloft.

Nothing happened.

I took a deep breath and focused all my concentration on the paper and read the prayer a second time, adding, "Amen."

Again, nothing.

"It's a big step, Josh," Digger said. "Maybe you're just not ready for it."

Annoyed, I held out the hilt to Digger. "Why don't you use it? You can recite the words properly, I'm sure."

"I can," he replied. "But the blade works better in the hands of a righteous man."

"It would appear that I am not a righteous man."

He looked over at me and spoke softly. "You are, Josh. You merely lack faith."

A car appeared in the distance, and Digger lifted the rifle to his shoulder and looked through the scope.

"That's him," Digger growled.

"If you shoot him, Willow could get hurt. Can you shoot out the tires?"

"That doesn't work," Digger said, his one eye looking through the scope. "I'll try one shot into the engine block, and if that doesn't stop the car, I'll take out the driver."

As the vehicle drew nearer, the driver must have realized who we were, because he sped up. It became clear that he was not going to stop.

"Once I stop the car, you get the girl and the voodoo doll," Digger ordered. "You must get the doll as well. Am I clear?"

"Yeah," I said.

As the speeding car drew closer, Digger gripped the hefty rifle tightly, his gaze fixed on it. He fired the rifle, the report echoing off the nearby hills.

The car still headed straight for us.

"We're running out of time," I pointed out.

"I know."

There was a second loud crack, and the vehicle was close enough that I saw the driver as a hole appeared in the windshield and his head snapped back. His hands went to the left, and the car veered off the road and into the trees, where it struck a large oak.

As I sprinted towards the vehicle, my heart raced. I flung open the passenger side door to discover Willow sitting there, bewildered, with a limp air bag sitting in her lap. The sight of blood on her clothing heightened my initial panic. Upon closer inspection, I realized that the blood belonged to the driver.

The young African-American man behind the wheel had suffered a fatal gunshot wound. There was a large hole in his head, exposing brain and bone through the bleeding wound.

I pulled the small boot knife to cut the webbing of Willow's seat belt and free her.

The doll was on the floor. The dead man stained its white dress with blood and gore as well. It had a sewn face that attempted to resemble Willow and a lock of curly dark hair tied in a ribbon to the doll's head.

"We have to go," I said, and pulled her from the car, the doll firmly in my other hand.

She stumbled a bit, trying to orient herself. "How did I get here?"

"What do you remember?" I said as I helped her up the embankment.

"I was in your room, sleeping in your bed," she said, looking around. "Where are we?"

"On a road somewhere in Texas, I think."

"We're near the Texas and Louisiana border," Digger said as he approached. He had the rifle on his shoulder and looked up and down the road in case any other cars were driving by. He reached out his hand. "Give me the doll."

I passed the doll to him and devoted my attention to supporting Willow, who was still unstable. Awakening from a spell because of a car accident could have bewildered anyone.

Digger untied the lock of hair and blew on it, so the hairs flew up and over the stream. He then took the doll and plunged it into the water, pushing it down to the bottom of the stream.

"Look away, Willow," Digger said, and I carefully turned her so she wasn't facing the stream.

I looked over my shoulder. "Why does she need to look away?"

"It's the doll," Willow said. "To break its power, you must put it in water and not look at it again."

"Are you okay?" I asked her.

She met my eyes. "I think I am… now."

She gently put her arms around me and pressed her lips to mine.

"Okay, you two," Digger said, stepping away from the stream. "I have a funeral to attend this afternoon, so we need to get back to Warren Rock."

I looked over at the car crashed on the side of the road. "We can't just leave him there. We have to tell the police."

"Tell them what?" Digger said. "That some guy used a voodoo doll to kidnap your girlfriend, and we teleported here to shoot him? How do you think that will go over?"

"But wait, I touched the car. My fingerprints—"

"Yeah, so being two hours away and seen by witnesses would be a good idea," Digger explained, and handed me the rifle. "Besides, I haven't had breakfast yet."

He pulled the tube from his pocket and extracted the scroll.

"Both of you grab each of my arms, hard," he ordered. "And close your eyes."

Digger repeated his peculiar incantation, prompting a powerful gust of wind to hit me hard in the face.

Then, solid ground was underfoot again.

I opened my eyes, and we were in the back of the motel, from what looked like the same spot as when we'd left.

Willow fell to her knees and vomited. I felt queasy, but stayed upright.

Digger looked at me. "Got your sea legs?"

I nodded wearily. "I'm okay."

He handed me the keys and the rifle. "Run to the truck, stow the rifle, and get a bottle of water for Willow."

I nodded and ran around the corner to follow through on his request. In mere moments I was back with one of the small bottles of water Digger kept stashed. He helped Willow to her feet, and I offered her the water. She took it gratefully.

"Okay, now we're going to get some breakfast," Digger said. "You'll both feel better if you eat. Then all of us have to take a nap. We have to get ready for that funeral this afternoon."

"I have nothing to wear for a funeral," Willow said, still unsteady on her feet.

"Right now we need to eat, and then all of us need to rest. What we just did is very draining."

We strolled to the small diner attached to the motel, and I found I was ravenous. Digger ordered us a big breakfast. When the food arrived, it looked like enough for six people. What surprised me was that the three of us finished it.

We headed back to our rooms, and Willow seemed a lot better, walking without hesitation or confusion. We stopped in front of my room.

Digger looked at me and then at Willow. "You might as well go in with him."

She flushed at this. "I hope I do not disappoint you."

"Are you kidding?" Digger bellowed. "I'm happy for both of you. But later, move your luggage into the room. I can save some money by renting only two rooms from now on."

Willow and I went in, and once alone, I kissed her, and she pulled back hesitantly.

"I am nervous," she sighed and held me at arm's length.

"You don't have to do anything you don't want to."

"I have heard… the first time… can be painful."

I whispered in her ear, "I will stop when you tell me to. But for now, I would like to do for you as you did for me last night."

Her eyebrows raised. "Really?"

I smiled as I removed my belt with the Lahat Chereb, and took my boot knife and placed them on the bureau. "Let me show you."

I went slowly, kissing her, touching her, caressing her, and waiting until she removed a piece of clothing before moving on. Letting her know her desires controlled the situation. I removed my boots and socks, but kept my clothes in place.

With aching slowness, we moved to the bed, and with time, I had her down to nothing but a pair of panties. She reached to caress me, and I swatted her hand away, which made her laugh.

"This is all about you, only you," I told her.

Soon, she was gloriously naked, and I moved my head into her lap to lick and suckle her as she had for me.

At first she was tense, and each touch made her jump a little. But as I continued, she relaxed, and soon her fingers were clawing my hair as she sighed and moaned.

In the afterglow, we lay together in bed, her naked and me still fully clothed, sleep pulling at us. Whatever magic was used to teleport us across the state in the blink of an eye had tired us both out.

On the verge of sleep, she said to me. "You came to rescue me. I feel like a princess."

"Don't sneak off anymore, okay?"

She held me close. "I never want to be away from you again."

We fell asleep in each other's arms.

# NINETEEN

An insistent knocking on the door awakened us, and still dressed, I groggily opened the door to find Digger holding two styrofoam cups of coffee.

That didn't surprise me.

What did shock me was that it was dark out and the lights outside the motel were lit.

"What time is it?" I asked. "Did we miss the funeral?"

Digger nodded, and I watched him speak. My hearing aid was still in the charger, but I could read everything he said. "You did, but I was there. I had to make it look like I was putting the dirt into the grave until everyone left. We might be up all night, so I let you two sleep. You and Willow need to get ready. Meet me at the truck in a half hour." He handed me the cups. "This will help."

I nodded, trying to get my head into the game. I stumbled back in, shut the door, placed the coffee on a makeshift desk in the room, and turned on a lamp.

Willow was sitting up, bare-breasted and gorgeous in the lamplight, and a flood of desire washed over me.

I sat on the bed, moving the coffee to the bedside table, and kissed her. She returned the kiss with equal ardor and I moved my hand down her back.

She pulled away, and I watched her mouth. "We have no time for this. We must wash and dress and go fight vampires."

She rose from the bed, completely naked, and headed to the bathroom to take a shower as I got my hearing aid in place.

I went to the sink to wash up a little, and she stepped out of the shower and into the room to dress.

"You stopped yourself," she said, putting on her bra. I was grateful I had put in my aid as she turned away from me. "You did as you said, and only pleasured me."

"I want you to feel safe," I explained. "I want to make love to you. But I can wait until you're ready."

She put on a black blouse. "You truly are a good man." She then looked down and asked. "You would do that thing... you did for me... again?"

I smiled. "Any time."

Her smile lit up the room. "That gives me something to look forward to."

As she finished dressing, I put on my belt with the Lahat Chereb and the Taser, though I wasn't sure if it was a useful tool to bring. So far, I'd had no luck making it work. I decided it was more of a relic I carried that reminded me of my father.

I put the knife into my boot.

Digger stood by the truck and smiled knowingly at us. "I was afraid I'd have to come and knock on your door several more times before I'd get you two out here."

Soon we were driving the dark roads, returning to the cemetery where we worked so hard the previous day.

"I should let you know. I talked to some of the townspeople today. Things might be more complicated than I planned," Digger said.

"What do you mean?" I asked.

"Just be ready for anything tonight, okay?"

"That's not very helpful," I pointed out.

Digger looked at Willow in the rearview mirror. "Have you heard from the spirits today?"

She shook her head. "No, I have not."

"Take a few minutes while we drive over," Digger advised. "Calm your mind and see if anything comes. We can use all the help we can get tonight."

Willow leaned back in her chair and closed her eyes.

I glanced back at her. Did she really get messages from spirits? It appeared so after that attack the previous night. When we first met her and she was possessed, she had appeared to be so powerful, and she sure handled that stick pretty well. I wanted to protect her, but she seemed far more capable of defending herself than I was.

We pulled up to the chain-link fence; the headstones illuminated by the truck's headlights.

Once he shut off the headlights, we were in almost utter darkness. "Come on, I have lanterns in the back."

Willow took a deep breath and opened her eyes.

"You okay?" I asked.

"Yes," she said, looking serious. "But you must be careful this night."

I frowned. "Why do you think that?"

She spoke through gritted teeth. "It is what the spirits tell me."

Digger's lantern did little to dispel the gloom all around us. I put my hand in Willow's and drew her next to me.

Digger handed us both crucifixes and six-inch tall crosses that appeared to be made of silver.

"Put the crucifix around your neck and the cross in your pocket," Digger said, as he kissed a rosary and put it around his own neck.

"You know I don't believe in these things," I told him.

"It doesn't matter. A great holy man blessed them, and his faith is strong enough even if yours is not."

Willow and I did as we were told.

Digger handed a lantern to me and another one to Willow.

"You take these," Digger said, passing me a long wooden stake and a wooden mallet.

"You're going to put this through his heart?" I asked.

Digger nodded. "Only if he rises. And we will have to work fast if he does."

He took out something that resembled a small pistol and put it into his pocket. He tossed Willow her fighting stick.

She easily plucked it from the air. She swung it over her head, spun it, and held one end as if ready to attack.

Digger nodded at the display. "We need to arm ourselves, and you're pretty handy with that thing."

Digger grabbed a stake, which he put into one of his oversized jacket pockets.

We made our way to the open grave, and I held the light out over the pit so we could look in.

At the bottom was a shiny new casket, covered with flowers and a thin layer of dirt.

"Sometimes a vampire tries to convert someone, and it doesn't take," Digger said, looking down in the hole.

"What do we do if nothing happens?" I asked.

He shrugged. "We fill in the grave."

"Be alert," Willow warned. "The spirits are unquiet here."

Digger and I raised our heads to look around, taking a step back from the grave.

A figure moved out of the darkness, and Digger held up a hand to let us know to stay where we were.

"Who's there?" Digger shouted and slipped one of the silver crosses out of his pocket. The bright metal gleamed in the light from our lanterns.

The approaching figure raised her hand to block her view of the cross. "Relax, it's just me."

The woman stepped into the light. It was Clem's assistant, Claire, who met us at the door of the ranch the previous evening.

"Can you put that away, please?" She flinched away from the cross.

Digger put the silver object out of view into the pocket of his jacket. He held up the lamp to shine it on her pale face. "Claire, what brings you out here?"

"Clem wanted to make sure everything went according to plan." She stepped to the grave and peered in. "You know, he might not rise — sometimes it doesn't take."

"We were just discussing that possibility," Digger replied, keeping himself between Willow, me, and the woman. "Maybe your informant at the morgue misinterpreted the signs. It happens."

A tiny smile appeared on her face, not enough to show her teeth. "Yes, it does. I think Clem is overreacting to the entire thing. We've been able to keep everything under control so far."

Digger countered her as she moved. "And yet, here you are."

"Like you were drawn here," Willow said.

The woman's eyes moved to Willow, and she appeared angry. "Still an innocent, I see."

"I see much surrounding you, too," Willow said, and took a step forward. "I sense betrayal. You wear the stink of it."

"You don't understand," the woman said, her eyes focused on Willow.

"Then tell us," I challenged.

She looked us over. "Clem and Serenity think it's fine to raise cattle for their own use, but it is not the way of our kind. We are predators who must find worthy targets."

"And the blood of humans is too sweet to ignore?" Digger said.

"Yessss," she hissed.

The little woman moved so fast, she was almost a blur. With her mouth open wide and fangs gleaming, she leapt over the open chasm of the grave, lunging for Willow.

Willow was prepared and swung her stick before the woman even launched herself. With a resounding crack of wood on bone, it knocked the attacker out of the air and into the open grave.

Digger and I both pulled out the silver crosses and held them up, as all three of us stepped back from the trench.

"Now what do we do?" I yelled.

"Stay back," Digger shouted in reply.

In the lamplight, a cloud of smoke rose out of the grave, floating above the open pit.

"What the—" I gasped.

The cloud moved right at me and I found myself engulfed in a swirling veil of noxious grayness. The stench of decomposition and death saturated every breath, seizing hold of my lungs as I choked and coughed. I tried to move away as my skin erupted with beads of blood, leaving a gruesome coating on my body that was quickly absorbed by the fog. I shrieked and spasmed, wracked by unbearable torment as my skin continued to rend and bleed.

"Mist form," Digger yelled, and pointed his small pistol directly at me.

I wanted him to shoot me. Anything to end the pain.

I screamed again, my eyes clenched shut as I waited for the force of a bullet — but it drenched me with a chilling spray of water. I gasped, choking on blood and water and terror.

I fell to my knees and coughed, but the mist no longer surrounded me.

"What was that?" I gasped.

"Holy water." Digger waved the pistol. "That was a vampire in mist form. The cross doesn't work when they don't have eyes."

Willow helped me to my feet as she held her fighting baton in her free hand.

"Back-to-back," Digger shouted.

We pressed our backs against each other, scanning the surrounding graveyard. Digger held his water pistol, Willow held her battle baton, and I pulled out the Lahat Chereb and the silver cross.

I focused on the sword and muttered the Hebrew prayer, but the hilt remained just as it was — no fiery blade, nothing.

I slipped it back into the pouch and pulled out the Taser, and held out the cross as well. I didn't know if a Taser would work on a vampire, but it was worth a shot.

"Let's move to the truck. We need better weapons for what we're facing," Digger ordered.

"Just what are we facing?" I asked.

"An experienced vampire, and a new one about to emerge," Digger told me as we moved as a unit toward the truck.

We reached the back of the vehicle, and Digger handed me the squirt gun.

"You see that lever? Up sprays a mist, down shoots a stream."

I saw a flash of movement to my right and fired a stream of water but hit nothing.

There was a creaking noise from the depths of the grave.

The sound of a coffin opening.

# TWENTY

Grating bumps and clunks resounded out of the hollow pit.

I was sure our adversary would use this distraction to attack, but I saw nothing move in the darkness outside of the light from our lanterns.

She must have transformed into something other than mist. I was certain she was lurking in the dark, waiting for her creation to rise from its resting place so the pair of them could attack us.

The only sounds were the occasional hoot of an owl and the rustling of leaves in the wind. Suddenly, a hand emerged from the dark soil, clawing its way to the surface, followed by another. Soon, a head with a receding hairline and a face filled with madness.

The eyes were wide, and the slack-jawed expression revealed the former mayor. From the look on his face, I could tell he was little more than a creature of primal urges, craving with animalistic instinct. Drool dripped from his open mouth and his teeth had elongated into a pair of impressive fangs.

Dirt and debris marked his suit from crawling out of the grave. He glared at us with cold, blatant desire.

Digger was getting something from the back of the truck as Willow and I stood guard with our crosses aloft. He yelled, "Clear!" and Willow and I ducked out of his way.

With a commanding presence, Digger showed off his extraordinary wooden crossbow. It featured a solid stock skillfully fashioned from timber and resembling a rifle butt that rested against his shoulder. They adorned the front of the weapon with a metal bow and stirrup, and intricate religious symbols decorated its entire length. As I observed the crossbow, I noticed a tightly pulled string secured by a metal clip. There was a short wooden arrow fitted into a slot, its tip menacingly sharpened.

As the man leapt forward, Digger pulled a metal trigger beneath the weapon. The deadly arrow shot forth, striking the revenant right in the chest with significant force and sending him tumbling backward to the ground.

"Nooooo!" moaned a voice, as the woman jumped out of the darkness behind Digger. She wrenched the crossbow out of his grasp and, with one blow, sent him flying. She lunged for me, her fangs extended, and her hand reached for my throat, ready to crush my windpipe.

I barely had time to fire a blast from the squirt gun, but my aim was true. She screamed as her eye burst into flames with a hissing noise. With a scream, she fell away, one hand over her smoldering eye, as she disappeared into the darkness again.

I looked down at the mayor with the wooden arrow through his heart as a small trickle of blood came out of his mouth.

"Eyes up," Digger hissed, rising to his feet, the empty crossbow back in his hand.

"How can we hit her? She moves too fast."

"Give me a stake," Willow ordered.

I had been carrying the mallet and a sharpened stake but had dropped them to the ground during our first encounter. Looking all around us, I grabbed it, then handed it to Willow.

She glanced at Digger. "Cover me?"

Willow took two steps away from us, then turned to face us. With a nod to Digger, she held up the stake and closed her eyes.

As I moved to Digger, he reached into one of his pouches and retrieved a metal tool that resembled a lever. He deftly attached it to the frame and the string of the crossbow. He pulled back the lever, causing the string to snap into place. After dropping the tool, he inserted another wooden bolt against the taut string.

I looked over at Willow. "What does she think she's doing?"

He raised the loaded crossbow and rested it on his shoulder; the arrow pointing into the darkness. "Shh. Let her work."

She had her eyes tightly shut and was as unmoving as a statue. Why was she just standing there? If the vampire lady jumped at Willow, she didn't stand a chance.

I started forward, but Digger put an arm out in front of me. "Stay here. Trust her."

I glanced at him and then turned my attention to Willow.

What came next happened so fast I could hardly see it.

With a jolt, Willow's eyes flew open and her hand swiftly rose, twisting in readiness. Simultaneously, the vampire woman sprang out of the shadows above, presumably from a tree in the cemetery.

As she leapt down to Willow, descending towards her prey, she landed directly on the pointed tip of the wooden stake which was held exactly in the correct position. It impaled her in the chest as her body collapsed to the ground, pinning Willow beneath her.

The stake poked out of the woman's back, the sharp point penetrating all the way through her black dress.

Digger put down the crossbow and the pair of us ran to Willow to pull the unmoving vampire off her.

Willow sat up and rubbed her arm. "That bitch fell on me."

I touched her face. "How did you do that?"

"I let the spirits of the loas guide me. They told me when she would jump and from which direction. I only had to put my hand in the right place."

Claire lay on her side with the stake piercing her from front to back. "You said the stake doesn't kill them?" I said.

Digger shook his head. "No. A stake in the heart only paralyzes them. If we were to bury them, eventually the wood would decay and they would come back. But it would make an unpleasant few decades for them."

He picked up the crossbow. "No, we have to behead them to kill them completely. And we have to do it now, while they can't move."

He trudged back toward the truck as Willow and I followed.

He pulled out the Hunga-Munga, which he offered to me. He handed the hatchet to Willow.

She frowned. "You wish me to behead the devil woman?"

Digger stepped close to whisper. "Take the hatchet and move out of the way."

Willow took the small axe and took a step to her right, just in time for Digger to raise the crossbow in one fluid movement and release the bolt. The feathered stake flew up through the air and struck something in a tree near the grave with a resounding 'smack'. A woman in a white dress fell out of the tree on the far side of the grave, slamming to the ground.

"Another one?" I cried out.

Digger lowered the crossbow and studied the graveyard. "Yes, but that's it."

He put the bow into the back of the truck and pulled out a chamois bag that had four pockets sewn into it, one of them already filled. He took the silver cross from me, kissed it, and put it into another of the pockets, followed by the cross from his jacket.

"We won't need these anymore," he said and folded the leather pouch twice and returned it to one of the many hiding places in the drawer of his truck. "Keep your crucifixes on for now."

We moved toward the fallen bodies, and I asked, "Who was the woman in white?"

"Not sure. She just showed up. Maybe Claire converted her as well. I did some checking today, and some of the townspeople talked about seeing a lady in white in this graveyard. I was on guard for her."

"Don't you think letting us know there was another vampire was important?" I demanded.

As we skirted the burial plot, Digger approached the prone figure cloaked in white and pivoted her gently, allowing us a glimpse of her visage. The woman, graced with an alabaster complexion and a cascade of vibrant, red locks, was truly beautiful.

Digger frowned and leaned in to look at her. "I am not sure if she's a new convert. My guess is that this Claire woman fed her and got her past the blood lust. Maybe brought her as back-up."

Willow looked around. "The spirits are most disquieted by this one."

"Should we behead her as well?" I asked.

Digger shook his head. "The spirts are probably upset that the vampires took one so young. I think with the help of Clem and Serenity, she might become part of that community and not be a menace."

"It would be nice," Willow relented, "to save someone from this night."

"I agree," I said.

Digger took the hatchet from Willow. "You watch over her. We're going to take care of the mayor and Claire. We'll take her to the ranch where they might help her."

Willow nodded and sat on the ground next to the woman, while Digger and I set to work.

It was a grisly job. With the Hunga-Munga's sickle blade in hand, I began the daunting task of severing the mayor's neck. Despite my lack of experience, I persisted, delivering a series of brutal blows until finally, I separated the head from the body. The sight of blood and gore left me feeling drained and on the verge of being sick.

Digger, as if mocking me, severed Claire's head with a single blow, and there was little blood at all.

I went into the grave and opened the coffin lid. Digger lowered the mayor's headless body to me and I returned him to the cushioned bed from which he'd risen.

"Leave room at the feet for the head," Digger yelled down to me.

"What about the woman?" I asked.

"Stick her in the coffin as well." Digger answered. "There's room enough."

I created space where I didn't think it was possible by maneuvering the body so that the shoulders were at the top of the box. Then I received the severed head from Digger and carefully placed it at the mayor's feet. However, when he handed me Claire's head, I noticed it had transformed. Its face was now covered in wrinkles, much of its hair had fallen out. The eyelids had receded into the sockets, while the lips pulled away from the teeth, leaving nothing but a skin-covered skull.

"What happened to her?" I asked. "She's all withered."

"She's been dead for over a hundred years," Digger explained. "Time and decay are catching up to her."

The body he gave me was a skin-clad skeleton draped in a loosely fitting dress. It barely occupied any space inside the coffin, such was the desiccated state of her remains.

I closed the lid, stood upon the coffin, and Digger helped pull me out of the grave. "Let's get the girl in the truck bed."

Willow rose. "No, she must ride in the back seat with me."

Digger frowned. "Are you sure? If that stake should come loose…"

"She lost her life. Must she lose her dignity as well?" Willow argued. "We cannot throw her in the truck bed like she is a tool. If she is to regain her humanity, we must treat her humanely."

"All right," Digger said and turned to me. "Josh, you take her feet, I'll — humanely — take her upper body."

We carefully carried the fallen girl and placed her in the back seat of the truck, with Willow helping to manipulate the body to get her in.

I noticed Digger was pretty winded at this point. "Are you all right?"

"Sure thing," he said with too much cheer. "I got a great workout."

I looked at the woman in white with the arrow in her chest and no blood. "We're going to take her to the ranch?"

"Yes, but first we have to fill in that grave," Digger insisted.

"You're kidding. Can't we do that tomorrow?"

"We have to get it done. Then we'll sleep, and we can leave town tomorrow," Digger said and looked at Willow. "I'm concerned there might be others after you, and if they are aware we stayed here, we want to get as far away as possible."

We went to the bed of the truck, and Digger handed me a shovel.

It took about an hour, but as we filled in the grave, the night creatures' sounds gradually resurfaced — the hoots of owls and chirps of katydids and crickets. It made a comforting background noise that persisted as we shoveled dirt into the grave. It was soothing to know that the animals were no longer afraid.

We filled the grave with dirt and compacted it before placing the sod back, leaving the site a few inches above the level of the ground. Digger had an impeccable accuracy in determining the required soil compression and depth.

Exhaustion from the battle overwhelmed me, drenched me in perspiration, and filling the grave covered me in grime. I also had memories of decapitating another human being in my mind, haunting me.

Digger drove as we made our way toward the ranch. In the rear seat, Willow held the head of the young vampire woman on her lap. Exhaustion hit me like a ton of bricks, and I laid my head back, closing my eyes. Even though I slept all day, I still felt as though I could hibernate for a month after the ordeal we just survived.

As we drove off the main road, we steered onto the extended driveway leading up to the ranch's grand entrance. Digger and I were pretty filthy. I couldn't help but contemplate how our vampire host would react to two scruffy gravediggers standing in their exquisite foyer.

We left the comatose woman in the back seat while Digger rang the bell.

He had to do so several times before Clem answered the door.

"Hey, Digger!" Clem said, all smiles. "Didn't think I'd see you tonight." He peered through the open door of the truck and caught sight of the young woman in the white dress. However, his gaze immediately soured as he noticed the sharp wooden stake piercing her heart. "Who's that?"

"A new vampire," Digger told him. "I think the vampire who's been killing the townspeople converted her."

"Did you figure out who was doing it?" Clem asked.

Digger met his eyes. "It was Claire. She showed up and attacked us."

Clem frowned. "Claire? No, she was in the office working…" His voice faded as he realized Digger was telling the truth. "Well, ya'll come in," Clem said.

Digger and I moved to get the white-draped body, but Clem said, "Wait, leave her there until I can get things ready for her."

He held the door as Digger, Willow, and I went in.

We walked into the spacious living room as Serenity met us, coming from rooms beyond. "Clem, what was — oh, we have guests?"

Willow made sure her shirt collar covered the crucifix.

"Digger says it was Claire who was making the new vampires," Clem said.

"Claire?" Serenity said and shook her head. "I am… surprised.

"They saved a new convert, though," Clem said. "She's got a stake in her heart, but she is still in one piece."

Serenity closed her eyes and shuddered. "A stake, how dreadful."

Digger didn't miss it. "Ever had that happen to you, Serenity?"

She nodded. "Someone staked me once, long ago. It was quite... unpleasant."

"It was the only way I could think to bring her to you, safely," Digger said. "I have no desire to bring any pain to you and yours."

She forced a smile. "Of course not, Digger. So, the vampire maker was Claire." She looked at Digger and me. "You had to...?"

Digger's face was like stone. "We did what we had to, ma'am."

I noted that the casual 'Serenity' was now the formal 'ma'am.'

Serenity, however, reached out and touched Digger's arm. "Of course you did. Now you understand why we needed outside help. It appears Claire had been giving us false information since the start of all this."

Clem went to the back of the bar and unlocked another refrigerator adjacent to the one containing our water reserves from the evening before. He extracted a plastic bag filled with blood, which had a layer of frost on the surface. The bag had a white label attached, bearing the letter 'A' in bold — presumably indicating the blood type.

"There may have been someone influencing her, pushing her," Digger said.

"Could it be the person you captured?"

Digger shook his head. "I don't think so. She seems young, and I would guess she is a new convert. It would be best if we left before you removed the stake."

Clem nodded. "We have to warm the blood before we can give it to her."

Serenity frowned, still looking at Digger. "Do you think we can save her?"

"Hard to say," Clem answered.

"She didn't attack us, so I think she fed recently enough," Digger said. "But we didn't speak to her. You two would know better than anyone if you can rescue her."

Serenity sighed. "I hope so. We had to destroy those new vampires, and now Claire… it's a lot to deal with."

"We'll be at the hotel until morning," Digger said. "If you need anything, send one of your staff with a message."

Clem handed Serenity the blood bag and walked with the three of us to the door. "We'll transfer funds to your account tonight. Should show up by tomorrow."

"It's fine, Clem. I wish I could have told you it was an out-of-town visitor doing the killing, instead of one of your own."

"It had to be someone local. But Claire? I didn't see that coming." He stopped at the doorway and spoke quietly. "I should warn you there is a lot of talk about you going around certain… circles."

"I've heard some of it," Digger said.

"Have you heard there is trouble brewing in Chicago?"

"Yes, I'm headed there tomorrow."

We stepped out the front door and looked at the open back door of the truck.

The back seat was empty.

The girl was gone. The wooden arrow was lying on the floor of the truck.

"What the hell?" Digger exclaimed.

Clem frowned. "You sure it was a vampire? Ain't no vampire can un-stake themselves."

"Now, I'm not sure of anything." Digger responded.

"We will keep an eye out, see if somebody glimpses her," Clem said, as he looked out into the darkness.

Digger's jaw set. "I'll come back if there is any more trouble, no charge."

"Appreciate that, Digger."

Frowning, Willow took hold of the arrow and scrutinized it.

"Go with care, Digger," Clem said, as we all got in the truck, started it up, and drove away.

We traveled in silence as we rode back to the hotel over the dark roadways, lit only by our headlights.

"There is something on this arrow, but it is not blood," Willow said from the back seat, the arrow still in her hand. "It is slimy."

I turned to Digger. "Slimy blood? What do you think that creature was?"

"Not sure. It worries me."

"And you're heading to Chicago tomorrow?"

"Yup."

"And you were planning to tell me... when?"

"Tomorrow," he said, his eyes watching the road as we drove. "I might even ask you to come along."

"Might?"

"Well, if you ain't busy."

Now it was my turn to stare ahead at the road before us. "If so, things have to change."

"What are you talking about?"

"No more secrets, no more mystery, no more hiding stuff from me or Willow."

"I only did that to—"

I interrupted. "It doesn't matter why you did it, or why you think you needed to. I don't care. I only care that you're not telling us everything."

"What makes you think I know everything?"

"Be honest with us. Tell us the risks and the dangers up front. I refuse to walk blindly into another one of these situations. If you can't agree with that, I can't go with you."

Digger was silent for a few minutes as we continued to drive. I felt no need to speak either. I made my situation known, and it was up to Digger to respond.

He finally said. "Can we talk about it tomorrow?"

"Yes — you tell me everything you know. Then I'll decide if I want to come."

"Fair enough," Digger said as he pulled into the parking lot for the motel.

We got out of the truck, Willow, and I went into our shared room. I folded up my dirty clothes and took a shower. Then I lay in bed in boxers and a T-shirt as Willow showered. I removed my hearing aid and enjoyed the silence of the room.

She came out of the shower wearing only the large towel and looked at me.

"I could take the chair," I assured her, sitting up.

Her mouth formed the words, "Can you understand me without your earpiece?"

"Yes, I understand you perfectly."

"I heard what you said to Digger," she told me. "That you might leave."

"You could come with me," I told her. "If that's what you want."

"I do not know, the loas are not telling me yet," Willow said with a shy smile. "But I know I want to be with you."

She dropped the towel and exposed her glorious naked body.

I sat up further. "Willow, we don't have to do anything, you're a vir—"

She stepped forward and placed a finger over my mouth. "Tonight, I am a woman with the same desires as any other woman."

In the dim light, I saw the roundness of her bare breasts, the curve of her thighs.

"Those people pursued us here because they needed a virgin to use. Think of that. This will protect me, protect us, when I am no longer any use to them."

She stepped close and grabbed my T-shirt and pulled it over my head and we kissed again, our bare chests touching each other, flesh against flesh.

She pulled back. "I want you to love me."

She lay down on top of me, and I didn't resist.

We spent a great deal of time kissing and touching, sensually exploring each other's bodies. Odd visions floated through my exhausted mind: a graveyard, a menacing vampire, and a woman in white.

Our movements were leisurely and deliberate, as we discovered each other's preferences and took our time.

We became one, and there was some pain for her, but she encouraged me to continue. We moved in unison, moaning, crying out, and overwhelmed by a shuddering finish.

We lay on the bed, the pair of us fighting to regain our breath, our bodies still entwined.

She touched my face, and I whispered, "Willow, I'm falling in love with you."

Her gaze softened, and I watched her mouth as she spoke. "As I am with you, my good man. But the loas are warning me."

"About me?" I worried.

"No, about what we must face in the next few days," Willow said.

I wanted to question what she meant, but weariness engulfed me. We dozed off, naked, entwined in an embrace.

# TWENTY-ONE

I woke up the next day, finding myself alone in bed once again. With the help of my hearing aid, I soon noticed the sound of water in the shower. I made out her sweet melody as she sang to herself in the bathroom.

As I donned my underwear and T-shirt, Willow emerged from the bathroom completely nude, not even bothering to wrap herself in a towel. Instantly, my jaw went slack as she radiated a sense of vitality that was simply irresistible. Her face was alight with unbridled happiness, making her all the more alluring.

She smiled at me. "It is a compliment that I get such a reaction every time from you."

"You're beautiful," I said and moved close to kiss her.

She laughed and held me at arm's length. "I'm starving, and sore."

I immediately became concerned. "Are you all right?"

"Nothing that any other woman hasn't had to endure. I am sure Digger is waiting for us."

I sighed and nodded.

Shortly after dressing, we walked hand in hand to Digger's room.

"You two ready to eat?" he asked. As always, he was in jeans and a shirt with his peacoat and that floppy hat of his. We followed him to the restaurant for the motel. We sat in a booth with cushioned seats of cracked and worn vinyl and ordered breakfast.

The restaurant was fairly empty, as it was late morning.

"So," I started, "what's in Chicago and why are you going there?"

"Technically, it's a town just outside of Chicago—"

I glared at Digger.

He held up his hands in a surrender pose. "Okay. The point is this, Josh, you looked into what happened in Portland, right?"

"I did," I said, which got a quizzical look from Willow. I turned to her and spoke in a low voice. "My father and Digger fought a possessed man who was offering human sacrifices at an old fort."

"Oh, my!" Willow exclaimed.

Digger nodded. "There is a convention starting in a couple of days. Calls itself Para Con. It's for people who believe in ghosts and the supernatural. They come together to hear lectures about ghost hunting, and buy products from vendors—"

"Marie will be there," Willow said, brightening. "She has a booth!"

"I know. I asked her to be there. She will be one of many vendors from all over the country," Digger replied. "I wanted her to go ahead of us and scout out the place."

"Are you planning to go there to make connections, meet people?" I asked.

He looked grim. "I have to go there because I believe Gremory will be there."

I stopped, the demon's name freezing my blood. "But I thought you… and my father…"

"Your father and I cast him out," Digger said. "But I knew she would return. It was only a matter of when. She tried to return using Thomas Neill in Duivelsmeer. That's why I needed to kill him."

We stopped talking as the waitress set our food in front of us.

"That was the demon who took my father's hand," I told Willow. "I would be more than happy to be part of some payback to him."

"Her. It's a female demon." Digger said, while eating. "I thought you might."

"If she shows up. Will it be VanWry again?"

Digger shook his head. "No, VanWry is dead, and he was merely a vessel. Gremory will have taken a new vessel."

I forked eggs into my mouth and chewed thoughtfully. "That means you have no way of recognizing the person she's using."

"Not by the face," Digger said, as he bit into his toast. "But with Willow and Marie to help, we should be able to track him down."

"Okay, give me the bottom line," I said and glanced at Willow. "What will her presence mean, and what is the danger to us?"

Digger took a bite or two more before he answered. "The risk is — always — that you could lose your lives."

"If he gets into this place and we don't get involved, what happens?"

"Gremory seeks to open the gates of Hell."

"And that requires human sacrifice?" I asked.

"Yes, and it will take a large number to accomplish the deed. Think of all the people that survived in Portland. If VanWry had killed them all, Gremory would have achieved her goal. She would release ancient deities and creatures that could bring about the end of the world."

I released Willow's hand, and we ate in silence.

"VanWry had the ghouls to help him," I said. "Will this new person have the same?"

"Probably," Digger said between bites. "And in a convention where people dress up, they might go unnoticed."

"The undead usually only come out at night," Willow stated.

Digger nodded. "That's true, but they can come out during the day if they are in a dark enough space. VanWry took people hostage, kept them as prisoners in a building with no windows. The ghouls could watch the prisoners, even during daylight hours."

"You think this could be worse than Fort Gorges?" I asked.

"It could be," Digger said, his eyes going from me to Willow. "So, are you in?"

I glanced at Willow. "You want to fight this demon?"

Willow sighed. "Yes, and I want to be there to keep Marie safe."

I faced Digger. "Hordes of ghouls, a bunch of people who believe in the occult, and a demon-possessed person with a sword, who will probably recognize us as a threat and want to kill us?" I exhaled deeply. "How could I miss out on that?"

Digger smiled, and Willow hugged my arm.

"Don't forget the new rule," I said, and pointed at Digger. "You hold nothing back — you tell us anything and everything before we face off against this guy."

Digger's expression looked like pure innocence. "Of course."

"It hasn't been the way you've been doing things. I expect surprises from the bad guys, but not from you."

This made Digger smile. "Yes, sir."

# PART THREE:

# FACING

# DESTINY

# TWENTY-TWO

An hour later, we set off on the road with our possessions stowed in Digger's truck. He had arranged his mystical gear and grave-digging equipment with great care, making it easy for us to access and retrieve what we needed quickly.

On an impulse, I kept the leather belt with the pouch containing the *Lahat Chereb* around my waist, but returned the Taser to the back of the vehicle.

Once again, Digger harnessed the power of the Ley lines. We made our way toward Lufkin, Texas, and then took a little-known country road. In a sudden flash of lightning, we found ourselves on the fringes of Kansas City, Missouri.

"That was very interesting," Willow said excitedly. "I could hear the spirits speak to me as we traveled from place to place."

"Really? What did they say?" I asked.

"They were worried that I was moving too fast," she said and chuckled.

"The important thing," Digger said, "is it allows us to complete our journey of fifteen hours in less than eight."

Even with the time savings of the Ley lines, it took several more hours before we finally pulled into a massive hotel near the town of Bourbonais, Illinois. It was in a bustling area with many corporate offices and various hotel-convention centers. Boasting a lineup of top hotel chains, Digger navigated us to the exact one.

As we drove into the lot, our attention was grabbed by a bold LED billboard on the front of the establishment, showcasing a colorful advertisement for the ParaCon convention.

"I take it this is where the convention is being held?" I said.

"Actually no. They hold the actual convention about ten minutes from here in an abandoned mental asylum in Manteno."

"An asylum?" I said. "That's kind of creepy, isn't it?"

Digger raised an eyebrow. "I think that's the point."

He dropped Willow and I off at the front door and went to park the truck as I went to the main desk to pick up our key cards.

As I checked in, I noticed that the reservation was only for two rooms. A fleeting thought crossed my mind. I wondered if Digger had booked it with the expectation of traveling alone with me? Or had he expected that Willow and I would become a couple by the time we arrived?

I considered asking him, but I doubted I would get a straight answer.

After I checked in, they gave me a glossy brochure with bold letters in dark tones with the image of a skull that read:

**Windy City ParaCon**

**Where the terrors come out to play**

The brochure advertised the show's location at the former Illinois Asylum for the Criminally Insane, along with a detailed history of the site. Additionally, I received a map outlining the route from the hotel to the asylum, as well as a schedule of all the convention events.

We joined Digger at the truck to get our luggage. Willow brought her suitcase and her fighting stick, while Digger brought his big old duffel bag.

The accommodations were lavish with our suites featuring a comfortable work area, plush sofas, and padded chairs. In Digger's room, two queen-sized beds provided plenty of space, while my shared quarters with Willow boasted a spacious king-sized bed. A standout feature was the oversized jacuzzi perched on a faux-stone base complete with ornamental pillars at each corner. Another door connected the two suites, making me ponder just how much the rooms had cost.

"Leave the adjoining door unlocked, just in case," Digger suggested. "We don't know what we're facing and might need to move fast. Do you have the Grimoire?"

"It's in my computer bag," I said. I'd had little chance to study it over the last few days.

Digger nodded. "I needed it when I confronted VanWry all those years ago, and I might need it again."

"What do I do with it?" I asked.

"I think it will be safer with you. Take it out of the computer bag and hide it as best you can, in case someone gets into your room."

"Do you think that could happen?" Willow asked.

Digger exhaled heavily. "I'm not sure. But they will think I have the book and will search my room. If you have it, at least we have a better chance."

"All right," I said.

"Good. Now you two should get some rest. I am going to the asylum and look around."

I almost volunteered to go along, but Willow looked at me with a smile.

"Okay. Good night, Digger," I said, and Willow and I went through the connecting door and into our room.

Without a moment of hesitation, Willow turned the faucets to fill the large Jacuzzi. "I could use a bath after the hours in the car."

"We both could," I said, and gestured at the large tub. "It looks like we can both fit."

"One way or another," she said with a smile.

I removed the overlarge book from out of my computer bag and held it up. "First, help me find a place to hide this."

We both studied the room carefully. I immediately dismissed the obvious places: under a table or under the cushions of the small sofa. Those places seemed far too obvious and exposed.

I grabbed a pillow, pulling the pillow case off. I slipped the book into the empty sheath of cloth, and then carefully inserted the cloth-covered volume between the headboard and the mattress. It just fit, but looking down, it appeared to be part of the bed. I put the other pillows on top of the gap between the headboard and the mattress and hid it pretty well.

"That should do it," I said, and turned to find Willow clothed in a fluffy bathrobe.

"You better get undressed if you want to share the bath," she teased.

I shed my clothes with lightning speed as we entered the inviting warmth of the water with the soothing jets. Gently, we explored each other's bodies with soft kisses and gentle touches. We moved together at a slow pace to accommodate Willow's tenderness from her first experience.

As I slumbered peacefully, Willow startled me with a sudden touch on my lips, urging me to stay quiet. Without my hearing aid, I had no clue why she was so alarmed.

I noticed a silhouette moving around the room.

Willow emerged from under the covers, and I scanned the room for a potential weapon. With caution, I moved to the bedside lamp to either turn it on or throw it at an assailant.

As I flicked on the lamp and sprang out of bed, catching sight of Willow brandishing her baton and Marie writhing on the floor in pain, holding her leg.

I saw Marie's mouth move. "Ow, child — you hurt me."

Willow had struck Marie on the leg in the dark.

As Willow and I were in the buff, she swiftly grabbed a bathrobe to cover herself while I hastily donned my pants. I put in my hearing aid.

Kneeling beside Marie, Willow apologized profusely.

"What were you doing, sneaking in here in the middle of the night?" I asked and glanced at the clock, which read: 2:05.

"I mixed up some special oils for you." She pulled out two small bottles from her pocket, each filled with a golden liquid and equipped with an eyedropper top. "Since I was next door, I thought you should have them for tomorrow. I was just going to put it on your dresser and leave."

"You were in Digger's room?" I asked, a bit shocked. After all, she was my mother.

"Of course, honey," Marie said in a dismissive tone. "And don't look at me that way. I am a grown woman, and Digger and I are both adults."

I felt myself get hot with embarrassment.

She went on. "Trouble is, Digger hasn't shown up yet."

"He hasn't?" I said, with another glance at the clock.

"Nope, that's why I figured I'd drop off the oils while I was thinking of it." She rose to her feet and both Willow and I tried to help her, but she waved us off. "It's okay, nothing broken, but I'll have a lump tomorrow. I'm going back to the room and see if I can get some sleep."

"If you're sure you're all right," I said.

With a feeble nod, she proceeded to the door connecting our chambers, hobbling slightly before exiting.

I closed the door, then turned the lock to seal it.

Willow followed me and looked over my shoulder.

"You are suspicious?" she whispered.

"Aren't you?" I murmured back. We stepped back from the door and I pulled her close to me. "That story she gave us. That's no reason to go sneaking into someone else's room."

Willow didn't look happy about my concerns. We approached the headboard and removed the pillows to inspect the Grimoire.

It was undisturbed.

I looked at Willow. "Should I go out and search for Digger?"

"Where would you look?"

"I don't know," I said. "I guess we should see if we can get some sleep."

"I can't," Willow complained. "Now my mind is racing with worry."

"How can I help?"

"I need to distract myself from these thoughts," she murmured, discarding the bathrobe and reclining unclothed on the bed. She stretched deliberately, a sensual showcase of her curves. "Do have any suggestions?"

"One comes to mind," I told her as I joined her in bed.

Upon awakening at around eight in the morning, I was relieved that Willow had not disappeared this time. Instead, she peacefully slumbered by my side.

The entire time I spent with Willow — excluding the moments when we were fighting off a bloodthirsty vampire — felt like my ideal honeymoon. We filled our days with companionship and intimacy, which I hadn't experienced with anyone to this extent before.

Digger was leading me to confront the demon responsible for severing my father's hand, yet I struggled to even ignite the *Lahat Chereb*, let alone wield it against any threats.

The possibility of a greater threat loomed over me. With Gremory in the picture, not only was my life at risk, but the lives of Digger, Willow, and even Marie hung in the balance. Was it my duty to vanquish monsters, or was there a larger purpose in store for me? And what was the mysterious destiny that my father hinted at?

"You look so serious." Willow's eyes sparkled in the dim light of the room.

I smiled. "Thinking about serious things, I guess."

Her hand caressed my chest. "Like what?"

I pulled her close. "Like, I want to be with you, but I know so little about you."

"Well, you know I am Haitian, that I know how to stick fight, and that I get messages from the spirits. I am also glad I waited to be intimate until I met you."

"What do you want to do, I mean, with your life?"

"I want to use my gifts to help others," she said, raising herself up on one elbow. "I want to meet a man, raise a family. What do you want?"

"At this moment, I'm not sure. I wanted to be a journalist, but I didn't like what I saw. I want to help Digger, but it looks like I'm not very good at it."

"You need to stop thinking about what you can't do, and open your mind to what you can," she said and lay back. "And if you could do it with me, I would be happy, too."

There was a knock at the outer door of the suite.

"Who's there?" I said as I slipped out of bed and grabbed my trousers, fumbling my way into them.

"Room Service," came a voice behind the door.

Exiting the bedroom, I went out to the front room of the suite. I opened the door and a man with a cart brimming with food entered. He deftly unloaded plates with their contents concealed under covers, as well as a coffee pot accompanied by four cups and saucers. I went for my wallet; glad I had left it in my pants. To my surprise, the man shooed away my attempt to pay, stating, "All taken care of by the guest next door, sir."

As the man left with the empty cart, Digger appeared in the doorway.

"Did I get enough food?" he asked.

"For an army," I suggested.

"Put on a shirt. I'll uncover our choices," Digger said.

As I made my way toward the bedroom door, it swung open and Willow emerged. Dressed in a chic ensemble of black pants and a frilly blouse, she gave my backside a playful pat as she walked by.

I went into the bedroom and pulled on a shirt, but I could hear them talking.

"Digger, did you find Marie last night?" Willow asked. "She was looking for you."

"Yes, she stayed in my room. When did you see her?"

"About two in the morning. She snuck into our room."

I came back into the room to see Digger frowning.

He looked over at me. "You had a visit from Marie last night?"

"Yeah, and she got the worse of it. Willow hit her leg with that stick of hers."

Digger nodded. "I noticed a lump on her calf. She's still sleeping."

"Marie said you weren't in your room," Willow stated. "Where were you?"

"After visiting the site of the ParaCon, I talked to the staff here about any unusual requests by the convention guests," Digger admitted.

"Anyone ordering 'Zombie Chow' or something?" I joked.

Willow frowned. "Zombies don't eat."

"There were a few odd requests for the guy running the convention," Digger said. "Robert Gibbons, he's the organizer and a lecturer. He claims to be a paranormal investigator and does events like this around the country. He's been getting deliveries here to the hotel, that then get moved to the asylum for the show."

"I don't know," I said. "Lots of conventions have papers and materials shipped to the hotel and then to a site."

"How about a box the size of a coffin?"

Willow poured her own cup of coffee, but now stopped with it halfway up to her lips.

"A coffin? Do you know what was in it?" I inquired.

"Maybe papers," Digger said. "Maybe one of the undead. Or maybe it's just a damn decoration."

"All of those are a possibility," I pointed out.

"It could be a zombie or ghoul, even a vampire." Willow said.

Digger poured himself a cup of coffee. "Which begs the question, is the thing inside that box controlled by Gibbons, or is it controlling him?"

I dished out some of the food onto one of the extra plates. "How do we find out?"

"He has a lecture at noon," Digger said, and glanced at his watch. "They open the vendor area at about nine-thirty. We should head over there and check out each booth."

Willow and I nodded in agreement.

"I'm going to wake Marie, but I have to ask a favor."

We both looked at him.

"Don't tell her anything we find out. Keep everything we discover between the three of us."

"What's wrong?" I asked.

"Maybe nothing," Digger concluded. "But you have the book, so anyone who comes into your room uninvited has to be looked at carefully."

"You think someone is influencing Marie?" I asked.

Digger shook his head. "Probably not."

"I have a way to find out," Willow said.

Digger lifted his eyebrows questioningly. "You're going to ask the spirits?"

"Yes, but I will also offer to help her at her booth. That way I can see if she's acting strange."

Digger ran his hand through his short white beard. "That might be a good idea. You could also see what's going on in the marketplace, and since you're working at a booth, no one will notice you."

"What should I do?" I requested.

"Look around with me, see if we can find out anything. Then, read your book. It is the one thing we know the demon wants. Did you hide it well?"

I shrugged. "Well enough. Why didn't you leave it in your truck?"

He smiled at this. "They know I'm here. By now, they've gone over my truck with a fine-toothed comb. That's why I didn't want the book in it."

In contemplative silence, we consumed our meal for a brief interval, absorbing the weight of Digger's proposal. It chilled me to think that an entity inhabiting a body was fervently seeking Digger's ancient book of magic.

Digger looked at his watch and assembled a plateful of food and another cup of coffee. "I'll wake Marie. Meet me in the garage at 9:15, okay?"

Without waiting for a response, he headed out the door, food and coffee in hand.

Willow made sure the door was secure and looked at me.

"I am worried for Marie," she said.

I nodded. "I'm worried for all of us."

Willow dressed in her ruffled blouse and pants, and I had on a casual shirt and black pants, so I looked suitable for walking around the marketplace.

Digger was standing in front of the truck as we arrived. He was not in his jeans and peacoat, but wore a black suit with a white shirt and no tie.

"Wow!" I said. "It appears you actually do own a suit."

He grumbled in annoyance, "Dire situations require hard choices."

"Did you style your hair?" I said, enjoying making him uncomfortable for once. "I think you trimmed your beard."

"Let's go," he muttered.

As we drove out of the lot, I asked, "What is the story of this place? Do you know?"

"I spent half the night researching. It started out as a grand estate with a lot of property. The owner had no heirs and donated it to the state, which turned it into an asylum in the late 1800s for severe cases."

"Severe?" I asked. "What did they think was severe?"

Digger shrugged. "Murderers, rapists, and other criminals who were mentally unfit. Through most of its history, a lack of knowledge of mental health turned the place into a hub of torture."

"What would they do?" Willow asked.

"Treatments included ice baths, electric shocks, purging, bloodletting, straitjackets, and even lobotomies."

"Jesus," I muttered.

"The state finally closed the place in the 1970s," Digger said. "Nothing could be done with it, as a group got the main building registered as a historic landmark. Then out of the blue, last year, the state allowed a developer to lease the property."

"To do what with it?" I asked, surprised by this.

"Restore the historic parts and turn it into a venue for hosting shows and events. This is going to be the first event to take place there."

"Have they restored it, then?" Willow asked.

Digger turned us down a long driveway with a huge sign that welcomed us to the Windy City ParaCon.

"They fixed up the meeting rooms and the space for the vendors is functional. But for this event, it's all pretty rudimentary," Digger said. "I sneaked into areas that were still a mess."

"What are those like?" I asked.

"Pretty rough," Digger said. "But the ParaCon insisted the show had to be there. So, they're making it work."

As we came over a small hill, a colossal Gothic Victorian edifice stood before us, its somber stone walls reaching up toward the foreboding clouds above. Towers and turrets protruded at curious angles, defying the laws of physics. It enveloped the grand circular driveway, and the newly resurfaced parking lot with an eerie aura. Sunlight seemed to be devoured by the mansion's black shingles, leaving it aglow with a disconcerting luminosity. Ivy-clad walls and contorted gargoyles added to the ominous atmosphere.

I stared up at it in wonder. "I can see why they wanted it here."

"There are spirits here that are unhappy," Willow said from the back seat.

"I believe you," I said.

As we parked within newly painted lines of the parking area, the bustling lot was rapidly filling. The three of us emerged into the gloomy weather, gazing once more at the immense structure before us.

"We won't find out nothing, standing around here," Digger said and headed to the entrance where several smokers were standing about.

As we entered the building, the sight of a monstrous door immediately struck us, imposing in its size and solidity. As we stepped through it, we found ourselves in a spacious foyer, where several card tables stood. They marked each table with paper signs bearing the letters "A-H", "I-P", or "Q-Z", and there were short lines for each. Three women sat behind the tables, their faces grotesquely painted with zombie makeup. Dim sunlight filtered in from nearby windows, and it was difficult to discern whether their faces were authentic. I stood behind someone in pale makeup and a long cape.

The faux zombie women welcomed us warmly, providing us with name cards and lanyards, as well as another schedule of events. We made our way through a set of large glass doors into the building's lobby, which was already bustling with numerous people.

Signs on easels guided people toward the various rooms for the differing events, but we focused on finding "The Marketplace." Following the clear directions, we soon walked through a second set of glass doors. The space we entered was undoubtedly the main ward of the building's past.

They transformed it into a vast open area with red-carpeted runners creating aisles where vendors set up booths of various sizes. Electricity went to each booth through a series of overhead cables and heavy extension cords hung down for the vendors to plug in equipment.

Although it was only the first day and the room had just opened, it was already brimming with energy. We walked past various booths partitioned off with pipe and drape curtains, taking in the different offerings.

We walked past booths selling oils, herbs, incense, and spell kits. We also came across dowsing rods, as well as Ouija boards fashioned from genuine cherry wood. At other booths, there were electronic gadgets like ghost-detectors, EMF meters, night vision video-cameras, and an unfamiliar object named a 'spirit box.' There was even a booth featuring aquariums and even 'Spirit Guide Fish.'

We eventually reached the compact kiosk that Marie leased for the event. It bore a banner that read 'Direct From New Orleans.' She artfully arranged all of her offerings, which included potions, oils, candles, and various other wares. We found her engaged in a lively conversation with a man regarding one of her unique oils. She made the sale, and after he moved on, she turned to us.

"What are you three up to?" Marie asked. She looked happy that she'd already made one sale that morning.

"Looking around," Digger said. "Trying to get a feel for the place. Have you seen Gibbons?"

"The man in charge?" Marie said and looked around. "Yes, he walked through a few minutes ago, when they opened the room."

Willow spoke up. "Marie, would you like me to help you here at the booth? I know many of your oils and potions."

"That is a fine idea, child," Marie admitted. "It also doesn't hurt to have a pretty young lady here. Are you sure it's no trouble?"

"None," Willow said. "It will be fun."

"I'll bring you both lunch in a few hours," Digger offered, and the pair of us headed off to find the elusive Robert Gibbons.

As we passed more booths with other merchandise, I saw a tall man in a suit and a great head of hair, walking with a smaller man who carried a clipboard and was jotting notes as they went.

We soon caught up to them, and Digger called out, "Mr. Gibbons?"

The tall man stopped and turned to watch us approach, as his assistant continued to scribble on his clipboard.

"May I help you?" Gibbons said in a deep voice.

Digger offered his hand. "Yes, sir, I'm Everett Hill. We spoke about security at the convention."

Gibbons frowned. "Ah, yes, I remember talking to you a few days ago." He glanced around the room. "As you can see, no cause for alarm. In fact, most of the attendees haven't even arrived at this hour."

"I have it on good authority there may be some kind of trouble over the next few days. Is there a time I could meet with you and go over my concerns?"

"Look, Mr. Hill, I'm a busy man with a convention to run, and lectures to present." He glanced back at his assistant. "You can meet with Mr. Manning."

The skinny man stepped forward and held out a card. "Clyde Manning, Mr. Gibbons' assistant. I could fit you in later today, around four PM at the convention office here at the asylum — but only if you have evidence of a credible threat."

"I do," Digger stated. "And it could happen as soon as tonight."

Manning glanced at Gibbons with concern.

"Tonight is the big party." Gibbons said dismissively. "Everyone in costume, drinking, dancing." He chuckled. "The only worry is if somebody overindulges."

Manning moved close to Gibbons and turned away, covering his mouth. I couldn't hear what they said or see it.

Gibbons nodded to Manning and looked over at Digger. "We have to check the marketplace and make sure we set the vendors up correctly. Catch my lecture on developing a paranormal investigator business." He glanced at his watch. "It's at noon."

"We'll be there," Digger said. "Thank you for your time."

As the pair wandered off, Digger's jaw grew tight. He obviously did not care for Mr. Gibbons.

I spoke up. "Do you think Gibbons might be the one Gremory has possessed?"

"I'm not sure," Digger grunted. "But willingly or unwillingly, he's doing her bidding."

# TWENTY-THREE

D igger stopped at a booth loaded with knives, swords, and blades of every description. Several of the knives had a wavy blade, and I picked one up.

"That's an *athamé*," Digger explained, as he pointed at several blades made from quartz or stone.

I pointed at the light-colored stone knife and asked, "What is that?"

The shopkeeper drew close. He was a heavyset man with a wild brown beard and shaggy hair. He wore a tunic that hung over his trousers. "That's a Selenite Chakra Athamé," he announced. "Selenite is a protective stone that taps into pure divine light. Those symbols carved into it represent the chakras. It's the perfect tool for healing or enhancing your psychic abilities."

It was clear that he rehearsed that speech countless times, but it failed to leave an impression on me. Was this the standard level of discourse for the entire event? After what I witnessed, the cosmic woo-woo didn't do it for me.

Digger picked up a pair of short knives with metal handles, as well as the blades. He checked the edge with his thumb and then asked. "Silver throwing knives?"

The large sales agent nodded and went into his spiel. "Yes, solid silver, meticulously checked for balance and spin. Enough weight for a twenty-foot throw, but light enough to allow you—"

"I'll take them," Digger said and pulled out his wallet. He paid the man, who wrapped the blades in paper and gave them to Digger.

"Don't you already have enough knives?" I asked as we walked away.

Digger shrugged. "Never hurts to have another weapon. I'll need to consecrate them, of course."

"Of course," I grinned.

As Digger completed settling his purchase, I moved toward the back of the vast hall, where an enormous pair of double doors drew my attention. Next to them were immense windows divided by metal frames into dozens of square glass panels, rising far above me. The only part of the windows that could open were a casement approximately ten feet off of the ground.

Through one of the small glass panes, I glimpsed out at a sprawling courtyard. There was a group of men, hanging heavy steel cables and electrical wires overhead. A large step van sat within the space, its access allowed through a gap between the decaying buildings. Men hurriedly unloaded items from the van. They were assembling a stage, and the workers were putting up backdrops and lighting.

Despite the orderliness and the busy group, I couldn't shake the feeling of unease as I surveyed the scene. The rundown buildings loomed menacingly around the courtyard, their dirty and missing windows hinting at something deeply sinister.

Digger approached, putting the wrapped knives into the left breast pocket of his suit and looking out the window with me. "That's where they're having the opening night party tonight."

"Really? Looks like they still have a lot to do," I said.

"Let's head out to the first lecture. I want to get to know the speakers in case any of them are being used by the demon."

As we departed the Marketplace and made our way to the lobby, we scanned the signs to find the correct meeting room. They renovated the hallways immaculately. There was dark yellow tile running waist-high on the wall, above which was a freshly painted and refurbished surface. The ceiling fixtures, sleek and contemporary, provided excellent illumination.

"So, this was a place for the criminally insane?" I said.

"That's right."

I frowned. "Did they just let them wander about freely?"

"No. I told you, I was here pretty late last night, checking the place out. There's an entire wing of cells with heavy metal doors. I doubt they'll have any events in that part of the building."

We stepped into a large room, where a cluster of attendees sat on folding chairs, waiting for the lecture. Our gaze shifted to a raised platform with a screen flashing the words "Energy Reading."

A man by the name of Brian conducted the session. During the class, he shared details of his life and chose random attendees to 'read' their energy. He offered extensive and often overblown insights. The last segment centered on the idea that everyone possessed latent abilities that we could each develop with effort. Brian suggested his book would help unlock our potential, and at only nineteen-ninety-five, it offered a bargain price.

After departing the first lecture, we ventured into a different gathering place. Inside, a woman donning black attire reminisced about the Victorian era, expounding on the methods employed during séances which took place over a century ago. Beginning with proper séance manners, she then delved into the possible outcomes and how to execute your own séance safely.

Of course, she also offered a book that could help for only thirty-nine, ninety-five.

After that lecture ended, Digger and I walked through the halls, heading to the next meeting room.

"Anything?" I asked.

"Yeah, these folks are boring."

"I mean, do any of the speakers seem dangerous?"

"Only to our mental health," he asserted. "I got a vibe off some attendees, but I'm not sure."

"A vibe? Are you psychic as well?"

"Mine is the voice of experience. Plain old observation and deduction. There were Satanists in the last room."

"Was it the guy all in black with the heavy eyeliner and the sleeve tats?"

"Him? No, he's harmless. It was the guy in the open shirt, vest, and loafers who sat next to him."

"I barely noticed that guy."

"That was the point."

As soon as we entered the third meeting space, we saw Gibbons getting set for his presentation. He was sitting comfortably on a raised platform accompanied by various tech gadgets I saw displayed at Marketplace's stalls. Behind Gibbons was a screen:

## ROBERT GIBBONS
## PARANORMAL INVESTIGATOR

The room filled up quickly, and Digger and I stood in the back instead of taking a seat.

"Good morning to all of you. My name is Robert Gibbons. I am going to take you through some of my experiences as a paranormal investigator. I hope to share with you how you can be a part of this exciting field."

With an innate gift for sales and public speaking, Gibbons captivated his audience by sharing firsthand accounts from the field. He showcased various gadgets on his table, expertly showing their purpose and utility. The capabilities of each device awed the visitors. There was a voice recorder that captured ghostly whispers. Gibbons demonstrated an electromagnetic field sensor that he claimed detected otherworldly presences.

With an enthusiasm that set him apart from the previous lecturers, he exuded friendliness and extensive knowledge. As he wrapped up, he invited attendees to join his online course. This course would equip them with the fundamentals of paranormal investigation, and ultimately prepare them to become skilled ghost hunters.

The notion seemed foolish to me after what I'd gone through. If these individuals encountered what I did, they would be smart to run for the hills instead of investing in his web classes.

Gibbons glanced at Digger and I and then moved into the crowd and spoke to people as the room slowly emptied.

I stayed next to Digger. "Is that what all this is about? Sell a course and make you think you can chase ghosts?"

Digger shrugged. "Ghost are pretty easy. I don't see anyone having a hard time with them. If it makes people happy, I figure there's nothing wrong with that."

"But doesn't it put people in danger of facing the things you're fighting?"

"Sometimes. Face it, Josh, there are few people who can deal with the things we've taken on."

I felt honored that he included me in his private club. However, Digger's observation held truth. Very few possessed the fortitude to endure the savage monsters we'd recently encountered. I yearned to expand my knowledge and gain Digger's level of bravery to combat them with confidence.

"There's a lunch break now, and I want to examine some more things in the Marketplace."

"Okay, while it's daytime, I want to go back to the hotel and read some of that book."

"There's a free shuttle bus between the convention and the hotel. I'm sure you can get a ride back there with no problem."

We went our separate ways, and I headed out front, where a shuttle bus just arrived, dropping people off. I got on and in a few short minutes, was back at the hotel.

"How late do the shuttle buses run?" I asked the driver.

"Tonight they run all night," he explained, "because of the party."

Upon returning to my shared room with Willow, I retrieved the hidden pillow-wrapped package from between the mattress and headboard. Carrying it with me to the front room, I settled onto the sofa to explore its contents.

I opened the book and noted that the front cover had an inscription I hadn't noticed before: *Hic est liber benedixitque.*

It was Latin, but I didn't know what it meant, so I moved on.

I went back to the section about creatures and noticed that there were additional notes on some pages. One page told of pouring salt into a grave and saying certain words to stop a ghoul from rising. Someone had added notes in the margins like, "Speak with authority," "Believe it to make it work," et cetera.

I turned to the back of the book, and for the first time, noticed a warning. The page I turned to stated that the spells in the last section were to give enough knowledge to stop anyone from attempting them. It warned never to use or speak them. According to the page headings, some of these spells included: *Summoning of Demons; Freeing The Old Gods;* and *Calling Forth Destruction.*

I went back to the section about creatures, wanting to avoid any spells that brought forth destruction of any kind. Back in the safer part of the book, there was information on how to stop a *Banshee*, techniques to calm a *Draugr*, and even a ritual that cast out a *Skadegamutc*.

As I delved into descriptions of mythical beasts such as the Furies and Empousa of ancient Greece, my eyelids grew heavy. I carried the book with me to my bedroom and, with a sigh of relief, I kicked off my shoes and removed my hearing aid. I lay on top of the bed and lay down to continue to read. Soon the words blurred, and sleep swept me away, the book slipping open down my chest.

I found myself in a dream, standing in a vast white space. In front of me stood a colossal book that dwarfed my size. As I reached for the cover, it emitted a grating sound like an ancient rusty door.

As I gazed at the enormous sheets of paper that towered over me, strange entities materialized before my eyes. There were the familiar ghouls and zombies I had previously confronted. But there were also bizarre creatures resembling ancient beasts. A few were diabolical and crimson, while others bore bat wings and lengthy snouts brimming with sharp fangs.

As the room filled with every possible nightmare, I recoiled in terror. My belt held the bag containing the *Lahat Chereb*, and as I retrieved it and felt the hilt in my grasp, a piercing scream shattered the air.

Suddenly jolted awake, I sat upright in bed. Because of my hearing impairment, I knew the shriek was a figment of my imagination.

It was late afternoon; the light had shifted; the room was darker, and Willow stood next to the bed, her hands over her eyes.

I jumped to my feet and held her.

"Are you all right?" I said.

I pulled her hands away. Her eyes were red and inflamed.

Her lips moved and said, "The book…"

I glanced over at the exposed volume resting on the bed. It was open to that title page with the odd Latin words: *Hic est liber benedixitque*, and they glowed a dull red. I swiftly shut it and secured its peculiar clasp before reaching for my hearing aid.

"The book?" I asked, as I put the device in my ear. "It hurt you?"

"What?" she said, and she shook her head as if waking from a dream. "No, I… came here… to see you."

I picked up the heavy book. "But you said, 'the book.' Is there something about it that upset you?"

Her eyes were no longer red, and I saw a curious expression cross her face. She blinked several times and said, "No, I came to see you."

I lay the book on top of the bed and glanced over at the digital clock on the bedside table. It read: 5:45.

"The marketplace closes at seven," Willow said. "Marie and I wanted to let you know to join us afterward."

Her eyes went to the book, and she stared at it. She was acting strange. "Are you sure you're all right?"

She met my eyes. "Yes. Why don't you head down to catch the bus?" Willow said. "While I straighten up the room?"

I chuckled. "It's a hotel. Someone else straightens up. It's almost six. Why don't you go help Marie and we can meet there once the marketplace closes? I want to read a little more before the sun sets."

With a longing look, she fixed her gaze on the dense book, gave a small nod, and started walking toward the door.

"How about a kiss?" I ventured.

She turned, leaned forward, and gave me a quick peck. Then, with one last look at the book, she headed out the bedroom door and into the front room of the suite.

At the sound of the hotel door shutting, I sighed and went into the bathroom to relieve myself. First Marie came in late at night, and now Willow showed up unexpectedly, both of them acting oddly. Was someone controlling them? Unsure, I thought it best to bring my suspicions to Digger's attention.

I came out of the bathroom and looked at the table where I placed the book.

It was empty. The Grimoire was gone.

I flung open the door and scanned the hallway. I could see two girls, one with blonde hair and the other with a bold purple hue, entering a neighboring room. Neither of them had anything but their purses. It was impossible for them to be the perpetrator. Besides, how could they have gotten into my room?

I quickly found the leather pouch that contained the *Lahat Chereb*, and even pulled it out and held it. I secured the belt tightly around my waist and replaced the artifact inside its pouch.

Leaving my hotel room, I knocked on Digger's door, hoping to find him inside. Failing to elicit a response, I made my way to the elevator.

I retrieved the schedule of events from my pocket and scanned it once more. Besides the grand opening dinner, tonight's festivities included a costume competition. Most participants were likely in their rooms preparing their gory ensembles. This realization heightened my anxiety, because having people dressed as zombies next to real zombies would make it harder to tell who to fight.

I caught the shuttle and made my way to the asylum. The day had taken a turn for the worse, and ominous clouds loomed overhead. The clouds were thicker and even darker than in the morning, threatening to disrupt the night's festivities.

Which might be a good thing.

I headed into the Marketplace, and as I predicted, it was pretty slow. There were a few individuals strolling around. They weren't the committed attendees who dressed up in elaborate and difficult costumes.

As I walked toward Marie's booth where Willow and Marie awaited me, I searched for Digger. Marie greeted me warmly and seemed untouched by what I sensed in Willow. A smile graced Willow's lips, giving the impression of her usual self.

"Have you seen Digger?" I asked.

"He had that meeting with Gibbon's assistant at four," Marie said. "Isn't he in the room?"

"I knocked on the door, but I didn't get an answer."

"I'll call him," she said. "I have to go outside — there's no service in here."

"Really?"

Marie casually dismissed it with a wave of her hand. "Too much metal in the walls, I guess. Why don't you help Willow?"

Marie bolted away. Meanwhile, Willow arranged petite oil bottles on displays. She organized them on an unadorned shelf alongside various elixirs and mixtures.

I stood next to her, but Willow didn't look at me, her attention focused on the bottles. I helped her place the oils, making sure the labels faced out. "Is anything bothering you? You seemed strange in the room before."

She smiled, but there was no happiness in her eyes. "Why are you questioning me?"

"I just thought you were acting odd, and I wanted to know if anything was wrong?"

She returned her attention to the bottles of oil as she placed them on the shelf. "No, nothing."

Clyde Manning, Gibbon's assistant, strolled past. He was a recognizable figure with his clipboard in hand and scribbling on it.

I moved away from Willow to stop him. "Mr. Manning?"

He glanced up from his clipboard and seemed surprised I was bothering him. "Yes?"

"I'm Joshua Bennett, I work for Mr. Hill. He met with you at four?"

Manning glanced at his watch in annoyance. "He asked for that time, and then he never showed up. I decided his concerns were probably unfounded, and he lacked the courage to tell me."

This disregard toward Digger incited a sense of anger within me. Through clenched teeth I said, "I can assure you, Mr. Hill does not lack courage."

Manning shrugged and stepped around me to go on his way, giving me a dirty look as he went.

I returned to Willow.

"He said Digger never showed up," I said as I picked up a bottle of oil and looked at the label. "I'm worried."

"I am sure Digger is fine," she said, continuing to stack the bottles.

Marie returned, pushing a stray lock of hair back into place. "He's not answering his phone."

I frowned. "That's not like him."

Marie shrugged. "I'm sure it's fine. We have to shut everything down. We still have to get into costume."

"Do we have to go back to the hotel?" I asked.

"No, we can get changed here," Marie suggested.

I looked at what I was wearing. "I thought I'd go dressed like this."

Marie laughed. "No, we all have costumes. Come now, it will be fun."

I mustered a grin, yet the foreboding sensation lingered that tonight's events would be anything but amusing.

# TWENTY-FOUR

Marie pulled out several black hanging bags from behind her booth, looked them over, and handed one to me and one to Willow.

"Come, I found a place where we can change," Marie said and led us to a doorway on the side of the Marketplace room I hadn't noticed before. The heavy wooden door creaked open, revealing a dimly lit curved hallway that stretched out before us. The walls of yellow tile went to the ceiling, where the paint was cracked and peeling.

Then I saw the cell doors.

They painted the heavy metal doors in green; the paint marred by splotches of rust. The open door lacked a handle on the inside, clarifying that these were for patients who had to be confined. A narrow window with bars was the only way for a patient to peek outside into the hall.

Marie pointed at two of the empty cells. "We can change in those."

With a lump in my throat, I ventured into an unoccupied cell that had once confined numerous prisoners, forsaken by society.

Within the dreary confines, I found a couple of chairs and a solitary lamp in the corner, powered by a long extension cord. Its feeble glow barely illuminated the musty cell.

Willow joined me, and opened her costume bag, and retrieved a lengthy white gown that evoked memories of the classic film, *The Bride of Frankenstein*. The dress boasted a square neckline, draping open sleeves accompanied by underlying sleeves, cleverly layered to resemble the appearance of mummified bandages.

She didn't seem excited by it, and this surprised me. From what I knew of her childhood in Haiti, I guessed she got little chance to play dress up for Halloween.

I hung my costume bag on a hook embedded in the wall near the window before unzipping it. Inside lay a sleek tailcoat sporting a mock shirtfront, a flowing cape, and a recognizable half-mask, similar to the one worn by The Phantom of The Opera.

"Where did these costumes come from?" I asked.

"Marie arranged them for us," Willow said.

"Willow," I said, "I think we should put the costumes on over what we're already wearing."

"If you say so," she replied. "Why?"

"In case anything happens tonight," I explained. "Did you bring your fighting stick?"

"I left it at the booth, but I see no need for it," Willow said, without emotion.

I stared at her again. "Are you sure you're all right?"

"Stop asking me that." She scowled. "I am fine."

I nodded and got dressed. I tried to run through my mind what I could do if something happened.

Digger said I lacked faith, and at that moment, my need for faith was dire. Although I had acquainted myself with Digger's Grimoire, I only retained a fragment of its knowledge. The only weapons I possessed were the Lahat Chereb which I could not activate, and the small blessed knife in my boot. I decided that f nothing else, I could use the golden hilt as a bludgeoning weapon.

I was wearing sturdy black pants and a long-sleeve shirt which fit under my costume easily. I hung the pouch with the golden hilt outside my clothes at the base of my spine and also checked my small blade to make sure I could access it easily.

I pulled on the cape, which hid the belt pouch, and secured the elastic band for the half-mask around my head, anchoring it snugly to my face. "How do I look?"

"Good," she said. She had pulled the dress over her own clothing. Even though it was formless, little more than a cloth bag, she filled it out in all the right places.

"You're quite fetching yourself," I said, smiling.

She made a small curtsy. She seemed normal now. Had I worried about nothing?

The pair of us walked into the shadowed hall, and I called out, "Marie, are you dressed yet?"

Adorned in a sleek black dress and a petite cape, Marie strolled down the corridor with a witch's hat clasped in her grasp.

She smiled. "Oh, you both look so good!"

"Thanks," I said. "Do you have any idea where Digger might be?"

Marie gestured, distracted. "I don't know. He will find us at the event. I think he just went on ahead of us."

It was odd that Marie and Willow weren't displaying any concern for Digger. This immediately set off warning signals in my mind. However, if they were under some kind of influence, the wisest choice was to comply with their actions.

"I'm sure you're right," I said, attempting to sound casual. "We'll see him at the party."

After the time spent in the wing designated for prisoners, stepping into the well-lit Marketplace was a relief. As we strolled through the convention room, I pulled us over to Marie's booth.

"Willow, get your fighting stick," I said.

"Why do I need that?" Willow asked, annoyed.

"Yes, this is a party, not a battle," Marie said.

I thought fast. "It's a nice accessory to your costume," I suggested.

This seemed to satisfy them, and Willow pulled her stick from behind one of the displays.

We made our way toward the exit, two security personnel sealed off the Marketplace room, using stanchions to limit access.

The lobby swarmed with hordes of individuals adorned as vampires, ghouls, zombies, along with an assortment of superheroes and characters plucked out of Sci-Fi and fantasy. A fellow garbed as Captain Kirk moseyed by, alongside his companion wearing the haunting garb of the Corpse Bride.

Meanwhile, a chap outfitted in a zombie ensemble tottered about with half his face grotesquely gnawed away.

That one was a little too real for me.

Glancing at the thronging multitude, I couldn't help but feel ill at ease. A considerable number of individuals wearing clothing resembling the undead had arrived. They far exceeded the number of participants I had encountered at the conference.

A surge of individuals flowed toward a second massive chamber designated as the ballroom for the night. We merged with the crowd. Upon entering the room, I caught sight of a set of double doors that revealed the substantial courtyard I had seen through the windows in the Marketplace. The area outside emanated music and flashing lights. As opposed to lingering within the ballroom, the assembly ventured outside into the courtyard. My unease grew as certain figures resembled zombies and ghouls a little too well. They gestured for the attendees to move to the outdoor space.

We stepped through the doors and into the courtyard. A grand stage crafted from metal scaffolding greeted us. They adorned the finished stage with elegant, dark maroon curtains. Positioned on both sides of the stage, four men garbed entirely in black with hoods covering their faces beat upon four massive wooden drums. Eight large speakers amplified the sounds of the timpani. A great number of people had gathered, spreading out to form a vast semi-circle around the area.

As the drums grew louder, I turned off my hearing aid, took it out, and slipped it into my pocket.

It was a wise decision to have the event at the isolated asylum, far from any neighbors. The sound of the amplified drums would make any nearby residents call the police if they held it anywhere else.

A microphone occupied the forefront of the rectangular stage. Positioned at the back of the colossal platform, a technician controlled the lighting and sound with dual consoles.

Directly in front of the stage was a large, oblong, rectangular stone.

I stopped walking, shocked to see the stone: six feet in length, four feet in height, and broad enough to accommodate a sizable person. It was a match for the very stone that Miss Scalia and Kelly described to me. The one they claimed to have seen in Portland, Maine.

The same stone altar where VanWry sacrificed people for the demon Gremory.

It seemed impossible that it could be the same object. Its weight was likely too great and transporting such a colossal thing from an island in Portland, Maine, to the outskirts of Chicago would require considerable effort. My rational mind refused to believe it.

Taut metal cables ran overhead, crisscrossing the space above the sacrificial stone.

Willow sensed it when I tensed up. I turned to read her lips.

"What is it?" she asked.

"That big stone in the center of the stage. It looks like an altar."

Willow appeared unconcerned.

I went on. "It means the demon Gremory is here, and she's going to use that stone to kill people."

People packed the courtyard when a man took the stage, dressed entirely in black with a hood that left only his mouth and chin visible. His attire was gothic, complete with tall leather boots, a studded belt, and multiple medallions attached to chains around his neck.

I was positive that he was Robert Gibbons, the mastermind behind this conference.

I moved to Marie. "Is there any way to stop that man?"

She frowned, but also seemed unconcerned. "It's just a show, Josh. Don't take it so seriously."

The figure strode toward the microphone, and from the way people reacted around me, I assumed the crowd was erupting with excited cheers. Everyone appeared enthralled by the extravagant spectacle marking the start of the gathering. The undead assistants, whether authentic ghouls or simply actors in makeup, closed the doors. Those led into the grand ballroom, and shut off one route of escape.

I shifted my focus toward the roadway between the renovated edifice and the run-down structures, the entry point for all the gear. Stationed there was a group of roughly ten shabby minions, positioned in front of a towering chain-link fence that obstructed the passage.

There was no way out.

The applause died down and the hooded man moved to the microphone. My hearing aid was off, but I could read his lips.

"Tonight we shall empower the ancient entity, and she shall reward us beyond our wildest dreams."

Enthusiastic fist pumps and cheers I couldn't hear came from the guests. It seemed unlikely that any of them comprehended or were interested in what he'd actually said.

After all, it was a party!

The man continued. "And we shall make an example of he who defied us."

The crowd reacted with more fist bumps, but a sudden movement caught my attention. As I turned my head, my eyes fell upon a bound man suspended upside down from one of the overhead cables. Multiple ropes combined with thick metal chains wrapped around his arms, chest and legs, securing him in place. They tied his legs to a wheeled device attached to the cables. Two ghouls were using a pair of ropes to wheel him as he hung inverted. They moved him down the cable toward the courtyard and the menacing stone.

It was Digger.

Digger's bruised and battered face silenced the once jubilant crowd. His black suit appeared worse for wear. At that moment, the crowd wondered if the event was simply for entertainment or something more serious.

When the ghouls reached the large stone, they skillfully lowered Digger using a pulley system. They carefully positioned him to lie on the rough surface, still entwined in ropes and chains, trussed like a Thanksgiving turkey.

He lay there, motionless.

I looked up at the stage, not wanting to miss anything the man said.

"He shall be the first sacrifice, but he shall certainly not be the last," the man exclaimed, and went to the technician at the side of the stage. The man handed him a long curved sword in a scabbard.

I looked over the crowd, and there were doubt-filled faces and people talking. Unease rippled through the crowd as the mood shifted from celebration to fear. I glanced at Willow and Marie, but neither of them took their eyes away from the stage, their faces like statues.

The man on stage waved to the drummers, and in unison, they paid their respects with a deep bow. The four men, each using only one drumstick and the palm of their free hand, pounded out an eerie rhythm on the colossal drums. All around me, I saw people cry out and cover their ears in pain. The drums were so loud that even without my hearing aid, I could feel the rhythm coming in waves against my skin.

I turned to Willow to tell her to get ready with her stick, as we might have to fight our way down to the stone to rescue Digger.

Willow, however, had dropped her hands from her head, as had everyone I could see. Now she, Marie, and the entire crowd stared up at the man on stage, wide-eyed and unmoving. The unusual drums seemed to have enchanted the crowd in a spell, rendering them wide-eyed and motionless.

Digger lay on the stone, not even attempting to struggle free from his bonds.

On stage, the man was talking again. "We must give some of you to the demon, but it will be a sacrifice that brings you joy."

I moved between people toward the stage and the sacrificial stone, looking for someone — anyone — not affected by the drums.

As I moved, I threw off my cape and my fake tailcoat, not caring where it fell and reached into the leather case on my belt and pulled out the *Lahat Chereb*.

Now or never.

I chanted the Hebrew, unable to hear myself, and over the loud drums no one else heard me either. I held it up as I finished.

Nothing happened.

I repeated the blessing… still nothing.

By now, two ghouls noticed the drums did not freeze me in place and moved toward me. Apparently, the drums didn't affect them either. One drew near, reaching for me, and since I had the golden hilt in my hand, I fiercely hit it on the side of its head, causing it to stumble back. A second creature moved toward me, revealing a menacing maw of razor-sharp teeth.

Now I was quite certain — it was a real ghoul.

After days of my work with Digger, my muscles had toughened up. With all my might, I delivered a powerful blow right to the monster's face, using the hilt, causing it to stagger backward.

Wasting no time, I ran to the sacrificial stone, turned and faced the crowd, my arms outstretched and holding the *Lahat Chereb*, trying to protect Digger. They all had their eyes fixed upon me.

The mesmerized crowd advanced toward Digger and me, fury etched on their faces. The man on the stage incited them to attack me. Worse, he could have even ordered them to rip me to shreds.

The look in their eyes convinced me they would do just that.

# TWENTY-FIVE

The group was moving toward Digger and me in the same clumsy, stilted way I had seen zombies walk. Yet unlike zombies, their eyes were wide and filled with hate.

I held up the hilt with both hands, ready to bludgeon the attackers, but I doubted I could do much. The crowd would soon overwhelm me.

People surrounded us, shambling toward us, murder in their eyes. I glanced at Digger, maybe to say goodbye.

Although bound head to foot, his face bruised and beaten, he had one eye open and I saw his lips move. The drums were beating, and I was sure the demon-possessed man was yelling orders, but none of that distracted me. He looked at me without fear and the words he said were, "Have faith."

If these were his last words to me, they weren't helpful.

A sudden realization struck me. I did possess faith. Maybe not the faith of a specific religion or practice. But I had faith in my father when he fought to protect me all those years ago. Digger's guidance gave me faith, and I had learned from his wisdom. There was faith in my love for Willow, and I believed without a doubt that it would stand the test of time. I even had faith in Marie, my newfound mother, and the undying love she bore me. These things all the people around me had given me, I took on faith.

A peculiar peacefulness overtook me, pushing the fear aside. With unwavering conviction, I knew I possessed everything required to rescue us.

With every bit of conviction I owned, I spoke the words.

The hilt emitted a scorching flame that dazzled in its luminosity, stretching for three feet into a single, edged blade. The spectators retreated in amazement, while the ghouls attempted to shield their eyes.

Most of the ghouls moved back, cowering in fear of the flaming weapon. But one broke rank and lunged toward me. I swung the blade at its decaying head and cleanly sliced it off.

Using the comparison of a hot knife through butter simply would not do justice. It was as if the blade passed through thin air, effortlessly and with no barriers. My arm moved fluidly, unhindered by any resistance. The head of the ghoul now lay on the ground and the body fell away, no longer animated in its undead state.

A second ghoul was reaching out for Digger, its jaws agape with menacing teeth. I acted quickly, driving my blade straight through its chest. The sharp flames cleanly sliced through the creature's body, emerging from the other side. With a swift upward movement and a deft side cut, I sliced through its body and the head tumbled to the ground.

As I faced the unmoving crowd, all attention on the blaze of my sword, an internal struggle plagued me. These weren't zombies, but real living people under someone's control. I had no wish to harm them, but the puppet master looming over them might command an attack. If I liberated Digger, what would happen?

As I retreated, my feet met the unyielding stage behind me. Suddenly, one guest charged at me, sporting a beige coverall and a backpack reminiscent of the Ghostbusters' attire.

On instinct, I raised the sword, and it went right into his chest. I screamed as I did it.

He fell back and stumbled. I braced for a gruesome injury and bleeding wound. However, to my astonishment, there was no sign of harm — no singed spot on his jumpsuit. After blinking multiple times, he gazed directly into my eyes and mouthed the question, "What happened?"

I got close to him and yelled, "Are you all right?"

He nodded and said, "If you can stop those drums."

The Lahat Chereb didn't injure the man, but it had broken the control.

I thought back to Miss Scalia's testimony to me. She saw my father use the flaming sword to kill the ghouls in Portland. She never said he used it against the prisoners, and it was because it didn't hurt living people.

Digger used it on VanWry, who burst into flames, but a demon possessed him.

My father's weapon gained newfound reverence as I realized it could only be used against the shadowy threats of the undead, rather than fellow living beings.

It could, however, break the hold the drums created in their minds.

But for how long?

With a flaming sword in hand, I charged ahead, swinging it wildly at the crowd before me. They dispersed, allowing me to carve my way through them. Each time I grazed someone with the blade, they all had the same reaction: shock and then a look like they were coming awake.

I sprinted toward Willow and Marie, moving with the sea of people, who went from advancing toward me to stumbling backward to get away.

As I approached, Willow brandished her fighting stick and lunged at me. Despite being slowed by the spell she was under, her strikes were quick and precise. With a sweeping motion, she aimed the stick at my head. Reflexively, as I learned long ago in fencing class, I lifted the flaming sword to parry the slice, even though it was intangible. To my amazement, the fiery weapon stopped her fighting stick as if it were a solid object.

With a few steps backward, I positioned myself to attack and marveled at my weapon. I only needed one thrust to break Willow's enchantment, but I was too busy defending against her ferocious strikes. Thankfully, the fencing classes my father forced me to take in high school paid off. I parried her blows, though the impact reverberated through the hilt and down my arms.

As I stepped back, Marie made a desperate move toward me, inadvertently blocking Willow's next strike. Reacting quickly, I aimed the blade toward her shoulder, causing her to flinch in pain. Her momentary discomfort dissipated as her gaze refocused, though she seemed to be surprised by her location.

As I retreated from Willow, I brandished my blade to fend off the encroaching throng. Multiple individuals lunged at me, including a ghoul. When I sliced through its neck, the head came clean off.

All of this while defending myself against Willow's practiced strength and speed.

I wanted to call out to her, but I knew in her spellbound state, my words would be useless, as she couldn't hear me over the noise of the drums.

As she twirled her stick from one hand to the other, I parried her once more, wincing from the strain in my arms. Suddenly, I failed to block and her stick slammed against my head, causing a flurry of stars to appear before my eyes as I crumpled to the ground.

Willow retreated and prepared her final assault. While I was on my knees and dazed, my view of her movements limited. My mind raced as I envisioned a strike from above that could end my life or render me helpless. Without hesitation, I blindly plunged the fiery sword upward and into her sternum, and her mouth fell open in a cry I couldn't hear.

Willow fell to the ground. Despite feeling disoriented and struggling to clear my head, I rose to my feet. I swung my sword wildly to protect myself from potential assailants.

As Marie rushed over to lend a hand, a ghoul charged toward me, its razor-sharp teeth exposed. Swiftly, I pushed Marie aside and swung my flaming sword, cleaving the creature in half. The decaying innards spilled out onto the ground in a revolting, putrid heap of black liquid, devoid of any blood.

Willow was sitting up, and I helped her to her feet.

"What happened?" she mouthed to me.

I realized that the noise would drown my voice out. Retrieving the blessed blade from my boot, I handed it to her and then pointed to Digger, who was still bound on the stone altar. I then pointed to myself and the drummers. Fortunately, she comprehended my message to free Digger while I dispatched the drummers. She swiftly made her way through the crowd with the help of Marie. Several onlookers attempted to block their path, but Willow swung her fighting stick and Marie used her fists to get past them.

I focused my attention on the drummers.

As I charged forward with my sword, swinging it wildly, people retreated in fear. I decapitated a duo of ghouls who attempted to halt my progress. The fiery sword kept the audience at bay as I urgently made my way towards the drummers on the sides of the stage. They continued to play their mesmerizing beat.

I reached the first drummer, and uncertainty consumed me. My instincts kicked in and I swiftly thrust my sword right into his solar plexus.

What happened next shocked me to the core — the drummer ignited into flames.

These were not merely mindless ghouls, but something else. My attack shocked the other drummers, their gazes fixed on me through the holes in the hoods that covered their faces.

It was only then I noticed that they all had red eyes.

The man on the stage had watched me and my attack. He pulled the sword from its sheath and headed toward Digger and the stone altar. I was worried, but I saw Willow mount the stage, swinging her fighting stick and moving to meet the man.

I needed to focus on my task, lifting the sword high and chanting the ritualistic incantation once more. Suddenly, the blade ignited with an intensifying radiance and increased heat.

The demons couldn't handle the situation. Two of them on the opposite side of the stage abandoned their drumsticks and fled, their black robes flapping behind them. The one remaining drummer in his hooded cloak came at me, his padded drumstick raised like a weapon. In one swift motion, I slashed where its head should have been, resulting in the creature igniting into flames, melting, and collapsing to the earth.

I moved to the man behind the elaborate light and sound board. He also wore a hood, and I swiped the flaming sword at him and he fell. It surprised me that his head did not come off, nor did he burst into flames like his demonic brethren did. Instead, the figure sat up and pulled off the hood that hid his face.

It wasn't a demon at all. It was Robert Gibbons. He appeared bewildered, as if he just emerged from a hypnotic state.

I knelt to him and said, "What happened?" in a quiet voice. I assumed that without the drums I didn't have to yell, but without my hearing aid, I couldn't tell.

"This isn't the way I planned this," he said, looking around at the outdoor stage, the lights, and the setup. "I was working, and my assistant came into my office and waved a medallion. Then everything went black."

It suddenly dawned on me who the man on the stage wearing the mask could be. It made sense that the one leading the creatures and pulling off this elaborate scheme was none other than his assistant, Clyde Manning. He had been possessed by Gremory!

I looked to the stage and saw Willow circling Manning, her fighting stick raised. While I had been fighting the demons and freeing Gibbons, she skillfully prevented him from using his sword to harm Digger.

Despite her valiant efforts, I saw Manning's sword had already damaged her fighting stick, leaving chunks missing from the wood. Willow was relentless in her defense, blocking and parrying Manning's advances with her impeccable skill. He continued to come at her full force, undeterred by the blows from her stick.

As Marie wielded my short knife to slice through the ropes, freeing the chains that bound him, Digger writhed in a desperate struggle to break free.

I gazed at the crowd. With the magical drums silenced, they were no longer a mob, but merely bewildered individuals. Yet, coming through them, a pack of ghouls advanced, shedding their fake persona to reveal their true intentions. Unnoticed by Willow and Marie, the ghouls infiltrated the throng. They displayed their razor-sharp claws and decaying faces with sharp teeth. The masked attendees recoiled, frantically making their way to the door in a desperate bid to reenter the ballroom.

I dashed across the stage, circumvented the battling Willow, and vaulted off, my flaming sword above my head. Within moments, I sliced through two menacing ghouls attempting to reach their master. My fiery blade severed their skulls with graceful, efficient strokes, and their bodies collapsed. Nothing more than lifeless, headless shells.

Manning lunged toward me, only to be repelled by Willow. She brought her fighting stick up in a blow under his chin that knocked the half mask from his face. Unmasked as Clyde Manning, his expression contorted in rabid fury. He raised the sword in the air, and looking over at Digger, he dove to bring it down on the old man's neck.

Glittering in the courtyard lights, the blade arced up and descended. Willow had no blocking options from her position, and I stood too far away to intervene.

I saw the blade come down and stop, and both Marie and Willow's mouths opened in shock as I ran with the Lahat Chereb high over my head.

Digger held the chain between his hands, stopping the blade from striking him. He wrapped the chain around the sword, immobilizing it.

Willow struck Manning on the back of his head, knocking him forward. With amazing strength, he pulled the sword free from the chain and turned to Willow with his eyes both a fiery red.

Before he could strike, I jumped up on the stage and thrust my burning sword into his chest, all the way to the hilt.

His body ignited, his mouth fell open in a scream I couldn't hear and flesh dissolved into nothingness, his head fell back, wailing in agony. Soon, the once-massive black cape drifted down to the ground, charred and vacant from the ordeal.

Marie assisted Digger in his attempt to break free of the chains and ropes binding his feet. With my blade in hand, I sliced through the restraints with ease, freeing Digger's feet, but leaving him unscathed. When he motioned toward the gathering crowd, I took notice of two ghouls closing in on us.

I raised my weapon just in time, as a ghoul was a mere three feet away. I slashed at the head, cutting it cleanly off.

From his pocket, Digger produced a small leather-bound book. Opening it, he read aloud phrases I couldn't follow by reading his lips.

Whatever he said, it brought the advancing ghouls to a halt.

Extracting a plastic vial from yet another pocket, he emptied its contents onto the giant altar stone. Reciting his incantations and spilling the liquid, it changed into a purple mist that expanded over the stone and down onto the ground. When it reached the approaching ghouls, they succumbed to its power and fell to the ground.

The mist grew thicker, spreading across the courtyard. As it cleared, I noticed that the ghouls, along with their clothing, vanished.

Digger spoke some words over the Lahat Chereb, and the flaming sword was nothing more than an empty hilt again. I stowed it safely back into my pouch before taking my hearing aid out of my pocket, switching it on, and fixing it into my ear.

As my hearing returned, an unusual sound filled the air. Initially, I mistook it for gusty winds or the gentle lapping of water, but soon I recognized the source: the sound of applause.

Digger, with scratches on his forearm from escaping the ropes and chains, and a hell of a swollen eye, stepped forward to take a bow.

My attention was drawn to a sudden movement at the periphery of my vision, causing me to pivot on my heel and instinctively reach for the pouch containing the Lahat Chereb, ready to employ it if necessary.

However, it was merely Robert Gibbons scaling the platform in a disheveled state. As the audience erupted into a louder round of applause, Digger gestured toward Gibbons, attributing all accolades to him. The overwhelmed event planner took a wobbly bow.

Digger took hold of our hands and led us in a final bow. The doors to the ballroom came open, and the guests ceased clapping to file inside.

Despite being at a considerable distance, I discerned the comments of attendees by reading their lips. They lauded this as the most exceptional convention they had ever been to, with many nodding their agreement and complimenting the "show."

Digger sat wearily on the stone. "They don't know how close they came to becoming human sacrifices to Gremory." He shook his head. "I'm getting too old for this."

Willow looked at me, her eyes bright. "You made the sword light."

"I found my faith," I admitted.

"I am so glad to hear that," Marie said, handing me back my small knife. "My son, you were magnificent!"

Digger, still unstable, smiled as well. "I knew you had it. You just needed to find what you really believed in." His eyes went to the two women. "How long were you under his influence?"

"I am not sure," Marie said. "Longer than I would like to believe."

Willow nodded. "The last thing I remember was at Marie's booth this afternoon."

I looked at Willow. "Do you remember coming to our room? Waking me up?"

She shook her head.

"Once you left, the Grimoire was gone."

This made the old man raise his head. "That's not good." He looked around the courtyard, rapidly emptying of conventioneers.

"I think I know who to ask," I said, approaching Gibbons who appeared to be in a state of shock while perched on the stage's edge. "Where's the book?"

"What are you talking about? What book?"

I paused. I considered the possibility that he was being honest. He had fallen under the control of the demon, just like the rest of guests.

"You have an office here in the asylum?"

He frowned. "Yes. It's on the cell block, where they kept the difficult patients."

I recalled the cells where we changed into our costumes. "Off the Marketplace room?"

"Yes."

"Good. You're going to take us there. Now."

"What? But I can't—"

I pulled the small blade from its sheath and held it to Gibbons' throat. "I said… now!"

# TWENTY-SIX

Together, led by Gibbons, our group of five strolled through the makeshift ballroom filled with people talking loudly. Guests stood in lines at the buffet tables, helping themselves to food before searching for an available spot to eat. A lively DJ was playing music, adding to the festive atmosphere.

Gibbons had revived from his experience and was becoming his annoying self again.

"Threatening me with a knife," he blustered as I pushed him ahead of us. "I'll see you get brought up on charges, young man."

"Keep moving," I said and gave him another push, wishing that he'd been the possessed one. I would get a great deal of satisfaction seeing him melt away with the Lahat Chereb in his gullet.

As I glanced over my shoulder, I noticed Marie and Willow were helping Digger walk. Despite her small stature, Marie served as a sturdy crutch for my bigger comrade. Willow also took some of his weight as he shuffled along the corridor in his tattered suit. The three of them staggered forward with unwavering resolve.

As we arrived at the entrance to the Marketplace, Gibbons acknowledged the security guard with a nod. The man removed the stanchions to grant us access. He turned to go the opposite direction from the cells where Willow, Marie, and I had changed clothes, and I stopped him.

"That's the wrong way. I saw cells over that way," I said, and pointed.

"There are more on this side, and that is where my office is," Gibbons said, annoyed.

We followed him through the Marketplace, and he opened another door into a dimly lit corridor that seemed to stretch endlessly. Years of neglect were obvious from the condition of the walls. The cell doors were rusted, and some were bent, with chains and shackles still attached. There was no carpeting in this hall, so the sound of our footsteps echoed off the cold stone walls.

Gibbons stepped to the second green door. "This is it."

He reached for the doorknob and I stayed his hand. With a gesture, I motioned to Willow to take the other side of the door so the pair of us framed it. Digger and Marie moved away so that someone could not see them through the open door.

I pulled the Lahat Chereb from its pouch, then nodded at Gibbons.

He looked at me as if I was insane, and opened the door and stepped in.

"You're back, are you?" a woman's voice said. "What happened out there? What went wrong?"

Gibbons stepped in. "Yes, you see—"

Before he could speak another word, Willow jumped into the room, her fighting stick sweeping up in an arc, and I leapt in, the prayer for the Lahat Chereb already on my lips.

Both of us froze, unable to move or speak.

They arranged multiple tables in the spacious room, stacked with heaps of papers, forms, and brochures. Overhead, plastic ties held extension cords running to the machines positioned on the desks.

Droplets of water from a visible pipe fell continuously into a vibrant orange, five-gallon paint bucket near me. There was a small couch, only large enough for two people to sit.

In the corner was an open coffin.

I could not move a muscle. I could only move my eyes and peripherally, I could see Willow next to me, also frozen in place. Beyond Gibbons stood a lady garbed in white, her fiery red locks framing her face, while she held Digger's Grimoire open in her hands.

I knew this woman.

She was the elusive vampire in the white dress, the one Digger took down with a crossbow in Texas. She was the same one who had vanished from the truck while we were conversing with Clem and Serenity.

Why was she here? We thought she was a new vampire who knew very little. How did she get here? And how did she get the Grimoire?

"You two might as well come in," she said sweetly.

With a gesture at Gibbons, the man flew across the room. She threw him with such force; he knocked a chair over. Without walking, but dragged by invisible force, Digger and Marie slid into the room.

"Who are you?" Digger croaked.

As she spoke, she addressed him by name. "Are you unable to recognize me, Nekrotháftis?"

With a graceful sweep, she lifted her skirt, drawing his attention to her leg constructed from gleaming gold. Despite its mechanical design, it was a perfectly formed woman's leg, possessing all the beauty of a natural limb. She continued to unveil her body, revealing her other leg, which was covered entirely in soft brown fur.

"Empousa," Digger hissed, still held up by Marie, but it appeared they were both as immobile as Willow and I. "It isn't possible. Zeus sent you to the underworld eons ago."

I had read about her in the Grimoire just that afternoon. I wracked my brain trying to remember anything I read, but at that moment I drew a blank.

"Van Wry returned me to this plane that night in Portland long ago," she boasted.

I recalled Julia Scalia's account of the woman in white she saw on that Halloween night over twenty-five years ago, I also remembered the story the waiter shared about the men who encountered a paralyzing woman in white at Fort Gorges. Both times, it must have been this woman.

"I didn't know he released you," Digger went on, and I saw the fear in his eyes. "You're a demi-goddess. You've been at peace with humans for centuries. Good lady, what mission could be so important that you needed to return?"

His language was shifting into that polite and flowery form of speech he'd used with Papa Legba. This worried me. Throughout the battle with Gremory and even when he was on that altar, I hadn't seen fear in Digger's eyes, just a grim determination to free himself.

Now, Digger was scared.

"I came back to this plane years ago with one purpose," she stormed. "To release the Goddess Hecate from the underworld. That was why I helped Gremory possess the foolish mortal Van Wry and gave him the ancient spells. That is why I helped these fools this night. And you have stopped me both times."

"But, fair Empousa, Hecate would bring about great destruction—"

"What do I care of that? You mortals have forgotten the older gods. Hecate would humble the fools who think they run this world and bring endless night to you lovers of light. Look at humans, walking about unafraid of the night and the gods of old."

She closed the book and sealed it with its metal fastener. "I have your Grimoire and I can use its spells to unleash Hecate. I shall make her the one true goddess."

She looked at me with contempt. "I have spent years searching for this one. I sent Lamia to destroy him, but she never returned."

I could move my mouth, and I croaked, "Why me?"

"Hecate perceived, even before your birth, that you were the only one that could stop us. Since you were born after I arrived on this plane, I could not track you. But I could track your mother. I sent zombies to distract your parents while I attempted to steal you when you were six months old, but your mother stopped me that night."

She glared at Marie. "I cannot tell you how many years I visited New Orleans and your mother seeking you or Digger as he buried the undead, but I never located you. Finally, I realized the only way to find you was if you sought Digger and your mother. I finally located you in that dreadful little town where Digger found you."

"You sent Anastasia to me?" I asked.

She shook her head. "No, my Vrykolakas was there to lead Digger on a merry chase, but her hunger got the best of her. She helped me find you, though."

"The new vampires in Texas, that was you, too?" I threw in.

"I convinced the Claire woman to create vampires, as another way to achieve the sacrifices Gremory needed to release Hecate. But those bumpkins she worked for foiled my plans. Upon your arrival, though, I decided to kill you all. Then, as I waited to strike from high in a tree, the Nekrotháftis shot me and paralyzed me!" she raged. "It took all of my strength to free myself."

It was clear now. The one behind the scenes pulling the strings and directing Digger and I to solve the emergencies she had caused had been Empousa. We had been her unwitting puppets all along.

She stepped away from the book and put one finger against my cheek, took a drop of sweat and, with a long tongue, licked it off her finger.

I grimaced.

"Digger, you will lose another of your apprentices. There are enough people to sacrifice here so that Gremory shall finally have her army and free my mistress."

She spoke a few strange words, and Gibbons sprang up like a marionette pulled by its strings. His face twisted into a dark expression, his eyes turning red like the demons I faced before.

"Ah," Gibbons said, his voice distorted in the same way as Manning's, when the demon Gremory possessed him. "Let me kill the gravedigger. Allow me to make him a sacrifice for you, Empousa."

"No, Gremory!" the creature insisted. "I will have the apprentice first. While the others watch."

Her countenance underwent a striking transformation, as if lifting a veil. Her features became exquisite, her vibrant scarlet locks gleaming. From her toes up to her thighs, her limbs evolved into a stunning human form, exuding an alluring pallor.

She stepped toward me, undoing the belt with the pouch that contained the Lahat Chereb from around my waist and handing it to Gibbons. She took my arm, and all at once, I was free to move with her.

"So young man — Joshua, is it?" she said in a musical voice that was as intoxicating as her lush, full body. "Come and sit by me."

I attempted to glance back at Willow and my friends, but she took one finger and forced me to look at her. Her full, wet lips went into a pout. "Don't you want to look at me?"

She drew me over to the small couch, only large enough for the pair of us, and she led me to sit down on it. She pulled me into an embrace, giving me the most exciting kiss I ever experienced in my entire life. It wasn't just a kiss; it was the kiss. The one that filled me with a desire so strong it pushed any other thoughts out of my head.

I fought to focus. I had read about her in the Grimoire. She had the power to transform her appearance, and I saw that firsthand. What else? She came out of the underworld, so someone had killed her, and as Digger said, it was Zeus. What was he the God of? Thunder and lightning? Where could I get lightning here?

I tried to think, but all I could do was drink her in with my eyes. She was unparalleled in her beauty, with every inch of her body measured to perfection. Even Hollywood's biggest stars would pale in comparison, as she filled my thoughts with alluring images.

Empousa had a weakness. What was it? Something about insults, but I couldn't be sure.

She reached down and opened the front of her white dress to reveal the most perfect set of breasts I ever witnessed, and every other thought went out of my head.

She sighed and said, "Am I not beautiful?"

She was. In fact, the word 'beauty' was too tame for this heavenly creature. I thought of nothing but touching those breasts, kissing them, and joining with her again and again.

There was an odd taste in my mouth. A taste similar to a rotted tooth.

This instantly made my head clear, and I focused on that bitter tang. The waiter told me that the paralyzed men at Fort

Gorges cursed the woman who had led them astray, insulting her even though they couldn't see her. I recalled that in the Grimoire, it said slander weakened Empousa.

I had nothing else — it was worth a try.

Yet, looking at her, my longing surpassed any emotion I'd ever experienced before.

"No," I said aloud, forcing the words out. "In fact, you are damn ugly."

Her eyes grew wide, and she yanked her dress closed, hiding away the bounty of her bosom. "Don't say that."

"I shall slay him for you, my queen," Gibbons yelled and stepped closer.

She gestured for him to stay back.

Her smile returned, sunny, and pretty, and she whispered. "You want me, admit it."

I desired her intensely, with an insatiable passion that knew no limits.

"Want you?" I slid away from her, and it felt like scouring my skin with sandpaper. I forced the words through my clenched teeth. "Some ancient skank with a bunch of dumb parlor tricks? No way."

Her hands went to cover her ears. "Don't say that."

I dimly realized that Willow, Digger and Marie were moving — slowly — but that meant the paralysis was fading. I needed to keep going.

"Cover your ears all you want, you old toad. I can sign it to you if you can't hear it." I rose to my feet and hastily signed that she was: "A dumbass whore and a shit for brains bitch."

She jumped to her feet with a roar. "No. You want me, you need me."

I went on, using every insulting word I knew, as she held her ears and screeched louder.

Gibbons, possessed by the demon, grabbed me and whirled me around to face him, his red eyes staring into me as he growled. "I shall rip your throat out, mortal."

"Oh, will you?" said Willow as her fighting stick came up and smacked Gibbons on the side of his face, breaking his grip on me, and the man fell to the floor.

My insults had disrupted the creature's concentration and broke the paralyzing spell. Digger stood next to me, facing Empousa. Her womanly façade was changing, shifting, gaining size and substance.

Digger looked at me and moved his lips silently to tell me, "The insults will only slow her down. They won't stop her." He then spoke aloud, "You're an ugly old monster, a hideous hag."

The white dress was moving as if bones were shifting underneath it, and her breasts were vanishing. The pale white flesh altered to a grotesque gray as the form under the dress ceased to look female at all — she now resembled a large slug.

I looked around for a weapon, any weapon strong enough to fight her. I looked at the extension cords overhead and the five-gallon pail half-full of water, and an idea struck me.

"You think anyone would find you appealing, you ancient slut?" Marie said, freed from the paralyzing spell as well.

"Stop, stop!" the hideous creature shrieked. Her hair was gone and her features, though still approximately human, were sexless.

Wobbling jowls hung from her as her nose grew wider and seemed to melt.

The thing on the floor was more like an overlarge blob fish, unformed and becoming less attractive with each passing moment, but I clearly saw two legs, one of gold and the other covered in brown fur.

I remembered Digger told me that gold was a very conductive metal, and Zeus could fire lightning, right?

The she-thing rose, her body now distorted and wrongly formed, and yelled out, "You won't escape me, Nekrotháftis."

A circle, like an unholy mouth filled with a thousand sharp teeth opened on the creature and it leapt at Digger, the fiendish maw attaching itself to his neck.

I wasn't sure where the Lahat Chereb was, but without hesitation, I grabbed the pail of water and threw it at the creature. This shocked her so much that she released Digger. On his neck was a round wound about the size of a silver dollar, gushing blood.

I grabbed a hanging extension cord, sliced it with the small blade, and threw it at the golden leg connected to the monstrous thing. She screamed as electricity flashed up her leg — instantly shutting off all the lights.

Emergency lights came on, and I saw the pouch containing the Lahat Chereb sitting on the floor. Muttering prayers under my breath, I pulled it out and held it aloft — its sacred flame lit up the dim cell like an oasis of holy illumination.

At the same moment, Gibbons rose, grabbing Willow by the throat.

"Surrender, mortal," the red-eyed creature screamed.

Without a moment of hesitation, I pushed the fire blade right into Willow's sternum, making her eyes grow wide in shock. The blade continued harmlessly through her body and impaled Gibbons, who, with a yell, let her go and fell away, the blade's magic casting out his demonic counterpart.

I turned to Empousa and aimed the blade for what I thought was her head, and brought it down. Blood exploded into the room and I struck the bulky, misshapen body with the flaming blade several times. Parts of her fell like meaty slabs of whale blubber in chunks onto the floor. The only unchanged thing was the one golden leg, which lay detached from its owner.

Digger's wound was still bleeding profusely. I had to cauterize it, as Digger had done to my father's wrist the night he lost his hand.

I refocused my mind. "Digger, you know what I have to do."

With a prayer on my lips, I applied the fiery edge to his open wound. Before the blade passed harmlessly through human flesh. This time, an unpleasant sizzle filled the air, along with the odor of charred skin. Digger's response was only a feeble, guttural cry.

I pulled the flaming blade away to see that it had sealed the wound. Not knowing the proper incantation to halt its enchantment, and now feeling I held a much more dangerous weapon, I released my grip. It plummeted to the concrete floor, extinguishing its flames as it contacted the ground.

I sat on the floor and took Digger into my lap. The office was in chaos with the corpulent corpse looking like a dead worm. There was a strange black slimy liquid that appeared to be her blood all over the room. The disgusting smell of it overwhelmed my senses.

"Get help," I said to Marie.

She ran from the room.

Digger looked up at me and tried to speak, but nothing came out.

Willow knelt next to me and put her arm on my shoulder.

"What the Hell happened here?" a voice said.

My hand went to the Lahat Chereb on the floor and Willow raised her fighting stick. It was only Gibbons getting up, black blood all over his clothes, his hair wild, but his eyes were no longer red.

It relieved me that the Lahat Chereb hadn't melted him, like it did Manning. I assumed that since Empousa forced the demon Gremory to possess him; it didn't have the chance to corrupt his soul. At least, no more corrupted than it was already.

I looked down at Digger, but he was unconscious.

# TWENTY-SEVEN

T he three of us waited in the hospital as they treated Digger for loss of blood and the damage done to his jugular that required surgery. There was the hazard of a stroke since the wound was so near the brain and the damage created the possibility of a blood clot.

Marie rode over with the ambulance. Willow and I took the shuttle to the hotel and since the danger was past, put the Grimoire into the room safe. Then we took a cab to the hospital. After the night I'd had, I didn't want to risk driving Digger's truck for the first time at night.

After several hours, and little information from the doctors, Marie suggested we return to the hotel. Exhausted from our near-death experiences, we did as she said and got an Uber to take us back.

Although the conventioneers had returned to the hotel, they were still roaming about in costume and filling the bars. My hand kept going to the *Lahat Chereb* still in the pouch of my belt as I passed by people in zombie makeup. I soon decided they were far too jolly to be actually undead.

We got back to our room and undressed for bed. Willow kissed me, and I was glad that she tasted of nothing other than a good, clean woman.

As we lay down, she reached over and caressed me unexpectedly.

"Are you too tired?" she teased.

"Not if you aren't."

"When do you plan to ask me to marry you?" she asked.

I sat up. "I-I — where did you get that idea?"

"The *loas* told me you are my betrothed," she said and raised her eyebrows. "You don't want to marry me?"

"No, it's just…" I attempted, but found words failed me. "I know nothing about having a wife—"

"No one does, you silly man. The point is for us to learn together," she said, and got up. "But if you don't want to—"

"I didn't say that," I replied. My mind raced with things I should bring up and arguments I could make, but they all seemed pointless. Then the truth struck me. I was in love with this woman, and I wanted to be her betrothed. In a way, I had known it that first night.

I didn't have a problem with that.

I looked deeply into her eyes. "Willow, will you marry me?"

She looked away. "Well, I don't know…"

My mouth fell open in shock and she faced me, laughing. "I guess you'll do."

We both laughed as I fell into her arms.

The next day, while the Windy City ParaCon went on with its meetings and lectures, all the guests were bragging about the great 'show.' We told Marie of our engagement, which got kisses for both of us. All three of us went to the booth at the convention, and then I escorted Marie to get Digger's truck and visit him in the hospital.

On our way from the Marketplace to the parking lot, I had a run in with Gibbons. He followed us out, complaining about the fee he had to pay to remove the rotted creature from the room.

"I have to use that place for an office, and the smell was still there," he complained.

I paused and turned to him. "You still have that metal leg, right?"

"That thing? What use is that?"

"It's pure gold, and a couple thousand years old," I told him. "I think that will take care of any debt we may owe you. Besides, if it weren't for Digger and our friends, your convention would be the epicenter for the greatest mass murder of all time."

Marie chimed in. "Yes, you should thank us for saving your sorry ass."

"That leg is really gold?" was all he could say.

We turned and walked away.

I drove Digger's ungainly truck to the hospital and was nervous each time I took a curve. When I parked it in the lot, I was afraid I might hit the vehicles on either side of me.

On the way in, Marie and I met the surgeon who treated Digger. Her name was Dr. Elizabeth Miller, a forty-five-year-old woman with a lean build.

"I had to replace the vein in his neck with one from his leg," she explained to us.

"Is he going to be all right?" Marie worried.

She shook her head. "We won't be sure for several days, because of the possibility of a stroke. He'll be here in the hospital for a week, maybe two."

"I will take him back to New Orleans when they release him," Marie said as Dr. Miller walked away.

"Is that the best place for him to recuperate?"

"Of course, with me taking care of him! What else? You think he should be in that big, ugly house in New York by himself?"

I looked at my feet. "I think you know best." I hesitated for a moment, the next words new and difficult for me. "Momma."

She looked at me, tears in her eyes. "Then you believe me."

"I did the day you told me," I admitted. "It just took time for me to accept it." I took her hand. "I'm so glad you told me."

"As am I," she said.

I smiled. "But I have concerns about this man you're dating."

She paused, confused, then realized I meant Digger. She barked a laugh and hugged me for all she was worth.

After waiting a while, we visited Digger, laid up in the hospital bed. This once robust individual, who gave off an air of invincibility, appeared frail and elderly with his pale complexion. It was as if the burden of a lifetime had finally caught up to him, causing him to appear weighed down.

Bandages encircled his throat, and I was sure that the scarring would be terrible — but he was alive.

"How you doing, Digger?" I asked.

He hissed, "Can't talk."

I put my hand on his shoulder. "You don't have to. Just mouth the words, don't speak them. I can read your lips."

He nodded, then grimaced, as this movement apparently hurt.

"Is the creature dead?" he mouthed.

"Yes, I killed her with the *Lahat Chereb*. Then I used it to close your wound."

"Hurt like hell."

I chuckled. "I bet it did."

His face took a serious tone. "When can I get out?"

"You're here for a week, maybe a little longer. Then we have to wait another week before we can drive you back to New Orleans."

"I will take care of you," Marie insisted.

He glanced over at her with affection. "I might like that."

"You get some rest, Digger. We'll visit tomorrow."

He grimaced, and I thought it was his attempt at a smile. "Thank you, Josh. Your father would be proud."

We rose to go, but when I reached the door, I said to Marie. "I have something private I want to ask him."

"I'll wait in the lobby," she said.

I returned to the chair, which got Digger's attention. "Digger, my father and the way he died — he had a round mark on his neck. Do you think Empousa did it?"

He considered this. "She was looking for you, and I guess she found Ephraim. If she wanted to push you to seek me out, killing him would be the surest way to do it. Plus, she probably wanted revenge for stopping the release of Hecate in Portland. So, yes, I think she killed him."

My jaw was tight. "Then I did what I vowed — I avenged my father."

Digger nodded. "Yes, you did. If you wanted to, you could go back to New Jersey, and never think about these things again."

I stared at him. "But there are other sons who lost their fathers to these monsters. Other people who lost friends or loved ones. Who is going to avenge those people?"

Digger grinned. "That's how I got into this business."

I smiled. "I'd like to hear that story someday."

Digger leaned back. "Maybe someday. I'm tired right now."

He closed his eyes, and I headed out. I had a couple of tasks left to complete that day, one of which was to call the hotel and request an extension for the two rooms occupied by Willow, Marie, and me.

I rode with Marie out to a shopping center in Willowbrook, Illinois — just a short seven-minute drive from the hospital for my next errand.

Driving us back to the convention, I headed straight for the Marketplace to find Willow. Along the way, attendees frequently stopped me to offer their congratulations on my "performance" the night before. Many of them couldn't help but inquire about the mechanics behind the flaming sword, asking, "How on earth did you make it shoot flames like that?"

As I made my way to the booth, I spotted Willow. When the current customer walked away, I approached. I stood in front of her, sank to one knee, and presented the engagement ring box I'd just purchased, with Marie's help.

"Willow, will you—"

That was all I got out before she pulled me to my feet, kissed me soundly, and said, "Of course I will, you silly man."

Marie gushed, "This is wonderful!"

Willow nodded. "The *loas* told me he was going to marry me."

I shrugged. "Who am I to argue with the *loas*?"

Marie folded her arms, cocked her head, and said, "Who, indeed?"

Two weeks later, Willow and I exchanged marital vows in an intimate gathering hall on the hotel premises. I had successfully persuaded Lizzie to fly out from New Jersey to attend the ceremony, and I also bought a plane ticket for Willow's aunt, Lovelie to be present on this momentous occasion.

This was wonderful for a man who did not have one momma growing up. Now, I had three, all in one place.

We found a man online known as an 'On-Demand Officiant' to conduct our service. He incorporated multiple traditions to suit our specific wishes, resulting in a splendid ceremony.

Lizzie had reservations about my decision to tie the knot with a woman I had known for merely a month. However, the moment she met Willow, they established an instant connection.

Even Lovelie smiled at the ceremony.

Best of all, Digger could be there. He was in a wheelchair and still weak, but he escorted Willow down the aisle and gave her away.

My darling made a beautiful bride.

We stayed another week at the hotel, our families returning home, while Willow and I enjoyed our honeymoon. Following her suggestion, I introduced her to the fundamentals of sign language. This allowed us to communicate in a way that other individuals could not easily comprehend.

Throughout that week, there were no supernatural beings, horrifying creatures, or walking dead to contend with. We enjoyed dining experiences at esteemed restaurants, and indulging in refreshing dips at the hotel pool. As newlyweds do, we also took ample time to engage in intimate moments in our private quarters.

As the third week came to a close, Digger, Marie, Willow, and I gathered in our hotel suite to plan our next move.

Digger was out of the wheelchair, his recovery remarkable, although still pale and weak. I located a heavy cane from the back of his truck. He relied on the walking aid as he made his way forward.

Marie gave credit to her potions. Who was I to argue?

"I should have figured it out it sooner," Digger complained. "I mean, a Lamia attacked when you were a kid, Josh, then in Duivelsmeer, it was a *Vrykolakas*. All these Greek creatures should have made me think of Empousa."

"She could change form and you didn't know Van Wry released her in Portland," I said.

"Anyway," Marie said. "How are we gonna work things out?"

"The way I figure it, between the four of us, we can cover everything," Digger said. His voice had returned, but with a new gravel to it. "I'll go with Marie to New Orleans, help her with the shop, and get my strength back."

Willow and I exchanged a glance. "Where do you want us?"

"You two can stay in my house in Airmont, New York, and oversee operations there. I'll contact the staff and make the introductions, and I can teach you how to run things. My staff are all good people, and the bookkeeping is all online, so I can take care of that. But I need someone up there to monitor things and be available for the 'special' calls."

Willow frowned. "Special calls?"

"You think just because Empousa and Gremory bit the dust that there aren't other problems with the undead? I think you two handle yourselves pretty well and you'll take my Grimoire with you. Between those spells, Willow kicking ass with that stick, and Josh handling the Lahat Chereb, you should be fine. I figure I'll switch to part time."

"Maybe you should think about retiring," Marie corrected, and put her hand through his thinning hair in a gesture of affection.

"I will. As soon as I'm sure Josh can handle everything. What do you two think?"

I looked at my friend and my new momma, Marie. I gazed at my beautiful wife, and I thought about my father and the stories that scared me so much as a child.

Could I do as Digger asked? Pose as a simple man, a common gravedigger, and yet be ready at a moment's notice to rise and fight off things worse than the monsters I'd already faced?

"I think it sounds like a fine plan," I said and smiled.

Digger nodded. "Good, 'cause I got an email from a friend of mine in New Jersey. They've been having a problem with an active skeleton. I figure this is the perfect first mission for you two. Here's what you need to do—"

As Digger went on, I smiled at my new wife, and signed, "I love you."

She signed "I love you, too," back to me.

My attention returned to Digger as I got ready for the next part of my new life.

# ABOUT THE AUTHOR

Known as the "Wizard Of Odd", Arjay Lewis is an actor, magician, and multi-award-winning author. I write tales of the strange and the horrifying.

I have spent my life as an entertainer, amusing people as a street-performer in the 1970s; a Broadway and casino artist in the 1980s; a party performer in the 1990s and 2000s; a cruise ship performer in the 2010s.

Stories have always been in my mind, and I have been writing since the 1990s. My reason to write is simple: to entertain. I write the type of books that I like to read: murder mysteries, strange tales of unnatural gifts, odd happenings and horror.

Please visit my web site and sign up for my mailing list to be "in the know" for upcoming books. Visit me on Facebook, Twitter, or my Amazon Author page.

And thank you for reading. You are the reason I write.

www.arjaylewis.com
www.facebook.com/arjaylewis
www.twitter.com/arjaylewiswrite
www.amazon.com/Arjay-Lewis

# ALSO BY ARJAY LEWIS

**Doctor Wise Series**
Fire In The Mind
Seduction In The Mind
Reunion In The Mind
Haunted In The Mind
Devotion In The Mind
Asylum In The Mind
Specter In The Mind
Vengeance In The Mind
Echoes In The Mind
Infection In The Mind
Justice In The Mind
Ritual In The Mind
Vanished In The Mind

**Horror**
The Muse
Kept In The Dark
The Vanishing
Digger

**Romantic Suspense**
*(with Debra Snow)*
A Study In Murder

**NYPD Wizard Detective**
The Wizards Of Central Park West
The Vampires Of Greenwich Village
The Werewolves Of Washington Square

www.ingramcontent.com/pod-product-compliance
Lightning Source LLC
Chambersburg PA
CBHW051517250626
47156CB00001B/125